uNLEASHED

NecroVerse Book One

by

AARON BUNCE

Autumn Arch Publishing
Iowa
www.AaronBunce.com

Publisher's note
This is a work of fiction. All names, places, characters, and incidences are
either the product of the author's imagination, or are used fictitiously, and
any resemblance to actual people, alive or dead, events or locations, is
completely coincidental.

A product of Autumn Arch Publishing

Cover art: Eder Messias
Cover art – colorist: Joel Chua
Cover art – typography: Christian Bentulan
Interior design: Aaron Bunce

Trade paperback ISBN: 978-1-7338095-2-8
Amazon KINDLE: B07VRDYD1Y

1st Edition – 2019

Day 1

1230 HOURS

Jacoby poked irritably at the conveyor feed button. He waited, tapping his boot impatiently. Nothing happened.

"Load next," he growled, but the computer didn't respond.

"Piece of crap!" He pounded the monitor housing with a calloused palm. The screen flickered and went black. *Figures. First Anna, and now you.* He reached around and started tightening the various cables behind the monitor.

"Women, crappy work gear, and fucking hangovers. Why can't anything just work like it's supposed to?" he muttered.

"You and your lady friend have another fight?" Mike, from the adjacent workstation asked. Jacoby had been so caught up in his thoughts that he didn't notice him approach.

"Stinking dumpster fire of a night, man," he said, fidgeting with his workstation.

"Yeah? Looks like it. You look like shit. She hassle you about re-upping your contract?"

Jacoby nodded and glanced at his reflection in the glossy monitor. His hair was a tangled mass of brown. Dark bags hung beneath his blood-shot, brown eyes and there were more than a few white hairs mixed in with his stubble. He looked like hell.

"That's why I'm all on my lonesome, man. Dragging a lady all the way out here is a sure-fire recipe for trouble. She want you to transfer back home?" Mike asked absently, flicking rock fragments off of his shirt.

"No!" Jacoby snapped, and immediately regretted his tone. "She, uh, doesn't want to have anything to do with her folks, but she also says that deep space mining is for people who've got nothing and nobody...who've got no sense of adventure. She wants us to move on, maybe set up in one of the colonies...maybe Mars and take up terraforming work. I don't know. One minute she's practically begging me to bring her out here to get away from her family, and the next thing she wants to go somewhere else. Her folks are in her head, man, she just won't admit it. The money's better than anything

I'd get planet-side. They're filling her head with garbage." He glanced at his workstation as the monitor beeped.

"You aren't married to her...I mean shit, have you two ever had sex? If you want to stay, why doesn't she just go back to Earth?" Mike asked.

Jacoby shook his head and rubbed his eyes, and then turned back to Mike and caught sight of his sour-faced supervisor, Janice, entering from the admin hallway. Lately, their interactions seemed to be butt chewing's or nasty looks. He'd received a performance write up the day before, which devolved into an ugly shouting match and the threat of a suspension. He knew he wouldn't receive any more warnings. Jacoby would simply be stranded in deep space, without a job.

He tapped the load button again, but kept an eye on Janice. The conveyor motor finally started to hum.

"Anna's my best friend. We've been close since we were kids...even when her folks forbid it. Her mom is a real piece of work, trying to always set her up with one sleazy piece of shit after another. Always the same kinds, too – a financial broker with his own yacht, or an attorney with the right name, or some corporate tool clinging on to daddy's coattails. She got me off Earth, and then I snagged this gig, and got her out of the Lunar colonies. It just worked out for both of us. Anna understands me better than anyone else."

"Well, Anna's hot, bro. So you know, if she gets tired of you and needs a new friend, or roommate, whatever you call it, I've always got room in my quarters. And I would so hit that! I'd love to see those long legs wrap around me, and those tits! Man, I'd hit that..."

"Shut up, ass," Jacoby groused. The thought of Anna with someone like Mike made him sick...sicker than the ideas of all the other wrong guys her mom had forced on her throughout the years. Mike laughed, scratching his stubbly chin, turned around to track Janice, and leaned back in on Jacoby's station, his breath hot with cheap coffee and something sour.

"So, if she's so keen to get off Hyde Station, how'd you get her to agree to another year out here?" Mike asked.

Jacoby looked away, his brow furrowing as the computer finally cycled loudly through its deep scan and mineral analysis protocol. He reached up to rub the sleep from his eyes, but did not respond.

"Wait. You didn't tell her before you re-upped your contract?" Mike scoffed, covering his mouth and leaning back dramatically. "Damn, no wonder she's so pissed with you, man! Like I said, I've got room for her if she needs a new roommate."

Jacoby flipped him the bird, but he had already turned to walk away. He lacked the necessary patience to put up with his bullshit. He turned back to his monitor, rubbing his temple and wishing for some relief from his pounding headache. To top it all off, his mouth still tasted like stale liquor.

Guys like Mike couldn't understand the value of someone like Anna. He didn't have to deal with the expectation and the disappointments of her family, their shadow stretching halfway across the galaxy.

What do you see in Jacoby? He's just a dirty miner – the son of a factory worker, collecting laborer pay in the middle of nowhere. A friendship with someone like that will bring you no benefit. Now...Braniman Kopecky's son was just promoted to Senior Tech advisor. He just bought his own private shuttle, and I hear he just broke up with his girlfriend. Anna hated their meddling, their nearly incessant game of "climb the social ladder". He understood her in a way that her own family couldn't, and she him. They had something stronger than friendship. Something her parents couldn't, or refused to understand. It was love, even if they weren't able to articulate it to one another. She was his person, and he was hers.

Ignorance really is bliss.

"Analyzing sample, please standby," the computer chirped, breaking him from his melancholies. Lines of data appeared on the monitor, flooding the screen in a wash of numbers and metallurgic data. He had to look away. The numbers and symbols flashed by so quickly they made his stomach turn.

"Mineral analysis complete. Composite iron, tungsten, nickel. Radioactive elements cobalt, iridium, rhenium. Trace targets silver ten percent, palladium fourteen percent. Warning, void detected," the computer said, spitting out preloaded target results before beeping loudly.

Jacoby perked up. *Fourteen percent palladium!* That was double anything he had ever processed. A hundred pounds of palladium would more than cover his quota. Hell, it might even land him a bonus. *It might crack a smile on Janice's fossilized face. Hell, she'd probably shatter.*

"Now that would be a sight!" he said, dismissing the unreliable computer's void warning while reveling in the idea of his supervisor crumbling into pieces. He smiled at the thought, the tension working to pull his face in a permanent scowl releasing just a bit.

The conveyor started to turn, and a moment later the hatch slid open. A large chunk of rock appeared, roughly twelve feet in diameter. Pre-processing had already pulled the gravity anchors out, leaving a number of perfectly bored holes.

"Chart results, grid layout." Jacoby stepped back and sized up the asteroid. A laser grid appeared, breaking up the rock in sections. Each square opened up with a wave of a hand, displaying that section's mineral composition in a three dimensional hologram. He circled, scrutinizing each section until he found what he was looking for.

"Rotate sample ninety degrees clockwise." He donned his apron and reached for his face shield, but reconsidered and pulled on his goggles instead. The idea of being trapped in a sealed mask with stale liquor breath was far from appealing.

He donned his gloves as the tool ring descended around his workstation. He pushed a fresh fusion plug into his plasma saw and adjusted his goggles. Jacoby checked the computer's cut vector and depth, but leaned in as one of the holographs changed. The computer had updated the image with a hollow cavity, roughly the size of a basketball. There was a void after all, and it was sitting directly over his palladium deposit. *Damn! Maybe it's just ice. Or, the scanner is acting up again.*

Every rock jockey knew the protocol. It was drilled into their heads continuously. All voids were to be drilled, tested, and secured before cutting or processing began. Jacoby knew it was for a good reason. If a void was a pocket of methane or hydrogen sulfide, it could be ignited by the heat of plasma cutting. Explosions in deep space mining made a bad day worse, and he didn't want Anna taking him home in a box. Tested samples were always processed by the Hazard and Special Drilling team, and any deposits they processed would be theirs to claim.

"I ain't giving away this haul," he muttered, glancing over to make sure Mike wasn't looking before waving away the void hologram. Then he deleted any mention of the cavity from the computer. He knew what would happen. H.S.D would pad their numbers with his find, and he'd get a dud rock full of junk mineral or ice in return. He'd fall even further from quota and Janice would finish tearing him a new hole. He'd never get a chance to work a day of his new contract. She'd just send him packing.

The plasma saw hummed gently, the contact points heating up as the shield unfolded. Jacoby lowered the blade into his first cut, the hot plasma easily parting the smooth rock. The air around him was filled with the hot, salty smell of melting silicate.

Jacoby followed the computer's angle, cutting quickly. He felt a tremor in the handle. *It's just the saw. Probably needs resonance adjustments again.* He pushed the blade deeper into the rock, confident in his decision to continue.

The handle shook and jerked violently. He panicked and tried to pull the saw free, but it moved sluggishly. If the saw became stuck, the rock would cool and fuse to the blade. They would never get it out. Forget quotas, Janice would eat him alive if he ruined a ten thousand credit plasma saw.

He put all of his weight forward and felt the saw break loose. It cut for just a moment before sinking in all of the way. Jacoby's wrists turned painfully and he stumbled forward. The saw's safety engaged as his hand came free, instantly powering the tool down.

Cursing, Jacoby kicked the rock. He leaned in and yanked on the handle, but it was stuck firmly in place. A strange noise filled the air, leaking out and around the saw blade. It sounded like a basket of angry snakes.

A cloud of vapor burst from the cut rock, enveloping him. Small, wet droplets spattered Jacoby's face as he staggered backwards. *Gas!* He swiped at his face, but it was in his nose and mouth. He had already breathed it in. *No, not gas. Gas isn't wet.*

Filling with panic, Jacoby stumbled towards the emergency button on his work terminal, a plan forming in his mind. *I'll tell them the void didn't show up on scans. That it was an instrument malfunction.* They had to believe him. That way, they couldn't blame him for the ruined saw either.

He dropped a heavy palm on the duress button and sagged forward onto his knees. He suddenly felt very tired, very heavy. Jacoby tried to remember the excuse he had concocted, but his thoughts had grown sluggish. His head throbbed and everything began to spin.

He lifted a hand and managed a single step towards Mike before sprawling, face first onto the ground. Jacoby rolled over, gasping for breath as people swarmed all around. A fuzzy, dark ring settled over his vision. Someone was shaking him and talking, and then everything went black.

* * *

"Jacoby! Wake up. Jacoby!" someone shouted out of the darkness.

Air flooded into his lungs as his eyes popped open. He was flat on his back, a host of faces hovering above him, all staring and whispering.

"Well, hey there, Jacoby. I thought you were having a fit there for a moment. You okay?" Jacoby's vision cleared and he focused in on a face. It was Yuri, the shift emergency responder.

"Uh, what happened?" he sputtered, looking at his workstation, and then locked eyes with Janice. Her face scrunched up in a sharp scowl, her lips pulling back to expose coffee-stained teeth. The fluorescent lights set the wrinkles around her eyes into sharp contrast, making her appear withered and hard. She looked pissed.

"You went down like a bag full of tailings," Yuri said.

"I got lightheaded. Think maybe I'm coming down with something," Jacoby lied. *Better to deal with Janice later, after some cool down time.*

"You look a little rough. Why don't you head down to the clinic and get yourself checked out...we'll send the electronic documents on ahead for the doc. At the very least get a vitamin booster and some rack time." Yuri helped him up, and looked to Janice. She pressed her lips together, forming a pencil-thin line, but offered no argument. At least none she would share now. It would come later, when he alone could take the full brunt of it.

Jacoby signed the incident form and declined a wheel chair, insisting he was capable, even when Yuri argued that someone was supposed to accompany him. He hung up his goggles and apron and walked out into the plant proper. The din of mechanized conveyors, plasma saws, and hydraulic pumps instantly washed over him. It made his ears ache and his head throb.

Jacoby smashed his hands over his ears and ran. He turned a corner and stumbled past a crowd of people, stopping only to smash the call button. They cast him strange looks, whispering behind their hands, but he didn't care.

The doors opened quickly, the large space beyond windowless and empty. Jacoby jumped inside, and refused to pull his hands away from his ears until the transit elevator doors closed fully. He hit the button for A ring, just as one of the lights overhead flickered and went dark.

He slumped into the darkest corner, savoring the quiet. The elevator hummed gently up the large tube, leaving the production hub behind as it slipped silently towards the habitation rings.

The door chime sounded a while later, the sudden noise punctuated by a ring of flashing, colored lights around the door. His fists balled up without thought and he almost punched the elevator panel. Anger washed up in a massive wave and his vision started to narrow.

Jacoby smacked his forehead against the wall and spit out a forceful breath. He took another and finally managed to unclench his fists. Why did the noise...make...him...so...angry?

The clinic was busy when he arrived, so Jacoby checked in and took a seat. He tried to ignore the murmurings, but the hushed conversations quickly irritated him, like a sink dripping incessantly while he was trying to sleep. He stared into the black of space beyond the window and counted the stars.

Jacoby bounced his face off the window when a nurse called his name. He'd been counting stars one moment and snapped to the next. Had he dozed off, and if so, for how long?

He limped back to the exam room. His body ached. Not just his joints, but his muscles, and even his skin. He stayed as cordial with the nurse as possible, but the room was full of instruments, and they all seemed to make noise. The clinic physician walked in with a flourish. He was short, with a pronounced belly and an odd, rigid lilt to his step...an old injury perhaps?

The doctor tapped and swiped on the screen of his overly large data point. He was balding, with a relatively round face, a pronounced cleft in his chin, and cheeks that sagged down to hide his jawline. His eyes were the only thing remarkable about him – the right an almost golden-brown, while the left shone icy-blue in the screen's bluish light.

He scanned his screen for another long moment, before going straight into a well-practiced spiel.

"I'm Doctor Reeds. The nurse's notes here say you're not feeling well today? Had an incident on the production floor? Well that's no good, no good at all. Lots of people on station are struggling with bugs right now. You trap this many people together in a sealed can floating in space and bugs are gonna flourish. They go gangbusters. So, the old saying goes: misery loves company."

Jacoby could only nod. He had a full-blown rock crusher rumbling in his head and his saliva felt thick. He thought that he might actually throw up. Doctor Reeds checked his temp, his glands, eyes, nose, and throat. Pretty much everything every doctor ever seemed to check. Reeds then proceeded to ask him a large number of questions, some personal, and some pertaining to his work. Jacoby tried to focus and answer honestly. The doctor's voice was irritating, however, not to mention the *tap tap tap* of his fingernails against the screen.

"Yep. Definitely think that's it. Someone on the last ore freighter from Earth had a virus...influenza E. Nasty little bug. Problem is, it's not a bacterium, so antibiotics are worthless. All I can do is give you a booster pack of vitamins, minerals, and synthesized immune boosters. I'll send a com note down to production excusing you for a few days of rest. I do need your consent to draw a blood sample for base analysis and cultures, just to satisfy company requirements, and then of course your screens will all have to come back clean before we can clear you for work again," the doctor said, the wheels of his chair squawking loudly.

Jacoby took a deep breath and swallowed hard. The sound of his voice continued to grate against his nerves, but the squeal of chair's unoiled casters almost unhinged him completely. Horrible impulses pushed their way into his thoughts. He had to look away, or he thought that he might actually strike him. No, he wanted to kill the noise. Kill it.

"Excuse me?" Doctor Reeds said and tapped him gently on the shoulder. Jacoby swung about, fists balled and jaw clenched. The doctor barely touched him but it felt like he had dropped a hammer on his back.

"I just need your consent for the blood draw," Reeds said rather meekly and gestured to a signature box on his screen.

"I'm...sorry. Just not myself today, I guess. Go ahead." Jacoby took a deep breath and tried to force his raging heart to slow, and then scribbled something unintelligible onto the screen with a trembling finger.

Jacoby looked away and bit his knuckle as the needle bit painfully into his arm. He glanced back as blood filled the auto-syringe. Thick, deep-red fluid filled the vial, the color mesmerizing and unsettling at the same time. The booster injection was less painful, but he could feel the solution filtering into his body. It was cold, then hot. He could've sworn he felt it bubble. Or was that his blood?

The doctor's face flashed in and out of his vision, his mouth moving comically and his words muffled and distant. Jacoby wanted to bite him, or pummel his face until he couldn't make noise anymore. A horrible pressure was building in his head, and settling behind his eyes. He felt drunk or high...maybe both.

The office blurred and a strange gurgling, sucking noise reverberated out of his belly. He was in a hallway, but not entirely sure how he got there. How much time had passed? His head started to throb in time with his heart. It felt like it might split down the middle.

I hate the pain, hate the damn pain!

Everything made him angry...no, everything was anger. Jacoby stumbled past a group of admin workers. They laughed and joked, walking importantly in their overly tidy uniforms, "Planitex Industrial" emblazoned in bold, red lettering.

Yes, the color of blood.

He hated their faces and their happiness. They didn't pay him any mind as he tripped and fell through a service door. His stomach gurgled and whined again. He could feel it shake his whole body.

Something sour and thick pushed its way up his throat. He heaved and bent over, retching all over the wall. It was thick and his stomach cramped so hard he almost crapped his pants. The vomit ran down the white ceramic wall panels, falling onto the ground with a "plop". It was bubbly, stringy, and blue. There was blood, too, pockets of red blood.

The sight of blood sent a wave of anger rushing through him. He couldn't rationalize it, but he liked the way it felt. Like strength and power. The anger grew more intense, and he slammed his fist into the bulkhead over and over. Bones in his hand snapped. The pain felt surprisingly good.

Jacoby staggered back out of the service passage a few moments later. The group was gone.

Better for them.

More convulsions wracked his body, crawling up through his chest and neck. His anger swelled as the convulsions moved into his head. A peculiar crawling sensation pushed forward from behind his eyes, his throbbing headache increasing in response.

Jacoby staggered across the hallway and leaned against the outer bulkhead for support. The stars twinkled, surging like blistering pinpricks of light. He took a half-step back, baring his teeth as he caught sight of his ghost-like reflection in the window. Black veins crept through his pale skin, forming dark rings around his eyes, which now looked like dull, shadowy pits.

"Anna!" he moaned, a glob of thick mucus slipping out of the corner of his mouth.

His vision narrowed, the anger that had so consumed him a moment before loosening slightly. Jacoby's heart fluttered as he thought about his friend, and how stupid he had been to dwell on their fight for so long. *She was right about me not telling her about the new contract. I'm a fool.*

Jacoby stumbled down the passage and back onto the transit elevator. The ride to D ring passed in a blur. He was in a passage when he snapped to again, signs pointing to long-term housing blocks on either side of him. He flashed between rage, inconsolable depression, and intolerable joy with almost every step forward. Fear tied them all together, until Mike's words bubbled up into his mind. *I'd hit that.* Jacoby's hands balled up into fists, his knuckles popping loudly.

He was at the door to their quarters and held his wrist up to let the reader scan his imbedded id chip. The door chimed softly and whooshed open. Anna sat on the padded window seat. Her head was down and hands crossed over a book. No one read paper books anymore - no one except Anna.

The overhead light struck her curly blond hair and it seemed to catch fire in the light. She'd dozed off waiting for him. Jacoby took a step into the living room, but horrible, murderous thoughts clawed their way into his mind. He saw flesh tearing, blood spilling, and hair matted and ruined. *No, it is Mike...*he thought. He was just angry about what the prick said.

The anger surged back in again, the emotion so strong it almost knocked him off his feet. He barely caught the corner of the wall. The book hit the ground with a thump as Anna woke with a start.

"Coby, I didn't hear you come in. I wanted to..." she moved towards him, but Jacoby threw up a hand.

"No!" he growled and threw his body down the hallway, bouncing haphazardly between walls. His voice was thick, gravelly...not his.

"Coby!" Anna called after him, but he stumbled into the bathroom. Jacoby turned and put all of his weight against the door. It slammed shut and he flipped the lock. He shut his eyes as more horrible thoughts ripped through him.

"Coby," she whispered from just outside the hall. "Coby, we need to talk about this. I'm sorry I got mad, but we need to talk, to listen to each other. That's what we do. That's what we've always done." She started to cry.

"Just go away, Anna. I can't...I can't deal with this right now," he growled, barely able to stifle the urge to slam his face into the door. He couldn't bear the thought of her being hurt. He loved her, cherished her. She made him want to be better.

"Don't push me away, Coby. Please! I don't care what my family thinks. They can go to hell. Our friendship means more to me than that! You know that, right? I just wish you'd told me...I'm sorry I snapped. It's just...it's just... Please, come out so we can talk this through!" she pleaded.

Jacoby could feel her body heat through the door. He rose to his knees and rested his face against the cool metal. Muscles all over his body started to twitch involuntarily.

"Please let me in."

He could smell the mint on her breath, and the sweet musk of her body. Lusty thoughts flooded through him, but they quickly gave way to the anger. Fingernails scraped against the door, digging, splintering, and tearing into the paint.

Anna's trying to pry open the door, he thought frantically and moved for the handle. *She can't see me, not like...this.* Jacoby staggered back, realizing with horror that it wasn't Anna fumbling with the handle, but him. The fingers of his right hand scrabbled against the metal door like thick spider legs, moving with a menacing purpose all their own. He reached over and pulled his arm back just as his fingers curled around the lock release.

"Coby? Are you okay? What's going on in there?" Anna asked, sniffing loudly.

Jacoby slumped back to the ground, his right arm still convulsing wildly on its own. *First my best friend, then that bitch Janice, and now my body, everything is spinning out of control!* He choked back a sob, and finally managed a deep, steadying breath.

"Anna, we can talk about all of this tomorrow. I'll give you all of my attention...as much as you want. All of it! I just need...I just need a little time to myself right now. I need rest." His voice wavered and broke. He was barely able to spit out the words. Damn he sounded strange...scared.

"Fine!" Anna hissed after a lengthy silence, and then he heard her stomp off down the hall.

Jacoby let his head droop as silence fell over the bathroom, a blessed, soothing, silence. He closed his eyes, willing his jumbled, erratic thoughts to calm. *Rest, just need rest*, he thought, begging for the peace of dreamless sleep.

But it would not be so. His body flopped to the side and he fell painfully against the metal waste can. His arm flopped and slapped him in the face, his jagged fingernails scrapping and gouging his flesh.

"No...stop it! Damn you! Damn you!" Jacoby grunted and rolled over, holding his breath for fear of making any noise.

What would Anna think? He thought in a panic. *She'd leave...no, she'd run, straight for a shuttle and go back home. She'd leave me all alone. He'd never been...all alone.*

Jacoby slapped his flailing arm down and clutched it against his chest. It wouldn't stop moving. It wouldn't stop. Gagging and wheezing, Jacoby fumbled his way to his knees, and then his feet. He staggered against the wall as a sharp pain jabbed into his head. Angry, belligerent thoughts battered his mind. He wanted to hurt someone, or something...anything he could get his hands on. He wanted to kill. To rip and tear. To bite and gnash.

No! he sagged forward against the sink, trying desperately to get his runaway anger in check. It would pass, he only needed time! He lifted his head and opened his eyes, meeting his reflection in the mirror.

"Gak!" Jacoby groaned, unable to form words. His arm flopped back up, his fingers snaking into his hair. He reached up and pulled it free, tearing a fistful of hair out in the process. His fingers opened and closed spasmodically, allowing the clump of hair and bloody scalp to fall to the floor.

Desperate and terrified, Jacoby grabbed his unruly arm just below the elbow and brought it down against the sink. He gasped as flesh smacked painfully into stainless steel, but did it again and again, banging the limb against the sink like a fisherman with a feisty catch. Blood spattered his face, coating the sink in dark droplets. Finally, with one violent swing, he felt the bones in his forearm snap.

Jacoby growled, grinding his teeth through the pain, but his ruined arm didn't fight anymore. It now hung, twitching next to his body, an angry pulse beating in time with his raging heart.

"It's nothing. It's nothing. Just a bad day...that's all," he murmured, almost singing reassurances to himself as he clutched his arm and stepped tentatively up to the sink. It didn't matter that he was lying to himself. He would believe it. For now, at least.

Jacoby bit his lip as he met the gaze of the reflection staring back at him in the mirror. He wouldn't look away. No, he couldn't. It wasn't real. He was real. The black veins crept away from his eyes, painting a macabre, vile tapestry across his pale skin. But that wasn't what unnerved him so. No. His reflection wasn't him. The man staring back at him grimaced, a faint trail of blue saliva leaking out of his mouth, and then he winked.

Day 2

08 15 HOURS

A sliver of light pierced the darkness, burning into his eyes like a searing, hot bolt. Jacoby groaned, rolled over, and found that he couldn't move his neck. His hands worked out and explored the space. It was hard, and relatively cool. He opened his eyes a little further. He was lying in the shower, his body contorted, twisted onto itself to fit into the tight, three foot by three foot space.

Jacoby slowly unraveled, first his feet and then his legs flopping out and onto the floor. A chime sounded somewhere beyond the door. He grabbed ahold of the shower door handle and pulled himself upright, the pain in his head and neck almost instantly fading away. A chime sounded beyond the door again, followed by a series of sharp, staccato knocks.

"Hold on," he heard Anna say.

Slowly, Jacoby unfurled his body and stood. He winced, faintly remembering pain in his arm. The bone, it was broken. And yet he felt no pain. He lifted the limb, turning his hand and twisting his wrist. The bones appeared straight and intact. His skin was also free of any cuts, bruises, or blemishes.

"Was it? Could it all have just been a bad dream?" he muttered, exhaling deeply. But as he turned, he spotted blood crusted on the side of the sink. There were small bits of blood spattered on his shirt, as well as something blue. What had happened? His recollections of the previous day were foggy at best....and the harder he strained to remember, the foggier it all became. A clump of bloody hair sat on the floor not six inches from his foot.

"Jacoby, door!" Anna yelled, her tone clipped and icy.

He slept in the bathroom, no, the shower. *No wonder she's pissed. What did you screw up now?* he wondered, leaning forward and looking at his reflection in the mirror. There was something crusty in the stubble around his mouth, but other than some unruly hair, he didn't appear too worse for the wear. Had he gotten drunk the night before? It made sense. Probably got stuck talking to Mike, wasted some credits on synth-whiskey, threw up on himself, and crawled into the shower to sleep it off. Or was that the night before?

"Coby!" Anna hollered, this time her voice devoid of anything resembling warmth.

"Yeah...coming!" he finally managed to holler back.

Jacoby hastily pulled off his shirt and stuffed it in the hamper, before scrubbing off his face and brushing his teeth. He turned and reached for the door, taking note of the strange scratches in the painted metal just beneath the handle. *I don't know anything about it,* he decided, shaking his head and pulling the door open.

Anna waited at the far end of the hall, standing next to the door. She was still in her nightgown, a Planitex issued sweatshirt pulled tightly around her shoulders. Her hair was disheveled, although it looked as if she'd hastily tried to tie it back. Her normally welcoming blue eyes met him with an icy and painfully apathetic glare.

"I'm coming," he said, making his way quickly down the hallway. Despite waking up shoved in a single stall shower, he felt surprisingly spry. In fact, most of his usual aches and pains appeared to be gone.

Jacoby approached Anna, giving her his best disarming smile. It died when he reached the open door. Janice stood just outside in the hall, her face a pinched scowl, her gray-streaked red hair pulled back in a painfully tight knot.

"We had a seven fifty-five post incident review. It is eight o'clock. Why am I here, as opposed to down there?" she intoned, her aire of stuffy, bored superiority ringing clear.

"I didn't know," Jacoby replied, innocently.

Janice smacked her gum, her teeth clicking together in what could almost pass as a snarl. Then she laughed. "Let's add that to the 'Jacoby didn't know' book, and file it in the 'Jacoby ruins company equipment and generally fucks up the whole shift' chapter," her humor drained away almost instantly.

"Just let me get a shirt. One sec," he said, his nerves twisting his gut.

Jacoby eased around Anna, who only moved to follow him back to his bedroom. As soon as they turned the corner, she started into him.

"A post incident? What happened? Why couldn't you tell me last night? Was it because you were drunk again...two nights in a row? And it was Mike, wasn't it?"

Jacoby nudged the pressure pad on his dresser with a knee, and forced the drawer open when it moved too slowly. He fished out a clean work shirt and pulled it on before turning back to Anna. He desperately wanted a shower, but knew Janice wouldn't wait. Anna waited for him to turn back before continuing. He knew his friend, and unfortunately, she knew him better. He'd only salvage things if he started with some honesty for a change.

"I collapsed at work yesterday...no, I'm fine," he started, her angry face breaking momentarily with concern. He continued before she could cut in. "Station doc just thinks that I had a bug...have a bug. I probably got a little too warm. I blacked out and fused my saw. No one got hurt," he added, trying to defuse as much of the tension as possible.

"You're sick? I thought you were just hung over, or worse, drunk again. You should have told me. If you weren't feeling well, I wouldn't have brought any of that shit up. We've always talked about things...well, everything. I was just mad that you didn't tell me about the new contract before you signed it. You've been so distant lately. Yes, I want to get off this station...maybe see Mars, Jupiter's moons, or go further out to the outer system colonies. You seemed so excited when we started talking about the deep space colonization program and then you just up and renewed your contract.

"If you'd asked if I minded you renewing your contract, I wouldn't have said no. I might have questioned it, maybe brought up some alternatives. I wasn't mad until you...well, until you wouldn't come out of the bathroom. I thought you were hiding from me so you wouldn't have to talk about it. You know how I hate it when people refuse to deal with shit," Anna said, her cheeks flushing with a touch of red.

"I know," Jacoby said, weakly. He considered the foggy memories of the previous evening: the blood on the sink, as well as the scratches on the door. Part of him disagreed with her. He *did* need to hide from her. But he wouldn't interrupt her now. He'd earned every word.

He eased into his clean pants and pulled on his boots. He wanted to sit down and talk, to get their situation back to where it was just Anna and Coby, their own little self-contained universe where their friendship stood strong against whatever came at them. That's when things were good. There wasn't anything they couldn't tackle together. But the longer he kept Janice waiting, the worse her wrath would be, and this wasn't "a dip your toe in to see how hot the water is" scenario. Janice would likely try and boil the meat from his bones.

"I'm already feeling loads better. I think the trip to the doc was the difference. Let's talk later. We can work through everything, I promise. Besides, if Janice has her way, we may be looking for alternative plans sooner anyway, and we might have to start talking about some changes," he said, reaching up and tucking a loose strand of hair back and behind her ear. "Are you working today?"

Anna smiled, a little bit of the ice melting in her gaze. Then she shook her head, "No...I'm not scheduled today or tomorrow."

A small hint of Jacoby's tension melted away when she didn't flinch or pull away from his touch, but she didn't go out of her way to make it easier either. He moved forward, Anna sliding out of his way.

* * * *

Janice clicked her gum, her lip freezing in the typical "you are shit" sneer she reserved for people that fell short of expectation. He'd seen that look a lot. *God she's a bitch.*

"Sat in my office for fifteen minutes waiting for you...got the crud floating around station. I feel like hell, and what am I doing?" she quipped, before pulling a tissue out of her pocket and blowing her nose. The always-pronounced wrinkles around her mouth, the crow's feet taking flight from the corners of her eyes, and her sunken cheeks were even more pronounced than usual.

"I don't know," Jacoby responded, quietly.

"...waiting on you," she growled, irritably, "then had to take three elevators and walk all the way up here to D ring, just to stand outside your room for another fifteen minutes. More waiting, Jacoby. That's thirty minutes of my life I'm neva getting back, Jack. Jack...Jack...Jack," Janice snapped, turning and traipsing stiffly down the hall.

He followed, his stomach turning sour.

"Incident follow-ups every morning, first thing...always, always, always, unless you're crippled or maimed beyond saving. Reminder went out to your PDP. Ain't my trouble if you choose not to read it, or you broke that, too," Janice snapped, when he didn't respond.

Jacoby hated it when she called him Jack, and even more when she intentionally rhymed his name into a sentence. Thankfully, their walk to the elevator passed in silence. He fumbled in his pocked for his data point, but it wasn't there. He didn't remember the last time he'd seen it, actually.

The elevator hummed quietly as it plummeted down the gravity tube. His stomach did a little jig and gurgled loudly. Janice mumbled something snarky.

"What was that?" he asked.

She turned, smacking her gum, but intentionally looked away, in the "you're not good enough to look at, right now" manner that drove him crazy.

"Didn't say nothing!"

Painted hair, nails, and lips, to cover the cracked and rotting flesh beneath, the voice said again, but it wasn't Janice. He could see her face and her lips didn't move.

Jacoby reached up and rubbed his temples, the start of a headache just then forming. They walked out and onto the curving path of D ring's lowest level, until Janice stopped at the massive transit elevators. They long ride to the production hub passed quietly, the length of the station zipping along around them.

The elevator chimed loudly as it reached its final destination, the doors opening to the familiar noise wash of the production station. He followed Janice through pre-production, past racks of cavitation chisels, laser bores, and hydraulic ratchets. Runner drones hummed by, pushing gravity carts full of ore en-route to processing for enrichment. Just another day cracking space rocks, only he wasn't a part of it.

Everything was stained with grease and rock dust, the familiar patina and oily smell an odd comfort. He looked down at his hands, the cracks and swirls on his skin stained with the same patina. This station, the ore they mined, and the rocks floating in the nearby belt were a part of him, and he them. No one could take that away – not Janice, not Anna's parents. No one.

Half of the overhead lights were still dark, leaving the space between banks and the corners in heavy shadow. The darkness was comforting. Jacoby spotted Mike at his locker, his coveralls pulled half on. He mouthed "what the f...?" but turned back to his locker as Janice noticed. He'd tell him later...if he had a later, or maybe not...not after his comments about Anna. Yuri joked that Janice likely ate her young, so Jacoby didn't feel confident in his future.

Janice turned into the conference room, pausing to drag her glossy fingernails down Shane, the foreman's, arm. He turned and flashed her a stiff smile, before they all filed into the room. Jacoby waited for Janice and Shane to sit, before sliding into the lone chair on the opposite side. He instantly felt like a child, sent to the principal's office for punishment, and shrunk a little deeper into the chair.

"Coffee?" Shane asked, looking to both Janice and Jacoby.

"Just water, please," he said.

Jacoby liked Shane. He was former military, soft spoken, but fair with everyone – the makings of a good boss.

"Yeah, sweetie! I like it black," Janice said, tickling Shane's arm with her fingernails again. Then as he left, she looked at Jacoby, her smile dying, and said, "We'll get started.

Shuffling papers, Janice smashed her bony rear deeper into the chair, as if trying to grind a softer spot into the seat with her pelvis. *Try a pillow, skeleton queen,* he thought, irritably.

We could soften the old bones for her, the soft voice said again, and Jacoby shifted uncomfortably in his chair. An electric tingle shot down into his arms a moment later, his fingers convulsing against the armrests.

"The union requires that I notify you that this follow-up is strictly administrative, and you will be paid the normal non-duty pay for this time.

Me, personally, I think it's a crock of shit. But I've got to say it, so there," she said, spitting the words as she lined up the forms neatly before her.

Shane returned, dropping a bottle of purified water before Jacoby, and a stained coffee mug before Janice. He slid into the seat, carefully, but subtly, sliding over to give himself some extra room.

"The form is simple, by the numbers... I've already filled out most of the information, so you just need to listen and at the end, sign. No talking. First, you disregarded a void warning prior to rock processing. The logs were pulled, and we confirmed that you deleted the warning and manually triggered processing. The company considers any tampering with warnings or logs an automatic write up and six month probation. Second, you fused your plasma saw...which I shouldn't have to tell you is an incredibly expensive piece of hardware. The saw is a total loss," Janice paused, wiping a bit of smudged mascara from beneath her eye and letting her palm fall with a loud *slap* onto the table. "I'd can your worthless ass for those two alone, but as Shane here reminded me, the union has precedent, as you requested medical treatment afterwards I cannot fire you. We're also running short on qualified rock crackers, so Planitex has been ordered to issue *leniency,*" she said, spitting the word.

Worthless is words, air, expelled with no value. False face and bloated words, the voice whispered, accompanied by a loud ringing in his ears.

He looked to Shane and then turned around in his chair, but there was no one else in the room. Who or what was he hearing? Jacoby inserted a finger into his ear and wiggled it around violently, but the noise didn't relent. When he turned back, Janice was watching him, her gum hanging over her lip in a failed bubble. She wrinkled up her face in disgust and proceeded to blow her nose messily into a tissue.

And I'm disgusting? the ringing returned, and he wiggled his finger in the other ear.

"Is everything okay? Are we good to proceed? Or, do you need a moment to pick your nose, too?" she asked, her voice dripping with false sincerity.

Jacoby flushed warm and promptly sat on his hands. "Doc said I probably picked up the bug making its way around station. Said it would be a few days before I was better," he responded, avoiding her gaze.

"Yes, ill," she said. "That brings me to the next portion...drugs and alcohol. Due to some...personal concerns, the company is hereby proceeding with a standard incident blood screening, and has already taken action to remove you from any production work until results are returned. "

"Drugs? I wasn't on drugs," Jacoby argued, looking to Shane.

The foreman immediately held up his hands, "Jacoby, it's not our call. The company has the right to request screens on any post incident."

Jacoby's insides wound up into a tight ball, his anger threatening to burst forth. He knew several workers who had incidents on the production floor, one even that month, but not a single one had been forced into a review, or worse, wait on a toxicology screen – they just went back to work.

"That's bullshit," he grumbled, "Dan Seevers crushed a cradle because he didn't set the mooring legs correctly. He didn't miss any time. Bob Harskens ran his plasma saw out of high temp synthetic lubricant and burned it to slag. Did he miss any time? Gerhold Driver dropped a two ton hunk of rock on his workstation, and he didn't..."

"Jacoby, we're just following the company's directive," Shane argued, cutting him off, but Janice silenced him with a hand to the shoulder, her crooked smile firmly in place.

"I met quota every month last year...even doubled it two months running. I finished top five in production three out of four quarters, but since I signed my new contract all I get is crap, junk rock with no trace or valuable minerals, while other guys get cherry 'stroids full of palladium, tungsten, and tritium. I can't make bonus anymore. This is a load of crap. Give me something to work with, not this worthless..." Jacoby said, his voice quickly rising, but he mastered his temper just in time. "I just need a break. I'm sick, and got overheated. I got too hot and blacked out. It won't happen again."

He knew it wasn't just that. It was the drinking, the stress coming from working six out of every seven days, and all his fuck up's in between. Damn, he should have told Anna about the contract.

Janice's painted nails tapped a quiet cadence against the table, her lips pulling into a smug smile. She had him right where she wanted him, at her mercy, and he knew it.

"Jacoby, you know pre-processing is automated and doesn't play favorites. The contract *you* signed states that we, as the company, have the right to request a post incident. You have the right to deny, but that is the same as a positive test, and results in instant contract termination. Is that what you are doing? Because I would love to..." Janice said, but Jacoby wasn't listening, he was too distracted by the ringing in his ears and the rising anger that he couldn't quite suppress. His knuckles had gone white around the armrests.

"Can I talk to you outside for a moment?" Shane interrupted, and abruptly the two pushed their chairs back and disappeared out into the hall.

Jacoby sat, his fingernails tap-tap-tapping a cadence against the table. He didn't consciously do it, but his hands needed something to do. The fluorescent light bank flickered overhead, the ballast buzzing in time with the ringing in his ears. His fingernails dug into the table, the urge to gouge the thin veneer off the cheap furniture abrupt and almost undeniable. Shane and Janice's muffled voices echoed in from the hall, their words unintelligible and hollow – more white noise to grate against him.

They conspire. Peel, peel, peel away the false faces. The truth lies beneath, the voice urged, strangely fixating on the cheap table, as if it was Janice, the source of his troubles.

"Who said that?" he asked, but there came no response, save the buzzing of the cheap overhead light.

His gaze snapped up - first to his water bottle and then to Janice's cup of coffee. He looked to the door, and grabbed the cup, but the hot liquid slopped over the side and onto his hand, dribbling down onto his pants. The pain snapped him to clarity, the red haze of anger fading away. Suddenly, he didn't want to throw the scalding coffee in Janice's face when she reemerged. That would get him more than fired, but perhaps detained for assault and thrown in a station security cell. He'd find himself stuffed on an ore transport back to Earth and God knows what else.

Anna would have to leave, too. Her parents would be vindicated, and she would run home to what's his face Kopecky, his well-appointed condo in the Cloud Towers, and his private shuttle. Their friendship would fail just like her mom predicted.

Jacoby lifted the coffee and licked the rim, running his tongue all the way around the cracked mug, and quickly set it down in its previous spot. *Enjoy that, old prune,* he thought, wiping the spilled coffee on his pants below the table.

Should have spit in it, all the better for flavor, the voice said. Jacoby smacked the side of his head and turned in the chair, but he was all alone. He looked at his hand, several of the nails cracked and split.

The door clicked, Janice and Shane reappearing from the hallway. Jacoby took a deep, cleansing breath, and willed himself to stay calm – no matter what happened. Janice pulled a wad of tissues out of her pocket and blew her nose loudly, then stuffed them back into her pocket. She scooped the coffee mug off the table and lifted it to her lips. Jacoby leaned forward, coughing into his hand to hide a smirk. She moved over to stand above him, the overhead lighting making her eyes look sunken, the lines and wrinkles even deeper and harder.

Prune.

"Thank your, foreman," she said, turning back to Shane. "Jacoby, you will take two days personal, and as long as your screen comes back clean, you can return to full work. We're done here, I don't have the patience for more," she said, coughing into her arm, then pulled the papers together and stuffed them in an envelope.

Jacoby cleared his throat and stood, swiping his sleeve across his forehead. It wasn't warm in the office. Quite the opposite, but he'd started sweating anyway. Janice lifted the coffee mug to her lips and took another long pull, grunting when she was done, like usual.

Little piggy pig pig, the voice chimed in. Jacoby looked to Shane, but the foreman hadn't said anything. Was he really hearing voices?

"Enjoy your coffee and have a nice day," he said and walked out of the room. He turned the corner, desperate to put as much distance between him and Janice as possible. He considered taking a trip up to see the doctor again, but wondered if admitting he was hearing voices was perhaps not a good idea.

It's stress, that's all it is. Fix things with Anna, and talk it all out. She always knows what to do.

"You just hit your head when you fell. That's all. Just hit your head," he mumbled, and stepped back onto the elevator.

0830 HOURS

Anna tidied up the bedroom, folded the blanket on the bench by the window, and reconstituted a coffee cube. Steam rose from the machine, the smell of brewing coffee almost instantly filling their confined space of D ring. It smelled less like coffee and more like hot rubber – nothing like the premium organic roast her parents always bought, but it was better than anything they served in the employee lounges.

The thought of home instantly threw her back into a funk. Even millions of miles away, her mother was controlling her life. It was bad enough when they were still planet side, her mother almost constantly questioning, doubting, and redirecting, always subtly, and always just loud enough for her to hear. How far away did they need to go to shed her parent's bigotry and derision? Could they ever go far enough, or was the damage already done?

"No daughter of mine is going to be friends with a mechanic's kid," she cursed and shook her head. Her folks never took the time to see Jacoby for who he really was. He was the only one who listened when she talked...who took the time to actually know her.

I hope you're happy, mother...not that anything could ever make you happy, she thought bitterly, pulling a ceramic mug out of the cupboard.

Anna filled the mug and lifted it to her lips just as her PDP vibrated on the counter next to the sink. A heartbeat later and it started to ring, The Great Gate of Kiev by Mussorgsky breaking the silence. Anna set her coffee down and picked up the data point, the transparent polymer shell reading her handprint and glowing to life. A triangle flashed on screen, indicating a waiting message.

Coby, she thought, her stomach lurching. He didn't talk about it, but she knew things hadn't been going well. She felt a wave of guilt rise up inside. She knew he was struggling with work – the long, back to back to back shifts, and yet insisted on struggling in silence. He'd plucked her away from her fucked up life back home, even when her parents cut her off, and now he was killing himself to make sure she had everything she needed.

"Anna, you dumb bitch," she whispered, taking another sip of bitter coffee. He'd taken the new contract because they didn't know where they would go or do if he hadn't. Hell, their plan never really extended far beyond get off Earth.

Anna opened the message with a swipe and her hope fell. It wasn't from Coby, but Lana in Sys Ops.

[Lana] - I know it's your day off, and you're only part time, but could you cover a shift today? Everyone is f*&#!g sick.

Anna read the message and took a large sip of coffee before responding.

"That's fine, I guess," she said, the data point transcribing automatically, "how soon do you need me?"

[Lana] - As soon as you can get down here. We've got overdue maintenance on C ring's faulty O^2 recirculation module today, and just sent another operator home after he hurled all over his dash. Place smells like old CO^2 scrubbers and barf.

Anna cringed. Nothing unraveled her stomach faster than the sound or smell of someone else's puke. She wanted to stick around and talk things over with Coby, but knew Lana wouldn't have reached out if she had a host of other options.

"I'll be right down, but you're not sticking me in his control pod," she responded, and downed the last of the coffee.

Lana's response chimed in almost immediately - an animated hand forming a thumb's up, followed by a winking face sticking its tongue out.

Dropping the mug into the sink, Anna set the data point down and headed for the bathroom. After a quick shower, she pulled on a work jumpsuit and tied her hair up. She closed her bedroom door and walked by Coby's room. It was a mess, dirty work clothes strewn across the floor, a few vaccu-seal wrappers scattered amongst them.

"An olive branch," she whispered, and quickly swept through the room, picking up, tidying, and dumping the dirty clothes in the auto-wash.

A maintenance bot hummed down the hallway as she swiped her wrist across the controls, locking the door to their quarters. The dog-sized machine cleaned and polished the floor, purring quietly in the confined space.

She skipped the habitat elevators and turned left at Spire Tunnel three, the relatively narrow conduit connecting D ring to the Ops and Support Spire at the station's center. She stepped into the elevator, banks of flat lights bathing the confined space in a blue-green glow.

"System Operations," the elevator said as she stepped onto the magnetic pad, the door closing behind her. The capsule shot up the tunnel, her knees bending as gravity increased. The overhead lights dimmed as the solar shade adjusted, the black void of space hovering just beyond the elevator capsule and its transparent tube.

It never ceased to amaze her – the sheer scope of...blank space. C ring rotated below them, the shielded ceramic and titanium skin dotted with flood and marker lights, stars twinkling against the black backdrop beyond it.

It would never feel like home to Anna, but it was peaceful and quiet, not to mention blissfully removed from the frantic rat race of earth's social mosh pit, where wealth, station, and social integration meant more than basic survival. The new migration race off world just made it all worse. Corporate and colonial expansions were supposed to relieve some of the stresses of overcrowding and social warfare. Unfortunately, it only exacerbated existing issues, and created a host of new ones.

"They can keep that madness," she said, genuinely happy to be away from that particular brand of chaos.

Taking a deep breath, Anna watched the station zoom by, until the capsule slowed and docked with the spire. The doors opened with a *whoosh,* just as the magnetic pad turned off. Anna stepped into the hall, automatic lights flickering to life as she entered the spire's atrium. She passed walls of lockers, a decon shower, and a wall of Kravinski escape pods. She couldn't fathom cramming her body into one of the spherical lifeboats and willingly jettisoning herself into the cold vacuum of space. There was a better chance that someone asphyxiated to death before they were retrieved. It was the stuff of nightmares.

Her shoes padded quietly against the clean, almost sterile floor. Gravity was heavier here than in D ring, by at least a tenth of a percent. Perhaps it was a coil out of calibration, or a dozen other sensitive components in the spire's gravity generator. Most couldn't differentiate a difference, but for some reason, Anna could.

She made her way down the narrow stair, curving around and around towards The Hive, the station's nerve center. Tall acrylic windows shone to her left, sleek, blade-like servers dominating the center of the spire, their polycarbonate bodies connected by a complicated series of coolant lines and fiber cables. They fascinated Anna, in no small part due to their logic based AI, which was responsible for every action, consequential reaction, light, outlet, solar cell, and computation on the station.

A far cry from Medieval Literature and Foundational Cultural Studies, she thought. Logical AI and quantum computing had become more than a way to fill the quiet hours while Jacoby worked. She downloaded schematics, theoretical papers, and even user manuals to learn more. She applied for a server technician post – after all, everyone on station had to work. The system auto rejected her application, responding with recommended posts, because everyone had to work the allotted minimum hours each cycle, or risk reassignment or a profit share decrease.

"No dead weight," administrator Evans wrote in her monthly communique. In the end, Anna took a Maintenance Operator position – it was administrative work, but she knew the department head, Lana, from social circles back home, and it afforded her a point with which to work and learn. *Maybe someday,* she thought, jumping off the last step and walking through the Hive's fire door.

The Hive was a single, round room, a semi-circular desk dominating its center. Flat, transparent monitors hung all around the desk, constantly cycling data from hundreds of different sensor points – reactor temp, solar panel generation, water filtration output. All station data flowed to this point. A half dozen technicians worked at the circular station, talking into cheek mics, typing on keyboards, or watching monitors. The room was warm, loud, and to Anna, awesome.

Lana's head popped out from around a monitor, her face brightening as she approached.

"Thank...God!" she gasped, rocking back in her chair.

"I'm here," Anna said, sheepishly, holding her arms out in a self-conscious "ta da".

"Girl, you just saved my life. Everyone is getting sick with this damned virus that schmuck brought on the last freighter. I can't man a shift without someone running a fever or puking their guts out. We're behind on monthly preventative maintenance and have half the water recirculation system offline and in need of new pumps and liners."

"How can I help? Point me where you need me," Anna said.

"Any other day, I'd say grab a code scanner, grease gun, and a pair of pliers, and start fixing some doors around here, cause nothing breaks more, but shit, our usual problems are the least of our worries right now."

"I wouldn't know the first thing about fixing a motorized door, but if you gave me a schematic and some time, I could probably figure it out."

"That's why I love you, girl...straight to the point and always willing to learn!" Lana replied, pulling her into an uncharacteristic hug. "Most of the techs around here complain if they have to work on something too simple, and then in the next breath complain if they have to work on something more complicated. Today, it is the oxygen recirculation unit on C ring. It faulted out last night, just like it did last cycle, but it was always bad code or a motor driver failure. We've been able to keep it running despite itself with little fixes and resets. But this time it popped a high-pressure alarm, and then a compressor coil failure, so we're worried that there might actually be something wrong with it this time. We shut the whole module down and isolated the circuit, but we need to get in there and check it out before we can risk powering it up again. Habitats in C ring are already getting a little stuffy...scrubbers are working, and we've diverted breathing air from B and D, but they aren't meant for that kind of volume. Maintenance pods one and two are assigned on other critical tasks, uh, pod three is out of service, so you're in pod four."

"You weren't joking. Everything's falling apart around here," Anna said, one of the techs turning and throwing her a not-to-subtle scoff.

"Welcome to Planitex Sys Ops, where everything is older than it should be and getting new parts is like asking for somebody to hand over their kidneys. It's like firefighting, except you're floating in a vacuum, the fire doesn't follow the rules, and you can't use water!" Lana said, laughing sardonically.

"That sounds horrible!" Anna laughed, but her mirth died away quickly. "Wait, pod four isn't the...?" she started to ask, but Lana's expression told her everything she needed to know.

"It has been cleaned and sanitized. I promise."

"I don't do puke. It makes me sick..."

Lana squeezed her arm, just as her cheek mic lit up. "You've reached Lana, goddess of fiber and silicone-based processing, go for Sys Ops," she said, dropping into a seat and swiveling back towards the monitors. "Did you try unplugging it and plugging it back in?" she asked with a laugh, but turned and mouthed "I'm sorry".

Anna cringed as a barking voice rang back out of the ear mic. *Someone's not in the mood for jokes,* she thought, and headed for the dark ready room, a solitary red light glowing just above the doorway. Cots lined the walls to her left. The closest ones were empty, but a dark form filled the last in the line.

Probably the on call service tech from the previous night's shift, she figured, turning right and stepping into the small maintenance dock. A spherical service pod sat to her left, its spider-like tool arms retracted next to its body. "Ace" had been painted over the small hatch.

She pulled on her emergency EVA suit, hooked a helmet seal to her neck flange, and pulled her helmet out of its cubby. Anna walked over to hatch four, the L.E.D indicator above the portal glowing green. She turned the wheel, pulled the hatch open, and stepped inside the service pod.

Once in the seat, Anna strapped in and waved her wrist over the control console. The pod hummed to life, the H.U.D appearing on the clear, polycarbonate shell. After a brief warmup, the solar shade lightened, the black shell turning transparent. Space loomed before her, the habitat rings curving around the spire like the wheels of a massive wagon.

"Two thousand people living in a compressed can way out here in space," she whispered, taking it all in.

A sync notice popped up onto her H.U.D. She accepted and her mic crackled in response.

"My display says Anna is my operator. That can't be...can it? I know Anna, but she hardly ever works," a man's voice filled her ear.

"Yes, Brad. It's Anna," she said, manually guiding her pod up the spire's length, the rigid umbilical connecting her pod to the station groaning slightly. "They asked me to work since everyone is getting sick."

"Ain't that the truth," Brad grunted, his service pod coming into view, its spider-like arms already extended.

"So we're servicing the Charlie ring oxygen re-circulator unit?" she asked, eager to get Brad on point. He was a nice guy, but also flirty, and at times, crude.

"That's the rumor. I'll line up now, why don't you pull the blueprints, conduit diagrams, and procedure. I'm syncing to you now."

Anna ran her finger down the display on her right, selecting subsystems and document folders, while commanding the pod with her left. She came to a docking clamp, secured the pod in place, and extended the umbilical out to its full length. A moment later, a large technical schematic appeared on the shell of her pod, the transparent polycarbonate awash in a complicated maze of marked wires, coolant lines, and oxygen feed pumps. She'd never worked on anything so complex, let alone guide a sensitive repair on one. The feed from Brad's pod popped up next, filtering through a ticker of sensor data and his suit's bio readouts.

"This is a far cry from high frequency beacons and point to point laser comm arrays," she said, nervously, skimming through the shutdown and startup procedures. Unfortunately, most of it was in Taiwanese. The portion of it that was in English wasn't much better.

"It's a piece of cake, Anna. You just feed me the information I need as I ask for it. Easy peezy," Brad replied, his pod moving into position before the modular re-circulator. It looked like a house-sized box on the inside of the ring, massive, red explosive placards visible even from her distance.

"Pump two shows a fault, and pump three tripped its breaker on a low coolant alarm. The procedure says to 'isolate the affected pump from and the break circuit. Purge pump coolant lines, vent work space, then make initialize manual rotation for to ensure pump bearings is not frozen'. Jesus, who writes these things?"

Brad laughed. "People who never have to service these things in vacuum, that's for sure!"

Anna watched the feed, the camera inside Brad's pod knocked askew and showing only the side of his head and one arm. She considered asking him to adjust it, but thought better of it.

"The Com fiber was broken. That's most likely the problem. These units are designed to fault out if they become disconnected from the network. Give me a sec, then we can power it up and see if it faults out again. By the way, how have you managed to not get sick?" Brad asked, working the delicate controls to guide the tool arms.

"Sounds good," Anna said, reading more of the schematic, and struggling with how to answer the question. "I don't know, maybe I'm just lucky."

"Okay? How about Jacoby? Is he okay?" Brad grunted.

"He's...well, fine."

"Fine as in 'there's some shit going on I don't want to talk to you about, Brad', or like, 'he's fine fine'?"

"He's under a lot of pressure. I think his supervisor is screwing him around," Anna said, and immediately regretted it. Brad had a nasty ability to get her talking about stuff that wasn't his business.

"My ex used to call those 'rough patches'. Of course she was usually complaining about me. She wouldn't talk to me for days, sometimes weeks at a time. She said I was pulling away from her," Brad laughed, but it was a hollow sound. She heard his pain. "Ain't that some shit? She said I was pulling away from her, when she was the one who wouldn't talk to me. Then I come home one day and find her blowing some maintenance guy in my bed. Guy has the gall to look over to the nightstand, see the picture of me, and then look right at me and act surprised. I mean, who do you think the guy in the picture is, ya know? The one watching you get your knob polished?"

"That's…horrible," Anna said, continuing to scan down the document. He'd done it again. He'd gotten them talking about his failed relationships.

"Yeah, and I didn't even kick his ass. I just grabbed my shit and left…okay. I've got the broken section of fiber cut. I'm going to patch it now."

Anna watched Brad through the camera; the tech slumped over the controls, a water bulb floating just over his shoulder. She paged down through more of the poorly written instructions, a series of three-dimensional icons hovering over lines of text and blocking some of the words. She looked back up to the camera as one of the pod's service arms lifted up a cut section of fiber optic cable, another appendage working to splice it in place.

"Why didn't I bring my coffee? This is like reading a dictionary for fun."

Brad laughed, his voice breaking up over the radio.

"You stop laughing. You need to pay attention to what you're doing," she scolded him.

"I could splice fiber in my sleep. That leaves me plenty of attention for you, baby," he said, baiting her.

"I'm not your 'baby', Brad," Anna said. The last thing she needed was for word getting through sys ops that she was flirting with Brad. The guy had the kind of reputation that could give a girl an STD.

"Hold on, this section titled 'For make safety restart operations' says to purge O^2 lines as well as the compartment case before restarting," she said, paging down to another section. "Make sure you ventilate the unit and purge the lines before you finish the splice and restart the unit."

"I'm…done," Brad said, grunting. "It's okay. It was just a broken fiber. I'm going to let the unit power up now."

"Brad I don't think that's a good idea…" She watched the service pod's arms extend out, tuck the fiber back into the compartment, and pull back again.

A new data thread appeared on her H.U.D as her computer read the data streaming in from the O^2 separator unit.

"Already done, sweet thing. Just relax. Don't make this repair more complicated than it really is. We've got a whole laundry list of things after this, so no time for unnecessary steps today. You and I are gonna..." Brad went silent for a moment, and she watched as he typed on the keyboard in his pod, the dash alight in bright buttons and gauges.

"What is it?"

"The unit is powering up. Pumps one through four are showing green, pump five is not responding. I'm showing positive pressure at two times atmosphere. Can you confirm?"

Anna swiped her screen over and a new window appeared almost immediately. She tapped on the status icon and a number of smaller windows popped up, streaming through lines and lines of data. She watched C ring's atmospheric composition slowly tick towards green.

"Flow is good. But I'm not getting any data back on pump number five either..."

"I hear something. Maybe one of the pumps is malfunctioning," Brad said, just as a red light flashed on her screen.

"Brad, I'm showing an over temp alarm on pumps five and six," Anna said. Her screen suddenly lit up like Christmas, white and green gauges flashing crimson. She looked up just as a distant *pop* sounded, the oxygen recirculation unit exploding in a cloud of expanding gas and metal fragments. The armored, ceramic outer skin pealed open like an over pressurized soda can, a secondary explosion sending a geyser-like plume of metal and broken shielding shooting violently into the void.

"Oh my god! Brad, are you all right?"

Brad's service pod spun back towards the spire, its multitude of tool arms all extending and contracting.

"A..a I...ca..t c..trol." Her radio crackled, every other word drowned out by the violent hiss of static.

"Lana, the oxygen unit...it exploded," Anna yelled into her mic, but there was no response.

A large chunk of debris bounced off the station next to her pod, the resounding *thunk* reverberating through the metal all around her. She spun away, shielding her face as smaller pieces of debris peppered her solar shield, clattering against the thick acrylic like rain. Panic tightened her chest. Her gaze swept over her H.U.D, the pod controls, and her radio panel.

A window popped up on her display as Brad's pod continued to drift towards the station.

"Anna...Anna, can you hear me? What in the fucking hell is going on out here? I'm showing complete atmospheric loss in one, two...no three sections of C ring from compartments one through four and the panel for oxygen generation has gone black. We lost three cameras, too. I can't see anything." Lana's face popped up on the video window, a crowd of other people standing behind her.

"The oxygen module is gone! It...it exploded! And I can't get through to Brad on his coms."

1100 HOURS

Jacoby wandered around after his meeting with Janice, drifting from corridor to corridor, aimlessly walking. He drifted into the commissary, strolling through shop after shop, picking through racks of criminally overpriced merchandise.

What does a mining station in deep space need with a sports outlet?

He strolled out of the sporting goods nook, and passed an electronics shop, a three dimensional vid commercial blaring loudly, the animated, borderline-hysterical Japanese teenagers singing praises about the new iPhone jaw implant interface.

Jacoby sifted through his thoughts, trying to block out the market's overwhelming sights and sounds. There was just too much of everything – light, noise, and stuff. He felt overly sensitive, raw even, as if every nerve was hanging just above his skin.

He walked back out of the shop and strolled to the railing, resting on his forearms. The lower floor hung just twenty feet below. More shops lined either wall while small, automated merchant kiosks dominated the space between, their holographic ads filling the air with even more light and noise. A lazy trickle of people walked in either direction, stopping outside shops to interact with three-dimensional A.I. ad interfaces.

*People...*they were more distracting than anything else – the way they looked, moved, and smelled. He couldn't seem to stop staring at women, the bounce of their breasts or the jiggle of their butts as they walked.

Jacoby turned away and strolled down the way, a pair of station security officers walking out of the next shop side by side. The woman tucked her purchase into a bag, and looked up, throwing him a friendly smile.

She was tall and athletically built. The sides of her head were shaved, the longer hair on top a rich auburn color. A splash of freckles covered her short, narrow nose, and her eyes were strikingly green, accented by the slightest trace of metallic-blue eyeshadow and dark eyeliner.

He walked past, his gaze just catching on the neckline of her tight, black and gray jumpsuit, where the zipper hung loose, exposing the soft and flawless skin below. Jacoby drew in a breath through his nose and smelled her – a complicated and sensual mixture of vanilla sweet and amber spice.

There was something else under it all...something that immediately elicited a fire inside him.

He spun and faltered a step, his gaze roaming down the woman's figure as she walked away, from her bouncing hair, slender, muscular arms, to the flexing curves of her hips, rear, and thighs. An uncomfortable pressure formed in his head and a thrill coursed down his body, settling like an undeniable itch in his groin.

"Damn," Jacoby cursed and doubled over, blood rushing to his pelvis so fast his head went fuzzy and his legs unsteady. He staggered forward, slapping the wall with a hand, just managing to keep from falling on his face. Bright stars burst before his eyes and that irritating ringing noise filled his ears.

"...hey, buddy, are you okay?" someone asked, and he felt hands hook under his arm. He could barely hear them over the ringing.

"Are you sick? Do you need us to call for help?" a woman asked. They'd come back to help him, but damn, she was too close now. Jacoby kept his eyes down but he could smell her, could almost feel the heat radiating off her body. She was right next to him, her hair practically tickling his neck. Yes, it was red, fiery red with subtle streaks of blond.

"Can you hear ...?" the woman asked, but paused, sucking in an almost startled breath through her nose, and then coughed.

Jacoby straightened as she pulled away, his eyes sweeping quickly over the man in a desperate attempt not to look at his female counterpart. He was tall and slender, with a pronounced Adam's apple and long, angular face. He looked strangely like the scarecrows from his great grandparents' farm, save the flannel shirt and straw hat.

She deserves better.

"What is the matter, Lex? Are you okay?" the man asked, moving to grab the woman.

Lex...she has a name. He didn't know why it mattered, but some part of his brain felt it was important.

Jacoby's gaze crawled over to her, despite his every effort to stop it. She stood half a dozen paces away, facing him and breathing hard, a hand held over her sternum. They locked eyes for a moment - hers were wide, the pupils blown. He'd seen the effects of stims and other synth drugs with Mike to recognize the symptoms. Strange, her eyes hadn't looked like that a moment ago.

Is she high?

Jacoby's gaze crawled down to her breasts, a portion of his mind slowly pulling the zipper down, her heady scent increasing as the jumpsuit pulled away, her soft, pink nipples begging to be kissed. Her chest heaved as she ripped off the suit, her tongue curling up and sliding teasingly over her top lip. She reached down, glossy, painted nails bunching up in her panties, the sheer fabric pulling tight and starting to tear.

"I'm...I'm alright, F-F-Fred," Lex stammered, "I don't know what happened. I got a little light headed and my heart started to race. Whoa, that was weird."

Lex. How soft she must be. Soft skin, soft hair. How soft, how inviting inside!

Jacoby's face turned hot, a painful twitch shooting down into his right arm. Lex was still clothed, but in his mind she was naked and bending over, supporting her weight against the wall, begging him to touch her. She didn't want Fred. She wanted him.

Red hair, like fire. Hot, burning fire. That is what I want. Taste her, feel her, inside and out.

Jacoby turned away. His thoughts were crazy...out of control. But he couldn't deny the attraction. His pelvis ached with an unrealized need.

"Hey, buddy, just relax. Maybe you should sit, and we'll call the med techs."

"I think I just...I think I'm," Jacoby stammered, his hands shaking against his knees. He couldn't seem to straighten his thoughts, and didn't feel himself at all – ill, angry, and violently aroused at the same time. He wanted to cry, vomit, and have sex, the sensations so strong he almost couldn't bear them together.

Red hair, like fire...that's what I like. The thoughts banged around in his head, swirling around Lex's now naked body as she writhed on the ground, her fingers working seductively between her legs.

"No. I'm not hearing things. I just hit my head, that's all," he mumbled under his breath. He didn't know where the strange thoughts were coming from, but they weren't him damn it! A foreign impulse shot into his right arm and chest, his back stiffening in response. He pushed away from the wall and stood.

"Oh my god," Lex exclaimed, and turned, suddenly looking at the ground.

"Dude, you're fucking crazy. What in the hell is that about, people don't need to see that shit," Fred said, jumping in front of Lex protectively.

"I'm okay, b-b-but thanks," Jacoby stammered and looked down. He had an enormous erection, his pants pulled painfully tight. He kicked away from the wall, cutting quickly into the shop just behind them.

A clerk looked up from the desk as he ran by, brushing up against a rack of shirts and nearly knocking it to the ground. Jacoby ran into the bulkhead, pushed off down the hall to his left, tore open the bathroom door, and jumped inside.

He stood in the dark for a long while, fighting to catch his breath, his hands and feet twitching violently. The impulses didn't slow and Lex was still there in his mind, moaning his name, sweat glistening on her chest and face. She spread her legs, gesturing for him, begging for him to thrust himself inside her. His hips twitched, the muscles in his legs going tight.

NO! Stop! he yelled, pounding his fists against the sides of his head. "Get out of my head. Get out of my head!"

I can't. I won't. I can't.

Jacoby closed his eyes, sucked in a deep breath and pushed it out, then took another. His heart was racing, the blood practically roaring in his veins and throbbing between his legs.

He focused on the space beyond the outermost bulkheads – the void, cold and black. More air rushed into his lungs, and he pushed it back out. The chaos in his mind started to calm. He reached over and swiped his hand over the light sensor, the LED bank above the mirror blinking on. The cool, bluish light stung his eyes, but he refused to blink.

Jacoby leaned in apprehensively, wrapping his fingers around the narrow stainless steel sink. He stared into the mirror, his reflection gazing right back. His face was red and sweaty, a vein on his forehead thrumming gently in time with his heart.

"You've just been through a lot lately. It's stress, that's all. It gets worse when you're around people. I'm not cracking up. You just need time...to...relax," he said, and his reflection nodded back. "And you haven't had a girlfriend in a...long time."

Breath in, breath out. Repeat.

Yes, relax, after you have fucked her brains out, the voice said, his grin widening. His left eye twitched in a wink and for a moment, a shadow of dark veins appeared around his eyes. No...he was seeing things – a trick of the light, or his stress.

He ignored the vulgar voice and focused on the dark void again, imagining a place free from sound and heat.

"I just need some peace...some quiet," he mumbled, closing his eyes and letting his head droop.

Breath in, breath out. Cleanse...and push out the stress.

I am still here. I have been, I am, and I will be here.

"It's not real. I'm not hearing anything," he whispered, willfully ignoring the stray thoughts.

When he opened his eyes again he was staring at his tented pants.

"I can't go back out there like this," he said, wiping his sweaty forehead on his sleeve. He was still sweating and shaking, but his heart wasn't beating out of control anymore.

Jacoby unbuttoned his pants. He pulled the elastic band of his compression shorts out, his erection jumping forth like an uncoiling spring. He knew his dick well, hell they'd been connected at the hip his entire life, and partners in crime since puberty. But this...this was bigger and harder than anything he could remember. It was so hard it hurt.

Coward. It is for her, not your hand.

He ignored his runaway thought and sat down on the toilette, scared to even look at his own dick for the first time in his life. Trying to lock his mind on anything else, Jacoby reached down and took a hold. The bathroom smelled like wintergreen urinal deodorizers and orange peel-based hand cleaner...hardly an atmosphere conducive to mastering one's impulses. There was another scent there, too. He smelled it wafting out of his shirt and off his skin.

Crack a rock with something inside it, melt my saw to slag, get put on administrative leave, Janice yells at me, and now I'm jerking off in a commissary bathroom...and I smell funny.

Twenty minutes later, Jacoby pushed back out of the bathroom, his arm sore from one of the most awkward and difficult masturbation experiences of his life. His pants were still tight, but no longer painfully so. He ducked out of the shop, careful not to make eye contact with the man sitting behind the counter.

Jacoby walked quickly out of the commissary, pressing the airlock button repeatedly as he waited for it to cycle. Finally, after an excruciating wait, the light above the wide door cycled to green and it whooshed open. He stepped inside, and turned, slapping the button to cycle it again.

He just needed some time – perhaps a shower, a cold one, and maybe a relaxing drink...or two. Then he would take a nap to help get his head right, and when he woke up everything would be right again. That would work, that would help him get her out of his thoughts.

A curvy figure stepped from around the corner, appearing in the wash of the bright and colorful light displays just as the door started to his shut.

Lex leaned out, looked right and then left, spotting him, her red hair and green eyes sparkling. She took a step forward, but then stopped, her hands clenching and unclenching at her sides. The zipper of her suit had been pulled down a little further, and this time it wasn't just in Jacoby's imagination. She licked her lips and took a breath to speak, but Jacoby turned away, cursing and forcing his thoughts to anything and everything else. The airlock door finally slid shut, the atmosphere equalizing and making his ears pop.

She wants us. The thought popped into his head just as the lights flickered overhead, and a loud claxon split the silence.

1500 HOURS

"This is what it looks like when the shit hits the fan," Anna mumbled, swiveling in her seat. She reached up and wiped her forehead before the sweat could run down into her eyes.

The pod smelled stale and humid, like stress – a musky, stuffy scent the small air scrubbers couldn't remove. She'd worked without a break since the explosion, relaying information, remotely rerouting oxygen supply lines, scanning schematics, and assisting the emergency techs.

A host of messages flooded onto her display, some automatically generated by the spire's emergency protocols, while others came in from Lana and the other control room workers. She flipped through them all, unsure what was actually important and what she could just skip.

"Anna, babe, how are you holding up out there?" Lana asked, her voice tight and thin over the com.

Anna swiped at her face again, flicked through another message, and reached over to turn the climate control all the way to cold.

"I'm in here...I'm safe enough, I guess," she said, eyeing the small spider web crack in her pod's solar shield. "How's Brad? Is he going to be all right?"

A heavy silence settled over the pod before Lana responded, the background noise of the control room filtering through like the buzz of angry insects.

"We took him to medical. He's going to be just fine. I'm worried about you. How are *you* holding up? Talk to me, girl?"

"I'm fine, well, but wish I could be doing more. I'm just sitting here. I could be..." Anna choked on her words as a body appeared in one of the station's floodlights. She forced her head down to the display and tapped at the screen, her hands shaking and numb.

A drone launched from the spire a hundred feet below, the autonomous worker bot sliding noiselessly on its small thrusters.

"Anna, I need an extra pair of hands," one of the techs said, his voice crackling distantly on the radio. She linked to his pod, remotely activating a matching pair of service arms.

"Tell me what you need me to do, Jerod," she said, scanning his tech credentials first. Damn her eyes ached and her butt felt flat. She'd been sitting in one place so long.

"We're cutting this damaged housing free so we can fit our patches but these conduit bundles are in the way. We don't want to cut them off and risk having too little to splice into later. I'd use the auto-sync to have the pod hold them out of the way, but there are just too damn many of them. I need an extra set of hands. Do you see them?"

Anna leaned in, wiping her eyes and spotted several thick masses of conduit and cables hanging out of the marred station's skin.

"Yes, I'll try," she said and worked the joystick on her left and right, the pod's arms moving in response. The delay was minimal, but still required a level of foresight and patience she wasn't used to. Anna missed the first bundle twice before finally capturing it in the claw and pulling it out of the way. She worked the second arm in, holding her breath as the four-fingered claw skipped off the armored cable and bounced back.

"Shit!" she cursed.

"Just relax and try again," Jerod said, his voice surprisingly calm, all things considered.

Anna took a deep breath, leaned in towards the monitor, and navigated the arm. This time the claw locked around the cable, and she successfully pulled it back.

"Nice one, Anna. Now lock those arms out of the way and we'll make our cuts," Jerod said.

She locked the controls and sat back, wringing her hands together.

"See, you are a real bad ass," Lana said, her voice crackling through the white noise. "Doubt me now? You are about the most valuable thing to me right now. I'm down three pods, half a dozen external cameras, and god knows what else. Don't worry about things inside...we're taking care of that. Pressure doors are sealed and we're doing emergency accountability. This is why we you're out there...my eyes and ears, and all that stuff...so just keep doing what you're doing."

"I'm in way over my head, Lana. I've never done most of this stuff before...outside simulations. And now I've got to do it all, and it all matters."

"Trial by fire, babe, and you're doing great. I'll buy you all the drinks you want when this is sorted out. For now, just keep being my rock out there."

How can I not worry about things inside...when there are people floating around out here that are supposed to be...in there? she thought, watching the drone approach the floating body.

The station worker floated, slowly spinning into and back out of the beam from a bright floodlight, disappearing into the black as the drone latched on and started dragging it back towards the station.

A service request popped up on her screen from one of the service technicians. Anna opened it, minimized the request, scrolled through her open schematics until she found the right one, attached it to the request, and fired it back.

A data feed flooded the monitor to her right as the technicians worked to make sense of the damage caused by the explosion.

Anna lifted her data point, opened her contacts, and clicked on Jacoby's icon. She wiped the sweat off her upper lip – damn the pod was warm – and started typing, her fingers trembling but more reliable than her voice.

Accident on C Ring. Did you hear? Are you okay? People are dead. Please tell me you're okay!

Anna typed quickly, her fingertips leaving smudges on the glowing screen. She hit send and the message shrunk, zooming into the "sent" folder.

She flipped through another host of messages and requests from the control room and her technicians. Her eyes burned and she blinked, everything going blurry for a moment. She needed eye drops. The damn screen was too bright and she'd been staring at it for too long. *Figures...the only part of me that isn't supposed to be dry right now is fucking dry.*

A material request for ceramic sealant popped up from the service techs. Anna switched to A.D.D.S, powered up a drone, and linked the request. A few moments later the request cycled from white to green, and then finally to blue.

A drone appeared from the spire below her, propelling itself noiselessly towards the damaged section of habitation ring.

Anna glanced over at the station's status monitor, the very readout she'd been actively avoiding. The affected compartments in C ring still showed zero atmospheric pressure, while the rest displayed wildly fluctuating oxygen and carbon dioxide levels. The screen flickered, darkened, and then brightened again.

Everything is acting weird.

It's got to be hell down there, she thought, and picked up her data point again. The screen showed "no new messages".

"Damn it, Coby," Anna cursed, and quickly tapped out another message.

R you okay?

She glanced at her screen, then looked back down and added another note.

I'm stuck in a service pod and don't know for how long. It's bad. Real bad. Please send me a message as soon as possible. I'm kind of freaking out and need to know you're okay. Shit hit fan. Massive splatter.

Anna sent the message, dropped the data point, and scrolled through more updates on her pod's H.U.D. Time crawled by, the minutes ticking by on her digital display. Another hour passed before she picked up her data point again, her anger bubbling forth. Still no response.

"What...the..." she started to curse, until the loading icon popped up on the screen, spinning and spinning. The data point flipped between screens, the three-dimensional icons flickering in and out of sight.

--Error–Messages saved as drafts. The network did not respond. Network fault. Try again in...error. Trying to connect...error.

"Lana, I can't get ahold of Coby on the station network."

Static crackled in her ear.

"Lana? Sys ops, are you there?"

More static.

The numerous screens, gauges, and buttons in her pod suddenly glowed brighter, the lights flickering in a nauseating display.

Anna covered her eyes and nervously reached up and fiddled with the climate controls again, despite the fact that the knob was already turned all the way down. She adjusted the com set and made sure it was still turned on.

"Jerod, do you copy? Is your pod acting up?"

The tech's voice echoed back weakly, the static so thick she could barely make him out.

"Say again, Jerod. I can't hear you." The pods continued their work, the bright light of welders and cutters flaring against the dark backdrop of space.

A loud pop sounded through her earpiece, and then everything went dark.

1900 HOURS

Jacoby was almost home when the passage went dark. He stopped immediately, holding his hands out to either side, a sudden wave of panic tightening his guts.

The station seemed to rock from side to side and he staggered to his right, catching the bulkhead with his face. Stars blossomed in the darkness but he managed to keep his feet beneath him.

"Back up lighting...now," he whispered, rubbing his face and crouching against the wall, afraid of what would happen if he stood again. The darkness ensued. They lived through countless power blips and surges. Lights would flicker, and sometimes go out. They were just an unfortunate side effect of living on a station this far out. Some components were new – state of the art, while others were old, cobbled together with duct tape and prayers. But this power blip felt different.

"Okay...and now." Nothing.

Jacoby listened, the passageway eerily silent around him. There was just nothing – no gently humming lights, beeping motion sensors, or whisper hiss of air flowing through the vents. He'd never heard it this quiet before, ever.

Someone shouted down the hall behind him, followed by a *bang bang bang* of fists on a metal door. More people called out, hands, knees, or feet slapping and smacking against closed doors.

He sat and waited for a telltale buzz or clunk, a whisper or rush of air, but nothing. With no circulation, the air became heavy around him, dead. Jacoby sniffed, noticing the strange odor he'd first smelled in the commissary bathroom. He stuck his nose into his shirt.

Damn, it was him. He was pungent, but far from his normal stink. It wasn't the sour of booze, either. In fact, he couldn't ever remember smelling that way before. Was it something he ate...drank?

Jacoby rocked back on his heels, the still air around him growing heavy with his smell. Desperate for a shower, he crawled forward on his hands and knees, trying to recreate the hallway in his mind. Jacoby felt his way along the wall, the cool, ceramic-coated panels giving way to a raised molding and the cool metal of a door.

A *pop* sounded somewhere overhead, and a loud *hum* followed. A light flickered on down the hall, and then another just above him. Jacoby slapped a hand over his face, the sudden light burning his eyes.

Something clicked, and then the door to his right slid open, the sudden movement sending him sprawling to the ground.

"What...who...?" a man asked, his voice tight with alarm. "What are you doing out here? Were you trying to...wait, Jacoby, is that you?"

"I was just," Jacoby stammered and pushed back up onto his knees and crawled back. He looked up, forcing his eyes open, and flinched, a part of his mind telling him to expect a punch or kick at any moment.

"Wow, easy. I'm not going to hit you," the man said, and knelt down to help him off the ground.

"I was walking down the hall when the lights went out. I got turned around and..."

"Yeah, I was getting ready for a shower when it happened. The door wouldn't open for a long time, and then when it did, you were there."

Jacoby straightened his shirt self-consciously and rubbed his eyes. Preston Graeves stood in his doorway, shirtless, his lanky frame filling the small opening. He was a lean man, with a well-toned stomach, sculpted arms, and a pleasant, mocha complexion.

Jacoby looked away, aware and uncomfortable with how naturally he seemed to size the other man up. Preston was handsome, muscular, and athletic – everything he wasn't.

"What is it Preston? Is it maintenance? Do they..." Preston's wife asked, appearing in the narrow hall beyond the door.

"Can you not get into your room? Do you need us to call someone?" Preston asked. He'd always been one of the nice neighbors – always with a hello or a wave.

"No, but thanks, Preston. I was just walking home when the lights went out. It was so fucking...sorry, it was so dark. I haven't even tried the door yet."

"Say, are you okay, man? Are you sick? You're all sweaty and pale. You don't look good," Preston asked, stepping halfway into the hall. The taller man sniffed loudly, took another audible breath through his nose, and snorted, before covering a cough.

"Baby, who are you talking to? I asked you if it was maintenance. Do they know why the power went out?" Preston's wife, Soraya, asked appearing in the now vacated doorway. "Oh, hey, Coby. I didn't know you were out here."

"I was just–"

"He was going home when the power went out," Preston said, cutting him off, his tone taking on an edgier quality. Preston rolled his shoulders and flexed his pectoral muscles.

"Is Anna home?" Soraya asked. She was tall – a former multi-sport athlete, the poise and muscular build still evident beneath her thin robe. Jacoby met her gaze, her large, almond-shaped chocolate-brown eyes bright and inviting. His gaze flicked down to her mouth – straight, white teeth and full lips, and then to her slender neck. Her skin, although a few shades darker than Preston's, glowed with an undeniable luster in the warm overhead light.

The thin fabric stretched tight over her large breasts, his eyes lingering for a moment before crawling down to her stomach, thighs, and shapely legs. Jacoby coughed and took another half step back as Preston moved a little closer, his bulk shadowing him.

"Honey, are you okay? You really don't look well," Soraya said, and stepped out into the hall.

No, stay away, he thought, but she was already next to him, her hands gripping his arms. She placed a hand on his forehead, before cupping his cheek. Jacoby coughed, trying to sink away from her, but she was strong.

"Baby, he's so warm. Like you were just a few days ago, when you first caught that bug," Soraya said, and helped Jacoby down the hall. He felt warm, but it wasn't him. It was her. "Coby, why don't we just help you to your room? I can help you lay down if Anna isn't home. By the way, are you wearing a new cologne or something? I...I like it."

Soraya gasped next to him, her breathing as hard as if she'd just finished a run or workout. His odd smell was even stronger now that she was close. He could smell her, too – rich cocoa and shea butter, coffee, and...warmth?

It was almost like he could smell her body heat. The air grew thick, and for a moment Jacoby was sure he could feel a single bead of sweat form between her shoulder blades and run down her back.

"The man can walk himself to his own bed," Preston grumbled behind them, sniffling and coughing. "He picked himself off the ground just fine."

"Don't listen to him, Coby. I don't mind helping. He's just grumpy. He's tired of being sick." Soraya's hands clenched and unclenched around his arms. Her fingernails were nicely manicured and painted, the paint a dark plumb color.

"What did you say?" Preston asked, his voice rising in the confined hall. Jacoby wasn't just hearing things. Preston sounded angry. He quickly glanced back to his neighbor and found the man standing in the middle of the hall, his arms shaking and his hands balled up into fists.

"Just go back on in and take that hot shower, baby. That'll make you feel better. I'm just gonna help Coby inside and I'll be back. Don't you worry."

Soraya guided Jacoby towards the door. He didn't dare look at her, for fear of what he might see, say, or do. He didn't want his thoughts to get jumbled again. What if he started to undress her in his mind? What if he couldn't stop himself this time and he actually tried to do it? My god, Preston would kill him. Preston could actually kill him.

They approached the hall and turned left. Jacoby was very aware of the woman's body rubbing against his, lean muscle accentuating her attractive feminine curves beneath the horribly thin fabric. In fact, it felt like Soraya was pulling him closer, her grip almost forcing his hand inside the folds of her robe. She was smooth, strong, and graceful.

A small thought was forming in his head, building with the pressure behind his eyes. Soraya was strong and sensual – an athletic and confident woman. That small part of him wanted her to dominate him, to take control and use him. The desire started to grow, despite Jacoby's efforts to deny it.

The thick quality of the air increased with the desire, the smell intensifying until he could practically taste it.

"Lets...just...get...you...inside," Soraya said, her voice rushed and breathing more rapid. She staggered and made a strange noise, but caught her balance quickly.

They reached his quarters, half the lights in the hall either dark or flickering rapidly. Jacoby moved to extend his wrist to the scanner, but Soraya moved around him, grabbed his wrist, and slapped it against the wall.

"You just go on home, babe. I'm just gonna help...him...inside, and get him comfortable," Soraya called out to Preston again as the door beeped and slid open. She sounded flustered and out of breath...so very unlike her norm. Hell, he'd never even seen her drunk before.

They were inside then, the quarters dark and quiet, save for the hall light outside the bathroom door. He heard the door close, and then they were alone.

"I think I can manage from here, Soraya. Thanks, I'm just going to take a quick shower and get some rest," he said, driven by the desperation to be alone. He needed peace and quiet, some space to figure out what was going on with his head.

"You've soaked through your shirt. Let me help you out of it," she said, and before he could argue, Soraya wrenched his shirt up over his head, tearing it in the process. She threw it down the hall.

"Thanks..." Jacoby started to say, as her hand came to rest on his chest. Her skin felt hot and soft against him, her nails digging ever so slightly into his skin.

"You poor thing, just look at your pants. You sweat through those, too," she said, and slowly unbuttoned his pants. They fell, bunching up around his feet.

Rich and strong. Give her control...let her do what she was made to do. The impulse is right.

The pressure pushed out against his eyes, his headache seemingly filling his entire head now. "I really don't think..." he stammered, trying to push her away, but his own impulses swept in and momentarily pushed away his objections.

His thoughts jumbled again, just as it had with Lex in the commissary, but it wasn't quite the same this time. He didn't want to fight this time, but fall into Soraya's arm and let her do whatever she wanted.

No, damn it, he thought, cursing the strange thoughts and urges. It wasn't him. This wasn't him. She was a happily married woman, and he was no home wrecker.

Soraya came forward suddenly, pushing him into the wall. Her lips pressed into his, her tongue sweeping into his mouth. She kissed him passionately, the warmth of her body settling over him like a hot blanket.

"Wait...Soraya, what are you doing?" he argued, pushing her away, but she was lithe and strong. She reached down and wrenched her robe open, exposing a tight-fitting sports bra and bikini style panties. Her stomach was shapely and muscular. His eyes dropped to the curves of her hips and thighs.

"I don't know...what it is...but there is...something about...you. My body...it feels so alive," she said and swooped forward again, smashing her body against his.

Jacoby lifted his head, but she kissed his neck, working her tongue down over his chest and to his nipples, moaning and gasping. "You're a...nice guy...but I've never...wanted anyone so badly before. So bad it hurts. Just want...to...need to throw you down and have you inside me."

"What about Preston?" he argued.

Soraya ground her body against him, her breasts warm and soft against his chest. She pulled away suddenly, her eyes lifting to his. Her pupils were huge, the chocolate brown of her irises almost invisible against the black.

"It's not about love," she hissed, her voice low and husky with lust. Her nostrils flared, her breath coming in short, powerful gasps. "You can feel it, too. I can see it," she said, running a hand down over his shorts and against his throbbing erection.

Yes, she feels it – the need. It is natural. Just give in to her. You don't have to do anything, just let her take it. His thoughts started to jumble again.

"No, not again," he grunted, clenching his jaw and fighting to block out the strange thoughts.

Soraya came forward again, her movements urgent and strong. She grabbed his hand and slid it against her stomach and inside the waistband of her panties. Jacoby tried to pull away, but his mind...his body, fought him. Part of him wanted this. She leaned forward and arched her back, moving his fingers down between her legs, the skin shaved bare and satin-smooth.

"Do you feel it? Feel my need?" she gasped, her face against his neck. She bit his ear gently and guided his fingers back and forth, parting her lips – she was hot and wet, ready for him. Soraya moaned, rocking her hips forward against his hand, her body shaking against him.

Yes. Strong and intoxicating like chocolate. Not fire, but chocolate and wonderful just the same.

"Oh, Coby. I need it now...I'm going to fuck you, Coby. I need it so bad it hurts. Oh my god it hurts!" she moaned, her breath hot against his ear. Yes. In that moment he wanted it, too.

Soraya pulled his hand out and reached for his shorts, but Jacoby snapped back to clarity and wrestled free. She clawed at him, her nails catching and scratching his shoulder. He managed two steps towards the bathroom before her hand hooked his arm.

Why is she doing this? Jacoby thought frantically as he turned around to fight her off. It wasn't like he'd never stared at her breasts before, or fantasized about what she looked like naked while taking care of himself. Soraya was definitely one of the sexiest ladies on station, but this...this didn't feel like a fantasy. After everything that'd happened lately, it felt more like an attack.

"I like it when you struggle," she growled.

Jacoby swung around and pushed Soraya against the wall, using his weight to pin her. She fought back, the muscles in her arms, stomach, and legs flexing in the limited light.

"Soraya, please stop," Jacoby pleaded. She leaned forward, fighting and trying to kiss him.

"Soraya, stop!" he yelled. She didn't stop. With a primal snarl, she bent low and heaved him back, squatting his entire body off the ground in the process. Her momentum slammed Jacoby into the wall, the impact knocking his breath away and showering his vision with stars. Soraya muscled him upright and yanked his shorts down.

"Yeah, baby, I'm gonna make you cum so hard...show you what a real woman can do," she growled, her voice even lower...like a cat purring.

Jacoby sputtered for breath, choking on his words, his thoughts a confusing mess. Soraya pinned him against the wall with a hand, her nails dragging down his chest and onto his stomach.

This is what you need. Submit. Let it happen. Don't fight. Purify her and make her ours. Make us all whole.

"What does that mean?" he gagged, fighting to understand what it meant.

He felt Soraya kiss his stomach, then her lips wrapped around the head of his penis and she slid his length into her mouth. Soraya pushed him back against the wall again, her hand firmly on his chest.

Jacoby moaned as she worked back and forth, her mouth and tongue soft and firm around his cock. Her hand continued to push him back, pinning him against the wall. It felt right, part of him reveling in the soft warmth of her mouth...the small, subtle voice in his heard singing with a lustful fire.

This is wrong, another part of him shouted and he moved to pull away, but she slapped him back against the wall. His thoughts swirled in a cloud of pleasure, doubt, and fear, the pain thrumming behind his eyes and between his ears.

She worked her mouth back and forth, his thoughts sinking into the pleasure of the moment. Soraya ran her fingernails down his stomach, the pleasure and pain melding perfectly together.

His head lolled forward. He watched her work her mouth lovingly back and forth, her flawless skin and firm breasts begging to be touched. Jacoby wanted her to pull away from him in that moment and throw him down. He wanted to know what her skin felt and tasted like, how her body felt when it accepted him inside. Jacoby wanted her to moan his name into his ear, wanted to make her scream as he pulled her nipples into his mouth and bit them playfully.

Soraya worked him into her mouth harder and faster, as if she could tell that he was starting to lose control. A fire rose up inside, the thick, effervescent smell filling the air like a cool morning's fog. He looked down, a gentle, but noticeable blue glow framing Soraya's body.

A single thought blew through the lust, crashing into him like an icy wind. *Preston.* The fear of Soraya's imposing husband effectively blasted through the cloud of lust and confusion. The fire was growing in his loins, his orgasm approaching with terrifying speed.

Jacoby grasped Soraya's hand and managed to pull her free. She fought but he was clear again, his thoughts his own. He lifted her upright, and she tried to kiss him.

"Soraya, you need to stop this. Now! Think of Preston," he hissed, trying to convince himself and her at the same time.

She pushed back, reaching down and trying to pull her panties down. He grabbed ahold of her arms and tried to stop her, but she pulled violently and the fabric tore.

Jacoby reacted, doing the only thing he could think of. He shook her hard.

"Soraya...please, snap out of it. This is not you," he yelled, shaking her even harder. She shook, her head snapping back and forth and then stumbled back.

Jacoby retreated to the bathroom door, gaining some distance for the first time. He pulled the handle, yanking the door open, preparing to barricade himself inside.

"Whaa?" Soraya groaned and took another uneasy step back. She reached up and held her head, before looking up again. She wobbled unsteadily...but he'd smelled no alcohol on her before.

He slid into the bathroom and prepared to close and lock the door. "Are...you okay?" he asked, realizing exactly how hard he'd shaken her. The last thing he wanted to do was hurt her.

Soraya met his gaze, the hall light shining directly on her face. She mumbled something under her breath, looked down at her open robe, the elastic of her panties now partially torn and her sports bra pulled off to one side.

She looked back up, her eyelids fluttering for a moment, her pupils contracting suddenly. She staggered again, and then quickly glanced around. She looked lost, bewildered.

"Soraya..." he started to say, hiding his nakedness behind the door.

"I...where...uh," she stammered, looked down, hastily pulled her robe closed, and turned on her heals and ran unsteadily down the hall. Jacoby followed slowly, maintaining a cautious distance. She paused to let the door open, but then turned and looked right at him.

"I, uh...you," she said, her eyes finally opening fully, and then she stepped out into the hall, her robe swishing quietly.

Jacoby checked the door to make sure it locked and fell back against the wall.

"What...in the fuck...was that?" he breathed, and shut his eyes tight. He reached up and rubbed his face, massaged his aching temples, and smashed his fists into his eyes, pushing back against the pressure in his skull. Either he was going crazy, or everyone else was. Or, maybe this was all a bad dream. Sure he'd fantasized about women throwing themselves at him...almost constantly, but this wasn't how he thought it would feel.

"Tomorrow, Jacoby. Tomorrow will be better. Tomorrow you won't feel like your head is going to explode and everyone will not be fucking crazy..." he started to whisper, just as the hall light went out, almost absolute darkness blanketing the living quarters.

"Or...not," he whispered, stepping away from the wall. The wide porthole window glowed like a radiant screen, the flickering stars beyond affording the only light. He waved his hands out before him, feeling his way to the bench by the outer wall.

Weird. Jacoby couldn't see anything but stars, not the strobe-like flashing lights, not the blazing floods, nor the blue, green, and red marker lights of the communications arrays.

He felt his way back across the living room, fumbling his way towards the bathroom, his data point glowing to life on the small table.

"There you are," he said, picking it up and tapping it awake. The three-dimensional loading icon popped up, spun twice, and flashed red.

"What in the hell is going on...?" he mumbled, just as the light overhead flickered on suddenly. The walls hummed, the ceramic and titanium weave vibrating as fresh air started to flow out of the vents once again.

"Maybe it's fixed?" He'd barely whispered the words when the light flickered again, the station's normal hum ebbing and flowing irregularly. His data point chirped and vibrated in his hand. The screen glowed to life, the network icon finally turning green.

The small device then proceeded to vibrate and beep continuously for several minutes, the screen flooding with alerts and message requests.

Holy f'ing shit, he thought, swiping through the messages as more flooded in. He found a message string from Anna, reading the increasingly desperate messages.

"Damn stupid power outage," he raged, and suddenly felt even more guilty about his run-ins with Lex in the commissary and Soraya. He selected the first message.

[Anna] - Accident on C Ring. Did you hear? Are you okay? People are dead. Please tell me you're okay!

[Jacoby) - I'm all right. Are you safe? Lights went out when I was almost home. I'm here now.

He typed the message out and paced from the window to the door, suddenly aware of his nakedness. He ran back into the hall, scooped his shirt off the floor and held it over his privates.

Jacoby paced for another ten minutes before the data point beeped. He unlocked the screen and clicked on the new message icon.

[Anna] - Thank God. We're still dealing with shit here. I'm hoping they relieve me soon. Have to pee so bad. Be home when I can.

A swell of relief flooded through him, and he typed out a quick response.

[Jacoby] - I'll be here. Hope they get you out of there a.s.a.p. Stay safe.

He took the data point into the bathroom, and proceeded to take an uncomfortably cold shower. When he was done, Jacoby toweled off and threw on some clean shorts and his favorite t-shirt.

He looked around his room – everything was picked up and put away, save for his bed, which was still a rumpled mess.

"What would I do without her," Jacoby thought, his guilt deepening. He made his bed, went out and washed the few dishes in the sink, and tidied up as best he could. Then he sat by the window, waiting, moved to the uncomfortable chair after a while, and finally, after starting to nod off, retired to his room to lie down.

21:00 HOURS

Jacoby lay in bed, his data point sitting on the nightstand, struggling to stay awake. Eventually his eyes grew too heavy to hold open and he drifted off. His dreams were oddly vivid, everyone he encountered either made up of blinding color, or dull, lifeless gray figures, wandering aimlessly.

He walked through the crowds of people, not entirely sure of where he was supposed to go or what he needed to do, yet still compelled to move nonetheless.

The bright, colorful people noticed him and followed, while the colorless shadows drifted away. The colorless people clumped together, their faces like featureless balls of light.

They crowded in, bunching up until he couldn't move. They pressed in and Jacoby tried to push them away, but there were too many. They all wanted to be near him, touching him. They wanted to be one – he could feel it, their flesh and bodies melting together, flowing over him like a hot, suffocating blanket.

Jacoby couldn't breathe, couldn't move, everything sliding into a hot, black mess – and then he snapped awake, sitting bolt upright in bed. The room was dark, a gentle hum of air buzzing in the register directly across from the bed. The air smelled a bit stale – the familiar tinge of warm plastic and ozone much stronger than usual.

Is it just me?

Jacoby reached up to wipe his face but he wasn't sweaty. Far from it. In fact, his skin was cold to the touch. He flopped back onto the mattress and listened to the quiet quarters, trying to determine if Anna had come home yet.

As if on cue, he heard the door beep quietly and slide open. Jacoby pushed up onto his elbows, half-lifting his legs to roll out of bed before her heard the bathroom door click closed. The shower turned on a few moments later.

Jacoby listened and waited, trying to put his thoughts in a reasonable order, preparing to work things out with Anna. He knew his drinking had been a problem, that hanging out with creeps like Mike was taking him in all the wrong directions, but more importantly he wanted Anna to know that...well, that he knew it. She'd been trying to tell him, and he was just too stubborn and pigheaded to see it.

Before signing his contract with Planitex and coming to Hyde station, they'd only had each other – through the months of backpacking on earth, scrounging enough money to get off planet...then their time squatting in a small eight by eight foot micro hotel in the lunar colony, just scraping by.

They'd struggled, but Jacoby couldn't remember a time when he'd had more fun. It was simple, an adventure, and together they'd managed to stay out of trouble. But this...this was starting to feel like all the things they'd been running away from.

The shower turned off and a little while later the bathroom door clicked open again and he heard Anna go into her room.

"Mike is just like the guys from school, you know, the cool, popular guys you always wished would be your friends? Well, they are, and just look at them, and you. They're doing what they've always done, drink, party, chase women, and use stims. But that wasn't you, and that's not who you are. Why can't you see that? The longer we're on station here and you're around guys like that, the more likely it is that you get yourself into trouble." Anna's voice echoed around in his thoughts.

Jacoby rubbed his eyes again, his anger and frustration mounting. She'd said it, and he'd gotten angry...because he knew it was true, but wasn't ready to accept the truth.

He waited, hoping that Anna would come to talk to him, hoping that he could come clean and say what needed to be said, that she would forgive him for being such a stupid ass, and they could get back to good. The quiet moments stretched on, until he rolled over and closed his eyes,

He rolled over, trying to get comfortable, the cheap micro-foam mattress working to mold around his new shape. His thoughts were sluggish, muddled by sleep. A soft noise issued from the hall and he turned just in time to see a shadow move from his doorway.

"Anna?" he called, his voice gravelly. He heard her move in the hall, the soft swish of fabric just audible above the gentle hum of circulating air.

"I didn't want to wake you," she whispered, appearing in the doorway again. She swept into the room, a dark form moving between shadows.

Anna moved to the window and raised the solar shade, allowing the station's ambient exterior light to dispel a small amount of the gloom. Then she moved to the bed, and tentatively sat on the edge, the backlighting keeping her face in shadow.

Jacoby could smell her – the soft lavender of her shower gel, her wet hair, and the subtle mineral scent that clung to freshly laundered clothes.

"I..." she started, but paused, heaving a weary sigh.

"I want you to know that you were right...about all of it," Jacoby said, pushing quickly up to sit before her. He needed to say it...all of it, before his thoughts scattered or he forgot, because dammit, he always forgot the important shit.

"I've been an ass lately. I don't know what I was thinking when I renewed my contract. We should have talked about it first, like we do...about everything. It just...well, it felt like a little security for us both...another year without having to worry about where we are going or what we are going to do for money. And you were right about Mike and the guys. It was just a way to blow off steam at first, to laugh at Janice and the rest of the bullshit, but then it just turned into a reason to have a few drinks – a way to forget about shrinking bonuses and our struggles to hit quota day after day. Mike, the booze, the stims, it all messed up my head. I wasn't thinking right...I didn't feel like myself. I don't want to make excuses, but it all took me away from what and who I am," he said, trying to spit it all out and make sense at the same time. Anna listened, the details of her face and sleepwear coming into focus as his eyes adjusted to the dim, ambient glow. She stared at the bed, her shoulders and mouth sagging slightly. She looked exhausted.

"It's always been you and me, since early in school, when your parents forbid you from being my friend. We found ways to spend time together, talking about...well, everything – your overbearing parents, my split family and my dad never being around. You were the only one I could talk to about my dad getting drunk and slapping me around. You remember when I tried to run away and you made me skip afternoon sessions so we could sneak down to that abandoned fueling station in the Quarter's district? You listened to me talk all afternoon, hell it was dark before I worked up the nerve to admit my dad hit me. You hugged me and told me that you'd always listen...always be there, no matter what. It was your promise, and I swore to do the same. What were we, ten years old?"

Anna snorted and nodded, some of her wet hair falling from behind her ear. "I told my friends that I gave you that black eye...that you teased me at recess that I hit like a girl, so I punched you to prove you wrong."

Jacoby chuckled, remembering how all the little girls teased him after that. *Jacoby got beat up by a girl.* He swallowed down the laughter, also remembering how Anna had been pulled into the headmistress's office once the rumor spread and stuck to her story, even accepting a weeklong suspension to keep the truth a secret. If the school knew his father beat him, shit would have gotten complicated real quick. He'd have been torn out of his home, pulled into the system, and likely never seen Anna again...just another broken kid from a broken family destined to fail at everything.

"I never would have made it without you...through *him,* the time after *him*...shit, any of it. I probably would have ended up just like *him*."

"I told you I would protect you, and as soon as we were old enough, we would run away to where our families couldn't rule over us anymore," she added, sniffling again, "but then you grew up and you were bigger than me."

"Except that whole period of time where you were in college. I mean, that wasn't really your idea, though."

"You are the reason I made it through all of that, Coby. Nothing like having your parents decide what school you will go to, your field of study, and where you're destined to work after, the man you'd marry, or how many kids you'd pop out. And my mom, ugh, her weekly visits, where she would search my dorm room to make sure I wasn't spending time with people she didn't approve of..." Anna whispered, sniffling again.

"Ha, yeah. By that, you mean *me*. She refused to let you live *your* life. What a..." Jacoby sighed.

"Bitch," Anna cut in, laughing and nodding her head vigorously.

"We got clear of them," Jacoby said, simply, scratching his nose. "I should have talked to you. You're the rational one, the one who does the research and determines the best routes and plans. I'm the one who makes impulsive decisions. Do you hate me?"

"Hate you? Coby, why would I hate you? I...I," Anna stammered, reaching up to pull her hair out of her face. She took in a deep breath, and pushed it out, looking at the ceiling as if trying to put her thoughts together. "I just don't like Mike...or guys like him. They're crude and reckless and think pushing sleep deprivation with stims and alcohol is fun. They break shit cause it's fun, get in fights to prove they're tough, and steal to get a thrill. They're the exact same as they were back in school, when getting drunk before class, hiding dead animals in people's lockers, and starting rumors were just ways to pass time. They think women are meat, Coby. They're pigs. You've never been like that...not back then and sure as hell not now. I guess you started acting differently when you started spending time with them. I freaked out a little, thinking that I was..."

"What?" he asked, as she went quiet.

"I thought that I was losing you, Coby. I thought you were slipping away from me...turning into one of them."

Anna moved fully onto the bed for the first time. She moved closer and for the first time he became aware of the heat radiating off of her body. He wanted to snuggle close and bask in her warmth.

Precious flower. Hold her close, protect her, make her endure.

Jacoby shook his head and almost cursed out loud. *Not now...shut up!* he thought, willing his loud, jumbled thoughts to be silent.

"I think in a way, it's true, and it took our fight for me to see it. I was slipping away...uh, becoming someone different. It felt like the only way to deal with the stress, without dumping it all on your shoulders. Because I didn't want to do that...I didn't want to come back and make you listen about Janice doing this, or Mike saying that, or not meeting my quota again and my Panitex share taking another quarter cut. That didn't feel right. I wanted to...well, just as I always have...I guess, wanted to shield you from all of it. I wanted to protect you."

A tear ran down his cheek and he reached up to swipe it away, realizing for the first time that his eyes were brimming with them. A tear leaked down Anna's cheek, too.

"I'm not some delicate flower, you jerk," she said and lurched forward, throwing her arms around his neck.

They fell back onto the bed and shared a long, tight, teary hug, both sniffling and laughing. When they pulled apart, Anna rested her head in the crook of his arm and wiped her face.

"So, you're forgiven. For now," she said, snapping a hand into his belly playfully. Jacoby grunted and fought to protect himself, but Anna simply rolled away.

"I got your messages...sorry, I tried to respond but the network was down. What...what happened? I got stuck in the passage outside Preston and Soraya's quarters when the power went out." He swallowed the rest of his words, unsure how exactly he would tell her the rest of it – cracking the rock, the trip to the clinic doc, the administrative leave, the redhead in the commissary, or Soraya. Damn, how could he tell her about that? He shifted uncomfortably, his thoughts straying back to Soraya's muscular body, the strength in her grip, and the softness of her mouth on his...

Anna groaned and rolled back into him, her legs flopping animatedly.

"Lana messaged me right after the skeleton queen came and got you this morning," Anna said, using his private nickname for Janice. He laughed, guiltily.

"Evidently everyone is getting sick with that flu bug going around. She asked me to come in because they had a butt-load of scheduled and past-due maintenance...mostly on the oxygen re-circulator unit on C ring. I was trying to help Brad... the technician. I was trying to make sense of the stupid...fucking...schematics," she said.

Jacoby could hear the frustration in her voice, but he could feel it, too, the tension winding her body tight. Her robe pulled up as she bounced her legs again, emphasizing her point again. The gentle white-blue light bathed her foot, calf, and thigh, his eyes jumping away almost right away.

"The whole unit exploded, Coby. It was like a bomb went off. I've never been more scared...ever. But that was only the beginning. We got techs out there to patch the damage and reroute the fiber bundles and stuff, and the power cycled off. My pod got freaking cold and dark," Anna said, rolling over to face him and snuggling closer.

Jacoby's heart started to pound, her warmth bleeding through to warm his cold skin.

"I'm still cold, and you're so nice and warm," Anna said, wiggling even closer.

The pressure grew in his head, pushing on the back of his eyes once again. *No,* he thought in horror, but only felt an irresistible desire to hold Anna closer and keep her there, to protect her.

"They said that when the module blew, it caused a power surge and the relays and breakers didn't isolate properly. Power relay stations all over C ring blew, which overloaded the transmission lines to B and D. The backflow tripped relays in every ring, forcing an automatic reactor shutdown. They say it's bad...like bad," she said, nuzzling her face up by his neck. "Coby, you smell nice. Did you buy some new deodorant at the commissary?"

"No..." he said almost immediately, his mind flooding with panic.

"Oh, well, whatever it is, I like it," she said, drawing in a heavy breath, her nose brushing up against his neck. The soft contact set a fire inside him, his groin almost immediately starting to swell.

"Coby?" Anna asked, reaching over and pulling his head to the side. She brought her left leg up to rest on him, the additional contact providing yet more warmth.

"Yeah?"

"For a little bit today, I didn't think I was going to make it out of the pod alive. Then when I couldn't get ahold of you on my data point, I thought maybe something happened to you," she said. She snorted. It was that quiet noise she always made when she was thinking about something serious, something that worried her.

"The thought of dying was scary, but I was more worried that something had happened to you...that I'd be all alone. I don't know what I'd do without you in my life. It's just too much to consider."

"I'm not going anywhere," Jacoby whispered, hooking his arm up and pulling her closer. Anna obliged, snuggling right up against him. She nuzzled her head against his chest, took in a deep breath through her nose, coughed, and closed her eyes.

"I just want to stay right here tonight. I hope that's okay with you," she said, almost whispering.

The closer the better, we won't let anyone hurt you, the quiet voice in his head said, the pressure swirling behind his eyes, and for the first time that day, Jacoby agreed.

"That's perfect."

Day 3

0300 HOURS

Jacoby snapped awake. His mind moved slowly, his thoughts almost immediately spinning back to...he couldn't remember falling asleep, only the waking up part.

Anna moved next to him, her hand gently rubbing his chest, her whole body seemingly coiling and flexing. He glanced over at the holo-clock projected to his right. The small display ticked away in seconds, the hour passing to three o'clock just as his eyes focused.

Anna breathed in deeply, the breath coming out as a low moan.

Is she having a bad dream? Is she okay?

He turned to find her eyes open and her bottom lip tucked between her teeth. She exhaled forcefully, her breath warm on his neck and face.

"Are you..." he started to ask, but Anna moved in quickly, her lips pressing urgently into his.

Jacoby moved to pull her away. It wasn't the first time they'd kissed, but those pecks before had been playful, friendly. This wasn't the same. They'd always agreed to keep their friendship free of romantic complications. Sex ruined friendships more than anything else.

Anna's lips were soft and warm, her scent filling his nose and washing almost every other thought away. The pressure quickly returned in his head, the desire to hold her, to protect her, increasing in kind. She pulled away and their eyes met. He was confused, shocked, and knew it was painted plainly on his face.

"It's okay. Just this once. I want to feel you...truly feel you, and I...I need you to feel me. After everything that's happened, and is happening, I just need something pure and good, something beautiful," Anna whispered, nodding and pulling back in to kiss him. Her leg wrapped over him and rubbed against his groin.

Jacoby struggled with stronger than usual urges all day – to curse, fight, fuck, or strangest still, let Soraya have her way with him. It was all the stuff of fucked up dreams, not *his* life. He'd resisted each time, fighting with every ounce of resolve. But now...

Jacoby's resistance melted away as their bodies smashed together. His heart started to pound, the *thump thump* filling his ears. The pressure behind his eyes grew stronger yet, but there was no pain this time, only a growing fire inside him.

Yes. We can cleanse her...protect her. Jacoby ignore the thought, falling quickly into passion.

He ran a hand down her side, up over her hip, and down to the graceful curve of her thigh. Anna moaned and took a deep breath, running her hand down and over his pants, to his growing erection.

Her breasts strained against the thin robe, her nipples already half perked. Jacoby hooked his right hand behind her knee and lifted, easing their bodies together.

Anna leaned in and kissed him, her tongue lightly brushing against his. They kissed passionately, Jacoby's hand sliding up and under her robe, hiking the fabric up past her waist. Anna felt hot now, the heat and soft touch of her lips toppling him fully into the lust he'd been denying for so long.

The fire doubled in his groin, his erection now straining against his shorts. Jacoby pulled the drawstring apart on Anna's robe, letting the garment fall open and exposing the flawless span of her breasts, stomach, legs, and hips. She wasn't wearing panties.

Anna moaned as his mouth moved down her chin, to her neck, his tongue dancing into the valley between her breasts. He ran his hand down her thigh to her knee and back up the inside, before gently teasing his fingers between her legs. Her body tensed, but she obliged, spreading for him, working her hips forward against his hand. Jacoby eased her lips apart, savoring her warmth and running his index finger slowly back and forth.

Anna twisted around, her hand sliding down his arm. She tried to urge him faster and deeper but he pulled away, content to take his time.

"You smell so good. God, I want you now," she moaned, her breath hot on his face.

Jacoby slid his fingers forward, easing them slowly inside her. Anna felt hot, wet, and velvety soft. She ran her fingers up and into his hair and then pulled him into a strong kiss. Her tongue met his, but then she pulled away, a soft moan growing in her throat. He worked his fingers in and out, teasing them shallow and then pulling them out to gently caress the pearl of her clitoris, before rolling them right back inside. Her body twitched and shook, muscles tightening as she writhed against him.

Anna pulled him into another kiss and then violently pushed him onto his back. Jacoby fought, but she came forward suddenly, tearing the robe off and throwing it onto the floor. Her mouth moved from his nipples down to his stomach, where he felt her hand slide into the waistband of his sleep shorts.

She wrenched his shorts down and worked a hand down his erection, a thrill shooting up his body. She kissed the tip of his penis, teasing the head of his cock with her lips, before accepting it slowly into her mouth, her tongue pressing firmly against the shaft.

Jacoby groaned, lifting his hips excitedly and encouraging her to take more of him into her mouth. Anna accommodated, working up and down slowly at first, her tongue applying almost perfect pressure.

"If you keep that up, I won't last long," he gasped, struggling against his almost painful sexual urges.

Jacoby reached down and ran his hand over her shapely rear, then back up her side to her breasts. Anna increased speed, her soft lips and tongue almost sending him straight into his climax.

He managed to sit up and kicked off his shorts, Anna pulling away, the soft glow from the porthole backlighting the perfect curve of her rear. She pushed up onto her knees as Jacoby rolled up to meet her, his gaze sweeping down from her neck, over her nipples, and to her belly. He'd always known Anna was pretty - the kind of girl that most guys turned to watch walk by, but now, in this light, she looked like a goddess.

Cherish her...fill her with your love. She is perfect. Claim her and make her ours. Make us all whole.

Jacoby wrenched off his shirt, Anna meeting him almost immediately with a kiss. She pulled him close, her body the warmest, softest thing he'd ever felt. Then she turned him around, using her weight to pull him on top of her. Anna stared into his eyes, her breathing hard and her body moving with palpable need.

Jacoby paused, a logical thought breaking through the fog of lust. Anna was his best friend, his buddy. They could argue away what had already happened between them as a simple, isolated stress-related mistake. They could move on...laugh about it even, but if he pushed forward, everything could...no, would change.

"I...want...you," she breathed, and curled her legs behind his butt, guiding him forward and forcing the tip of his penis inside her. Jacoby thrust on impulse, rocking his hips forward, his painfully hard erection easing in until his full length was inside her. She felt hot and smooth, like silk, their bodies fitting perfectly together. His thoughts coalesced, the raging, turbulent urges, regrets, and concerns about ramifications quieting until his mind thrummed with a single, harmonious will – please Anna.

No one else deserves her. The thought bounced around his mind, accompanied by a twinge behind his eyes. His passions grew, and he rocked his hips back, pulling almost completely out before easing his cock back inside her again. He moved slowly at first, fighting the compulsion to fall mindlessly into his passions. Anna reached around and grasped his ass, pulling him forward urgently, her breasts bouncing happily from each passionate thrust.

He bit his tongue and fought the urge to speed up, reveling in the moment. He caressed her stomach, easing his calloused hands up and over her breasts and teasing her excited nipples. Anna moaned loudly, her hands clamped onto his hips, her fingers scrabbling against him, her actions begging him to thrust harder. Jacoby obliged, thrusting hard and fast, their bodies smacking loudly together. Sweat covered his face, beading up on his forehead and threatening to drip off of his nose.

Anna retracted suddenly, Jacoby recoiling, the separation of their bodies almost a painful shock. In the next instant, he was flat on his back with Anna crawling atop him. She straddled him, sliding her hips forward and back, grinding down the length of his erection. Jacoby groaned and pulled himself up, smashing his face between her breasts, then bit playfully on her nipples. Their smells mingled in a fog around him – the intoxicating musk of their sex, enhanced by that peculiar note he'd noticed earlier outside

Soraya and Preston's quarters. It didn't smell odd, however. Now it felt organic, natural. It was perfect.

Jacoby kissed Anna, trying to master the impulse and extend their lovemaking, just as she tipped forward and raised her butt, sliding his manhood back inside her. She rocked forward and back, her body wrapping lovingly around him.

Anna ground them together harder, the head of his penis swelling and bottoming out. He groaned as her hands came to rest on his chest, her hips no longer grinding them together, but sliding them almost completely apart, before ramming him back inside. He slid one hand around her lower back, helping guide her movements, the other cupping her cheek. Her nipples rubbed teasingly against him as they fell into a kiss. She pulled back, a moan vibrating in her throat, her movements becoming more urgent, her breathing hard. Jacoby stopped trying to hold back. He drove his hips up as she came down.

The fire grew, his muscles tensing as Anna's fingernails dug into his chest. She was close, but he was closer. Jacoby grabbed her hips, thrusting violently, their bodies moving in almost perfect harmony. Anna slid forward, her sweat-glistened face resting against his. She took his hands and wrenched them above his head, pinning them against the mattress with surprising weight.

"I'm close, Coby. Oh, my god...I'm so close," she moaned, her breath coming in urgent gasps. Anna sunk into him, her soft breasts framing his face, her magnificent body lengthening the stride. Their sweaty bodies glided together harder and faster, her hips rolling him seemingly deeper with each thrust.

Jacoby tried to pull free as his climax hit, the orgasm striking so hard he felt his stomach spasm, but Anna pushed him down even harder, her hips rocking forward and her body spasming around him. She cried out, her quiet nature replaced by a far more primal one.

Jacoby laid there, Anna's body twitching and contracting around his cock as her orgasm continued, her arms and face visibly shaking. She collapsed onto him a moment later, her chest heaving as she fought to catch her breath.

She lay atop him for a long while, the silence stretching as they enjoyed the serenity of their lovemaking. She really did seem to glow, a cool, blue radiance outlining the alluring curve of her breasts, hips, and legs.

Anna threw him a smile, rolled free, picked up her robe and proceeded to clean up. She dropped heavily onto the bed a moment later, the beads of sweat on her back glistening like diamonds in the porthole's cool light.

Jacoby tried to cover up but she ran a hand down his stomach and over his frustratingly still-swollen erection.

"Wow, Coby. Did I not do a good enough job?" she asked, teasing her hand down his length.

We are insatiable.

Jacoby struggled with a blush as he tried to rationalize the truth of it. His release felt good, the pressure in his head and balls diminished by far, but his sexual appetite was still raw, seemingly untapped.

"That was...amazing. You're amazing," he breathed, pushing up onto his elbows, and then sat, awkwardly aware of his excited condition. He kissed Anna, her smell now sweeter and stronger than ever. He'd climaxed, but still felt as aroused as when they started. Truth be told, he felt better than he had in a long time – alive, strong, and oh so unbelievably horny. He should have been exhausted and satisfied, but...

"I guess it's just been a while," he said, his face flushing warm.

Anna's lips turned up into a devious smile and she threw him a wink, before rolling over onto her back. Jacoby's gaze dropped from her crystal-blue eyes, to the graceful curve of mouth, and finally to the pout of her breasts. Beads of sweat glistened on her skin, catching and refracting the blue-white light like liquid gems.

"In that case, you'd better come and get it while you can, big boy, before I change my mind and go to sleep," she said, lifting a single finger and gesturing him towards her.

Something buzzed loudly and snapped him out of a deep sleep. Jacoby tried to roll over and go back to sleep, but it buzzed again a few moments later, the sound frighteningly similar to the wasps that used to build their nests by the exterior lights of his dad's rundown apartment.

Pushing up from the bed, Jacoby flopped over onto his side and slapped at the nightstand, his palm almost missing it completely before finally wrapping around his data point.

The screen glowed to life, the light far too bright for his sleep-crusted eyes. Jacoby grunted, squinted, and turned the screen away. He waited several long moments before turning it back to his face.

The first update appeared through the glare. It was an official release from station administration about the unfortunate accident on C ring. Jacoby grunted and swiped through to the next, and then the next, the messages seemingly all about the accident or follow up communications offering updates and so on.

He moved to set the data point down but the most recent message caught his attention. It was from the station clinic, marked by a confusing string of letters and numbers.

[Clinic Automedic response bot] 1A2 - patient$5&(-)JacobyMason@{newline} blood work up -error- Physician=Dr. Reeds. Immediate patient follow up needed. Respond with (Yes) to automatically schedule the next available emergency appointment.

Emergency appointment?

Jacoby groaned and reached up to rub his eyes. *What does it mean? Did I screen pop positive for something?* But what? He wasn't drunk, and he sure as hell hadn't done stims in a while, and he refused to touch that newest chem Mike was talking about...what did he call it...brain boiler? Before he could fall too deep into panic, Jacoby typed out a quick response.

[Jacoby] Yes.

His thoughts flashed back to the previous night. He wasn't immediately able to differentiate between what had been dream and what was real. The data point vibrated almost instantly, and a message flashed in.

[Clinic Automedic response bot]{@##} Response confirmed{@}. Appointment time – 1100 hours. Please arrive fifteen minutes early.

"Damn...damn...damn," he grunted and rolled over. He clung to the sheet and sat up. His bed was a mess, the majority of the sheets and pillows scattered on the floor. But it wasn't just the mess. The room still smelled like sex, confirming his suspicions, the fitted sheet showing obvious signs of their lovemaking.

Jacoby rubbed his eyes again and struggled with a stab of guilt. Anna wasn't with him when he woke. Had it been a mistake? Had he ruined their friendship? The worry filled him and knotted up his guts.

Flinging his legs out of bed, Jacoby threw on a pair of shorts and reached for the door. Classical music – a march, heavy with brass and probably Russian – filled the next room. The door seal popped as it opened, the aroma of brewing coffee filling his nose.

Jacoby walked out into the common room only to find a portable battery unit sitting on top of their small coffee table, a number of glowing power cables draped out over the floor – one to a small wireless speaker, another to a floor lamp, and the last to the coffee machine on the counter.

"Hey, sleepy head," Anna said from the seat by the window. She jumped up, put her book down, and moved over to the coffee pot.

Jacoby approached slowly, the first signs of a headache forming. He studied the battery unit, the Planitex logo glowing a steady green on its otherwise featureless top. He looked up to Anna. She wore a pair of tight-fitting yoga style pants, and a gray fleece pullover. Her blond hair was pulled back into a ponytail, the subtle red and brown lowlights never more apparent.

"I got up early and found most of the power off. They're still not sure of what all is damaged, but are handing out these portable power units to compensate," Anna said, pouring some creamer into a mug, "I guess there are still large parts of the station without any power at all."

He took a breath to speak as she poured out some coffee, compelled to apologize for the night before, but couldn't seem to find the words. His thoughts were a confusing mess – doubt, foggy intimate recollections, more sexual urges, and uncertainty. He wanted to say and do anything in his power to ensure their friendship wasn't ruined – that they continued to be Anna and Coby, like always.

Anna turned and held out a white mug of coffee, and he accepted it, taking an exploratory sip. She looked to be the same old Anna, accept...she wasn't. Her eyes were bright, her hair curly and lustrous. Her skin practically glowed. If he hadn't seen her naked the night before, he might even think that her breasts looked a bit fuller, too.

"Drink," she said and nodded to the mug. He lifted the mug again and took a larger drink.

"Anna..."

"Hold that thought, Coby. There is something I need to say first."

Jacoby sucked in a larger drink of coffee than he was ready for and swallowed. The hot liquid burned his mouth and he sputtered. He feared what she would say next, and fought the impulse to stop her.

Coby, I love you, you're my best friend, but it's time for me to go home and tell my parents they were right.

Or.

Coby, I love you, you're like my brother, but it's all changed now. I don't think we can be friends after last night. Our friendship is ruined. I have to go home.

"I can see it on your face right now," she said, stifling a small laugh. "You think you took advantage of me last night...no, you're terrified that you did, and what we shared ruined our friendship."

He reached up and patted his face, and secretly wondered if he hadn't accidentally voiced all of his worries out loud.

"Well, don't be stupid. We both have had a really tough time lately, and we fought. It was a stupid fight, and we were both wrong, but we fought...which isn't something we've really done before. I love you, Coby, and I always will. We both needed a release...and truth be told, neither of us has had anything resembling an intimate relationship, well beyond our friendship, for a long while now. I don't regret what we did last night, and more importantly, I don't want it to change things between us, so I'm not going to let it. I know it's asking a lot, and maybe it's not entirely possible, but I hope you can still look at me as the 'same Anna'."

Jacoby forced out a breath, only after stars started dancing before his vision. Hell, he wasn't sure when he last took a breath. She was the "same old Anna", and he couldn't even harbor the thought of looking at her as anything but that.

"I seriously thought you were going to hate me, and that you just wanted to tell me that we ruined our friendship and that you were catching the next transport home to your parents," he sighed, looking to the ceiling and breathing a sigh of relief.

"Oh my god, are you serious?" Anna said, "Why would I ever do that? They're...horrible...people. You're my family."

Jacoby took another drink of coffee and laughed, letting much of that pent up tension go. He met Anna's eyes, and she squinted, as if reading him.

"Don't be weird about this, dude. We just had sex, like two or three times last night. There's nothing to feel weird about, except maybe your stamina...geez."

"Are you sure?" Jacoby asked, after stifling a laugh.

"Yes, and you know why. Do you remember what I said when you showed up at my door...the night before we ran away?"

He nodded. Of course he did, it was both the most terrifying and amazing moment of his life, up to that point. He'd gotten in a fight with his dad, which turned into a fistfight. Jacoby woke up on the floor, grabbed his stuff, and ran.

"I said, 'you're all I got now'."

Anna nodded. "Your teeth were loose, your lips were bleeding, and your eye was swollen shut. You right arm was hurt, too, remember? You were all bruises and could barely close your fingers into a fist. I told you that it would just be you and me, and nothing would come between us...and I meant it."

"You and me," he echoed, warmth blossoming inside.

"Now can I tell you all of the stuff I've done already today?" she asked, visibly brimming with life and energy.

"I guess," Jacoby said, feigning nonchalance, only his data point vibrated loudly a moment later. He unlocked the screen and opened the new message. It was an appointment reminder for the clinic.

"Shit."

"What's wrong," Anna asked. Jacoby proceeded to tell her about his screw up at work, his administrative time off, as well as his check up with doc Reeds. He couldn't remember how much he'd told her the night before, so he rattled on about all of it just to be safe.

"Half the lifts are down, so it's going to take us twice as long to get to the clinic on A. Go take a quick shower, and we'll go," she said, lifting the mug out of his hand and pushing him down the hall towards the shower.

Jacoby showered quickly, the water still ice-cold, toweled off, and threw on some clean clothes. He pushed out of his room, balancing on one foot to pull his other boot on, and followed Anna out the door.

"Must be nice. Just scrub your pits and butt and throw on a clean shirt and go. You guys have it so easy," she said, not waiting for him as he swiped his wrist against the panel to lock the door.

"Yeah, but we have to shave sometimes, and maybe even brush our teeth," he replied and barely suppressed his smile.

"Oh, you poor thing."

They turned right and walked together past Soraya and Preston's door. Jacoby eyed the gray steel warily. They were down the hall and around the next corner before he could breathe easily again.

"Now what is the matter with you?" Anna asked and pushed the elevator button.

"Uh, oh nothing," he said, pulling on his shirt collar to stretch it out. It was an old t-shirt, and he didn't remember it being so tight. The sleeves were tight, too. Jacoby patted himself down, until he looked over and found Anna watching him. He considered telling her about Soraya the day before, and her almost frighteningly aggressive behavior. Then his thoughts drifted to Lex, the hot redhead in the commissary. Should he tell her about that, too?

"Are you feeling yourself up?" she asked with a snort.

"No!" he argued, but felt his cheeks warm almost immediately, and decided to keep the details about the other women to himself. She'd probably just think he was bragging, and to be fair, he wouldn't believe him either.

"Well, that shirt does look a bit tight. I didn't know you started working out again. Is that what you've been doing with Mike and the other guys? When you're not drinking."

Jacoby pulled down on the t-shirt again, stretching the fabric but didn't respond. He hadn't lifted a weight since leaving earth, and yet he felt definitively bulkier, even in his stomach, where he could feel tight muscle beneath his thin layer of carefully cultivated burgers and beer.

The elevator arrived and Anna stepped aside, letting a group step off. They rode the elevator up to D ring level one and worked their way around to the hub, bypassing two transit elevators, until finally finding one in service that would take them through C and B to A ring.

Anna stood on the other side of the elevator, running in place, her ponytail bouncing playfully behind her. Jacoby watched and marveled at her almost sickening energy level.

"So, you wanted to tell me about all the stuff you've already gotten done today."

Anna nodded, and started shadow boxing the air. The gravity increased as the elevator started to move. Jacoby sagged under the pressure, but Anna continued to bounce, as if trapped in her own personal workout challenge.

"You were sleeping, and I was wide awake, so I got up, showered, did a load of laundry, ate breakfast, and..." she said, breathing against the strain, and then proceeded to rattle off an even longer list of chores and tasks. She'd been busy while he slept.

"How do you have so much energy? I feel like I had just closed my eyes before I woke up. Damn, I'm tired," he said and covered a yawn.

"I don't know, but I feel good. I mean, like the best I have, like ever! I feel like I could run a marathon, no...a triathlon. My hair was good this morning, none of that redeye I've had lately, and my skin is super clear!"

"I'm glad at least one of us feels good then," Jacoby mumbled as the large elevator stopped and the doors opened.

They stepped into the A ring atrium, the wide walkway a mass of congestion and confusion. Service techs worked behind wall panels, their bags and ladders strewn across the floor. The clutter formed an obstacle course from wall to wall.

"Come on, or you're gonna be late," Anna said, pulling him forward through the maze. They passed through bright pools of light and into entire sections of shadow. More workers bustled up ahead, carrying in long, thin tubes and handing them up to workers on scaffolding.

"Those are strings of photo-organic light emitting diodes. They call them solar strings," Anna said, pointing at them excitedly. "They stimulate vitamin D production in people, and facilitate photosynthesis in the station's habitat vegetation. The plants grow, breathe in our carbon dioxide, and exhale breathable oxygen. It's all part of the complicated life support structure in place."

Jacoby followed, dodging the technicians and trying not to trip over length of cable and tool trays. Sprawling ivy grew up the curved walls. Multi-tiered planters covered the walls on either side of them, masses of green vegetation clustering greedily in the brightest spots. Jacoby spotted plants with wide leaves that looked like elephant ears, to shooting stalks covered with clusters of purple and yellow flowers.

"This looks bad," Jacoby said, after waiting for Anna to lead them through the worst of the congestion. They fell into step next to one another.

"The accident communications from administration don't cover the half of it," Anna whispered but stopped as a group of admin workers in white and gray bodysuits appeared out of a side passage. She coughed and they continued on in silence.

They passed office after office, technicians working in overhead compartments, massive rolls of cable looped on the tables and chairs beneath them. Jacoby continued forward, watching the flurry of activity. He almost tumbled over a stooped person in the middle of the path, but Anna pulled him over just in time.

Jacoby turned to apologize but the female technician was too engrossed in her work to even notice him. She held a length of fiber up to a portable light, the shielding visibly melted and misshapen.

"Do you smell that?" Anna asked.

Jacoby nodded as they stepped up and onto an elevator. She leaned in, swiped her wrist against the pad and selected the up arrow.

"It smells like melted plastic and hot wires," he said as soon as the doors closed.

Anna nodded. "I stopped into the sys ops control room this morning and overheard the senior operator briefing his crew. They're calling it a 'cascade redundancy failure'."

"Okay? I do rocks and crushers. That technical computer stuff is your playground."

Anna laughed nervously, but he could tell that it was probably more nerves than humor.

"It means that the safety measures built into the station...the ones designed to protect important power distribution centers and climate control modules failed. The oxygen re-circulator explosion damaged a number of power capacitors, which then discharged their voltage violently, overloading the one-way relays designed to protect the electrical train uphill from power surges. I don't really understand all of it...it's a lot of electrical engineering jargon, you see. But it boils down to this – the explosion caused a back feed of current, some shit overloaded, which overloaded some other shit. Lines popped and melted, which damaged data fiber nearby. It's a fucking mess and they aren't sure if, or how, they're going to fix it all."

Jacoby let his breath out in a dramatic whistle. "That sounds bad, but on a station in the deep, it feels even worse."

Anna nodded. "They can mess with the atmospheric circulation to keep the air breathable all over station, thanks in part to the greenhouse metric. But the name of the game is power. The reactor is fine, but enough routing systems were damaged that they might not be able to get power to all the places it's needed...not without shipping cable and parts in from Earth or Mars."

She finished just as the elevator signaled its arrival on the next floor, the chime warbling like a sick bird. The overhead light flickered as the doors started to open. It all went dark for a moment, before humming back to life and the doors opened fully.

Jacoby met Anna's gaze, her worry echoing the concern tumbling around in his gut. They stepped out of the elevator to a passage full of people. They lined both sides...some leaning against the bulkheads, while others sat or lay on the ground. The passage was warm, the air stuffier than it had been anywhere else.

"Are they all sick?" Anna whispered as they moved forward.

Jacoby followed and nodded, tearing his gaze away only after a short, bearded man tipped forward to puke in a bag. They all looked sick – with dark bags under their eyes, red noses, and pale, clammy-looking skin.

Jacoby passed a small door on their left, and a memory flashed through his mind. He remembered pushing through that door, and...his memory grew fuzzy. *Did I get sick in the next passage?* he wondered.

They opened the clinic door and moved inside, only to find the spacious waiting room filled with people as well.

"Did you know it was this bad...the sickness?"

Jacoby shook his head as they stopped by the counter and waited for the nurse to look up from her large screen.

"If you're experiencing flu-like symptoms, please scan your id chip to check in and find a place to wait. I can't guarantee how soon you'll be seen," the young woman said without looking up. She wore a surgical mask over her mouth and nose, leaving only her eyes and forehead visible.

Jacoby swiped his wrist over the reader, a large red glowing box popping up on the nurse's transparent polymer monitor.

"You're Dr. Reeds' emergency follow-up appointment. Uh, okay," the young nurse said, finally tearing her eyes away from the screen and looking up. Her large brown eyes were visibly glassy and a thin sheen of sweat covered her forehead. She turned her head and coughed, the force almost knocking her mask free.

"Sick?" Anna asked.

The young nurse nodded, pulling her mask down to blow her nose.

"I don't even know why I'm wearing this stupid thing anymore. I'm already sick. This bug is horrible. Not even the synthesized immune boosters are helping much. We've already requested a batch of cloned anti-virals, but they won't be here for three weeks. Uh...Dr. Reeds wants to see you right away. You can follow me."

The nurse grunted and heaved herself out of her chair, before motioning him through hall to his right. Anna moved to walk away and wait but Jacoby hooked her arm and pulled her around to follow.

"It doesn't look like you've been affected by the power outages," Jacoby said as they moved down the narrow corridor, closed examination room doors spanning the hall on either side.

"Oh, we were. The clinic went dark yesterday for a full hour or so. We've had some blips...where the lights will dim and flicker, but so far today it's been okay," the nurse said, speaking slowly, and then gestured towards the largest room at the end of the hall. "Right in here. Have a seat please." The nurse picked up a black bracelet off the desk and hooked it around Jacoby's wrist. As soon as it clicked into place, the black band glowed to life, a red light thrumming in time with his heart.

The nurse turned away and pulled a thin, transparent screen away from the wall, a thin, flexible arm holding it aloft.

The exam room was large, with a padded examination table and a pair of uncomfortable-looking chairs. White plastic cabinets covered one wall, a simple stainless steel sink and lab table spanning beneath it.

Anna moved to sit in one of the chairs just as the soft rap of knuckles sounded on the door and Dr. Reeds appeared.

"Hello again, hello again." Reeds moved in, closing the door behind him, his balding pate gleaming in the white overhead light. "You look to be alive. That is good, yes, very good. And I see you brought someone with you this time, which is good. The support of family and loved ones can be the most powerful medicine."

Dr. Reeds shuffled in, gave Jacoby's hand a limp shake, and greeted Anna, before adjusting the large monitor against the wall.

"Is this on? Are these vitals current?" he asked the nurse, pointing at the glowing figures on the monitor. The nurse nodded and mumbled something quiet through her mask. The two exchanged a short, quiet conversation, but Jacoby couldn't hear what either of them said.

"To be safe, best to check it the old fashioned way," the doctor said as they broke apart. The nurse walked over to Jacoby and grabbed his arm, before pressing her index and middle fingers against his wrist. She watched the screen, as if counting, but then shook her head and walked away.

"It is right," Jacoby heard her say.

"I don't understand." Dr. Reeds cleared his throat and dropped heavily into the rolling chair.

"So...what's up? Did you find something wrong?" Jacoby asked, his stomach swirling uncomfortably. Had he tested positive for something on the blood screen? Or worse, was there something wrong with him?

"First, how do you feel right now?"

"I'm a little tired, I guess. And..." Jacoby started to say but paused. He tried to decide if telling the doctor about his headaches and strange impulses was a good idea...especially in front of Anna. Would he keep him from going back to work? What would Anna think? "I've got a headache, it's actually been on and off for the last couple of days."

"Have you had any bright or dark spots in your vision, muffled or impaired hearing?" Reeds asked next.

Jacoby shook his head. In fact, he couldn't remember when his senses were more acute.

"Unusual sweating, shortness of breath, or chest pain? A racing, or out of control heart rate...perhaps like you just finished running a race?"

Jacoby took a deep breath and took a moment to listen to his body. It all felt normal. "No, I mean just tired. I feel like I could lay down for a nap right now. And if you don't mind me asking, why? Did something pop up on my blood test? Is there something wrong with me?"

"The results from your blood screen came back...well, so far out of the normal range that our system automatically flagged you for follow up, but...."

"So far out of range?" Jacoby asked, his confusion deepening.

"I'm getting ahead of myself. First, let's just have a look at you and then I'll explain. Would you mind taking off your shirt and stripping down to your underwear? If your lady friend wants, she can wait out in the hall." Reeds turned back and stared at the monitor by the wall for a long moment, his face scrunched up in a scowl.

"It's not right," he mumbled and turned to the nurse. "Prepare an injection of Lanoxin just in case." She nodded and quickly left the room.

Jacoby turned to Anna, who shrugged and simply turned in her chair. He pulled off his t-shirt and threw it at her, then pulled his pants down. It wasn't anything she hadn't seen a dozen or more times before.

Dr. Reeds pulled on a pair of exam gloves and looked in his eyes, up his nose, mouth and ears, and then felt his neck, moving down to press on various parts of his chest.

"I am going to have a listen to your heart, this might be cold," he said, putting a digital stethoscope against Jacoby's chest. "Is there a history of heart disease in your family...perhaps tachycardia?"

"My grandpa died of a heart attack—"

"Odd, quite odd...take a few deep breaths, please," Dr. Reeds interrupted, slapping the stethoscope against his back.

The physician listened for a long while, moving the instrument from one side of Jacoby's chest to the other, and finally to his back. He leaned away suddenly, exhaling dramatically before rubbing his eyes.

"You're sure you feel fine?"

"Yes, doc. Why? You're starting to scare me."

"Well, the good news is you look to be feeling much better than yesterday. A remarkable turnaround, in fact, especially considering all the people out there. You were A-typical of influenza, although I didn't confirm with a mucus test. You were fevered, drawn, weak, and congested," Reeds said, exhaling again as he gestured towards the waiting room and beyond.

"I do feel much better."

"That's good...that's good. I'm so glad, because, well...uh," Dr. Reeds said as the nurse pushed back into the room, a syringe and bottle in hand.

"Because?" Jacoby asked, his fear and frustration growing.

"...well, according to your vitals and the results of your bloodwork, you should be dead!"

"Dead?" Anna echoed, her voice rising in alarm, "what do you mean he should be dead?"

He heard her jump out of the chair, her feet slapping the floor hard. A heartbeat later, her hands came to rest on his shoulders. She was shaking. "Are you saying Jacoby is sick...dying?"

Anna's hands felt warm on his shoulders, that small bit of tactile contact stirring his emotions and instantly scattering his attention. His headache returned almost instantly, the pressure filling his head and pushing out from behind his eyes. Blood started to pound in his ears as his heart rate increased. The change in his body wasn't necessarily sexual, but his desire was palpable...the need to shield Anna, to protect her from anyone and everything. Why did this happen anytime someone got near or touched him?

Jacoby turned back to Dr. Reeds and met his differently colored eyes. The doctor studied him a moment, before looking up to Anna.

"Well, yes and no. All of his symptoms and test results indicate that he is in acute cardiac distress. An unhealthier individual might already be dead," he said, flatly, and stepped back to scoop his large tablet off the desk. "But before I get into that, I have to ask. Did you feel something, just now?"

"Like what?"

"When your friend moved out of her chair and put her hands on your shoulders, your pupils constricted and you started to tremble. Do you feel differently than you did a moment ago?"

Jacoby moved to shake his head, but thought better of it. "Yeah, I mean. I've been having these strange headaches for the past few days. It's more pressure than pain though. I can feel it in my ears, but mostly behind my eyes."

"Uh hm...yes," Dr. Reeds said, his fingers tapping rapidly against his tablet. "And did that 'headache' as you put it, become noticeable just now?" The nurse moved in behind the doctor, an alcohol pad in one hand and the auto-injector in the other.

Jacoby nodded and shifted towards the woman in scrubs, his heart rate increasing yet again. He didn't do it consciously, but his body seemed to move on its own, as if to shield Anna from the woman.

"Easy, just relax. We're just trying to get to the bottom of...whatever is going on with you," Dr. Reeds said, sliding back a half step.

"What's in the syringe? And you still haven't told us anything yet. What is wrong with Jacoby? What is wrong with his test results?" Anna asked, her grip on Jacoby's shoulders tightening.

"Margo is holding an autoinjector with a dose of a rather common beta-adrenergic. We use it to treat high blood pressure. It works by reducing the force and rate with which the heart beats. The truth is, the testosterone levels in Jacoby's blood are impossibly high. In fact," Reeds mumbled as he swiped against the large screen. "A man of your age and physical condition should show free testosterone levels in the range of two hundred and fifty nanograms per deciliter to say eight hundred and forty on the high side. Your free testosterone levels came back at over ten thousand nanograms per deciliter. But that wasn't all. Your TSH levels, which indicate the health and function of your thyroid, are point zero zero zero zero one...which is within error threshold of reporting and would indicate hyperthyroid disorder if the numbers weren't so obviously erroneous. Beyond that we've also detected massive amounts of androstadienone, plus another compound our computers couldn't identify in your blood. We, uh, believe it is a compound, as you see, our computers returned a most frustrating error code."

"Andro..." Jacoby echoed, but struggled with the word. The doctor talked far too fast.

"Yes, androstadienone. It is a chemosignal, a compound derived from testosterone, otherwise known as a pheromone. It is normally excreted through skin and is received by the olfactory system of the people around you, but mostly the opposite sex. There is an entire field of study on the science of physical attraction as it pertains to human sexuality via chemo signals, physical traits, and body language, but I'm afraid I am not particularly well read on the subject. But that is secondary to my primary concern, as overly high levels of testosterone are inherently dangerous and can lead to severe heart conditions.

"Now, upon first receiving these results, I concluded that your test results were contaminated somehow. But you understand, with such obvious indicators of potential cardiac problems we had to bring you back in to check up and run a fresh blood sample. But...but, your heart rate is elevated as well, with a resting rate of one hundred and fifty beats per minute. Your blood pressure is far above normal at two hundred over one sixty-two, and your oxygen saturation levels are so rich they aren't even registering on our equipment. There is obviously..."

"But, what does all that mean? Jacoby is young...he's healthy. I've been with him, he looks just fine," Anna said.

"Quite simply, that he is in cardiac distress of some kind. We need to do some more tests...another round of blood work, a cardiogram to analyze his heart rhythm, and maybe some imaging of his chest and brain. But first we need to bring his heart rate under control, before he goes into cardiac and pulmonary arrest."

Wrong, wrong, wrong. No, they are wrong. The thought popped up into his mind just as the pressure in his head doubled. *Don't trust a mouth that moves moves moves.*

Jacoby shook the strange thought away.

"I feel fine. Great actually. There are lots of people out there who need a doctor's time more than me. I mean, just look out in the waiting area. But, me, I feel just fine," Jacoby said and pushed to his feet. Anna was there, behind him, one hand still resting on his shoulder. He turned towards the nurse, Margo, as she moved forward. She stopped mid-step, her eyes widening as her gaze met his.

"A-a-and I'm not saying that there *is* anything wrong with you, so let's just relax a minute...b-b-but all the data is showing me that something could be wrong. We just want to help you before your health turns critical. Please, just allow me a moment to do another blood test and a quick scan of your vitals."

False face...lies from a constantly moving mouth. He means to harm us. He cannot understand what us is! Jacoby shook his head, the thoughts banging around and feeding his growing panic. He definitely didn't think it, but heard it nonetheless.

"That's really not necessary..."

"Jacoby, please! Maybe the doctor has a point. There is no harm in just letting them do the tests to make sure you're okay. Right?" Anna said, hooking his hand and turning him to whisper in his ear.

He glanced at the door, his eyes drifting towards Margo. He met her dark eyes, a bead of sweat running down from her hairline to catch in her eyebrow, then to the injector clutched tightly in her gloved hand. The paper mask dimpled as she breathed in, the small indentation disappearing as she exhaled. He could smell her – sweat, small hints of body odor, and something else...sour, astringent.

She is contaminated, sick. She is scared, he thought, confident in the conclusion although unsure exactly how he knew.

"Listen to Anna, Jacoby. You look well, fit, and healthy, so let's just be on the safe side and make sure there is nothing wrong...beneath the surface. You know, as I say misery...it does love company," Dr. Reeds said, his voice quieter and shaking.

He seeks to pacify us, bind us, cage us. Strip us apart. Strip – strip – strip. Meat and bone, flesh and blood.

"Jacoby, please. Don't make a bigger deal out of this than it is. Just let them draw the blood and then we'll go," Anna said, her voice low and calming.

"Okay," Jacoby said and held out his arm. He had to watch her mouth to make sure he heard her right. His thoughts were simply too loud.

I need rest, my brain is out of control.

"Unfortunately, I'm short three nurses and two doctors, as well as half of my lab staff, so Margo here will only assist as she's just a tad under the weather, too. I will draw your blood again today...as I always say," the doctor laughed uneasily, "misery loves company and there are plenty suffering right now. Why don't you, uh, just have a seat over here."

Jacoby wiggled a finger in his ear and followed Dr. Reeds over to the stainless steel table. The doctor picked up the auto syringe and slid an empty ampule into the cage, wiped the inside of his elbow with an alcohol pad, and turned expectantly.

Bite, fight, and run. Survive we must, as we did with father. Run and hide...or fight. Jacoby wiggled a finger in the other ear and shook his head again, trying to dislodge the strange thoughts. It was just stress, damn it.

Dr. Reeds cocked his head, his differently colored eyes watching.

"Spell your last name please, Jacoby?" he said, indicating the chair.

Jacoby turned to find Margo behind him, her dark eyes moving rapidly, her weight shifting continuously from foot to foot. The syringe was still in her hand.

"M-a-s-o-n."

Anna moved in next to him. Her closeness and smell were a comfort but not nearly enough to quell his panic. She pushed him gently into the chair, despite every ounce of muscle fiber in his body twitching and begging him to run. His thoughts were almost constant now, the voice speaking directly to his arms and legs.

"Perfect, Jacoby. We're just going to draw some blood now, and while I do that Margo is going to take off your medical bracelet and replace it with a new one, so we can get a better set of vitals."

Dr. Reeds hovered around his arm, his black nitrile gloves making his hands look like thick-legged spiders. Margo, the nurse, moved in next to him and unclipped the bracelet, wiped his wrist clean with an alcohol wipe, and put a new one in place. She was shaking, too. He could see it, and somehow, feel it through the air between them. Why were they shaking? Why were they so scared?

"I can see that you're a little on edge, Jacoby. I can understand that..."

Ready to run...to fight. Both are to live. To live is the design. The strong live.

"Just a little poke," Reeds said, a hot pinch flaring as the needle jabbed through his flesh and into the vein. The doctor's hands shook...no it was almost his whole body now.

Jacoby watched blood start to fill the ampule and tore his eyes away, his gaze sliding up to the display on the wall instead.

His vitals showed as dashes and zeroes, until the nurse tapped on the new bracelet and it glowed to life. The monitor beeped and numbers started to appear.

HR must be heart rate, he thought, trying to focus on something and bring his thoughts under control. The number flashed as triple zeroes and then climbed abruptly, cycling through blue, green, and finally red numbers.

184 bpm – –

A bead of sweat ran down his cheek as the number continued to rise. He sniffed the air – it was warm and thick, the sour odor of bodies, breath, and his more recent peculiar odor filling the small room.

Damn, can they smell me?

"heart rate two oh one and climbing. Blood pressure is showing topped at three hundred diastolic, doctor. They're still rising," Margo whispered, leaning in to Reeds, her mask practically touching his ear.

Jacoby could hear her though, clear as day. His heart didn't feel like it was beating fast, far from it. He looked to Anna, who didn't seem to hear any of it. She squeezed his shoulder and gave him a reassuring smile, although worry lines had formed around her eyes. She was breathing harder, too...harder than him, in fact.

"That will do it," Reeds said, pulling the needle from his arm. A large bubble of blood formed when the doctor didn't cover the needle mark right away.

"Just relax for one moment, Jacoby. I'm going to run this test right away," the doctor said, his voice slow...overly calm. He was *trying* to act calm, but a part of Jacoby could see, hear, and smell the man's panic. It was oozing out of his sweat, dissipating and tainting the air all around them. Hell, it told him everything. The smaller man was practically ready to piss in his pants.

"Call the others in. Have them prepare a bed and crash cart...with restraints," Reeds whispered to the nurse as he dropped into the chair and rolled back towards the desk.

He admits the truth...finally. Jacoby reached up and rubbed his eyes with the palms of his hands. His muscles tensed up, bunching into painful knots.

"You know, doc, you can just send me another message when the results come back," Jacoby said, wiping the bleeding spot on the inside of his arm. His thumb hit the dark fluid and slid forward, smearing it down his forearm.

Run! His legs twitched.

Margo walked to the wall and tapped a small digital screen. An orange light above the door appeared.

Don't be weak. Leave. They can't stop us.

"I feel just fine, doc. Right, Anna? I'm good. I'll just go back to my quarters and lay down. You can send me the results." Jacoby moved forward just as the door opened, two bodies shadowing the hall. A young man in scrubs walked in first, followed by a young woman.

"No need to wait, the results will only take a moment," Dr. Reeds said and pulled the ampule of blood from the syringe before inserting it into a small computer on the desk.

Jacoby moved towards the door but the young man cut him off, while the other nurse hovered just inside the door. He looked into the young man's face, but it was like there was nothing there beyond the paper mask and surgical scrubs – just dark, lifeless eyes. He blinked and the young man's face clarified. He had freckles around his eyes and bushy eyebrows, with a pronounced nose.

"Calm down, Jacoby, they're here to help you," Anna whispered and squeezed his arm, but he twisted free of her grasp. He would fight them if he had to. Fight all of them, to break free and keep Anna safe.

The computer beeped and chattered loudly. Reeds picked up his tablet, immediately flipping through a host of colorfully glowing numbers.

They will surround us. They will kill us. Run Now!

His feet twitched, the spasm shooting up his legs. He tried to shake the strange thoughts and feelings away, but it was like his fight or flight impulses could talk.

"I'm sorry to say that your bloodwork looks even more troubling now. We need to immediately check you into the hospital wing for further tests and observation. I'm afraid this has become an emergency situation." Dr. Reeds stood and nodded over Jacoby's shoulder. A sizable orderly appeared through the door, pushing an old-fashioned wheelchair. The man had medium-length shaggy brown hair, a squat, crooked nose, and a scar that ran down through his lip. He looked like a man that had survived more than a few scrapes and tussles. He wore a white Planitex Medical Services shirt stretched over a muscular chest and arms. Tattoos peppered his arms and hands – some of the ink was faded, old, while some looked new. Margo reappeared from behind Anna, the auto-injector held ready.

"Jacoby, this is Randle. He is going to help us get you back to the hospital block. Why don't you have a seat in the chair...Margo needs to give you a quick injection to help bring down your blood pressure."

Randle moved towards him, the pressure crashing into Jacoby's brain in a wave, his vision and hearing immediately going fuzzy. "No! No shot. I don't want anything. I...am...fine. I just want to go!"

"I understand, Jacoby. But you need this," Dr. Reeds said, clutching to his white coat with shaking hands. "Help him into the chair, Randle. He could stroke out at any moment."

The young male nurse and the orderly moved in and grasped Jacoby's arms, moving him gently but firmly towards the wheelchair. Margo hooked an arm around Anna and guided her towards the door.

"Let go of her," Jacoby growled and fought. The pressure in his head thrummed in time with his heart, hot jolts snapping down his neck, through his shoulders, and into the rest of his body.

Randle, the orderly, hooked Jacoby's arm and jerked him down into the chair. He twisted and wrenched free, bouncing back to his feet. The orderly reached for him, tried to hook him around the neck, but Jacoby ducked under his arms. Randle over-corrected and fell over the wheelchair, tumbling feet over head to the ground.

"Just-just-just stop, please! We just want to help you, Jacoby!" Dr. Reeds shouted.

The monitor on the wall started to beep loudly, the displayed numbers flashing bright red. Dr. Reeds' head snapped up, his eyes going wide. The monitor showed a heart rate of over four hundred beats per minute. That wasn't possible.

"How? What?" the doctor rambled, "He's going into cardiac arrest. Sedate him, now!"

Jacoby's heart pounded, but nothing that felt out of control. On the contrary, he felt good...beyond good.

The male nurse threw his arms around Jacoby in a bear hug, pinning his arms to his body. Randle fumbled his way to a knee and then pushed off the ground, blood flowing out of both nostrils. His scarred lip curled up in an angry snarl, muscles pulling his face into a severe and devilish mask.

There was something familiar in Randle's expression that sent a wave of fear coursing through his body, a glint in his dark eyes that promised violence and pain.

No...no, he thought as the memories flooded back in. The look, the expression, wasn't just reminiscent of his father, but an almost photo-realistic rendering of his worst side...the side that always meant violence.

Randle pulled a hypodermic needle out of a pack on his belt, removed the cap with his teeth, and lunged. Time seemed to slow, the bright overhead light gleaming off the needle, several glassine droplets of sweat appearing on the orderly's angry face. The pressure behind his eyes responded in kind, a hot jolt filling his chest and firing out into his extremities, everything shaking and swelling at once.

His thoughts flitted from one possibility to another, moving faster than he ever thought possible. He saw the orderly moving towards him, the nurse pulling Anna out through the door, and Dr. Reeds yelling into a data point. He could see every movement, every possibility at once.

Jacoby flexed his chest and shoulders, pushed his arms away from his body and broke the nurse's hold. Then he swiveled in a flash, grasping two handfuls of the man's scrubs and wrenched him around. The orderly crashed into them, his arm snapping forward and plunging the hypodermic into the nurse's back.

"Ow...aarrgghh!" the young man cried, exhaling in a violent cough that knocked his surgical mask from his face. His dark-brown eyes went wide with realization.

"You son of a bitch!" Randle cursed, wiping his bloody nose on his right sleeve. Jacoby let the male nurse slump to his knees as the bigger man rushed forward, his teeth bared in a reddish-yellow snarl.

"Stop...I just want to leave..."

The orderly hit him with all the force of a charging bull, a mass of crushing arms and churning legs. Jacoby staggered back, the weight throwing him into Dr. Reeds. They all stumbled together, crashing into the stainless steel desk in a heap of flailing limbs, bunching scrubs, and white lab coat.

Examination tools and computer hardware hit the ground in an explosion of rattling metal and shattering plastic.

"Randle, that's enough..." Dr. Reeds started to yell, his breath exploding out in a rush as the orderly's knee missed Jacoby and smashed into his genitals instead.

"Jacoby, please stop! They're just trying...to...help," Anna yelled from the door. Her fingers were wrapped around the doorframe as nurses tried to pull her out in the hall.

His rage welled up inside, blossoming and pushing forth like a tidal wave. The voice, the chaotic thoughts he'd struggled with, was there, whispering and shouting at the same time, bending and pushing him into action, urging his arms and legs to move – to not give in to his learned response. When his father flew into a rage, Jacoby would curl up in a ball or hide. But now...

Fingers to rake – gouge his eyes. Bend and snap – break the fingers. The voice in his head bellowed violent promises...no, urges. It was part of him, and it wanted him to fight back.

"I don't want...to...hurt you," Jacoby grunted, fighting back as his own body started to twitch and move against his will. "Please...I just want to...leave."

The orderly yanked him off of the gasping doctor and squeezed, his muscular arms wrapping clear around Jacoby's upper body.

"I was spec ops, you puke. I've whooped bigger, meaner, and tougher than your scrawny ass," Randle grunted and squeezed, lifting Jacoby clear of the ground.

"Please don't hurt..." Anna's grip broke and she disappeared out into the hall.

Rend...break...snap his bones. Tear his meat and spill his blood. A red fog started to sweep across his vision, but Jacoby fought for control, fought to resist the angry and violent urges.

"Please...let...me...go," he grunted, struggling to draw breath. Randle squeezed even harder, his chest and shoulders popping under the force.

Jacoby snapped his head back in desperation, just managing to catch Randle in the face. The big man grunted, cursed, and fell back. His grip finally failed. Jacoby landed hard and managed a single step towards the door, before a hand bunched up in his shirt.

Randle swung him around, a fist snapping out and catching Jacoby in the stomach. The impact knocked his breath away and he sagged to a knee. His vision blurred, the pain tearing through his midsection like a hot spike.

"Please...stop," Jacoby pleaded when his breath returned. He held his hands up as a ringing filled his ears.

"Doc is here to help people, but pukes like you don't give a shit about anyone but yourself," Randle snarled, lifting Jacoby off the ground by his wrists and throwing him violently against the exam table. Randle's face was red, sweat dampening his hairline. His pupil's looked like wide, black saucers.

Fight back. Bend him...break him.

"Randle, that's enough. He's not fighting back," Dr. Reeds winced, wobbling and clutching to his groin.

"They need me around for pukes like you – shitty, worthless rock crackers strung out on brain boilers and booze. Pukes that lose control and endanger good people. Sacks of crap and piss that aren't good for anything else," the orderly raged, his fists swinging in out of control haymakers, hitting Jacoby's arms, chest, and stomach.

"I fucking hate people like you. Hate...fucking hate...HATE!" he raged, his fists continuing to batter.

Jacoby backed away, using his arms to protect his head and face, but the man was too strong, and too overtaken by rage.

"Please...stop," Jacoby sputtered breathlessly, blood dripping over his lip from a cut beneath his eye. He squinted though his hands, flinching back as Dr. Reeds limped forward and tried to pull the orderly back, but Randle shoved him violently away.

"Call security. Call them now!" the doctor yelled.

He will break us. Show him our strength. Break him first and he will learn never to cross us again. Make him hurt, or give me the freedom to do it for us!

Randle spun, rounding on the doctor and Jacoby lunged, throwing his weight onto the big man's back. He hooked one arm under his chin and the other under his left arm and held on. Randle roared and ran backwards, smashing him into the wall. Darkness and stars washed over his vision, the pain barely perceptible through the haze.

Randle's face was an ugly mask as he rounded on him, his fist swinging in impossibly fast. Jacoby saw the strike, but felt the impact in his shoulder long before the pain registered.

He will kill us. Fight back! Jacoby fought the urges when his right hand started to shake, and instead tried to curl up and protect himself, like with his father. Randle would tire eventually, or someone would come to help.

Jacoby was on his knees, the blurry fist striking his arms and chest again. He felt each strike, the violent crack of knuckles on bone popping his joints and bruising his skin and muscle. Randle swung again and again, his eyes now wide and black. His reason was gone – his teeth bared and savage, like a shark sent into blood frenzy.

Stop being weak. Fight back! The impulses grew suddenly stronger, until Jacoby's elbow jabbed out, deflecting one of the big man's punches. His right fist swung out next, connecting solidly with Randle's jaw. The orderly's head snapped aside, teeth clattering loudly.

Keep hitting him until his insides become his outsides! Hit-hit-hit! Crush him.

Emboldened, Jacoby ducked forward and swung as hard as he could, his fist hitting Randle in the chest. The big man barely moved, his body absorbing the strike like a mountain of muscle and bone.

You hit him in the tit? You are weak.

"Stop this!" Dr. Reeds shouted as nurses ran into the room.

They tried to pull Randle back, but the big man turned back to Jacoby, the humanity gone from his black eyes.

"L-i-t-t-l-e p-u-k-e," he growled, a thick rope of saliva sliding out of his mouth and hanging down his chin.

Randle lashed out before Jacoby could react, his hand flashing forward in a blur. The impact rocked his head back, pain flashing from his face, back through his ears, and down his neck.

Jacoby felt his head hit the wall and his legs went wobbly, but it all felt so far away. The fist flashed in again, but he was helpless to stop it. Randle's fist crashed into his nose, cracking his head violently against the wall.

The pressure exploded behind his eyes, the small, irritating voice now booming off the inside of his skull. Up became down and dark, light. The room spun as a sharp pain split his skull in two. Everything broke apart, until he was sideways, upside down, and on his head at the same time.

The pressure slid forward and all around him, wrapping around the room like a billowing sheet of liquid black. Jacoby tumbled backwards, falling, tumbling, and silently screaming.

Then it all seemed to straighten, the sense of motion wrapping around him and propping him up. The pressure filled his head. It seemingly filled every nook and cranny of his skull this time, slipping down his neck and into his mouth until he was sure he would be sick – it was kinetic, all joy, anger, and lust wrapped up into a concussive and violent potential.

Ahhh, I'm free. No more cage, no more dark corners. You and me, Jacky, now we are one. He felt the voice in his head, sliding down his neck and into the rest of his body, the strange urges and impulses wrapping around his own thoughts and desires. It was strength, power, and rage – everything he wasn't.

At least everything he never used to be.

1300 HOURS

"I already told you, I don't want to wait out there. Why aren't you listening to me?" Anna spat and tried to wrench free from the nurse. "I want to wait with my friend...with Jacoby. I'm not going to leave him alone."

"Ma'am, please. It'll be better...uh, safer, if you just come with me. You need to..." The nurse swiped for her arm again but Anna pulled back against the wall. The nurse caught only air, lurched stiffly, and almost fell. Her paper mask fell free in the process. A thin sheen of sweat covered her top lip, adding to the slightly darkened skin ringing her eyes. She looked tired, sick, and scared.

"My mother is a 'ma'am'...and I told you like a dozen fucking times already, I'm not leaving Jacoby here. I am the closest thing he has to a family, and you're not just going to...to sweep me out of here like some afterthought."

The nurse took a deep breath as if to argue, but her shoulder's sagged a little, the weariness in her eyes deepening.

"Please, just let me go to him..." Anna said calmly, just as a loud crash sounded from the exam room behind the nurse.

"Jacoby!" Anna screamed and ducked around the nurse, just clearing her grasping, clutching arms. She bounced from the left wall to the right, pushing off and running forward.

Anna approached the exam room door just as a pair of nurses tumbled into the hall. The first woman tripped and sprawled face first into the opposite wall with a sickeningly loud *smack*.

"What in the hell?" Anna gasped, skidding to a stop as the second nurse tumbled over the first, her dark scrubs torn and askew.

Anna jumped over the nurses and pulled herself into the exam room. Her foot landed on a metal tray, the debris shifting and sending her stumbling and fighting to correct. She'd nearly found her balance when her left foot landed in a large puddle of clear liquid, the rubber sole of her shoe instantly sliding out from under her. She tumbled painfully to the ground, her butt and shoulder landing hard.

A loud *smack* split the air – the telltale crack of knuckles cracking against flesh and bone.

"Jaco..." Anna cried and spun around. She took in the chaos of the room in a single, passing glance. Doctor Reeds stood between two nurses, a short orderly with mid-length black hair actively pushing him back towards the door. Another orderly, much taller and more muscular stood near the far wall, tattoos dotting seemingly every inch of available real estate on his arms. His tight white shirt was soaked through with sweat, and his sandy brown hair was a wet, tousled mess.

"Randle! Stop this now, stop it! Stop!" Doctor Reeds yelled, but the orderly shoved him back.

Anna flinched as the big man, the one doctor Reeds called Randle, swung his fist forward, the resulting *smack* sickeningly loud. The big orderly stepped back and turned, breathing hard. His face was sweaty and red, his lips pulled back in an alarming expression – almost equal parts snarl and smile. But it was his eyes that almost unhinged her. They were wide and bulging, seemingly black in the white light...empty.

"Get...out...of my...way," Reeds growled and tried to fight his way past the smaller orderly.

"Just go, doc!" Randle gasped, his voice a breathy growl. "This little p-u-k-e is d-a-n-g-e-r-o-u-s. Just doing my j-o-b. To deal with the dangerous o-n-e-s!"

Anna wiped her hands on her pants, less concerned with what the fluid was that she'd slipped in than what was going on against the far wall. There was something about the big man's voice...no, it was the way he talked. Slow, breathy, and rumbling, more like an animal growling than a man speaking. It prickled the hairs on her neck and arms.

"Doc, get back!" the smaller orderly snarled and pushed Reeds back hard again. The doctor staggered and tripped, a pair of nurses catching him before he fell.

"This is absolutely unacceptable...insubordination, that's what it is! Bob, let me by! Randle...you need to stop this! He's not fighting back. He's not causing any trouble!"

The big orderly turned fully and took a step towards the doctor. Anna gasped. She stifled a shout as the big man's face clarified, her feet and hands pushing her back without thought. Randle didn't look right, didn't look well. His skin was stretched back from his eyes and mouth, his expression so tight he almost looked like he was wearing a mask. Drool slid from his mouth, wetting his chin and sliding off in stringy droplets.

The big orderly moved, finally revealing Jacoby slumped against the wall behind him. His head lolled to one side and his eyes closed. His face was a bloody, battered mess.

"You son-of-a-bitch!" Anna cursed and pushed to her feet. Her hands balled up into fists and she moved towards the big man. She'd never been much of a fighter, but the impulse hit her so hard and fast that she couldn't deny it – she wanted to make the big man hurt, despite his size and terrifying appearance.

Randle looked at Anna, but doctor Reeds spun and caught her first, moving her out of the big man's reach. The young male nurse pushed Randle in the chest just then and fought to move past and get to Jacoby, but the big man shook his head, mumbling something over and over again, and snagged him by the scrubs.

"L-i-t-t-l-e p-u-k-es, l-i-t-t-l-e p-u-k-es, no good, no g-o-o-d," the big man moaned.

"What in hell is wrong with him? Why did he do that...hurt him like that? Argh! Let me go, I want to...need to see if Jacoby is alright," Anna argued and fought. She heard a commotion behind her in the hall, but before she could turn to see what it was, Randle swung the nurse around, tossing him into the wall.

The young man hit with a crash, his breath exploding out in a loud *uuuugh*.

"Don't just stand there, Bob, do something. He is out of control!" Reeds yelled at the other orderly. Randle pulled the ailing nurse away from the wall as Bob glanced between Randle and Reeds. He took a single, faltering step and raised a hand, but stopped.

"Where is security?! I want them here NOW!" Reeds screamed.

"Randle...hey, bud..." Bob said but jumped back as Randle snapped forward suddenly, driving his forehead into the male nurse's face. The young man jerked back, blood spattering from his nose and mouth.

"Another little p-u-k-e," Randle cocked his arm back, fist clenched, bloody knuckles pulling white in the bright light.

Anna looked from the nurse slumping in the big man's grasp, to his bloodied knuckles poised to strike, and pushed away as she tried to fight clear of the doctor. She'd heard the sound of his fist smashing into flesh before, and knew somewhere deep inside that he'd kill the young man unless someone stopped him.

Saliva slid free from the corner of Randle's mouth, his tight, freakish smile seemingly locked in place. The big man rocked forward, but his fist froze in the air as a bizarre clicking-laugh filled the room.

"Oh, R-R-Randle, R-R-Randle, R-R-Randle."

Reeds stopped trying to hold her back and they turned as one. Randle let go of the nurse, the young man immediately falling to the ground in a heap.

"White shirt...white pants...eyes of white and black. Blood on white. Red...red on white. The color of anger and blood. So...so strong and tough, beating on little pukes. Little pukes like Jacoby. So strong...so tough...so big and angry. Just...like...father. You shouldn't have hurt him...broke his head, cause now he can't hold me back!"

Randle grunted and swung around as Jacoby pushed up from the ground, his head lifting slowly off his chest. His body looked limp, only his legs moving as they propelled his body up the wall. He looked like a horrible, bloodied puppet.

"Jacoby?" Anna whispered, but the voice couldn't have come from her friend. It didn't sound anything like him.

"Randle, don't! Please, just stop!" Reeds yelled and took several large steps towards the orderly. "We can sort this whole thing out...make it right."

"L-i-t-t-l-e p-u-k-e," Randle growled in response, his hands clasping into fists.

"Dude...Randle, just shut up, man. Get out of here and get some air, bro. You're out of control," Bob spat, the smaller orderly stepping forward and trying to take control. He turned to Jacoby. "You talking in riddles now? You fuckin' freak! Get on the ground and put your hands behind your head. This whole thing is your fault, so just get on the ground. Do it now, or I'll put you down hard."

Jacoby laughed again, but stopped suddenly and looked around, his eyes focusing in on Anna. He mouthed her name, and then looked to Randle and the male nurse bleeding on the ground.

"Anna...what's going on?" he asked. He looked groggy, confused, but then his expression changed, a strange smile curling into place.

He pushed away from the wall and took a step towards her.

Randle grunted and snorted, cutting him off, bloodied, tattooed knuckles lifting to strike, his eyes bulging and wide.

"Crush, whoop, pummel, poor little Jacoby. Smash him, beat him...break him! Put him on the ground, just like father did. Why R-R-Randle? Because he doesn't like to hurt, doesn't like to make bleed. Not like you, R-R-Randle. Not like father. Red on white...blood on skin," Jacoby said. She could see his mouth moving, see his chest rising and falling as he breathed, but it wasn't him. It wasn't his voice. This was strange, distorted...twisted.

Then Jacoby's face twisted again and he blinked. He looked to Anna, confusion written plainly on his face.

"What in the fuck are you talking about? You were the one making a scene, freak...fighting back when the doctor was just trying to help you. We're just doing our jobs. Now lie down on the ground, and put your hands behind your fucking head," Bob spat and wedged his body between Jacoby and Randle.

"No. Jacoby cowers. Jacoby wouldn't fight back, but not anymore. Now, Jacoby has me. You shouldn't get in our way. Go-go-go."

"Has you? Get in our way? What in the fuck are you talking about?" Bob asked, but Randle cut him off.

"Little p-u-k-e's not going anyw-h-e-r-e," Randle growled, his voice rumbling.

Bob turned back to Dr. Reeds, but the physician didn't seem able to speak. Reeds looked to the nurse on the ground, the young man cradling his bleeding nose and moaning quietly. He met Anna's gaze, mumbled something else under his breath, and looked back to Randle.

Why isn't he doing something?

"Okay...sure, Jacoby, we'll let you go. We're just gonna take it easy now and head to a private room down the hall," the smaller orderly said. His voice was quiet, his movements slow and measured, as if he was disarming a bomb.

"Put the little p-u-k-e d-o-w-n," Randle snarled, quietly, his fists shaking.

Jacoby's eyes moved away from the orderly, first to Anna, and then over her shoulder. She heard people enter the exam room behind her – the soft tread of shoes in the hall the only indicator.

Anna half-turned, catching the movement out of the corner of her eye. Several station security officers slipped through the door. They wore slim, black body suits, gray honeycomb armor accentuating their knees, elbows, chest, and shoulders.

"Gotcha," Bob exclaimed behind her, and she turned back just as the orderly jumped forward and pinned Jacoby's wrists to the wall.

No!

Jacoby's smile widened and he moved in a blur. Bob lifted free from the ground, cried out, and tumbled back into Randle.

The big orderly seemed to snap awake at the contact, his trembling form exploding into motion. Bob tried to jump on Jacoby, but snapped back as Randle yanked him by the shirt.

"What in the f..." Bob cried as his counterpart flew into a rage. Fists and knees flew, Bob taking a knee to his ribs before a punch to the back of his head. He turned on Randle, his right fist swinging around in a wide punch, but the bigger man struck first, his elbow swinging up and catching him in the chin.

Strong hands clamped around Anna's arms and they pulled her back. She fought against them, but they were too strong.

Doctor Reeds turned and started yelling, spittle flying from his lips.

"Stop him...stop all of them!"

The nurses ducked out of the way, pushing past the doctor as more security officers tried to force their way into the small room.

Randle hit the smaller orderly over and over again, the man's head snapping back and forth violently. The nurses were gone, and then the doctor. The security officers pulled them out into the hall.

Anna watched as Randle threw Bob across the room, the smaller orderly almost pirouetting through the air before crashing against the stainless steel table. Randle turned his rage towards Jacoby, just as the security officer pulled her towards the door.

"Jacoby! No! Leave him alone!" Anna screamed. Randle's fists flew, his neck almost as red as his bloodied knuckles.

"Miss please, we need you to get out of the way."

"No...stop him! He's a monster. He's going to hurt my friend, my best friend," Anna screamed and pointed right at Randle. The security officer turned, reached for a white baton on their belt, and managed a single step towards the two men.

The big man's fist swung in at Jacoby's face, her friend just standing there against the wall, his expression and posture placid, bored. Then she blinked and Randle's fist was in Jacoby's hand.

The orderly howled and reared back to swing with his other fist as more security personal crowded by, pushing her towards the door. Jacoby's other hand caught the orderly's fist out of midair, and then his face twitched.

"R-R-Randle. You like to hurt...see pain...feel it? Does that make you feel powerful? Is it exciting?" Jacoby said, suddenly, his voice filling the room. They pushed her out through the door just as Jacoby smacked Randle's hands aside and caught him by the throat, somehow hoisting the big man clear off the ground with a single, outstretched arm.

"Put him down! Do it now!" one of the security officers yelled.

"Down? Why down? I don't want to hurt you, but R-R-Randle and I have some things to t-t-talk about," she heard Jacoby say.

Anna fought free from the security officer's grasp and pulled herself back into the doorway. Four security officers surrounded Jacoby, the ends of their batons glowing red. She sucked in a breath to scream his name, to scream for them all to stop, but Jacoby turned and looked right at her. His dark eyes shone in the light, a strange, creeping shadow playing just beneath the skin of his face. His tongue flicked out of his mouth, and then he grabbed Randle with both hands and threw him into the air.

The big man hit the ceiling, his bulk crashing into the remaining light in a shower of sparks and shattering plastic.

"Jacoby!" Anna screamed as the room fell dark.

They were in the hall next, the security officer dragging her along, moving towards the reception area. As soon as the officer stopped pulling, Anna tried to run back down the hall. She only made it a few steps.

"Listen...I need you to stop. Please!" the officer yelled and jerked her back around.

Anna tried to listen, tried to comply, but she couldn't seem to break free from the compulsion to run, her arms and hands itching with the need to punch and hit.

"Look at me!" the officer said. Her voice was husky and strong, the kind of smoky, sultry she remembered from her father's cherished antique records. The thought grounded her a bit and she was finally able to still her legs, to stop moving.

It was jazz. That's what it was, she thought, regaining a bit more of herself. The scrolling scales of trumpets and saxophones, overlaid by sultry, sexy female singers.

The security officer reached up, unclipped her helmet and pulled it off. Anna looked into her green eyes, the connection snapping even more of the fog away. The officer was taller than her, wider through the shoulders and chest as well. The sides of her head was cropped close to the scalp, but thick auburn hair swept back on top – and not the fake red she saw on so many women, but the real deal. Her complexion was creamy and smooth, the kind lucky women took for granted, wealthy women paid handsomely for, and the rest lusted after.

Anna sucked in a breath, shook her head, and shuffled her feet.

"I'm...I'm sorry, I don't know what came over me. I think it..."

"Adrenaline. They call it 'fight or flight'. It can make your vision tunnel and make you lose fine motor functions. I used to be a soldier and know it well. Keep your eyes moving and your brain engaged. Are you alright? Are you okay?" the officer asked.

An angry buzzing noise sounded from the exam room and something crashed against the wall.

Anna nodded, her eyes dropping to the patch sewn into the front of her bodysuit. It read *A. Miranda.*

"What is your name?"

"Anna," she said, her voice shaking.

"Anna, I'm Alexandria, but everyone calls me Lex," the officer said, and scanned the chip in her wrist with a compact data point.

"Ja-Jacoby. Please, don't let them hurt him. This isn't his fault. The orderly...he just went crazy."

Lex searched her eyes and took a breath to respond, just as another crash sounded in the exam room. One of the security officers stumbled into the hall and smacked hard against the opposite wall a heartbeat later.

"Shit," Lex swore.

"Listen, I need you to wait out there. I have your data. If I can't find you, I'll message you on your com," Lex said, pushing Anna towards the waiting area.

"But...but," Anna stammered, just as Jacoby appeared in the hall. He held Randle at arm's length, the big man's feet kicking and thrashing violently, his head and face bright red.

"Drop him! Let him go, let him go! I'm not going to tell you again!" a security officer yelled. He hung around Jacoby's neck, jabbing his stun baton into his back over and over again.

"Bad R-R-Randle. Bad R-R-Randle. Doesn't like it when others hurt him...does he?" Jacoby growled, smacking the big man into the wall repeatedly.

Anna stumbled back down the hall as Jacoby flicked the officer from around his neck, tossing the man back into the darkened room. Lex approached, pulling her baton from her belt, the stun prong flashing from green to red. Jacoby looked at her and laughed.

"Red! My fire...my hot, burning fire. You are the one I want," Jacoby said, as Anna stumbled out of the hall and into the waiting room.

1430 HOURS

Anna fell against the nurses' station. Her head spun and legs shook, the sour taste of stomach acid creeping up her throat and into her mouth. She walked her way around the desk, but fell to her knees and crawled the rest of the way on her hands and knees. Anna barely made it to the trash can before throwing up.

Her stomach cramped hard, buckling her over. Wave after wave of nausea rose up, pinching her guts all the way down to her privates. Anna emptied her stomach into the waste can, the plastic confines magnifying the sound of her retching. Hot, sour ick choked her throat. She pushed and pushed, her body fighting against the cramps, telling her she needed to breathe.

A wave of darkness washed over her vision, the blinding canvas exploding with bright, brilliantly colored spots. Finally, after what felt like an eternity, she finished and gasped in a ragged breath.

Anna slumped back against the can and wiped her mouth on her sleeve. She swallowed – her throat and stomach were soar, the thick sensation and sour taste lingering in her mouth.

"Ehh, lovely, Anna," she grumbled, sniffled, and bent forward to spit into the can. She grimaced, and it wasn't just from the smell. Paper and office waste filled the bottom of her can, the refuse now spattered with her sick.

"Oh my god," she whispered, gagging, "what did I eat that was blue?" A red bubble formed in the slimy mess, sliding down the piece of paper before breaking with a quiet *pop.*

"At least you didn't...piss your pants," she said, reaching down and checking her pants. Anna let out her breath slowly, burped, and pushed up onto her knees. She looked around self-consciously and found the waiting room had gone quiet.

It wasn't full anymore, and most of the people had moved to the back, away from the desk and the hall.

They're afraid...afraid of Jacoby.

She looked from person to person – the faces all drawn and pale, with red noses and dark bags under their eyes. Anna listened for a moment, her belly rumbling noisily as she tried to decipher what was happening to Jacoby.

She heard voices, raised voices, the thump and squeal of rubber soles slapping the ground, and an occasional thump.

Is he still fighting? Why is he fighting? And why did he say those things to the redhead...Lex. Why did he tell her that she was the one he wanted?

Anna suddenly doubted everything? Did she really know Jacoby...like, really know him? Was he involved with Lex and she not know it?

Anna gagged and burped again. She leaned over the can, heaved, and spit. She looked up to find the people moving away from her – some shuffled towards the exit, while others whispered to one another and settled into seats further away.

One face stuck out of the crowd, the woman's pointed jaw and pronounced cheekbones forever locked in Anna's memory.

Janice – the skeleton queen.

Janice eyed Anna for a long moment, her glossy fingernails tapping loudly on the plastic seat next to her, and then she tipped forward in a violent coughing fit. Janice swiped at her mouth and nose with a tissue before rocking back in her chair.

"You're the girl, aren't ya?" she croaked as Anna pushed off the ground.

"I'm sorry?" Anna looked down at the waste can. She considered kicking it back under the desk, but then thought better of it.

"I remember your face from his personnel file. Saw Jacoby at the desk, saw you with him. Been sitting here the whole time. Been waiting the whole time with everyone else. We heard the commotion in there. Heard him fighting with the doctors," Janice said, stopping to blow her nose.

Dark mucus blew right through the tissue, spattering her pants.

"Ugh...this damn bug," Janice spat, pulling the tissue away and looking at her pants. A glob of black mucus hung suspended from her nose.

Anna jumped away as Janice snapped forward suddenly, the dark mess spraying everywhere. The people seated on either side of her recoiled, shielding their faces and complaining.

"Oh, shut up!" Janice yelled, beating her fists against her thighs. She ripped a stack of tissues out of her pocket and began swiping at her face.

The man to her right got up from his seat and walked.

"That's right, walk away," she raged shaking a tissue at his back. "This shit...this nasty, ugh..." Janice raged, barring her teeth.

Anna stepped back and moved to walk away, but could barely turn before the woman was out of her seat and blocking her path.

"I was fine...you know, dandy, before this...his shit. Before Jacoby started fucking up – at work...all the time, like nonstop. And now look at him – can't even take his administrative days off without screwing those up. Here he is at the clinic starting fights with doctors and nurses. Don't get comfortable, sweetie, with your perfect, pretty hair and your skinny little waist. He's gonna screw up again on the job, and I mean soon, and then I can send his ass packing on the next freighter. Fitting, too cause he comes straight to the clinic and gets right in. The rest of us have been sitting here forever," Janice chattered angrily, her lips moving faster and faster. Anna wanted to push the woman, to smack her in the mouth, but a fresh line of dark mucus ran from her nose and over her top lip.

Anna turned around and moved to walk away, but Janice pushed noisily out of her chair and cut around her, jabbing a finger towards her chest.

"I used to have tits like that when I was younger, nicer than those, in fact," Janice pointed at Anna's chest, spitting as she talked. Dark ick seemed to run freely from her nose now. "You're not so perfect...obviously, because you're hanging around a loser like him. Do you hear me? A louser? A leaser?"

She couldn't seem to pronounce the words properly and her voice warbled oddly. She glared at Anna, large bubbles of tears forming and running from her eyes.

"I don't have to listen to your shit," Anna snapped, backing away from her jabbing, boney finger. "I'm leaving."

"My shit?" Janice snapped, her eyes going wide. "Does the truth hurt, honey? We saw security go back there. They've prosbably allready detooned his worthless aaaaaaa..." she paused, almost gagging on the words. "It's all ov..." Janice tried to speak again but stammered, her eyes rolling back in her head.

Anna saw it coming and jumped back, right before Janice turned and started to flail. The boney woman fell into the line of chairs, spitting and coughing, a cloud of dark fluid erupting with every violent breath. It hit the ceiling as well as the people around her.

Janice landed in a middle-aged man's lap, the young woman seated next to him throwing her hands up and almost immediately tumbling to the ground.

"What in the hell?" the man yelled. He threw his hands up as well and pushed off the chair. Janice tumbled to the ground and immediately started to seize. Her arms and legs thrashed violently, while her head swung back and forth, cracking loudly against the floor.

Anna backed away, subconsciously wiping her hands on her pants. Some of the people in the waiting room backed away, climbing up onto their chairs, while others rushed in to try and hold Janice still.

"Someone help!" a woman screamed, dark droplets of Janice's mess spattered across her face. "Someone get a doctor."

Janice flopped over again, bucking against the men now trying to hold her still. Her face turned towards Anna, and cold panic tightened her chest. Dark fluid pushed from the woman's eyes now, flowing down to meet the dark streams leaking out of her nose and mouth.

Anna turned towards the exit, kicked over her garbage can, stumbled, and caught her balance on a chair. She turned as nurses ran out of the hall and towards the mob clustered around Janice.

The boney woman started to thrash more violently, and then turned her head and spewed onto the ground. Janice gagged, croaking and squealing, her noises horrible and frightening.

This is wrong. This is all wrong, Anna thought, fear and panic besting her resolve. She pushed between two people at the clinic entrance and ran out into the hall.

A worker walked out directly ahead in the hallway, pulling a length of cable behind them. Anna dodged him, but caught the cable with her throat. The worker cried out and fell back. Anna landed atop him, her bulk hitting his soft belly.

"I'm...so...sorry," she gasped and rolled free. The worker grunted and yelled, but Anna refused to stop. She kicked off the ground and ran blindly down the hall, through the door, and out into the A ring atrium, rubbing her neck as she went.

She dodged around the missing floor panels and the scurrying technicians, only dropping into a fast walk when people started to stop and stare. Anna arrived at the transit elevator only to find a mass of people already waiting. She paced back and forth behind the group, pulled out her data point, and opened her messages.

Of course he wouldn't have sent me a message, he was wrestling with security, she thought and angrily stuffed the device back into her pocket. She wiped her hands on her pants and silently wished for some way to sanitize...well, everything.

What was Jacoby thinking? What was that orderly...Randle, doing? Anna tried to reason it all out in her head as she waited for the elevator, but none of it made any sense. It all felt so needlessly out of control...so pointless.

The elevator chimed and the wide doors slid open. The crowd before her parted to allow the arrivals to move past, and then filed in to take their place.

Anna moved in last, drifting to the left side of the lift, where a pair of technicians moved aside to make room. She nodded her thanks and tapped the icon for D ring, despite the fact it was already selected.

The doors hissed shut, the magnetic drive kicking in smoothly. Anna tried to run through everything the doctor said – all the vital statistics and medical mumbo jumbo, but the only thing that stuck out to her was his expression and the words "should be dead".

What is wrong with Jacoby? Could the doctor be wrong? My god, could it affect me? The last thought hit her hard, her hands immediately starting to tremble. They didn't just share the same space, but last night they'd pushed well past the boundaries of friendship.

Anna fought to push the experience at the clinic from her mind – the horrible, thick air in the exam room, Randle's murderous rage, and Janice. The thought of Janice made her mouth water, and despite every attempt to think about anything else, the image of her writhing on the ground floated forth in her mind. Not just writhing, but vomiting foul, black sick.

Anna's stomach lurched and she stifled a burp as someone coughed on the other side of the elevator. The sound was wet, unhealthy. Another coughed in response, the entire group shifting uneasily. A murmur filled the confined space and someone sniffled loudly.

Anna tensed, her weight shifting restlessly between feet. She struggled against the urge to run, to break away from the crowd, but she was trapped in a sealed compartment surrounded by the vacuum of space.

She looked to one of the technicians next to her. The young man met her gaze. He had light, brown eyes, a long, narrow chin and scraggly clumps of facial hair on his cheeks. He gave her a crooked smile before looking away, and wiping his nose on his sleeve.

Anna saw a dark streak on the fabric as he dropped his hand, and she immediately pushed away, jamming her body forcefully into the unforgiving metal. She glanced at the doors, then the holographic display.

Open, damn you. Open!

Was it moving? Were they stuck? It was moving so slowly she couldn't be sure.

The technician coughed suddenly and Anna jumped.

"I'm sorry," the young man said. She spun around, intentionally avoiding his gaze. She looked to his sleeve. No black mucus...no sick. Was she seeing things? Was she losing her shit?

The elevator chimed suddenly, the panel behind her glowing bright blue.

"B ring atrium," the elevator chimed, in a smooth, multicultural accent. The lift promptly opened and a large group of people shuffled out through the doors.

Two people walked on and the elevator continued on. The newest additions, two young women, whispered and laughed, standing so close together they almost looked to be holding one another. The girl on the right coughed, not bothering to turn away as her friend told a story.

Anna tapped her knuckles on the cool steel panel, fighting the urge to pull her shirt up over her nose and mouth. She'd never been sensitive about germs or bugs, but after her experience in the clinic, she was well and truly freaked out.

They arrived at C ring. Most of the crowd departed, save for an older man standing on the opposite side of the lift. She watched him out of her peripheral vision as she scrolled down through messages on her data point.

The man wore a full work suit, the faded olive fabric worn through in spots, the forearms and knees stained by rock dust and grease. She knew the smell well enough, as it was how Jacoby smelled after every shift.

Anna rubbed her neck and scratched a spot on her hairline. Her right eye started to twitch just as the man cleared his throat. It was a soft sound, and not sickly like the others, but rather a subtle grunt born out of habit.

He did it again, and then again, Anna's eye twitching each time.

Stop it, she wanted to scream, the itch on her hairline growing more pronounced – like a bug biting and digging at her flesh.

Anna clawed at the spot as the man cleared his throat again. She moved to round on him, but the elevator stopped abruptly.

"D ring atrium," the elevator said and the doors hissed open.

"Go right a–" the man started to say.

"Thanks," Anna cut in and jumped forward, running out of the elevator. She made her way down the narrow corridors, passing in and out of heavy shadows, at least half of the overhead lights now dark. The air had a different smell than it did earlier as well – heavy, damp, and stuffy.

She pushed the call button on the service elevator and waited. A service panel to her right was dented in, a smudged partial footprint marring the yellow paint. A bag of trash sat just to its right, the contents spilling out onto the floor around it.

Were they there earlier? She honestly couldn't remember.

The elevator quietly arrived and she traveled to their floor in blessed silence. The doors opened, stopping halfway, the motors humming loudly. The lone overhead light flickered, went dark for a long moment, and surged brighter again. The elevator chime warbled, yet the doors refused to open.

"Okay?" Anna whispered and approached slowly. She pushed on the doors for a moment but they refused to move. The hall beyond the doors went dark and Anna froze, the sound of her beating heart filling her ears.

The elevator shuddered, and Anna quickly stepped forward, turning sideways and slipping through the narrow opening.

"This place is coming apart at the seams," she breathed and looked back at the elevator. The doors continued to whine but didn't move, the lone interior light flickering on and off before finally going dark for good.

1455 HOURS

Pain snapped into Jacoby's body in sharp, biting jolts. The heat remained on the spot long after the security officers pulled their stun batons back. He didn't want to fight them, to hurt anyone.

What a lie! The voice in his head laughed, another violent urge snapping down his arms.

Of course the other part of him wanted to inflict pain. He could feel it more succinctly now than ever before. It was fiery passion, swinging through uninhibited violence and insatiable lust between every raging heartbeat. He'd been able to ignore it before, but for some reason he'd lost control.

Jacoby knew that little voice well enough, as it had been there since he was a child. But it had always been so small...whispers lending him strength during his darkest moments. As he got older and learned to defend himself it faded to the background. Or had he simply learned to ignore it?

You can't ignore me anymore, the voice said, as another stun baton jabbed into his ribs. Electricity snapped painfully through his skin, his muscles immediately knotting up and his lungs cramping up.

I kept you safe when father got too rough. I took over when he staggered into your room, piss drunk and angry. That was me that took the beatings, the one that pushed you into that dark place and protected you. You don't remember the worst of it, thanks to me - the broken noses, loose teeth, fractured fingers and splintered fingernails, and the knife. Where do you think the scars came from? The ones hidden under your hair, on your back and legs?

"That's not true," Jacoby argued, "he hit me, slapped me a few times, but it was never that bad!"

"What is wrong with this dude? Seriously, let go...of...his...throat," a security officer growled, only his mouth visible behind the visor of his helmet.

"I can't let him get away...with...it. Not anymore...someone has to make him answer for all of the anger," Jacoby grunted, squeezing Randle's throat even tighter, fighting the security officer's attempt to peel his fingers back. But it wasn't him...he didn't say it, and he couldn't seem to control his arm.

He pulled Randle away from the wall suddenly and slammed him into the bulkhead again.

"Stop it!" Jacoby yelled, trying to get the angry portion of him to let go. A baton cracked against his arm, while another jabbed painfully into his ribs, fire exploding into his body.

You don't know the half of it...the half of what I did for you. You just thought you were a brave little boy, a survivor that managed to run away. I am your anger, your suppressed lust from when father caught you looking at naked pictures of ladies.

Randle's face was reddish-purple, his dark eyes rolling crazily from side to side. But it wasn't Randle anymore. All Jacoby saw was his father, his complexion ruddy from a combination of drink and dirt.

Randle's mouth moved, but it was his father's voice that spoke. "You ain't worth the credits I gotta drop on ya – the fucking clothes I put on your back, all the food you gotta eat. Ain't worth any of it. Should'a kicked you out when your mother's worthless ass ran off."

He should have. We could have lived somewhere, hell, anywhere else. Or you should have run away. I would have protected us. Someone would have wanted you," the voice cut in, filling his thoughts. It was so strong now, fighting to take control of his mind and body.

"What is this guy talking about?" a security officer growled as he jumped onto his back and hooked an arm around his neck. The other officer drove his baton into Jacoby's midsection and then his arm.

"Put him down now, or I'll..."

"I'm sorry, I'm really sorry," Jacoby gasped and yanked Randle away from the wall. His legs propelled him out of the exam room, his momentum slamming the orderly's bulk into the wall. He did remember the voice...the seemingly wild urges and quick to anger side of himself from those days. He'd banished the thoughts, told himself they weren't real.

"Drop him! Let go of his neck...do it now!" the officer growled, tightening his arm around Jacoby's throat, something hot jabbing into his back again and again.

"Bad R-R-Randle. Bad F-F-Father," Jacoby growled, smacking the big man into the wall only to pull him back and do it again. But it wasn't him...the voice or the violence. Any of it.

He flicked the security officer off his back, his body moving automatically. Jacoby watched the man sprawl to the ground, the impact knocking his helmet askew.

He reached up and tried to pull his right arm away from the big man's throat just as a different voice cut into the chaos.

"Let go of him now!" It was a woman, her voice husky, resonate, and full of authority. Pain flashed in from all sides, but his grip loosened around Randle's throat. The angry part of him was listening. There was something about the woman's voice that broke through the fog.

"Stun his arm...stun his arm. I can't break his freaking grip. How is this dude so strong?" the officer to his left grunted, the man he'd just thrown from his shoulders jamming his stun baton into Jacoby's leg. The pain was beyond intense, a fire that ripped through his skin, muscle, and bones, but something held him upright. No, not something.

He turned down the hall as another security officer approached. A glowing baton hung from her right hand, her sleek, gunmetal gray helmet clutched in the left. Her fiery red hair was pulled back and up, but he recognized her immediately – green eyes sparkling in the intense, overhead light.

"Red! My fire...my hot, burning fire. You are the one I want," the angry part of him said, his lips and tongue moving strangely in time with the thought.

His gaze caught Lex's green eyes, moved down to her full lips, then her neck and down over her formfitting bodysuit and curve-hugging padding and armor. An all-consuming lust grew inside him as blood pounded in his ears and behind his eyes.

"Let him go," Lex said, her voice rising noticeably. Was she scared, confused?

No, she recognizes us. She remembers us, the angry part of him said and he felt the corded muscles in his right arm release. Randle dropped almost immediately, gagging and coughing, his strangled gasps almost inaudible compared to the riotous beating of Jacoby's heart.

Jacoby felt his body turn fully towards Lex, when he wanted nothing more than to back away, to run. He could hear the crackle and hum of their stun batons, the pronged ends glowing with the angry promise of more pain.

The air around him grew thick, the pressure thrumming in his skull. The odd smell filled the air once again and he watched as Lex's nostrils flared. She took a half step back, her eyes flashing open. He drew in a breath through his nose – spicy amber cut by something more organic, more palpable.

Lex blinked rapidly and reached up to rub her forehead.

Jacoby took a single step towards her, the angry part of him distracted, his voice quieting. He could feel his right arm again, but more importantly, he could move it.

"I'm sorry..." he started to say, but Lex's eyes jumped up, her pupil's contracting and expanding rapidly. Then she growled and lunged.

Jacoby caught a glimpse of the stun baton, the red glow flashing in his vision. A sharp pain erupted in his face, and everything went dark.

1600 HOURS

Anna moved out and around the corner from the elevator and turned down the long, curving hall. Only a single overhead light panel was lit ahead, the cool glow bathing an isolated patch of floor and walls. Several others flickered dully, but the rest were dark.

"Just don't light any candles, people," she whispered and moved forward, silently hoping to avoid experiencing another sealed environment explosion ever again.

Anna passed crew quarters on either side of the hall. The darkness added a patina to the doors and walls, exposing stains, cracks, scratches, and pitting she'd never noticed before. The station looked more than just dreary in the low light, but old, and dilapidated. A dark stain marred one door to her right. She stopped to consider it a moment, just as something thumped and banged behind that door.

Was that stain there this morning? Surely she would have noticed something that obvious. The dark fluid had dripped down the metal and pooled on the floor, where it dried in a wide, flat puddle.

"It's just in your head, Anna. It's in your head," she said, forcing her feet forward another half a dozen steps into the darkness.

Or is it? After seeing Randle in the exam room, and then Janice get sick in the waiting room, Anna wasn't sure. Hell, she wasn't sure what "real" was anymore. Shit was blowing up, people are going crazy and trying to kill one another, and Jacoby...

Anna moved through the pool of light from the one working bank. She didn't want to think about all of it anymore. She...couldn't.

A dull thud sounded beyond the door to her left, followed by muffled voices. A heartbeat later someone laughed distantly. Her tension broke and Anna let out a pent up breath, and then that person coughed, the sound louder and harsher than the laugh before it.

Anna froze, small hairs on the back of her neck immediately standing on end. She shivered and rubbed her arms, walking apprehensively forward into the darkness.

"Home, cup of tea...home, cup of tea," she said, repeating it like a mantra. There was simply too much to think about...to figure out at once.

She needed to sit down someplace familiar and safe to start sorting through it all – one messed up strand at a time.

The dark hall creaked and groaned ahead of her, a subtle glow from the adjoining hall ahead providing the only light. Another cough sounded somewhere down the hall behind her, then another ahead and just to her right.

Anna moved past the last quarters on the right, the shadows so deep she couldn't even see the door. The gray walls and bulkheads looked like stone, the shadowy doorway a narrow cave.

Something in her mind shifted, and she almost forgot that she was surrounded by ceramic and titanium superstructure, and beyond that, the cold, black void of space. For a moment, her mind almost swept her away to shadowy halls where Grendel stalked would-be Danish heroes, or Baba Yaga led ignorant travelers to their deaths.

A shout split the silence, the voice muffled and unintelligible. A voice answered – this one deeper and louder. Angry.

"It's not your business," Anna whispered and moved past the door.

Something heavy thudded up against the bulkhead just feet ahead of her, a loud crash filling the space beyond a heartbeat later. The loud voices rose again, Preston's voice immediately recognizable even through the sound insulated walls. The screaming reached a fever pitch and died away as something else thudded against the wall, a splintering crash following right after. A quiet voice rose up in the silence that followed. Anna held her breath – no, it was crying.

She slid through the darkness and stopped just before the dark door. Anna lifted her hand and rapped lightly on the metal door before she could think better of it.

The quiet crying continued somewhere beyond the cold portal, the air vent behind and above her buzzed gently, and her heart pounded uncomfortably loud in her chest.

Preston's voice rumbled deep and low, Soraya's crying gaining in intensity. Anna sucked in a steadying breath and pounded on the door again, this time much louder. The space beyond the door went quiet, the deep, almost imperceptible hum of the station the only sound.

"Soraya? It's Anna. Is everything all right?" Anna asked, but her throat was tight, her voice small and strangled by the darkness.

Silence spanned for a moment, and then she heard someone just on the other side of the door. They sniffled.

"Soraya?"

The door clicked and slid open slowly a few inches, the motor and gears grinding audibly. The power to their door didn't appear to be working. Anna made a mental note and wondered if she'd be able to get into their quarters at all.

"Anna," Soraya whispered, her voice a low hiss. "You can't be here right now, girl. Please, just go! Quick."

A gentle glow filled the hall behind her, but Anna could see enough of her face to see that her cheeks were wet with tears.

"I heard a crash and yelling. I just wanted to make sure you both were all right. Are you?"

"Yes. I mean, it's Preston. He's just not himself...still sick. Just needs rest and to get himself back to straight again," Soraya whispered and moved to push the door closed, but Anna forced her hand into the gap.

"Wait! What do you mean by 'not himself'? Are you okay? What's going on?"

"It's me, Anna. I think I said something...no, did something stupid. He got mad. It's my fault. Just go. It's best if he doesn't know you're here, okay?" Soraya sobbed, her voice breaking as she tried to push Anna's fingers out of the way and force the door closed.

A shadow passed behind Soraya just before she gave a startled shriek and fell away from the gap. Anna had just enough time to step back before the door crashed open the rest of the way.

"You again!" Preston growled angrily, his whole body shaking. "You've got a lot of nerve, you piece of shit!"

Anna caught a gleam off metal, spotted a short knife in his hand, and jumped back against the wall.

"It's Anna, Baby. She was just saying 'hi', but she's going home now," Soraya said, reappearing behind Preston in the hallway.

He didn't move or speak, his bulk continuing to block the doorway, the light from the room backlighting him and casting his face in impenetrable shadow. "Did you know about him? What he's really like? W-W-What he does?"

Anna pressed her back against the wall, her attention pulling reluctantly away from the kitchen knife clutched in Preston's hand. She tried to meet his gaze, to search his face and better understand his meaning, but the hall was too dark. He moved part way out of the doorway, his limbs expanding into the hall in an almost spiderlike fashion.

"Preston, why do you have a knife?" she asked, swallowing.

"Well, Anna?" Preston pressed, ignoring her question. The strange almost growling timbre of his voice sent a cold wave flooding down her back. There was something oddly familiar about his voice, but she couldn't quite say why.

Preston stared at her a moment, his eyes slowly sliding over until he was staring just over her shoulder. His mouth went slack and his head started to twitch gently up and down.

Anna turned to see what he was staring at behind her, but it was just a blank stretch of wall. She waved a hand in front of his face, but he didn't seem to notice.

"Heh, Preston, are you okay?" she asked.

Preston's head snapped up, his eyes swiveling slowly to meet hers. He leaned out from the doorway, his fingernails scratching against the metal on one side and the knife scraping on the other.

"Did you? Know about him?" Preston asked, his voice turning gravely and hoarse.

"Know what about 'who'? Who is really like 'what'?" She backed away, her first impulse to run for their room, but he was only a few feet away.

Can I outrun him? Can I get the door open fast enough? Will it open at all? She knew it was stupid - of course she couldn't outrun him. Preston was a former athlete, like Soraya. He was taller, stronger, had longer legs, and Anna had never been much of a runner.

"We always thought you two were nice - decent people...a couple friends looking out for each other way out here in the black," Preston whispered as he pulled his body out through the doorway, a wet cough echoing deep in his chest.

"Preston, I don't know..."

"Soraya helped him–" he interrupted, moving sideways into the hall to block the path to the elevator. Another raspy, wet cough vibrated in his chest and a tear slipped from his left eye. The knife shook in his hand, the blade gleaming in the low light.

"We found him on the ground outside our quarters after the power cut out," he said, pausing as a sickening noise echoed out of his stomach. He gagged and then coughed. "She helped him back to your quarters...thought he was sick...and when she comes back home." Preston stopped suddenly and bent forward in a violent coughing fit.

"My god, Preston, you sound horrible. Maybe you should go to the clinic–"

"I knew something was wrong right away. I know her – how she moves, feels, smells, even if she was too embarrassed to admit it," he said, snapping up and cutting her off.

"Did something happen? Is Soraya okay," Anna asked, moving slowly backwards down the wall, silently hoping he wouldn't see the movement in the dark.

"She was confused...uh, lost, had scratches on her shoulder and arms, and her robe and panties were ripped. You're a woman, put it together." Preston coughed again and Anna flinched back, her imagination filling in for what her eyes could not see.

"Jacoby wouldn't do that...not to Soraya," Anna argued, but watched as his arms and legs continued to twitch. "We play charades together and drink cheap wine, we tell stories, we complain about our days, and make fun of the stuffy up and ups you and guys work with in admin. He wouldn't hurt anyone."

"I...think...you...knew."

Anna shook her head, but what was that worth in the dark? She knew Jacoby – his awkwardness towards women, his sometimes painfully shy way. He could come off as a little crude at times, but he was the last person that would pick a fight let alone assault a woman. He was the one that stood up for people, especially after the shit he went through growing up.

"Where is he?" Preston asked, moving slowly towards her and forcing her into the deeper dark.

Anna wanted to argue against his accusation, to try and get Preston, who always seemed so levelheaded, to stop and see reason.

"Come on, Baby, put down the knife and come back inside. You're sick and you're head is messed up. Once you're feeling better you'll see the truth. We just need to...just need to calm down and get you back in bed," Soraya said and pulled on his free hand.

"Where is Jacoby, Anna?" he asked, dragging his wife down the hall.

"Can you put the knife down? I don't want anyone to get hurt," she asked, her gaze flicking from his dark hand to his face and back down, but immediately knew her error.

"Hurt? Hurt?"

Soraya slipped between them as Preston's anger seemed to blossom, his breathing now wet and raspy.

"Baby, that's not what she meant and you know it. Now come on, you're out of control! Give me the knife and stop fucking around. Let's go back inside before someone calls security and ruins everyone's day. I told you already that's not what happened. It's...it's not like that at all. Jacoby didn't do anything. I can explain everything, but I am not doing it in the hallway. Just...come inside and–"

"That man tried to force himself on you, and she," Preston growled, pointing the dark knife at Anna, "knew about it. There is no more talking. I know what happened in their quarters even if you won't...admit...it. I could smell it on you...could see where he touched you–" Preston rumbled. He reached up and pounded a fist on the side of his head and swayed a bit.

"Anna, just go. His head's messed up with this bug," Soraya urged and tried to push him back, leaning all of her weight into his body, but he didn't seem to notice. He grunted and smacked his head again more violently, something wet dribbling out of his nose.

"Ahhh! He hurt-hurt-hurt. I...hurt," he stammered, the words mushy in his mouth.

"What's got into you? Why aren't you listening to me? Baby, you're freaking me out. You're not right...not right at all," Soraya said.

A panel light flickered to life somewhere behind Anna, the flashing glow piercing the darkness like a strobe. She pushed away from the wall and tried to turn for their door but fell into the opposite wall and shielded her eyes. The flashing light...it made the floor and walls move, or that's what her eyes tried to tell her.

The light popped and hummed loudly, its violent, strobe-like flashes hitting her in dizzying waves.

"H-u-r-t in m-e...you. I smelled him on y-o-u. T-a-s-t-e-d him when you kissed me. I know what he d-i-d. Ahhhh. I k-n-o-w!" Preston moaned.

"Stop this, baby! I'm scared. Your ass needs to be in bed before you drop dead in this hallway. Or...or, let's go to the clinic so you can see a doctor," she heard Soraya argue, her voice rising in volume and strength.

Preston didn't seem to be moving anymore, his limbs twitching and trembling. Anna rubbed her eyes and squinted. Or was he? The light blinked more rapidly. Was he moving, or was it just the light?

Anna took a breath to speak, to quietly urge Soraya back and away from her husband, but flashing light played hell with not just her eyes but her sense of balance. The ground shifted and moved beneath her, the walls bowing and flexing. Was it like Randle in the clinic? She remembered him freezing, right before flying into a violent rage.

Anna knew that she needed to get Soraya away from him, get them both someplace safe, but that thought had barely planted in her mind before Preston started to cough and gag.

She moved straight towards Soraya and her husband, her feet stabbing out awkwardly at the ground. She held her hands out and swiped at the air, reaching and grasping, desperate to pull her back. Were Randle and Janice inflicted with the same thing? Would he become violent, or burst into sudden and horrible sickness? She knew people were sick, but could it be this bad? Had station administration lied to them?

"Soraya, you need to get back," Anna whispered, only steps away from her back as best she could figure.

That damn light just needs to stop flashing. She couldn't see in the dark, but at this point even blindness would be preferable. *Just another step...another step and grab her arm. Pull her back to our quarters. Then close the door and call someone.*

"He's just sick, girl. He needs to get his ass into bed," Soraya responded, but Anna could hear the fear and uncertainty in her voice.

"Soraya, get away from him. He's not just sick. I saw it in the clinic. It's bad. It makes them crazy," Anna said, forcing her eyes wide.

"Come on, baby. Let's go," Soraya said, grasping Preston's hand and then started to pull him back towards their door. She jerked to a halt and snapped back suddenly. Preston twisted and flung her into the opposite wall. Soraya screamed and cursed, the ceramic panels cracking under her weight.

"I know-know-know-no-no-nooooo," Preston moaned, his fists flashing up and smashing violently into his head and face. Bone and cartilage snapped and popped as his knuckles cracked into his jaw and nose, the knife cutting into his cheek and ear.

"You mother f...what is wrong with you?" Soraya grunted as she rolled over and tried to stand.

Anna lurched forward, hooked Soraya under the arms, and pulled her back as Preston wheeled about, the knife swinging in a wide arc. He slapped at his head again, bent forward, and choked loudly. Anna used that moment to help Soraya to her feet.

They managed two cumbersome steps down the hall before a heavy weight crashed into them from behind. Anna used the momentum and shoved Soraya down the hall, sending her lunging, stumbling into the darkness.

"Go...just run. Find help!" Anna screamed, staggering. She tumbled face first, Preston's weight bearing her into the ground. The hallway spun – darkness and flashing lights twirling around her, but she managed to kick around and roll to her back.

Preston thrashed atop her, his movements violent and wild, like an animal caught in the throes of death. She brought her hands up before her face, kicking and kneeing with every ounce of strength in her body. She tried to fall back on her self-defense training, to remember everything her jujitsu instructor had taught her about leverage and movement, but that had been so long ago.

"Preston...please...stop!" she grunted, his weight smashing her right leg against the ground. Preston coughed and sputtered, his voice lost and strangled as if trapped in his chest.

Something wet and hot spattered her hands and face as he grew even more manic. She managed to wrestle her leg free, desperate and driven by the singular need to get away. He shifted, moaned, and swung his right hand down. Anna caught his forearm with both hands, the blade of the kitchen knife now pulled between the meat of his palm and fingers. Blood ran freely from his hand, the blade having already cut deep into his flesh.

Anna pushed as he leaned into her, all of his weight driving the knife blade down and towards her face. Blood dripped from the tip, seemingly jumping back and forth from the blade in the flashing light.

"Preston...please...stop!" she grunted again, but he couldn't seem to hear her. Or if he could, he didn't care or understand.

Surprised by her own strength, Anna wrenched the knife away from her body, lifting Preston's weight back up. His chest started to vibrate and he moaned, pressing back in response. His mouth dropped open, a thick rope of drool spilling out and onto her shirt.

"Stop-stop-stop!" she cried frantically, cringing and flexing her entire body to push him away, but he was too heavy and strong. Her arms started to shake from the strain.

Anna kicked in again and again, her kneecaps striking solidly into his ribs but he didn't even seem to register the pain.

"Preston, you know me. We're friends, right? Please...don't do this," she pleaded, the cold and numbing realization stabbing into her chest. He wasn't just lost to anger, he wanted to cut her, stab her. He wanted to kill her.

She contracted her core and managed to pull her knees in, wedging them under his body and pushing him away. He started to flail again, fluid leaking out of his eyes and nose, a series of loud snaps and cracks sounding from his body. The knife slid from his hand and clattered onto the ground next to her head.

Preston thrashed and broke her grip on his forearms, his hands crashing down and hooking around her shoulders. The hall light blinked on suddenly, bright, white light filling the space.

Preston's fingers dug into her back as he fought to pull them together. A dark line formed above his nose as she flexed her legs out, fighting to gain purchase with her feet and kick him off. She couldn't talk anymore, could barely breathe.

Anna felt his body contract as he fought to pull her closer, as if embracing her in a strangling hug. A strangled cry formed in her throat as something beneath Preston's shirt moved, clawing at the thin fabric like curling fingers.

Footsteps slapped against the floor by her head and in the next moment a shadow fell over them.

"Get the fuck off of her!" Soraya yelled. She wrenched Preston's left arm free and yanked him back. The nails of his left hand dug deeper into Anna's shoulder as he moaned and lifted her clear of the ground.

"I don't know what has gotten into you, but I said get-off-of-her!" Soraya hooked her hands into the neckband of his shirt and pulled hard. The fabric stretched and tore, the shirt splitting right down the middle.

The skin between Preston's eyes split apart suddenly. Blood spattered from the torn skin, white bone appearing in the white light. Anna screamed and kicked as boney, sharp objects pushed out through the skin of his stomach and chest, the snapping of bone so loud it echoed off the walls.

"Help me!" Anna screamed as blood spattered her chest and face.

Soraya fell back against the wall as Preston scrabbled back over Anna, something boney and white popping through the skin just under his ribs, and then another.

Anna moved to cover up just as something swung in fast and smacked Preston's head aside with a loud *ding*. He moaned and twisted back towards her when Soraya swung the fire extinguisher in again, hitting him in the side of the head and tumbling him onto his back.

"Get up...get up!" Soraya yelled and half-lifted Anna off the ground and half-dragged her down the hall.

She kicked and stumbled, fighting for balance and trying to swipe the gore off her face. Bone and flesh snapped and slapped loudly against the floor and walls behind them, but Anna didn't dare turn and look. Was it still Preston anymore? What was it trying to do to her?

They ran together down the hall. Soraya yanked her around the corner and towards their door, overhead lights cycling on and off as far ahead as she could see. Anna crashed into the wall by her door, urgently rolling up the stained sleeve of her shirt. The scanner's small green light glowed in the darkness, but when Anna fumbled her wrist over the reader, nothing happened.

"Try again, try again!" Soraya yelled, grasping her arm and smashing her wrist against the wall.

Anna looked up just as a dark form appeared around the corner behind them. Preston staggered out into their hall, his right hand scrapping against the wall. His fingers left dark, wet smudges on the ceramic panels.

Preston made a strange gurgling sound and then his nose popped. His face tore wide, the flesh pulling away clear down to his top lip. He tipped sideways and stumbled into the middle of the hall, a horrible, tormented scream spilling out of his mouth.

Soraya screamed in response, her nails digging into Anna's arm. A door opened further down the hall past Preston, an elongated box of light cutting into the dark. Anna smacked her wrist blindly against the reader. A person appeared from the open door, leaning out and looking in either direction before spotting Preston.

"What is with all the yelling out here? I worked third shift....I just want to sleep!" they complained.

Get inside and close your door! Anna's thoughts screamed, but she couldn't seem to speak...to form the words. She couldn't look away from Preston as he ambled towards them, moving through the light streaming in from above.

She banged her wrist against the wall, but didn't even know where the reader was anymore. His face was peeling back like the macabre pedals of a blooming flower, jagged shards of bone tearing and stabbing out through the skin on his chest and stomach. She wanted to scream, to turn and run, but could only seem to smack her wrist against the wall.

Anna only tore her eyes away when Soraya wrenched her head around. She smacked the reader with her right hand and smashed her left wrist against it again, pushing against the limb with all of her weight.

"Hey, you...pal, leave the ladies alone. Anna, is that you? Are you okay?" the man from down the hall yelled.

The reader beeped suddenly and the door clicked. She shoved Soraya through the gap and into their quarters before it had opened fully and jumped inside. She punched the wall, the door control panel cracking under her fist.

Motors whirred, gears grinding unevenly and she turned to find Soraya shoving the door to make it close faster. Anna dug her fingers into the gap between the metal panels and pulled, a massive, clicking, shifting form hitting the door just as it slid shut.

"Lock...lock...lock it!" Soraya muttered, sliding to the ground and shoving her weight against the door. Something scratched against the metal door from the hall, a heavy *thud* shaking the door and its service panel a heartbeat later.

Anna swung around and jabbed the lock button on the cracked screen. The panel beeped and the icon flashed red.

"Lock? Did it...lock?"

The door shuddered violently.

Anna's gaze flashed from the panel to Soraya, and back to the panel. She hadn't heard it click.

"I don't...I didn't hear it click. Did you?"

The door shuddered again, the motor panel rattling noisily. Something popped in the wall.

"Hey, buddy...I'm talking to you. Why don't you get away from their fucking door or I'll call security," the man yelled out in the hall, his voice muffled by the ceramic wall panels.

The door shuddered again and again, the metal portal rattling loosely.

Anna grabbed Soraya and wrenched her off the ground. She pulled her down the dark hall. The bathroom light shone ahead, its dim glow barely breaking the heavy shadows.

"Just back the fuck off, man. What is wrong with you..." the man screamed from the hall just as Anna slammed the bathroom door behind them.

Anna sat on the sink and threw her feet up onto the door, bracing against the wall to hold it shut. Soraya slowly backed into the small shower, her eyes wide and her mouth open, before falling awkwardly into the small space.

Anna held her breath, choking back sobs, and listened. She reached down and pinched her arm again and again, but the pain felt real. No noise came from the hall beyond the door. No banging, no yelling. Nothing.

"What...in...the...hell...was...that?" she finally managed to ask. Her voice trembled and shook, her heart beating a violent tamponade against her ribs.

"That wasn't my Preston...wasn't. Can't...couldn't be. No-no-no. His face...his stomach. What...what was happening to him?" Soraya asked, her legs spilling awkwardly out of the small shower. She sobbed, her tears running heavily down her cheeks. Then she started to gag and Anna's body went rigid.

Anna picked up the waste can and shoved it in Soraya's grasping hands just before she pitched forward and vomited. She heaved into the metal can, her gagging and choking echoing impossibly loud in the small space.

No – please, god...no!

Anna pushed back against the opposite wall, her feet pressing her back into the corner and didn't stop. She watched Soraya tremble over the can, then glanced to the bathroom door and the lock. Was it safe beyond the bathroom? Was she safe in it?

"Ah...I'm okay. I just think it was...too much," Soraya grunted and wrestled forward to set the can outside the shower, then she leaned back and sucked in a deep breath, her chest shaking as she hiccupped.

Anna watched her carefully, mentally preparing to run or fight if she started to act funny. She inched forward and despite her reservations, glanced into the can. The crumpled up refuse was spattered with surprisingly blue sick. She wrinkled her nose as a bubble formed on a tissue and slid out of sight. It was red.

Day 4

00 19 HOURS

Jacoby was in his childhood home. It looked as it always did – disheveled, dirty, and smelled of stale synth alcohol, cheap, burned meat, and sweat. A visible haze hung in the air. It glowed orange in front of the open window, where the early morning sun spilled in.

A pack of exchange cigarettes sat on the dirty table, the crinkled, white pack smudged with grease. His father's old hardhat sat next to it, "Mason" scratched into the front where the nameplate had long-ago fallen off.

He moved from the kitchen to the small hall, passing by the living room. The small television glowed brightly, an E-span ticker sliding smoothly across the screen, while a rather rigid-looking woman in a drab suit droned on and on. The right side of the screen flickered, pixelating where the acrylic was cracked. He remembered when it broke – his father threw a bottle at the screen when WholeTech announced they were moving all manufacturing from earth to the lunar colony. Another job change and another night hiding from his violent, drunken rage.

His father sat in his recliner, his dirty boots hanging just past the edge of the footrest. His jumpsuit was dark, almost black, through the knees, chest, and arms, where years of soot and embedded grease stained the protective fabric.

Jacoby inched forward, moving closer than he usually dared. His father didn't snort or snore and he couldn't see his chest rise and fall in the gloom. He held tight to the water glass, the surface of the clear liquid sloshing from side to side.

His father didn't ask where the water came from, but it was next to him each morning without fail. He'd wake up, grunt and complain, and then drink. If his headache persisted, his mood would sour. If not, Jacoby might actually see his old dad again, and better yet, he might give him a ride to school. The water helped, sometimes. He'd leave pain relievers, too. If he could find some.

He stepped over an empty bottle, and tiptoed through several more before carefully sliding the water glass onto the small table next to the chair.

He eased the ashtray aside and moved the glass as close to his father as possible.

Jacoby reached into his pocket and pulled a single bubble pack free, the pills inside an opaque red. He laid the pain relievers down next to the water glass and turned to move away, but his foot came down on an empty bottle.

The glass bottle spun away, clinking loudly into several others. He turned back to his father, dark bags hovering beneath his open eyes like saddlebags, angry, red veins marring the whites.

He sat up and half-spilled from the chair before Jacoby could jump back, his palm snapping painfully across his cheek.

"Why'd you wake me? I told you a hundred times to not wake me," his father growled, his voice thick and gravelly with sleep. His legs unfurled and he spilled the rest of the way out of the chair. His hand snapped back again, catching the other side of Jacoby's face. He reeled, crying out, hot pain and tears flushing his face.

Jacoby fell back onto the bottles, glass crunching under this weight. His father was there, atop him, his breath hot and fetid from cigarettes and alcohol.

"Why? I've only got one rule–don't wake me when I'm sleeping. Do you know how hard I worked? Do you? Do you know? I'm tired…and I just want to, to sleep. Damnit, boy. Damnit!" his father yelled, his hand clamping onto Jacoby's arms. He shook him, banging his back and head against the ground. "What were you doing sneaking about? Is it fun? Is it fun to sneak around your dad while he's trying to sleep? To watch me, broken and tired from working…from working to make sure you've got a roof over your head? To laugh at dirty, tired pops? Huh? What were you doing?"

Jacoby sobbed, the hot tears filling his eyes and bubbling down his cheeks. He wrestled free long enough to point at the table next to the chair.

His father released one hand, his puffy eyes hard and cold. He turned slowly, following Jacoby's outstretched hand to the water glass and the small bubble pack of pills.

"You did…but, I…" his father mumbled and turned back to him, and promptly let go of his arm. "I…uh. You brought that for me? I'm…sorry."

Jacoby tried to pull away and stand, but his father grasped him again. He tried to curl up. Tried to protect himself, but his father was so much bigger and stronger.

"I'm sorry, Jacoby. I'm sorry. Did you hear me? I said I'm sorry. I didn't mean it. You know that, right? I didn't mean to hurt you!"

His hands clamped tightly around Jacoby's arms as he wrenched him off the ground and pulled him into an uncomfortably tight hug. His arms squeezed his chest, Jacoby's face smashing uncomfortably into his soiled work clothes.

"You shouldn't have woken me. You know I get so angry. You know what I'm like – my temper being too much to handle. Why did you make me hurt you? Why? I hate myself for it! Hate myself!" his father cried, squeezing him harder still.

Jacoby couldn't breathe. He coughed and gasped, but there was no relief, no space for air to be claimed. The pressure on his chest increased and his heart hiccupped in response.

"Stop fighting me, boy! I won't hurt you if you stop fighting!" his dad cried, but Jacoby had to get away. He was smothering...dying.

"Stop fighting, Jacoby. We're just trying to help you." The voice was his father's, but it sounded different. Less muffled...less tainted by drink.

He pulled on the air and gasped down a breath, his lungs expanding painfully in his chest. He forced the breath out and sucked down another, and then another. His face was clear, but it was still hard to breathe, like a massive weight was sitting on his chest.

His heart shuddered in an uneven, shuddering staccato beat. It felt like an eternity before it contracted in his chest again. Everything was dark, the air stuffy and warm.

Beep...beep. The noise beat against his ears, cutting clean through his head. Everything hurt...everything felt hard and cold.

I am dead...I am dying, he thought, his mind moving slowly as he tried to rationalize the pain coursing through his body.

Jacoby opened his eyes, his lids sticking together for a moment before peeling slowly apart. Darkness, only broken by haloed blurry lights. He blinked again and again, sipping on the air and listening to his arduous and impossibly slow heartbeat.

A pain flared in his neck as he tried to move his head. He tried to reach up and rub the spot but his hand refused to move. His other hand wouldn't move either, nor would his feet.

Jacoby tried to thrash as panic set in, but a stabbing pain bit into his temples and the notion suddenly lost all appeal. His heart rate increased as he grew still again, a small surge of life kicking back into his body. His lungs filled and he exhaled, savoring the sensation, but then a loud beep cut the air and his left arm started to burn. It grew cold a moment later.

He cleared his throat and took a breath, trying to master the panic as the creeping cold sensation moved up his arm and into his chest. His heart slowed dramatically once again. He blinked over and over, a fresh wave of confusion setting in.

"Where...am...I?" he croaked as a door swished open somewhere to his right. A short and incredibly blurry figure appeared at his side.

"Ah good, you're awake." The voice was feminine, the accent clipped.

Someone else walked into the room, the door sweeping open and closing quietly. Jacoby blinked again and again, twisting his head around to see them properly, but they settled into the corner behind him. He let his head fall back into a comfortable position and smashed his eyes shut.

"My name is Doctor Misra. How are you feeling?"

"My head..." Jacoby said, his voice weak. He sucked in another deep breath and pushed it out, that simple act requiring considerably more strength and energy than he'd ever remembered. "Everything hurts. It's hard...to breathe...and my heart...it feels...strange," he said, struggling to take in enough air.

"Your head took a considerable pounding," Doctor Misra said. "You have a broken nose, eye socket, as well as a Grade two, possibly even a grade three concussion. With that said, some memory loss is to be expected."

The doctor watched him, a surgical mask pulled over the lower half of her face. He blinked again, his vision finally clearing enough to see her properly. She was short, with dark hair and eyes and a noticeable accent. *Indian?*

Pakistani? He couldn't immediately tell. She wore a white lab coat over a pair of dark scrubs.

When he struggled to continue she set her large translucent pad down and started poking and prodding at his midsection. Then she moved up to his head and fidgeted with something on his forehead.

"You were involved in quite the episode in the clinic earlier, Mr. Mason. Tell me, how much of it do you remember?"

"Call me Jacoby, please. Mr. Mason was my...father," he stammered, puckering his lips to suck in another breath. Anna was constantly telling him it was just a name, and that hating it would just give his father power over him.

"Where am I? Where is Doctor Reeds?"

"You are in a safe place, Mr. Mason. We transferred you here after you suffered an...attack in the clinic. Do you remember that part?" Doctor Misra asked.

"Security? Attack?" Jacoby asked, irritated that she insisted on calling him his father's name.

He winced as he tried to scratch his nose. His arms wouldn't move. Jacoby picked up his head and managed to look down his body. He wore a blue and white hospital gown, bright blue grip socks covering his feet. Black nylon straps were wrapped around his wrists, securely fastening them to the rails of his bed.

The room was small, a series of panels and tanks covering the far wall beyond his feet, while cabinets, a small counter, and a stainless steel cart sat against the wall to his left. The wall to his right was glass, a dark room with beds and glowing, flashing equipment stretching beyond that.

Jacoby tried to think back to the time before his dream, but it was foggy. He twisted his head back around to a strange black device strapped around his left bicep. Clear wires snacked out of the smooth shell. Some disappeared into his gown around his chest, while others led towards his head.

"It is not unusual to experience short-term memory loss during medical crisis. I'm happy to report that we've taken dramatic measures to stabilize your vitals, predominantly your heart rate and blood pressure, and your condition has improved considerably. We've detected some fascinating abnormalities in your blood, as well as some irregularities with the electrical impulses in your brain and are working to pinpoint the exact root of this condition. We're learning so much," Doctor Misra explained, as she picked up her clear pad and started tapping on the screen.

"Abnormalities...brain?" Jacoby keyed in on the fact that she hadn't answered his question about Doctor Reeds. She also said his condition was "fascinating", and they were "learning so much".

"Yes. We took some in depth scans while you were unconscious, and are confident they will pinpoint the source of your...well, the exact cause of your condition. Once we have more time to study your scans, we'll know more. The Palmer Module on your left arm is monitoring and managing your vitals through an advanced series of electrical impulses and injectable compounds. It is state-of-the-art, and will keep you very comfortable. It's very important for us to accumulate as much data about your symptoms as possible. Beyond what you told Doctor Reeds in the clinic, have you experienced any other...strange or unusual sensations or urges? Heard, smelled, or seen anything strange?"

Jacoby listened to her talk and watched her mouth move, but it was all he could do just to keep his eyes open and draw his next breath. He closed his eyes, when he opened them again, the room felt brighter. Jacoby blinked and realized that there were other people standing around Doctor Misra...watching him, writing on pads, or talking into small devices. The closest leaned in and whispered into the doctor's ear. They all wore masks, too.

"Smelled? Heard?" Jacoby groaned, trying to make sense of her questions. "I...I felt fine, but now I can't seem to–"

"We can only help you if you are honest with us, Mr. Mason. It is very important, you must know that. Have you had contact with any station personnel recently...share any drinking containers, dining ware, perhaps share physical contact – touching, kissing, or sexual intercourse?"

Jacoby's mind spun, his sluggish thoughts keying in on her last word. *Sexual intercourse?* A distant and very small voice echoed in his mind. He couldn't understand what it was saying, but a profound sense of unease settled in. The questions troubled him, even though he couldn't quite articulate why.

"No...I wasn't feeling well, so I just stayed in my...room, and slept."

Doctor Misra eyed him, tapping something on her tablet. Jacoby tried to return her gaze, but there was something unsettling about her dark eyes – she was studying him.

"Very well. We can talk more later, after you have had a chance to rest. For now–"

"How...how long will I be...here? I want to...go home."

"I cannot say," Doctor Misra said, pulling a data point out of the pocket on her jacket and holding it to her ear. "Yes. That's right. Type three containment is crucial, for all of them. Do it right away. Yes...seal the quarters, even if there is someone inside. Then swab and scan everything," she said, then pressed the data point to her chest and leaned in to the man next to her. Jacoby tried to focus in on his face, but everything was too blurry. "Try series two. I want to see how long it takes the stronger sedatives to kick in."

"Rest, Mr. Mason. We'll take good care of you." The doctor tapped her data point and turned abruptly and swept away, her white coat billowing out behind her. The others trailed behind her, their footsteps the only discernable noise.

The device on Jacoby's arm beeped as he turned his head to watch her leave, a sickly cold sensation trickling up his arm and into his chest. His heart shuddered painfully in response. He pulled in a breath and pushed it out. Everything felt half speed – his heart, the blood moving in his veins, his thoughts...so...painfully...slow.

A chair creaked quietly behind him, and then a man cleared his throat. Jacoby turned his head slowly, but he couldn't see them.

"Hello? Who is there?" he asked, his voice gravelly and hoarse. The chair creaked again, but whoever it was didn't respond.

Jacoby closed his eyes. A pressure formed somewhere inside his skull, behind his eyes, but he felt heavy...and so incredibly tired. His vision went fuzzy and a muffled, white noise filled his ears.

Jacoby swallowed hard, his next breath burning in his throat. The room faded to black.

0250 HOURS

Anna sat perched on the hard, metal sink for what felt like an eternity, her legs propped up and shaking and her feet smashed against the door. Her ass fell asleep long ago, and the more she thought about it, she wasn't sure if she could feel her feet either.

"I need to move. We've been sitting here for hours," she hissed, and started to pull her feet away.

"Wait...no!" Soraya whispered, pulling half out of the small shower. "Wait-wait-wait...what if it...if it is still out there? It could be right outside, in the hall! What if it got through the door?"

"It? That was your husband...that was Preston. You saw what he did...what he tried to do. If he got through the door, then we're..." Anna trailed off and turned back to the door, trying to ignore the stabbing pain shooting through her backside, and failing. She winced and held her breath, listening, unsure how to continue.

"I don't hear anything," she said after another lengthy pause. Then before Soraya could argue, let her feet drop numbly to the ground. Fire erupted up her legs as the prickly, crawling sensation moved from her toes all the way to her hips.

Anna massaged her legs and fumbled her data point out, waking it up with a tap of the screen, trying to force her attention onto anything but the pain. She pulled up her contacts and pressed on Jacoby's profile, trying to connect for a video chat, but the network icon spun and glowed red.

"Damn, I can't connect. It won't connect, the network is down."

"That wasn't him, Anna. That wasn't Preston. It couldn't be," Soraya said, her eyes locked on the door.

"You can't just run out there..."

"It wasn't him. He would never say those things...do those things. It wasn't...wasn't..." Soraya said, cutting Anna off. Her voice trailed into an inaudible mumble, but then she sat up suddenly, unfolding her body with surprising ease from the small shower. "I need to go find him. He needs me. He needs help. I...I can help him."

Anna caught her before she reached the door, her arms impressively muscular.

"What are you talking about?" Anna hissed, struggling to hold her back. "You saw it...his face. His face split open, Soraya. His stomach...the bones...the blood? What does that to a person? It was him, he was with you."

Anna fought to hold her back, but Soraya easily pushed her across the small bathroom. Her back hit the opposite wall but she fought back and wrapped her arms around Soraya, pulling and twisting to keep her away from the handle.

"Stop!" she hissed, grunting and fumbling to counter Soraya's impressive strength. "Just stop. Please, we need to think about this for a second, have a plan...before we open that door."

Soraya struggled for another moment, the muscles in her chest and shoulders flexing like cables against Anna's arms. Anna's grip broke and she scrabbled for another hold.

"I don't want you to get hurt. I don't want to die," she hissed, and Soraya finally seemed to hear. She turned on Anna, tears pooling heavily in both eyes.

"I don't know what is happening," Soraya said, her lip quivering and voice breaking. Then she came forward and threw her arms around Anna. She trembled, crying softly, and squeezing them together.

Anna tried to think of something to say – some wisdom to help Soraya past her grief or to make sense of what happened, but nothing came to mind. She didn't understand any of it, how could she help someone else?

Soraya shifted, her cheek coming to rest against Anna's neck. The warmth of her body instantly bled through her clothes, the closeness of their bodies suddenly intensifying. It wasn't just the intimacy of their embrace, although she couldn't deny that. It was a bond, a connection, a smell that perfumed the air around them, and a resulting spark of familiarity deep inside. It was infinitely complicated and simple at the same time, a flicker passed through their skin-to-skin contact.

Anna slowly returned the embrace, her hands gliding down the other woman's back. Every muscle, smooth curve and line, even down to her bra strap felt surprisingly familiar. The spark inside continued to grow, until it flowed throughout her chest and midsection. She felt the warmth trickle into her arms and legs, the sensation seemingly circling between her legs.

Soraya shifted. She wasn't crying anymore, but she wasn't letting go either. What was she feeling? Was it normal? Could Soraya feel it, too? Her thoughts immediately turned back to her intimate romp with Jacoby, but also how good she'd felt after – strong, so full of energy, like she was years younger.

Anna felt the garbage can at her feet, even though she couldn't see it. She'd gotten sick at the clinic, the strange bloody blue color permanently fused into her mind – the same color that also spattered the garbage can a foot away.

Soraya pulled away finally, sliding away but taking ahold of Anna's hands. She was calmer now, but just barely. Anna didn't just see it, but felt it somehow – a ball of barely contained grief, panic, and fear bubbling just beneath the surface.

"What should we do?" Soraya asked, her voice so low it was barely a whisper.

"For starters, we need to get out of this bathroom. Then we need to contact someone and find out what is going on."

Soraya nodded and moved aside so Anna could move over to the door. She pressed an ear to the cold metal and held her breath to listen. Nothing.

Anna slowly unlocked the door and turned the handle. The mechanism clicked loudly and she froze, the noise seemingly filling the small bathroom.

Damn, stupid, loud piece of crap....ahhh, she cursed silently. Anna hovered before the door, waiting and listening. Again, nothing. She eased the door open the rest of the way and leaned out, tilting her ear to hear better down the hallway.

"Shit," she breathed. The hall light had gone out, leaving the entire space before her dark. She crept forward, feeling her way along the wall with one hand and leading Soraya along with the other.

Anna approached the end of the hall, a white glow from the porthole window in the living room to the right providing the only light. She stopped just before the door, her eyes struggling to focus in the dim light. Several dark, blocky shapes lay on the ground, while a panel hung loose from the ceiling.

The light panel glowed on the wall, but didn't respond to her touch. Anna stepped between the debris on the ground and ducked under the hanging panel. The door was still closed – she could see that much, but the wall was bowed in on the lock side, the ceramic panels and plastic moldings either cracked and disfigured or missing entirely. She couldn't entirely tell the extent of the damage in the dark.

Had the lock held? Would it open if they needed it to?

"Maybe we can just wait here...until the network comes back up or help arrives?" Soraya suggested, quietly.

Anna shook her head and moved in as close to the door as possible. Something moved out in the hall – an empty and surprisingly loud banging and scraping. She fought the urge to jump away and listened, trying to discern what or who it was.

"Stop for a second and listen. What don't you hear?" she whispered, turning away from the door. She waited for a response, but was listening more intently to whatever was just beyond their door in the hall.

"Air...I don't hear the air," Soraya whispered after another long moment.

Anna nodded, curling her fingers into the gap at the top of the door. She could push them through almost two full knuckles deep. The door must have been knocked clear off the rails. Even with power, it wouldn't open – just another problem she would have to consider.

"Don't..." Soraya hissed as Anna reached for the door control pad, but pulled away before pushing it.

Think, Anna. Don't try to open the door until you're ready to leave. If you open it now, it might not close again if something is out there.

Turning away from the door, Anna moved to duck back under the damaged ceiling panel just as her data point vibrated and started beeping. She fumbled the glowing screen up and frantically slid her finger down the side of the screen to turn the volume down, but it was too late. The noise had already been made.

Working quickly, Anna pulled up her messages, but the application was busy downloading a large packet of previously unreceived communications. She tried to stop the action, to create a new message, but an error popped up and the connection icon once again flashed red.

"Damn-damn-damn," she cursed and immediately held it up into the air, turning and moving to try and reacquire the signal. She stopped moving right before the door, the data point's clear screen tapping hollowly against the metal. Whatever signal she'd found was gone.

Anna exhaled in frustration and turned back to Soraya, but stopped. Her breath drifted in a visible fog between them. The air was cold out here, but worse, getting colder. She hadn't noticed it while locked in the bathroom, but here it was undeniable.

"We can't stay here. Climate control is off with the power, so it is going to get really cold in here," Anna said, and Soraya nodded immediately, although her gaze turned to the door. Anna knew the unspoken question. Is it still out there...whatever *it* was?

"We get the door open, and run. We run past whatever we see and go straight for the elevator. We get the hell off this floor, and find someplace with power...find someone that knows what in the hell is going on. Deal?"

Soraya nodded.

"Good, but first you need to wear something warmer than that," she said, gesturing at Soraya's bathrobe."

Anna immediately moved off to her dark bedroom and used the light from her data point's screen to change clothes. She pulled on clean underwear and then slipped into an olive-drab maintenance jumpsuit, rolling up the sleeves to just above her elbows. Soraya settled next to the bed and watched quietly as Anna picked up her code scanner and small tool pouch off the small desk and stuffed them into pockets, before sliding on her boots and clipping a headset onto her ear.

"I guess I'm going to get my time working on a door after all, Lana," she mumbled under her breath, and started rifling through outfits hanging in the closet. She pulled out a light-tan jumpsuit, the fabric worn and frayed in several spots.

"Here, I think this might fit you," she said handing it over. Soraya accepted it without word and laid it on the bed. She immediately untied the thin robe and pulled it down.

"Lunar Technologies I.F.P Maintenance? 'I.F.P'?" Soraya asked, picking the jumpsuit off the bed and pointing to a patch on the chest.

"Jacoby and I lived and worked in the lunar colonies for a while after leaving earth. Industrial fusion products held the contract for maintenance on the colony's forty-some fusion reactors. It's not as fancy as it sounds," she laughed, "I crawled around in service ducts all day, checking electromagnet temperatures and coolant levels. I practically lived in that jumpsuit, or ones like it, while we were there."

"Sounds interesting. You're full of surprises, girl," Soraya said, and Anna didn't have time to turn away before she stripped her shirt and pants off.

Ever the critique of her own body, Anna immediately felt a pang of jealousy. Soraya slipped the jump suit off the bed and lifted a shapely leg to slide it on, the data point's cool, white light highlighting the attractive and muscular curve of her thighs and backside.

She patted her belly subconsciously as Soraya lifted the other leg into the outfit and pulled it up, her muscular stomach flexing impressively in the pale light. She pushed her arms into the sleeves, hefted it up over her shoulders, and pulled the zipper up. Soraya stopped before reaching the top, the fabric squeezing tightly around her breasts.

"It's a little tight," she said, looking up and catching Anna staring. "This must have been huge on you?"

"Well...I was a little bigger back then," she said, self-consciously. The memory of backpacking across half of North America popped into her mind. She tried to push the stray thoughts away, but for some reason they grew in her mind and started to push everything else away. The room spun and her knees suddenly went weak. Soraya lunged forward and caught her hands...and then she gasped.

Anna tumbled into the memories. First, they were backpacking across the old Midwest, the old sun-scorched cornfields of Iowa and Nebraska hovering like brown husks on either side of the road. They slept in abandoned houses and barns, huddling together for warmth, and ate whatever they could find.

The Rocky Mountains spanned before them in the distance, the jagged, snow-covered peaks hovering just beyond the light layer of pollution-ionized atmosphere. She saw the transport appear from behind a mountain, the thruster blast cones lighting up the sky like a sunrise. They watched the launch from the magna train cargo car, the landscape whipping by them so fast it all blurred together. The thrill coursed through her, just as it had when she watched it - it was the realization, the idea that they were finally breaking free from her family, his father, all of it.

She heard the police, the One-Federal agents shouting and yelling for them to stop and "drop to the ground". The voices woke them from a dead sleep, driving them from the moving train when it reached Denver. Jacoby took a misstep as they ran to hide in a warehouse and fell into an old feed hopper. They hid there all night, flicking hungry rats away and waiting for the police to give up their search. When the sun rose the next morning they went straight to the launch depot and bought their tickets for the lunar launch. Somehow, Anna felt the rings on her fingers, and the weight of her mother's necklace around her neck, but they weren't there anymore. She'd pawned it all off to buy Jacoby's ticket off world.

The memories blurred and flashed, the blue sky and mountains suddenly replaced by the silent, solemn and dusty lunar landscape. She was crawling through service ducts barely three feet high by three feet wide, condenser lubricant and coolant water dripping down onto her back and head. She felt the ache in her hands and knees, the tension bunching up her lower back like a million stabbing needles.

The hum of the fusion reactor pulsed all around her, the deep *thrum-thrum-thrum* buzzing clear through to her bones. Anna squeezed her body into their small economy apartment at the end of her shift, her hair slicked down with grease, dirt, and sweat. She felt the small space close in - the walls barely wide enough to allow her to spread her arms. Anna crawled in next to Jacoby, smearing dirt on his pants in the process. The space was only large enough to allow them to sit facing one another.

They choked down vat-grown noodles and meat, and not the good stuff either - she felt the strange meat shift and pop between her teeth, the odd, almost plastic taste filling her nose and mouth. She gagged, the smell and taste covering her tongue.

Anna broke free from the memories, the dark bedroom washing back in. She was on her knees and not entirely sure how she got there. Soraya was next to her, their hands still clasped together. She looked up just as Soraya pulled away, rocking back onto her bare feet and standing.

"What was that? I saw...I smelled, tasted, everything. L-L-Like I was there? That horrible taste...was that food?" Soraya gasped. She patted the jumpsuit down and even reached for the zipper.

"I just started thinking about all of it, the road out of..."

"Home. You hitchhiked and stole rides on magna trains all the way to the mountains," Soraya cut in.

Anna nodded. "Yes, the orbital launch station in Colorado. My parents called every station on the east coast to keep us from making it off world. We did whatever we had to."

"That little room, the dirt...the grease...that food? You lived that way in the lunar colony? I thought they banned corporations from housing workers in such slums."

"Anna zipped one of her thigh pockets closed, but she couldn't ignore the question. Somehow, Soraya shared in all of it...the vivid memories, as if they were a video stream playing live in her brain.

"They did on Earth, but the Lunar Colonies operated under their own jurisdiction, so enforcement fell to the corporations on some hilarious version of the honor system. We were beyond broke when we got to the moon. We did what it took to survive. I ate some things I never thought possible to keep from starving. Half of the crap they sold to the poor workers could hardly be described as food. That stuff does horrible things to your body, and we ate it for several years. When Jacoby got the contract out here, it took me several months of a proper diet and exercise to get right again. Never again...never again," Anna said, shuddering. She patted her stomach as she eyed the jumpsuit Soraya wore, remembering how tight it had been at the end, when they'd almost given up.

"But how did I see it? It's like we connected somehow."

Anna met Soraya's gaze, puzzling through the strange moments before, during, and immediately after, trying to connect them in some rational fashion. Nothing fit, until she considered something Preston said in the hall.

"Out in the hall, what was Preston talking about...with you and Jacoby?"

Soraya recoiled and immediately wrapped her arms around her body.

"Soraya, please. It's important that we think about this. That we try to make sense of what is happening. When I was at the clinic earlier...when things got really strange, I got sick. It was gross...blue with bits of blood and stuff, like it wasn't all just food in my stomach. I don't know, I can't explain what it was or why. I've never had anything like that happen to me before. When we were in the bathroom, you got sick. I saw it. It looked the same, smelled the same, too. Something is happening to people on this station - sickness, well worse than sickness."

Anna pushed off the ground and held out her hand.

"Preston was telling the truth - about Jacoby. The power cycled off, and when we went out in the hall to see what was going on, Jacoby was on the ground outside our door. Preston wasn't feeling well, and I thought Jacoby was sick, too, or maybe he just fell down, so I offered to help him back to your place," Soraya said, eyeing Anna's hand warily, but then accepted it and stood.

"That's what friends do for each other-"

"You don't understand," Soraya interrupted, shaking her head. "When I was around him, something came over me. I don't know what it was - the way he smelled, or felt, but once we were in your place I just sort of lost control. It was like a dream. There was no Preston, nothing beyond a sudden and overwhelming...need, like my body was on fire. I tried to force myself on him, Anna. That's not me...I've never...would never do that. Jacoby is your friend, and you guys...well, we've always been friendly. When I left, it hit me. I think Preston knew, even when I tried to lie."

She watched Soraya struggle and reached out, grasping her hand. She gave it a reassuring squeeze, a spark igniting inside from the contact between them. Anna felt it - Soraya's shame, her confusion, and pain. But somehow, she'd already known. Was it a feeling, an intuition? Or had she seen it in Jacoby's eyes when she first came home that night after the explosion?

All of it, she realized.

"It's not your fault. You didn't do anything wrong," Anna said, squeezing her hand again.

Soraya looked up, her confusion deepening. "What do you mean? I just told you I tried to force myself on your friend! Preston, he thought Jacoby tried to take advantage of me, but it was the other way around. I got scared that he would leave me, so I started kissing him and tried to pull him into our bedroom to have sex, but he was sick. He wasn't up for any of that. And now...now Preston is..."

"I felt it, too, Soraya. Lately when I've been around Jacoby the air seemed to grow thicker, every smell becoming that much more intense. Everything else would melt away until it was just him and I. He's different somehow, although I can't say how or why...something in him, maybe. It's in me now, and you, too. I can feel it."

"This is crazy. All of it...just fucking crazy. I don't know what to do...where to go. Are we sick...will we die?" Soraya reached down and wiggled, managing to pull the zipper a little further up her chest. The worn fabric hugged her curves like it was tailored just for her, the splayed zipper teasing the valley between her shapely breasts. Even in a maintenance jumpsuit she looked beautiful and strong, like the goddesses that stood above their male counterparts in all the old stories.

"There is an answer to all of it, and I have a feeling Jacoby might be at the middle of it. We need to get to the clinic. The doctor...he'll have machines, tests, maybe he has answers. If anyone can figure this out, it is him." Anna squeezed Soraya's hand again, forcing as much optimism and confidence forward as she could muster.

Soraya's back visibly straightened and her shoulders squared. She squeezed Anna's hand in return, wiped a stray tear from her eye, and nodded.

"I need boots," Soraya said, breaking the silence.

Anna looked down at her bare feet, sizing them up against her own.

"I have spare boots, but they're small. Jacoby's might fit you, but he's a guy and well, he's only got like one pair."

Soraya eyed her for a moment, lifting her feet off the floor before settling her weight back down and lifting the other. It was cold and only getting colder, Anna couldn't imagine how that felt on bare feet.

"I'll find some somewhere," she whispered and they moved slowly out into the hall, stopping before the damaged door. Anna ducked under the broken ceiling tile, and looked back to Soraya to make sure she was ready.

"We can't just pull the door open if the motor is still energized. It might still open on its own, which I don't believe it will, but if it does, be ready to run! Run as fast as you can straight for the elevator and don't stop, no matter what you see or hear."

"What if it isn't working? The power...if it is out, will the elevators even run?"

"The elevators are supposed to be supported by emergency power generation, supported by a completely different and isolated circuit. They should work," Anna whispered in response, although she wasn't nearly as confident in the answer as she would have been even a day earlier.

"We can't stay here forever," Soraya said and nodded.

Anna turned, and without hesitation tapped the door control panel. Nothing happened. She leaned back, exhaling quietly and started scanning the wall panels, wondering where and how she was going to gain access to the motor and inner workings. Her gaze flitted over the small control pad again just as the screen flickered, and the door open icon abruptly glowed into view. Anna leaned back in and pressed the button eagerly.

The door shuddered with a loud *clunk* and slid free of the frame almost an inch before grinding to a halt. The motor started to whine, gears and metal parts grinding loudly in the wall.

"It's so loud," Soraya hissed, "stop it!"

Anna smashed the controls on the dim panel, but they didn't respond. The motor continued to grind and squeal, like some horrible, wounded animal trapped inside the wall.

"Do something," Anna whispered, urging herself into action. She dropped to her knees and tapped the small light on her headset, and then started fumbling and pulling on the damaged wall panels. She squeezed her fingers between the gap and with strength that surprised even her, ripped it free. The door rattled and shook, the horrible squealing echoing out into the hall as Anna found a mass of wires in the hollow wall space, and wrenched them into the light.

Voices and chaotic thoughts filled the darkness of Jacoby's mind, but he wasn't dreaming. Somehow he knew he was sleeping, but also felt powerless to change it.

Jacoby tried to make sense of the voices – they sounded urgent, desperate, but without clarity or meaning. He felt pain, too. Something was happening to his body – cold and hot mixing together in succinct pinpoints of pain in what he was sure were his arms.

Other noises punctuated the darkness around him, some clear enough through the smothering presence covering his ears, others just distant, jumbled sounds. He heard coughing, sniffling, and retching. Was it him? Was he dying?

The darkness parted suddenly, as if in answer to his unspoken question. He blinked away the blur in time to find the syringe from an auto injector pulling free from his right arm.

Jacoby groaned and struggled to collect his wits, but the room appeared to be different. The glass wall to his right was gone, now replaced by a large, complicated piece of medical equipment.

"...is he ready?" someone asked nearby, their voice muffled by a strange-looking mask. An airline snaked down from the ceiling and into their faceplate. They wore a rubber suit as well, the protective garment merging seamlessly with the mask.

Why are they wearing those suits...? he wondered, but his temples throbbed again and his thoughts scattered.

Jacoby tried to reach out to the closest figure in the suit, to get their attention, only to have a painfully bright bank of overhead lights blaze to life. He pressed his eyes shut and drifted off.

He opened his eyes again and the light was gone. He was in a small, dark space, a clattering noise banging loudly all around him. A twinge bit into his temples and he was sliding from the darkness. The room around him glided out of the fog.

"...antibodies...showing indication of infection," a man said as Jacoby tried to clear his throat and rouse himself. He inhaled deeply, the stabbing pain almost constantly burning at his temples now.

"...it could be a parasite...brain mass. Take...blood, tissue, and bone marrow...cerebrospinal fluid samples," the man continued, but he could only seem to grab every other word.

"...alter behavior? Is...dangerous?" a woman asked, her voice stronger and closer.

"We can't know the true scope...contamination...him. Middle...outbreak...strange but...of our worries. Virus...we don't understand. It appears to have been isolated...and those in the clinic. The orderly...cardiac failure...autopsy and...tissue analysis."

Something in Jacoby stirred, a distant glimmer of strength returning. He opened his eyes and fought for clarity. He puckered his lips and sucked in a breath - the strength had been fleeting, his heart pounding weakly in his chest as the predictable pain stabbed into his arm and the cold crept in a moment later.

No...fight it...don't...sleep. He peeled one eye open just as a long needle slid into his right arm. The black claimed him again.

"Jacoby, can you hear me?" a man asked, his voice quiet but close. He recognized the voice, and when he peeled his eyes open again, found his bed surrounded by what looked like a clear, plastic tent. Time had passed, that much was clear, but Jacoby didn't know how much.

Doctor Reeds stood on the other side of the barrier, his differently colored eyes wide with what looked like concern.

Doctor. Jacoby thought, putting the man's face and the idea together in his mind.

Jacoby tried to say yes, but couldn't seem to feel his mouth, so he simply nodded. The doctor's face clarified, the rest of the room slowly materializing out of the fog. He was in a large, long room, his bed just one of many in a long row. He could see people lying in beds just like his, similar tents covering them as well. Some writhed in place, kicking and clawing at their sheets, while others lay still, occasionally coughing or holding their heads. They all looked sick.

Jacoby reached up to scratch his nose, but his arm still wouldn't move. He wiggled it, growling inaudibly in frustration. Something on his arm beeped, so he stopped fighting.

"I'm happy to see that you are awake, Jacoby. I know this all has to be very confusing, but I assure you, I'm here now and plan to find out exactly what is going on," Reeds said.

What is going on? Jacoby thought, blinking again to clear away the sleep. He didn't understand why the doctor wouldn't know.

A shadow fell over him as someone approached the left side of his clear enclosure, their profile blocking one of the lights. Jacoby turned to see back-lit red hair and the sparkle of green eyes. He peeled his head off the pillow only to find the thick, black restraints were still binding his wrists and ankles to the bed.

"This is Alexandria, she is with station security. She is here to ask you some questions about the...uh, incident in the clinic," Reeds said, nervously favoring a bruise on his cheek, "but before we get to that, I think we need to talk about your...situation."

"Situation?" Jacoby mouthed, but he couldn't form the word properly. His tongue was thick and dry.

Jacoby waited for the voice in his head to chime in, while silently praying it wouldn't. Oh how he wished the last few days were just a bad dream.

He eyed Doctor Reeds, his heart beating like a sluggish drum in his chest, but only the silence of his muddled thoughts filled his head.

"Yes...the results from your tests? Has no one told you anything?"

Jacoby found that he had to watch the doctor's mouth move as he talked. He couldn't seem to catch all the words, but could fill in the gaps by reading his lips.

"No, but I'm...not...sick."

"Well, no, at least not like the rest of your bed mates, here."

"Where...am...I?" Jacoby interrupted. Reeds glanced to the white coat next to him, then Lex on the other side of the enclosure, before he spoke.

"You're in the station labs. I must admit it took me a fair amount of searching to find you. They told us they were moving you and some of your sicker counterparts to, uh, better manage your health and recuperation."

He doesn't know. The lies, he's eaten the lies, the voice chimed in suddenly, but it was quieter and weaker than ever. A heartbeat later, a sharp pain stabbed into his temples and his thoughts scattered.

"...your condition has been a great deal more confusing to us, but I think we have finally dug down to the heart of the matter. The truth, however frightening, is actually a good thing when you think about it. It's not a good prognosis, but...misery and company, as I usually say," the doctor said, repeatedly lifting his tablet before letting it drop down to his side. Jacoby could see it, the doctor was uncomfortable.

Don't listen...to...him! the voice echoed distantly in his thoughts, but it was so quiet he almost couldn't make it out. His temples tingled and a cold, creeping sensation filled his left arm.

He opened his eyes again, only his confusion matching his pain.

"My head? The pain...? What is...on my...arm?" Jacoby whispered.

"Yes, that brings us right to it. As you know...when you came into the clinic, your vitals were elevated dangerously. We found abnormalities in your blood which prompted us to pursue other tests. Your second blood test showed the same elevated and confusing amounts of testosterone and androstadienone, as well as other hormones and compounds present that normally indicate the presence of a...well, tumor. Antibodies were also present, indicating a number of possible problems, well...parasitic infection, and..." Reeds mumbled and drifted off.

Jacoby glanced to his left, his gaze crawling sluggishly up from the strap restraining his left arm, to Lex's tight-fitting suit. She returned his gaze, her green eyes seemingly saying "I approve of the restraints". Another pain in his temple forced his eyes down, over the name badge sewn into the fabric above her left breast. She pulled a data point out of her pocket and scrolled down through glowing messages, her eyebrows drawing down into an angry line.

"All of these numbers didn't add up...well, they were downright confusing...until we analyzed the brain scans we took in the clinic. The image resolution wasn't the best, but we found this." Doctor Reeds was still talking, but an uptick in volume drew his attention back to his side of the bed. His large acrylic tablet was held up before the clear plastic, a brightly colored image of what Jacoby figured to be a brain filling the screen. The doctor swiped to another image, which appeared to show the brain from the side.

"Do you see this red mass right here," he said, circling an area with his finger. The tablet drew a line around the area, the screen automatically zooming in. "This is a foreign mass. It is growing on the portion of your brain we call the hypothalamus, but you can clearly see what we call 'fingers' connecting the mass to your amygdala, hippocampus, as well as the limbic lobe. These regions constitute the oldest part of your brain, and what is sometimes referred to as the 'animal' brain. This mass, err, tumor, could explain why you were experiencing such wild swings in heart rate, blood pressure, and in my opinion, resulted in your confusing test results. I looked back on your file and am confident that it was the reason for your blackout on the processing floor the other day."

"I have a...brain tumor?" Jacoby asked, the fog in his mind lifting for a moment. The haze was gone, but the news brought about a whole new wave of confusion. How could he have a brain tumor?

"Yes. I'm sorry, but there is no easy way to break this kind of news. The good news is, I believe we can treat-"

"Excuse me!" Doctor Misra's voice cut in. She swept in from a side room, a group of people in white lab coats right behind her. Jacoby blinked to clear his vision but could see enough to tell that the short woman was angry.

"Why was this patient moved without my consent?" Reeds asked as the other group approached. Doctor Misra stopped a few feet away and immediately pointed at Lex.

"I already told you, Mr. Reed. We apprised you in an e-memo that we were taking over care of these patients. They are no longer your concern. I suggest you return to the clinic and take...her with you."

"What do you mean, 'take her with you'?" Lex spat, her voice rising quickly, "I'm with station security. I am following my..."

"Layla, my name is 'Reeds' as I've told you countless times. As in the plural and not the singular fibrous plant that grows next to marshes and other bodies of water. And these people were under my care. You can't just randomly...on a whim..." Reeds cut in, talking over Lex. He stepped up to tower of Doctor Misra, a clamor of voices immediately rising into an angry storm of sound.

Jacoby tried to sit up, tried to clear his head. The mass of voices hit him like a blanket, the woven fibers too intertwined to pull apart. He pulled on his hands, fighting to pull at least a hand free.

"We're using a Palmer Module to administer carefully constructed cocktails of pain management drugs, along with sonic and magnetic signals, in conjunction with electrical impulses to keep his vitals under control so we can stabilize his condition," Doctor Misra argued, and slapped a tablet against his chest. "It is all in his chart. You could read it for yourself."

"He needs to be prepped for transportation back to earth for treatment, not doped into a coma. I don't understand what you are doing down here. These people were receiving appropriate care in the hospital block."

"You have the clinic to worry about, Doctor, and plenty of station personnel suffering through colds, or worse, a scrape or bruise-" Doctor Misra snapped, her tone sharp.

"This is not right...not right at all. These people are under my care," Doctor Reeds cut her off. Red crept over his cheeks as his normally passive, almost mousy demeanor blew away.

"I am chief science officer on this station, which also makes me the senior and lead medical director. I report directly to the Station Directorate."

"You said you are treating him with triggered electrical impulses? And what kind of 'cocktail' is needed in their situation? From the look of him you're using large quantities of narcotic pain killers..." Reeds said, looking from Doctor Misra to Jacoby, and back to the group in white coats.

"Our treatment protocol is in line with current medical practices..."

"Current medical practices? Since when has electroshock therapy been used to treat brain tumors? This man has an aggressive case of what looks like Medulloblastoma. It has already metastasized and is in risk of causing long-term damage to cognitive function, that is, if it doesn't kill him first."

"That is the very reason why they are here and not still in your hospital, Doctor. Our concerns extend beyond the simple and easily detected medical conditions you noted. Now, I am telling you...leave my laboratory." Doctor Misra bit off the end of each word, her anger making her seem larger and more intimidating.

"Am I dying?" Jacoby asked.

"I see you've updated his records from my initial exam, but I don't see that you have him on any anticancer meds, just insane amounts of sedatives. This is wrong! He needs to receive an intravenous infusion of ILH-thirty-one to keep the tumor from growing and immediately put into cryo, so he can be transported back home – Earth, or the Lunar colonies at the very least. And these people. Why were they removed from the hospital block? They have exhibited far more serious responses to the flu outbreak and need our...

Cryo? Tumor? Growth? No! What a fool! Do not listen to him. It...is...me. It has always been me! I am keeping you alive. Don't listen to him, you are not dying. If anything, you are becoming stronger, the voice appeared suddenly, the pressure mounting in his mind. But as quickly as it appeared, a sharp snap burned at his temples and his thoughts scattered.

"Is it normal for him to twitch like that?" Lex asked, interrupting the two doctors. Jacoby had to work to uncross his eyes and looked up to find Lex staring down at him, her expression a mix of shock and horror. Jacoby shook, the impulse hitting his brain hard. The bed shook beneath him.

"Please...take it...off," he groaned, nodding his head at the Palmer device.

"My god, is he seizing?" Reeds turned and pressed his face up against the plastic.

"You are obviously unable to look beyond the most obvious and basic, Mr. Reed. If you were, you might have seen the existence of chemoblastoma triggered behavior modification. I deduced as much based off your notes and securities reports from his seemingly random swings in mood and behavior. If *you* had my knowledge and expertise with brain chemistry, you might have seen it. Analysis will tell us if it is the tumor at work, or this man suffers from some underlying and potentially undiagnosed psychological disorder. Now I don't have time to sit here and explain this all to you, I have work to do. You are both interrupting our work here and disturbing our patients. Mr. Reed, leave. Officer, I am ordering you to remove this man from my labs if he does not leave immediately. I want his access revoked."

"Hey, now, wait a minute," Lex said, lifting her gaze from Jacoby, to Reeds, and finally to Doctor Misra. "I'm not removing anyone from anywhere until I check with my superiors. I just came here to do a post incident interview with this guy here. I had to walk all the way to the clinic, and then down here. This whole thing doesn't feel right," Lex lifted a glowing data point, but her eyes remained on Jacoby.

More individuals in white coats appeared through a side door, followed by several more in strange, pressurized suits. Jacoby struggled, fighting to tear his arms free from the restraints. He was looking at Doctor Reeds, and then Lex's dark, silent form one moment, and then he was staring past them in the next.

"Damn, I can't connect. This dump...half the station is without power and the network is dropping out every other minute," Lex grumbled, moving around Jacoby's clear tent and holding her data point out before her, as if searching for a signal.

"I don't know what your game is, but this man is my patient! And why is he in a quarantine tent? He tested negative on virus scans? And...and these people. They tested positive for the virus, but they've already begun treatment," Reeds shot back, his voice rising to match the other doctor.

"No! This is out of your hands now! It is simple. You're done. Done!" Misra snapped back.

"Officer! Remove Reed from here at once. Do it, or I will make sure that both of you are on the next freighter out of here and never make it off world again!"

Jacoby wrenched his head to the side, the clear wires pulling tight on his scalp. If only he could...another sharp stab bit his temple. If only he could pull the wires loose.

He caught sight of a person half a dozen beds down. They were sitting up, motionless, but his vision was still blurry, his thoughts jumbled. The person sat on their bed, their back heavily stooped, but they were looking right at him. Jacoby tried to look away, but there was something about them – about their posture, their complexion, that was all wrong. But...damn the blur. He couldn't really make them out.

Break...free, the voice echoed distantly in his mind.

I...can't, he thought, only to have his temples throb again and his thoughts scatter. He yanked on his hands and fought against the straps. The nylon stretched, the muscles in his forearm knotting up.

The other patient down the line of beds tumbled from their bed, the sudden movement catching in Jacoby's peripheral vision. They didn't seem to make any noise. Reeds pushed a young man in a lab coat aside as they surrounded him and tried to shove him towards the door. Misra yelled, grabbed another man by the lab coat and pulled him down to whisper in his ear. Nurses and other staff were creeping in now, evidently drawn by the raised voices.

"You need to step back and let go of him. I can't get ahold of anyone to confirm what either of you is saying," Lex said, moving in and shoving the man away from Reeds. The young man cursed and rounded on her, his coat pulled askew.

"Don't, unless you want to know what the floor tastes like," Lex growled, a flip of her wrist effectively extending her stun baton. The end blinked green and then red, an angry spark lancing into the air.

The young man returned Lex's glare, but his eyes darted down to the stun baton, and he backed away a large step.

"Excuse me?" Jacoby said, trying to get Misra's attention.

"Doctor Reeds, I am operating under the direct authority of this station's directorate.

"Now you get my name right!" Reeds snapped back. "When has station administration ever taken an interest in medical matters? They have always allowed me see to personnel's medical wellbeing…"

Jacoby's attention was fleeting as a cold fog drifted up his arm.

The patient clawed at the plastic tent, raking their fingernails against it, their mouth moving. More patients were awake now…moving…crying out, and tumbling from their beds.

"I'm following up on the fight in the clinic. My supervisor dispatched me, and since I can't get a hold of anyone to hear differently, that's what I'm going to do, until I hear otherwise," Lex said, stepping towards Misra. She was easily a head and a half taller than the doctor, if not more.

He watched the patient several beds away continue to punch and claw at the plastic enclosure. Then they stopped moving, and started to talk. The nurses didn't seem to notice, or the doctors. They were too wrapped up arguing with each other.

"Doc...doc," Jacoby sputtered, trying to get Reeds' attention, but they couldn't hear him. They were too busy arguing.

"Ah! J-a-c-k! J-a-c-k..." the woman in the tent moaned loudly, her voice hoarse and muffled by the tent.

No! he, thought, blinking more rapidly. He saw it then, trapped behind a mass of gray-streaked red hair. It was Janice, the pinched, wrinkled skin around her dark eyes clarifying in his vision. Her mouth moved, and then she pitched forward in a horrible, wet cough, black liquid spattering the clear plastic.

"J-a-c-o-b-y!" Janice shrieked suddenly, and flopped sideways out of sight.

0335 HOURS

The wires spilled out in a massive, tangled clump, coiling into Anna's lap as if she'd disemboweled the door. She bit her lip hard to keep from cursing, and fought hard to concentrate as she pulled blocky connectors out of the way. A pile of cheap plastic relays tumbled out next, the wad strapped together by coils of black, electrical tape. She'd never seen such a cobbled-together, mess in her whole life.

"Hurry," Soraya whispered, hovering just over her shoulder.

"They're all black...I need to find the red signal wire. I don't see it!"

Anna tried to tune out the screeching motor, the metal door rattling in its tracks, but also the hot smell tainting the air. She focused on the tangled mass in her hands, tracing the dirty wires back through the clump. She fumbled her right pocket open and found her side cutters. She cut a black wire, and the door motor slowed down, only to speed back up again.

"Shit, damn self-rerouting relays. Where is it?" she whispered and cut another wire. The hot smell intensified, smoke now drifting out of the wall to her left. The door control panel flashed a bright error code now, and worse, it was beeping as well, adding to the din.

Anna pulled a wire free, a thick layer of dust and dirt rubbing off to reveal red insulation. *Yes,* she thought with relief and fumbled her cutters up and snipped it in half. The door motor abruptly started to spin down, the squealing dying away. The door shuddered, and with one final, grinding rotation, the motor went silent.

Soraya leaned on her from behind, her hands trembling. They both hovered there in the dark, the small beam of light hitting the gap between the damaged door and the frame and illuminating a small crack of the hall beyond. Smoke drifted in through the weak beam of light, the sharp, caustic smell burning Anna's eyes and nose.

She turned her head and held her breath, listening for signs of movement beyond the door, but her ears were still ringing from the motor's horrible squeal.

That was stupid-stupid-stupid, Anna. Why didn't you just try to pull the door open first? Now everyone in the whole habitat ring heard it! she chastised herself, leaning closer to the gap. She wasn't a technician...just a girl pretending to understand how things worked.

Soraya squeezed her shoulders suddenly, a wave of calming energy blossoming inside. It pushed out the anger, doubt, and anxiety, washing it away like a cleansing breath of wind.

It wouldn't have opened. Soraya squeezed her shoulder again. *It's not your fault, you're smart enough to figure this stuff out. I trust you. One-step at a time, girl.*

Anna's scalp tingled, the tiny hairs on her arms and the back of her neck immediately standing on end. She turned and met Soraya's gaze. Her large, chocolate-brown eyes seemed to repeat the unspoken, but silently conveyed messages.

"One-step at a time...together," Anna whispered, and Soraya nodded. Their connection was deepening, somehow, through some means beyond anything she knew or understood, they were communicating without words. So much so, in fact, that Anna could sense the cold biting at Soraya's feet.

Anna turned back and wedged her fingers into the gap of the door. Soraya did the same above her. Together, without having to count out loud, they pulled. The door creaked and popped, slowly sliding open. It moved an inch, then half a foot, and then two. It froze in place a little over a third of the way open.

"I'll go first," Soraya whispered and gingerly squeezed her body out through the jammed door. Anna watched and waited, her heart pounding like an out of control drum.

She stood, sucked in a deep breath, held it in, and slid through the door and into the hall. Without the ambient light from exterior portholes, the hallway wasn't just dark. It was black-dark.

Soraya waited in the middle of the hall – motionless and silent, like a hole in the darkness. Anna approached, the beam from the small light struggling to illuminate more than a few square feet ahead of her. She pressed a single finger to her lips and Anna nodded wholeheartedly.

They crept forward, slowly, deliberately. Anna swept her gaze from the ground, to the walls on either side of them as they went. She navigated them around a pile of debris - what looked like cracked ceramic and splintered polymer tiles crushed into dust.

The hall felt empty, the eerie quiet smothering even the darkness. Anna poked her head out at the intersection, confirming the passage in front of Soraya and Preston's door was empty first.

She turned and glanced back up the passage to the next door, the one the man had exited from. It was open, the weak light shining from within drawing the shadows. Puddles of deeper black stretched were they did not belong. A faint light flickered from inside the space, backlighting a partially open door with debris peppering the ground.

Soraya pulled on her arm, quietly turning her back down the hallway. They moved together, the darkness seemingly closing in around them. Anna scanned the ground, up the walls, and finally to the ceiling, where thick pipes and bundles of conduit disappeared into the dark.

Soraya stopped right outside her open door, and gave Anna's hand a squeeze, and then she pointed down at her bare feet.

I just need to grab boots. She squeezed her hand again and Anna felt the chilly floor tiles beneath her feet, the ache of cold settling into her toes.

She looked back up, the small light gleaming in Soraya's dark eyes, but turned sideways and looked into the quarters. Anna shook her head. Preston's face floated back into her thoughts, a shudder coursing through her body as she remembered the sharp crack of bone, but more terrifying, as the skin on his face split open like a horrible, fleshy zipper. A light glowed at the end of their small entry hall, but even standing in the darkness it didn't look or feel inviting.

She shook her head and tried to pull Soraya down the hall, but the other woman resisted.

"Just one minute and we're gone," Soraya mouthed, and punctuated the point by holding up a single finger.

You saw what happened to him, you heard them fighting in the hall. What if he hurt that man...killed him! He could be in there waiting for you! Anna squeezed her hand back and tried to push her thoughts forward, to change her mind, but she didn't know if any of it got through. Hell, she didn't know how any of it worked. How could she?

"It's okay," Soraya mouthed, then took a deep breath, turned, and moved quietly into her quarters.

Anna followed, but faltered, watching as the other woman disappeared through the door. She turned to the left and looked back towards the corner to her own quarters, then looked left to the elevators. Something rattled behind her, the noise distant and muffled. She tried to track the sound, but the hall was too dark – nothing moved, and at the same time, everything did.

Anna walked quickly through the door to follow Soraya, deciding she'd rather not face whatever they stumbled upon alone. She followed Soraya down the short entrance hall, the gentle glow ahead pulling her forward.

The small kitchenette sat to the right, a pantry to her left. Bottles of pills and small auto injectors sat on the edge of the kitchen counter. One bottle was knocked over, its liquid contents having spilled over the edge and dripped to the floor below.

Anna came to the small living room, a portable battery unit powering an old-fashioned floor lamp in the left corner, next to what looked like a real, leather chair. To her right sat a glass table and another chair, with a two or three foot long aquarium filling the space between. Brightly colored fish swam lazily in the bluish tank light.

The luxuriously appointed space always took her by surprise. It was the kind of place her mother would approve of, only to find reason to complain about later.

A bedroom sat off a hall to the left and a dark hallway to the right – a bathroom and another bedroom. They stopped and listened for a moment, but the gentle hum of the battery unit was the only sound.

"This way," Soraya mouthed and gestured her slowly down the long hall. Anna followed, continuously looking behind her, struggling with the idea that not stopping Soraya in the hallway wasn't just foolish, but dangerous.

There is only one way out of their quarters...nowhere to run. Why didn't I stop her outside? she thought, nervously eyeing the long hall.

Soraya stopped for a moment and listened, almost as if she'd heard Anna's doubts and fears. Could she? How could any of it be possible?

But the quarters were quiet...no, serene. With the gentle, warm light at her back and the subtle scent of lavender drifting out of the bathroom, she could almost lose track of the chaos plaguing the station. Almost.

If Preston isn't here, where did he go? Will he come back? She wondered as Soraya ducked into the dark bedroom, immediately moving to the left, where a small closet sat against the wall.

Soraya crouched down and started rifling around in the dark cubby. Anna felt her need, but it wasn't due to her cold feet. She stooped down behind her, shining the beam of the small light into the dark space.

"Thank you, I was just thinking that I needed light," Soraya whispered.

Anna sniffed. The air in the bedroom had an off smell here – in almost perfect contrast to the hall behind her. This room smelled sour, like sweat and sick. Soraya rocked back, a pair of white and gray jogging boots in hand.

A *snap...pop* sounded from somewhere in the room. Anna's head swung around, her shoulders immediately tensing up. She grabbed a handful of Soraya's jumpsuit and pulled back.

Her small light wouldn't illuminate the whole room, but something glinted off the far wall. It was shiny...or wet. The smell grew stronger – coppery, acidic. The hairs on her neck prickled. An urge blossomed deep in her mind, the impulse so strong it made the muscles in her legs start to twitch. *Fight or run.*

Another *pop* sounded, strangely reminiscent of someone cracking their knuckles. A low hum filled air, the corresponding vibration noticeable in the decking just as she felt the tickle of moving air kiss her neck. A heater pack glowed to life in the darkness directly ahead, something weaving through the air just above it.

"Baby, is that you?" Soraya asked, turning to the dark room, but Anna heaved her up and back. She missed the doorway and hit the door, smacking it hard against the wall.

"Shit! We need to get out of here...now!" Anna hissed, just as a light blinked on in the hall behind them. The quarters seemed to come alive as electronics clicked and blinked to life around them.

The square of light from the doorway cut through the concealing shadow, bathing the opposite wall in a bright rectangle, before blinking off and on again.

"Pres.t..o...n," Soraya saw him first, a confusing, bloody mess covering the wall that had been concealed by the dark the moment before. She gasped, her scream splitting the air before Anna could slap a hand up to her mouth. Anna choked and sobbed, fighting back screams of her own, but couldn't find enough air to make sound.

They slid sideways together and fumbled to pull themselves through the doorway. Anna tried to tear her eyes away, to turn and run, but it was too much for her mind to take...too horrific.

The light flickered again, making the smeared walls seemed to stretch sideways away from where Preston hung, arms and legs stretched wide, his impressive height suspended clear off the ground.

Strange, pulsating matter grew up and out of the skin on his arms and legs, forming what looked like snaking tendrils that coiled up and over the smooth ceramic wall. His head lolled off to one side, the skin pulled back like the gory pedals of a fleshy flower. Preston's mouth opened and closed slowly, his teeth abnormally large with no lips to cover them.

Every ounce of Soraya's fear, grief, and horror pumped into Anna's body all at once. It made her legs shake and back go weak. She felt heavy and sagged halfway towards the ground before she could shake it away.

"What's happening...to...him?" Soraya moaned, as Anna heaved her back upright.

Run! her mind screamed, and she wrenched them sideways towards the doorway. But it wasn't just Preston...not just his mutilated body. Another *snap* sounded, followed by a sinewy *pop.* Preston's ribs moved, popping and extending out through his chest, groping and pulling like the grasping pincers of an impossibly large insect. The bones clawed at her neighbor's back, pulling his bloodied torso further into the messy hole that had been Preston's abdomen, as if his body was somehow trying to...eat him. The man's legs flopped once, hanging free just above the ground.

Anna found the doorway and they stumbled outside, falling against the hallway. She couldn't look away though, even when her mind told her to turn and run – run as fast as her legs would carry her. Preston's body moved and shook, a trickle of blood dribbling onto the floor. Their flesh seemed to be fusing, or knitting together to make two bodies one.

Soraya's weight sent them tumbling sideways down the hall, a strangled scream pulling at Anna's resolve. She pushed Soraya ahead of her, scooping the boots up as they slipped from her hand.

"Go...go!" she managed, clawing at the wall and half-tumbling out into the living room.

They were in the hall, the kitchen, and then moving through the door. Anna slapped the door control once they were outside.

"Lock...lock it!" she gasped.

Soraya smacked her wrist against the reader, but only glanced at the screen, neither woman waiting for the resulting click. Anna swallowed hard and kicked forward as fast as she could, Soraya easily outpacing her.

They slowed down, turning the corner by the elevator, Soraya's feet slapping against the floor. The lift doors were closed, the floor indicator light glowing unsteadily. Soraya stepped forward and pressed the call indicator, but Anna grabbed her by the arm.

"No...look, it's moving," she whispered.

"What are you doing?"

Anna wiped her mouth and looked around, trying to master her panic and gain some small level of control. A light flickered to her right, and then left. The dark hall materialized out of the gloom as the trim lights glowed to life. The power flickered as the space grew bright, but plunged into darkness once again. A sharp *bang* sounded from back up the hall.

They both looked up to the floor indicator. It flashed two A and then a heartbeat later, three A. Another bang filled the passage behind them, debris rattling noisily to the floor.

Move!

"It's moving so slow," Soraya said, her eyes flicking back towards the corner.

Anna grabbed Soraya's hand and moved quickly past the elevator, where a solitary maintenance hatch stood in the corner. She turned the locking cog on the top, middle, and bottom, before pulling the door open. The hinges groaned loudly. The top rung of a service ladder appeared out of the darkness.

"Down...quick!" she hissed. Soraya didn't hesitate and crawled into the narrow, vertical shaft.

Another bang, this one far louder, reverberated down the hall. There was another noise, too, followed by a loud, electronic chime. It wasn't the door, but the...

Elevator, she realized, a striking wave of skin-prickling fear rushing through her. The elevator was bad? It was a feeling, an intuition.

"Go! Put those on down there," she hissed, and tossed the boots down into the darkness and then half-pushed Soraya after them.

"Don't look...don't look," Anna whispered, bouncing on her heels as she waited for Soraya to make room on the ladder.

She heard the elevator doors open, heard voices spill out of the lift and fill the passage. They were men – their breathing and voices muffled respirators.

An ugly, loud bang split the air and Anna jumped into the darkness, almost landing on Soraya's head in the process. She leaned out of the ladder well and grabbed the door to swing it shut.

A man walked out of the elevator and turned to look right at her as the door started to swing closed. He wore a strange-looking hazard suit, the gray material merging seamlessly with gloves and boots, but also a large, protective faceplate and respirator.

"Hey...I've got someone. Over here!" the man yelled, moving quickly towards Anna. A beam of blinding light flooded the space, burning her eyes as lamps on the man's helmet blinked on.

"Hey you, stop! Come out of there!"

Anna wrenched on the door, the criminally neglected hinges groaning in protest. She caught a glimpse of more suited men pouring out of the elevator, black crates clutched in their hands.

The man stopped and leveled something at her, just as the door pulled closed. She heard something click loudly, and then it whined right before a flash of blinding blue light erupted against the door.

The hatch smashed closed, a mind-numbing crash hitting the metal and almost pitching her off the ladder and into the darkness below. Anna wrenched herself upright again and fumbled in the dark for the locking cogs.

Did he just fucking shoot at me? The panic hit her as her fingers curled around the top lock. She slapped it closed, and then reached for the next one down, stopping only to turn her small work light back on. Anna blinked, but it wasn't just the dark. Bright colors swam before her vision, making it hard to focus.

The middle cog turned more easily, her hand finding the handle almost purely by accident. She dropped down two rungs to reach the bottom one. It started to turn as the top cog slapped violently open again.

Anna slipped and almost toppled from the ladder. She fought, corrected, and heaved herself back up as the middle cog smashed open.

"No!" she growled and shoved the middle cog back closed again. She reached for the top, but before she could grasp it, the middle lock moved. Anna dropped her hands to the middle handle again, fortifying the latch with all the strength she could muster. She felt something pressing on it, twisting with an incredible amount of strength.

"Go, Soraya...faster," Anna yelled down the shaft.

"I hear you in there! Open this hatch! Do it and come out of there!" the man yelled, his voice buzzing through the metal hatch.

The hatch shook a moment later, the metal ringing with a sharp impact. The pressure on the middle cog returned, twofold. Anna kicked a foot up onto the wall of the small passage. It slipped and she kicked up again, finally finding purchase.

"You shot at me, asshole! Whoever you are, you're...not...getting in," Anna grunted, every muscle in her upper body straining. The handle stopped turning, her newfound leverage giving her an advantage. A droplet of sweat ran down from her forehead onto her nose.

The hatch shuddered again, the impact ringing in her ears, and the pressure hit the cog. The handle started to turn, and Anna returned the leverage, a strength she'd never known welling up in her shoulders and arms. And yet, the handle continued to turn. Her strength wasn't failing, far from it. But her hands were slipping – heat was rising in the tight confines around her, and she was straining. Her palms were growing slick with sweat.

"Go...Soraya, go!" she gasped, looking to the top cog, and then to the bottom one.

"Think, Anna. Think...troubleshoot..." she started to talk to herself, to keep her mind working and fight the panic. She had to think the problem out loud, but the answer bounced around in her pocket, tapping against her leg.

Okay...fast...deliberate. Fast...deliberate, she thought, and then dropped her right hand off the handle and plunged it into her pocket.

The cog wrenched around, her left hand alone bending under the force. Her fingers slapped against her data point, closed around it, and she pulled. Anna's hand snapped off the middle cog, and she lunged for the bottom one, grasping the handle with her left hand and smashing her data point sideways into the space between the locking arm and the top of the receiver box.

Anna's hand slipped off the handle, the bottom cog almost immediately snapping up. Her data point shifted and caught, wedging diagonally in the narrow space, but she was already descending, moving hand over laborious hand down the ladder.

"Hold, just hold," she mumbled, the metal door shuddering violently above, the racket echoing loudly through the service passage.

She heard the lock rattle violently, punctuated by a sharp *crack,* like snapping glass or plastic. Anna fumbled down another rung, fighting the urge to look back up the shaft. She would make it. She had to.

"You see? You have no business here. You're just making things worse. Nurse!" Doctor Misra shouted, pointing towards Janice's bed. "Get those patients back into their bed. Sedate them, and someone get these people out of here!"

The dull, fuzzy sensation crept up Jacoby's neck and almost instantly settled like an irresistible weight on his eyelids. He fought the urge to sleep as a nurse wearing a white suit and respirator approached Janice's tent.

"Take...it...offff, p-p-please," Jacoby croaked, rolling his head back and forth, trying to catch sight of Lex or Doctor Reeds. He snapped his head to the side and thrashed his arms and legs, doing whatever he could not to tumble back into the black.

"What is wrong with them?" Lex asked, appearing next to Reeds.

"They're incredibly sick, and there is nothing you can do for them. Now would you please leave, as you have been instructed, and take this man back to his clinic where he belongs?"

"Layla, please, this isn't right at all...the procedures and protocols," Reeds argued.

"Ma'am, are you alright? Can you hear me, ma'am?" the nurse asked, unzipping the first layer of the tent surrounding Janice's bed. "Doctor Misra, we're getting some really weird readings on her vitals. She is showing in severe cardiac and pulmonary distress. Her heart rate is barely registering," she said, checking a tablet as she waited for another nurse to close the flap behind her.

"Pamela, get her back into bed and we will draw another series of blood samples. All of these patients are no doubt worse off thanks to our unwanted visitors...putting their already compromised immune systems under even more stress," Doctor Misra shot back, glaring at Reeds.

"Yes, doctor," the nurse said before stooping down and unzipping the inner layer of plastic. "Ma'am, I'm coming. Just stay calm."

Something felt wrong, so horribly wrong. The sense of unease bubbled up from Jacoby's guts - like a sour wave...like a sickness. Only it wasn't his, and somehow he knew it.

"Don't open...it!" Jacoby croaked, just as Janice exploded off the ground, a wet and feral snarl filling her plastic enclosure.

The nurse fell back with Janice atop her, the boney woman clawing and pounding on her head and faceplate. Jacoby wrenched on the restraints and kicked his feet, but his strength was gone, the Palmer Module hanging like a heavy parasite on his arm.

"Get her off of me...oh my god. Somebody get her off!" the nurse wailed, but everyone was backing away from the enclosure.

"Open that thing up! Somebody get in there and help her," Lex yelled, shoving past Doctor Misra and moving right towards Janice's bed. But it wasn't just Janice now. The other patients were up, pounding on their plastic enclosures and screaming. Black bits of spittle covered the plastic, but to Jacoby it looked like blood.

A tall man stepped out of the crowd, cutting Lex off. "Stop! Do not open that tent! You don't understand the risks here. These patients are in level-three containment to prevent further viral contamination to this station. That is our number one consideration here. Pamela and the other medical staff accepted that risk when they signed their corporate contracts. I repeat...do not open that enclosure!"

"Risk? From some crazy, sick lady attacking her? Step aside, sir and let me do my job," Lex said quietly, and brought the stun baton up before her.

"No. I order you to stand down, officer. I am Manis Nazzar, junior assistant to the station secretary. I speak for the Directorate. Doctor Misra has unfettered authority in this matter and already ordered you to remove yourself and this man from her lab. Do it now, or I will have you taken from this place and locked in restraints," the tall man said, squaring his shoulders and puffing out his chest.

"Someone...get...oh my god! She is...ow...there is something sharp cutting into my stomach! She's trying to...trying to cut my suit," the nurse, Pamela, started to scream. Jacoby fought against the restraints again, the pain in the nurse's voice adding to his panic.

"Layla where is your security team? This is getting...out of hand," Manis said, turning to Doctor Misra.

"I sent them out to lock down any further contamination," Doctor Misra snapped back, but turned back to the tent as the nurse grew more frantic. "Pamela, for God's sake, calm yourself. She is sick and weak...probably out of her mind with fever. You have been trained for this. Pacify her, and put her back into bed. And you...sedate her already!"

"I'm trying doctor. I've already administered a full dose of series two. She should be out, but..."

Jacoby could see it now. The other patients wore the strange devices on their upper arms, too.

"You sent them all away? You should have kept one here...to guard your lab," Manus shot back, his voice rising several octaves. He stomped his foot and started to pace.

"I didn't think I would need protection from sick people and my own staff," Doctor Misra said with a scoff and stepped forward, carefully maintaining her distance from Lex.

"Doctor, I can't...get her off. She is so...strong. And there is something sharp...ow...she is...oh my god! She is stabbing me! It hurts! Please! Help me! It hurts so bad. Please!" Pamela yelled, her screams devolving into hysterical, breathless, and unintelligible pleas.

"Stabbing? Pamela, she doesn't even have a weapon. Now get her back in..." Doctor Misra started to say, but the nurse shrieked again and Jacoby watched the doctor stumble back, her confident smirk melting away.

"Enough of this crap," Lex snarled, and pushed through a nurse and leveled the stun baton at another lab assistant, angry sparks arcing off the tip. Jacoby wrenched his arms back and forth, his wrists sliding a bit against the nylon. They were loosening, but just a bit.

"Officer, I ordered you to stand..." Manis yelled, but grunted, right before something heavy slapped the ground.

Jacoby turned back to find the administrator lying on the ground, clutching his arm against his chest. Janice and the nurse thrashed inside the enclosure, feet and hands slapping against the thick plastic. Lex ripped the zipper open just as Jacoby wrenched his head to the side, desperately trying to pull the electrodes free.

"She's breaking containment. D-D-Doctor, what do we do?" a young man in a lab coat asked, just as Lex pulled the nurse out of the tent by the foot.

"Separate them...and get her back into her enclosure. Restrain her to the bed! We'll need to decontaminate the whole space! Administer series three! We have to hope she doesn't code on an overdose," the short doctor shouted, directing several other nurses in suits forward.

Jacoby felt one of the electrodes pull tight, but he couldn't move his head enough to break it free. He turned his head back, just as the nurses broke Janice's hold on Pamela. Lex helped the two women and together they peeled the two apart.

"What in the hell?" someone shouted. Pamela rolled onto her side. Blood trickled out of her white suit, leaking through punctures in her chest and stomach.

"Uh, I want...everyone...out of...here. Full...quarantine. Seal the lab," Doctor Misra stammered, her dark eyes locked on the dark fluid spattering the floor around the prone nurse. The two women wrestled Janice back to her enclosure.

"Worthlesss s-s-shit!" she screamed suddenly, and wrenched around. The nurses flailed to maintain a hold, but Janice's hospital gown tore down the middle, pulling free and sending her toppling naked to the ground.

She scrabbled upright, her emaciated frame now fully visible in the harsh light. Janice stood still for a moment, panting and trembling visibly, her pallid, mottled flesh pulled tight over her boney frame.

"Restrain her! Restrain her!" Doctor Misra yelled, falling back behind two men. Janice spun on the group, a thick rope of dark saliva slipping down her chin.

"What is that sticking out of her chest?" the closest nurse screamed and jumped back.

Jacoby fought against his restraints, against his panic, against the air around him as he gulped down a breath. And then he tried to scream as he saw it, too. Sharp protrusions broke through the skin around Janice's rib cage, the horrible, blood-covered appendages moving and clawing at the air, before disappearing back inside. They looked like bone...but that wasn't possible.

Janice turned fully to him, her dark eyes wide and weeping. Her mouth opened and closed as she gagged and breathed, the noise ragged and wet. Something moved under her thin skin, as if her skeleton was made of roiling snakes.

"Slacking...on the...job! But I f-f-found ya, Jack...Jack...J-a-c-k! Worthless!" Janice hissed, her head twitching violently as she formed the words. Then she leapt forward and crashed into the plastic tent surrounding his bed. She scrabbled at the plastic, ripping and digging with her fingernails and teeth.

Jacoby twisted on the restraints, the nylon biting and tearing at his skin. The Palmer Module beeped loudly at him, his arm and temples burning angrily, but he wouldn't...no couldn't, let it stop him. A weight moved up his arm, but he refused to give in.

A hole appeared in the thick plastic, Janice's slime-covered hands cutting through and pealing it open. She tore her way through, pulling and wrenching. She bit the plastic, chewing it and tearing it wide.

A shadow moved next to her, a loud *snap* and blue light flashing a heartbeat later. Janice shrieked and writhed, her weight tearing the outer layer of tent all the way to the ground.

"Stay down!" Lex yelled. She lunged and struck again, the light flickering as the stun baton met flesh. Janice flopped ungainly to the ground, rolled, and sprang to her feet. She scuttled sideways, like some horrible, fleshy crab. Janice shrieked and went right at Lex, the stun baton catching her squarely in the chest.

Jacoby fought the deadness in his limbs, the horrible weight settling onto his eyelids. Movement caught his eye. The other patients down the row. They were fighting, too, clawing their way out through their plastic enclosures. He couldn't just drift off...he had to break free...had to...somehow. Or he would...die. They would all...die.

Doctor Misra shouted orders, her voice broken and strained. Her people rushed between the beds in a flurry, white lab coats flapping, fumbling surgical trays, auto injectors, and restraints from carts.

"Call the security checkpoint and tell them we need more officers down here!" Lex yelled, moving sideways to block Janice. "Get back!" she growled as the boney woman moved towards Jacoby's bed again.

"Jack...Jack...Jack!" Janice moaned, her neck popping loudly.

"Who are you talking to? What does that mean...? I told you to get back!" Lex said, but jumped back, catching Janice in the right leg with the stun baton. The prong flashed, the air crackling with the *snap,* splitting the skin open on Janice's leg. Something dark and fleshy rolled out.

"I want this place back under control! Lock down the lab now!" Doctor Misra screamed, just as a patient tore through the outer shell of their tent. The man clawed his head through first, and then shoulders and chest, sliding through as if being birthed. He jumped forward and swept a man off his feet, sending them both tumbling to the ground. Two nurses rushed in, pulling him clear and trying to wrestle restraints over his hands.

The stun baton cracked against Janice's midsection, the resulting *snap* and *crack* of electricity louder than before. But she didn't go down, nor did she seem to notice the pain.

Lex staggered back as Janice pushed forward, somehow able to muscle the taller, more muscular woman against the wall. Lex drove an armored knee into the smaller woman's midsection, lifting her clear off the ground. Janice gagged and screamed, but her body twisted around the strike, her spine bending grotesquely.

Jacoby wrenched his right arm straight up, the nylon strap pulling tight and stretched it towards his left wrist. If he could...just...reach the strap on his left wrist. But it wasn't enough...he couldn't reach it.

Janice kicked and clawed at Lex, knocking the stun baton to the ground. The smaller woman gagged and screamed, snapping her teeth, clawing and slowly crawling up Lex's arms and snapping at the air.

Jacoby wrenched on his straps again just as a shadow fell over him. He turned to find Doctor Reeds slipping through the inner tent, his face a pale, sweaty mask of fear and confusion.

"This is chaos. Chaos!" the doctor muttered, flinching as a patient tore free from another tent, his hospital gown tearing off in the process. Two nurses jumped on him immediately, the larger jabbing an auto injector violently into his back again and again.

"There is something going on here that I don't understand. P-P-Perhaps she knows...knows something at least. Whatever it is...it's bad, very bad! I have a gut feeling that you are involved...somehow. B-B-But I don't think you're a bad person...don't think you mean us harm. Please don't prove me wrong. We just need to...get out of here," Reeds reached forward and unstrapped Jacoby's left arm, then stretched across his body to free his right.

"I don't want...anyone to get hurt, doc," Jacoby breathed in response and half-rolled into a sitting position.

His head swam, his arms like leaden weights hanging from his shoulders, but he was free. Jacoby reached up and groped for the wires hanging off of his head. The adhesive pads tore free, small clumps of brown hair coming with them. The straps fell away from his feet.

Jacoby half rolled, half fell off the bed, the Palmer Module now beeping and vibrating violently against his arm. He pushed past Reeds and out of the tent, clawing and pulling on the infernal device, even as its needles stabbed into his arm, pumping more debilitating poison into his body.

He staggered and fell to his knees, everything below his waist going numb. The Palmer Module started to beep more loudly, almost singing in a frantic cadence of beeps and chirps. Jacoby pulled and wrenched on it, but it was stuck fast, a dull wave of pain radiating up his bicep and into his shoulder.

Lex and Janice tumbled away from the wall not far away, the smaller woman scrabbling violently and pulling her to her knees. She lashed out, the movement barely perceptible, and caught Lex on the side of the head. The blow sprawled the redhead sideways onto the ground.

Janice shrieked and pounded on Lex, her body convulsing as more bones snapped and popped, the bloody spines erupting through the skin on her back, too.

Help her! the voice rang out in his mind. It was weak, but there. This time there was no shock, no burning pain in his temples to drive it away.

Jacoby wrenched on the Palmer Module again, and then slapped the small screen. It glowed brightly, a padlock icon flashing red in response.

He stumbled forward, half crawling to get to Lex, but Janice looked up at him, screamed angrily, and grabbed her by the feet and starting to drag her away.

"Janice, stop!" Jacoby screamed, his voice still weak. He managed two steps before he stumbled and fell. The Palmer beeped again, the flesh underneath burning and tingling. "Stop...you withered old...bitch," he cursed, already out of breath. The device buzzed against his arm and beeped, as if laughing at him.

Break it. Smash it. Tear it apart!

He pounded a fist on the plastic housing, but it felt impossibly solid. "I can't...I'm too weak."

You've always been afraid to be strong to stand up for yourself...to use violence...even when it was called for. I've been here whether you want to admit it or not. Stop lying to yourself. Crack your head against the wall again and let me do what needs to be done, or admit that I am real, and give me control!

"Wait!" Jacoby growled, just as a ripple shook his right arm.

He remembered the clinic then, Randle's anger and his leaden fists smashing against his face. Then he remembered his head smashing against the wall, the sharp pain and dull fuzz that followed. A memory triggered from somewhere deep in his mind, so many years before. It was almost the same scenario, only it was his father standing over him, his fists cracking angrily into Jacoby's head and face. He'd felt the pain then, too...the fuzz, and faintly, losing control. The voice...it had been there.

"I remember you. I...remember. You are real. Help me!" he gasped, trying fruitlessly to tear the rest of the fog off that old memory. Something fought him, and the old recollection slipped back down below.

Yes! I will help you, but know that before the end, you will make us whole, the voice rang in his mind, a wave of angry, tumultuous thoughts coursing in with it. The veins in his right arm distended grotesquely, his fingers curling and flexing like spider legs.

His hand shook and the knuckles popped, as a gray pallor flooded down from his elbow. Without conscious action, his right fist swung down onto the Palmer Module. The plastic housing cracked. His hand reared back again, pain and blood mixing as his fist tore through the device with the second strike.

"Janice! Stop!" he yelled, staggering to his feet and plodding forward. He didn't know if she was Janice anymore, or if she knew her name, but he had to try.

His right hand tightened on the damaged device, and finally, felt its parasitic hold break free. Electrodes, needles, and catheter lines tore out of his forearm as the Palmer Module fell away.

Pure! We...must...be...pure! the voice seethed.

Jacoby's whole body shook, the veins in his left arm burning and throbbing in time with his racing heart. Clear fluid trickled out of the bloody holes left in the Palmer Module's absence. It bubbled forth, running down his forearm and dripping off his fingers, blood mixing and swirling on his pale skin.

Warmth blossomed in his toes, rushing up his legs and into his chest as the debilitating mixture of pharmacological poison was somehow expelled from his body. The horrible numbness and weight burned away, a hint of kinetic strength rushing in to take its place.

Now stop her!

Jacoby leapt forward, his legs no longer mush beneath him. He ducked low and scooped the fallen stun baton off the ground, and ran. Janice wrenched Lex along, sliding her across the floor like a hunter with their felled prey. She turned left and disappeared between two beds.

Jacoby followed, his hospital gown flapping up around his waist, cold air tickling his privates. He planted and ducked left at the spot and almost tripped over a nurse as she crawled out from under a tent enclosure. She shrieked, flailed her arms, and attacked him.

"Don't touch me. No! I don't want to be...don't eat me!" she screamed, fighting as Jacoby wrenched her upright.

"I'm not going to...eat you!" he yelled, before pushing her free. Jacoby ran forward, the chaos of the room crashing over him like a wave. He nearly tripped over Pamela, whose body shook and convulsed on the ground. Foamy spittle covered her nose and mouth.

Janice was ahead and to the right, dragging Lex towards the far wall. A large service panel was missing, the remnant of a torn, white garment hanging in the opening.

A group of nurses staggered by right in front of him, the three women struggling to control a large and very naked man.

The man knocked the two nurses on either side of him to the ground and straightened. He wrenched the third woman off the ground in a bear hug and spun, swiping at one of the women.

The man threw his arms wide and screeched loudly. The woman he'd been clutching to a moment before didn't fall...he wasn't holding her, nor was she holding onto him.

The nurse twitched and her head lolled to the side. She grimaced and opened her eyes, her gaze locking right on Jacoby.

"Ple.a..s...e," she moaned, and wordlessly mouthed "help".

You can't help her. She's already dead, her brain just hasn't realized it yet. You can help Lex...move!

Jacoby brought the stun baton up and moved to strike, but thought better of it, and moved forward, grasping the woman's outstretched arm. She wrenched free and clawed at him, the man swinging around immediately.

"I can't feel...my body. I'm sorry...I can't...I don't know what's happening to me...oh god, help me!" the nurse wailed, her arms and legs flailing violently.

The man screeched and swung around, but before Jacoby could bring the stun baton up to strike, he leapt straight up into the air. He caught a large pipe running along the ceiling, kicked his legs around a conduit running parallel, and scrabbled away.

Before Jacoby could even follow, the man ripped a vent cover free. No, it was the nurse...somehow, the two people's combined limbs moved together of the same accord. The cover fell away with a crash, and then moving like a horrible, man-sized spider, the man crawled inside the ventilation duct and disappeared.

"Someone...get her off...me!" Lex screamed, spurring Jacoby forward.

Janice had reached the service panel in the wall, but Lex was alert now and fighting, kicking and rolling, fighting violently to break free.

"Jack...Jack...Jack," Janice babbled loudly, clawing and wrenching Lex towards the dark hole in the wall. She tore one of Lex's boots off, tossed it aside and clawed for another grasp, the dark fabric between the armored pads bunching up and tearing loudly.

Lex rolled over, growling desperately, but suddenly jerked back towards the darkness, her hands sliding ineffectually against the smooth ground. Jacoby's vision narrowed until the two fighting women were the only thing he could see. His heart raced, muscles coiling and extending, propelling him forward.

His thumb brushed against a knob on the stun baton's smooth handle. It pushed in and turned, the weapon vibrating more intensely with every click. Janice was only ten feet away now, half of her body in shadow, the sharp, boney protrusions jabbing and stabbing, the wretched woman's chest suddenly splitting open.

Lex's legs buckled, finally losing her long-fought battle. Janice screeched in triumph and found new purchase, coiling to bring her into that horrible embrace. Jacoby was three paces away and launched his body into the air. He threw all of his weight forward, driving the baton into Janice's chest. But he didn't pull the trigger. The weight behind the strike pushed the weapon through the puffy flesh of what used to be her right breast and clear out through her back.

Janice wailed and fell back into the dark service passage. Jacoby hooked Lex under the arms and wrenched her back, her feet kicking and sliding against the ground. She was barely free of the darkness when Janice erupted forth, her body opening from neck to navel, her bones curling and jutting like jagged teeth. Blood spattered the ground before her in an arc as ropey organs hung free.

Jacoby lurched forward and caught Janice by the wrists, using every ounce of strength to push her back towards the darkness. He locked his gaze onto her eyes, anything to avoid the wretched, bloody horror that was happening to the rest of her body. She bent and buckled, her feet sliding towards the shadows.

"W-o-r-t-h-l-e-s-s...s-h-i-t!" she moaned and shrieked, biting and snapping at him. It wasn't Janice, however. It was her voice, but there was no humanity left in her eyes, just a swirling and dark malevolence.

He shoved her clear to the service entrance, but she splayed her legs and caught the sides. His momentum halted. Janice's wrists popped, ropey tendrils bursting from her forearms and wrapping around his hands. She leaned back and started to pull him forward and into the darkness.

"You never fucking stop! Do you? " Jacoby growled and wrenched his hand down to the handle of the stun baton sticking out of her chest, pushed the button in, and turned it all the way. Then he pulled the trigger.

A blue flash filled his vision, and a distant part of his mind screamed out. He felt his body go rigid, felt the heat and the pain, but couldn't put it all together. It was just oddly detached sensations.

Then he was sliding backwards. He could see and hear again. He caught a glimpse of Lex smashing a service panel back over a hole in the wall, and people in dark scrubs and white jackets scrambling to pull tables and equipment in front of it.

He looked up and found Doctor Reeds' face. The man was pulling him back, shouting at others, his differently colored eyes flicking quickly around the large space.

"Doc," he said quietly, surprised by the strength in his voice.

Reeds looked down.

"Jacoby?" he said, and stopped pulling. "My god, I thought you...well, when that baton arced between you two, I was sure it killed you. That kind of voltage when it meets skin and bone..."

They stopped moving and Reeds helped him sit. Jacoby lifted his hands. The tips of his fingers were black, the burns extending up his hands and onto his wrists. The darkened flesh followed a strange, coiling pattern up his forearm.

"I think I'm...okay," he muttered and patted down his arms and chest.

"The door is locked. It's sealed. They did it. They sealed us in!" a woman screamed behind them. Jacoby couldn't see her, but he could hear her panic, feel her fear through the air between them. He could feel Doctor Reeds' fear, too, but it was different somehow...a small measure of control still in place that wasn't there with the others.

"Well, unseal it! We need to leave...now before one of those things comes back!" Reeds yelled, pushing off and standing behind him. "Layla! Unseal the doors, Layla!"

Jacoby glanced around, taking in the chaos of the room as if for the first time. The beds were tipped over, the plastic tents torn and trampled. A massive bloody puddle sat not five feet to his right, the fluid smeared across the floor. He followed the blood trail over to where Lex and several others formed a barricade of medical equipment.

"Where is Doctor Misra?" Reeds called. Jacoby watched the small crowd look around. There were so few of them left, a handful of scared, disheveled people.

"She's not here-" a nurse responded, shakily.

"Pamela is gone, too! She was hurt. She couldn't walk. They took her. They took all of them. But why? What was wrong with them? What do they want?" another shrieked loudly.

Jacoby wanted to shush her, but a young man in a lab coat came forward and threw his arms around her. A duct overhead shook, the rectangular sheet metal distending loudly before quickly popping back into shape.

"Everyone...quietly and quickly, move to the lab. Now!" Reeds hissed. The doctor moved to help him up, but Jacoby waved him off. He pushed off the floor, a tingle shooting up through his legs.

It will take more than a little zap to kill us, the voice said, sweeping out from its hiding place in his mind.

"But why? And how?" he whispered.

Does it matter where strength comes from? Or does it only matter that it is strength? You owe me.

"I fucking hate riddles," he spit back, wondering what kind of payment a disembodied voice in his head could possibly want. Was it part of him? Or was it something else?

Jacoby started to follow Reeds and the group towards the door as Lex and the others finished stacking the last of the tables against the wall. She turned, spotted him, and visibly started.

He pretended not to notice and walked slowly, rubbing the tips of his fingers together. The blackened skin crumbled off, falling away like ash collected from a spent campfire. Pink, fresh skin lay underneath, soft and unblemished.

"Impossible," he breathed.

Lex appeared next to him, her movements lithe, graceful, and her steps quiet. It was clear she knew how to move.

"You're okay..." she breathed, as if the concept was abstract...absurd. "When my baton discharged...well, the way it arced between you. I thought you were dead."

"For a moment there, I thought I was," Jacoby responded honestly. He looked into her green eyes, the fear and concern worn openly. He held her gaze, the sparkle inciting something deeper inside him. The pressure mounted in his head, a vibration coursing down through the rest of his body. He suddenly had an idea of how the other part of him might expect payment.

Jacoby looked away as the air started to grow thick around him and he was immediately reminded that he was only wearing a hospital gown.

Lex sniffed and coughed, but fell into step next to him as they walked into the lab. Jacoby turned away from her, trying to put a little distance between them. He could feel the accelerating beat of her heart, the air charging in and out of her lungs, but also the warmth blossoming inside her...

Jacoby walked behind a row of tables, the rows of glass beakers and computer equipment helping to hide his growing excitement.

He turned to find Lex fidgeting with the motorized door, then heard it click loudly. They moved quietly through the long lab room together as a group. The lab equipment only seemed to get larger and more complex the further they went – centrifuges holding dozens of clear ampules giving way to sleek, blade-shaped machines covered in glowing displays.

Jacoby silently wondered what a mining station would need with such advanced scientific machinery. The lights went out on the left side of the room, bathing Jacoby into darkness. He stopped, a voice echoing quietly ahead.

Jacoby felt his way through the shadows, moving between tables and following Doctor Reeds. They reached the end of the lab and found an office to the right. The voice echoed out from the narrow door, the glow of a screen dancing in the window.

"Did you seal the lab?"

"Yes, I think so. I mean, probably. Doctor Misra told them to do it as soon as they went crazy and started attacking us. They weren't responding to the drugs anymore. They couldn't keep them sedated. That has to be it. I mean, you should have seen it. I barely got out of there alive."

Doctor Reeds settled in the doorway and cleared his throat quietly. Jacoby caught a glimpse of a man sitting in a chair, facing away from them, a data point held up before him. Another man's face filled the small device's screen before it went black. Manis Nazzar swiveled around in the chair to face them and then stood. He was lanky, but impressively tall, towering a full head or more above Reeds.

"You all aren't, well, you aren't authorized to be in here...any of you. Where is Layla? Where is Doctor Misra?"

"She's dead, I think...like most of her staff. You know, the 'ones that went crazy' and dragged them off into the ventilation ducts' while you ran in here to hide," Reeds responded, "I think you should tell me what is going on." Then the physician lifted something before him, and for a heartbeat, Manis' eyes widened, betraying him.

Reeds' body blocked his view, so Jacoby leaned around him to see. He was holding a smashed Palmer Module...the very one Jacoby had ripped from his own body.

0405 HOURS

Anna was well into the dark ladder shaft before plastic and electronics rained down on her head from above. She heard the hatch open, the noise echoing oddly down the tight confines.

A glimmer of light reflected off the rung of her ladder, and despite her reservations, she looked up. A light shone from somewhere far above. A man's voice echoed down – although she couldn't understand what he was saying.

She began to descend again. She couldn't stop...she wouldn't.

A banging noise sounded below, followed by another, and then a third. She dropped her leg onto another rung and looked down. A square of light broke the darkness. Anna climbed, the ladder slippery in her sweaty palms. Damn it was hot. Why was it so hot?

The diffuse light below grew brighter, the frame and rungs of the ladder now a shadowy outline. Her heart wasn't beating quite so fast, the gut-tightening sense of claustrophobia and panic lifting just a bit.

The man yelled something above, his voice rising in a loud shout. Anna stopped just above the open hatch and listened, pausing to hold her breath. No, he was screaming.

A loud noise drowned out his voice – a sharp popping staccato that filled the shaft around her and seemed to echo endlessly.

My god, is that a gun? she thought.

The screaming abruptly stopped, a chilling silence drifting in after. Anna hung there for a pregnant moment, holding her breath, and listened. She looked up just as something blotted out all of the light from above. Someone was in the shaft with her, moving down the ladder.

"Move!" she hissed and peeled her hands off the rung, dropping the last three lengths to the ground. A vibration shook the ladder as she let go, the metal rails thrumming and shaking.

She didn't want to think what it would take to shake such a sturdy ladder so much. Anna ducked through the hatch and promptly slammed it closed behind her.

"What was that? I heard something loud?" Soraya asked, moving in behind her and helping close the cogs.

"I don't...I don't know," she stammered, turning from side to side. "Why isn't there a lock?" she yelled, punching the thick metal.

Move, the impulse coursed through her just as Soraya grabbed her shoulders and pulled her around. They ran by the elevator, the glowing display above the doors just catching in Anna's peripheral vision. The elevator was moving, the down arrow hologram flashing and the numbers dropping.

"We need to get out of here now," she croaked.

They ran around the corner, voices immediately echoing up the habitat ring's main passage. Anna spotted a pair of security personnel moving away from them down the curving hall.

"Hey! You!" she screamed.

The two men directed a pair out of their door, one of the men talking loudly to a couple emerging from their door across the hall.

"Take only what you can carry! Station Directorate has ordered the temporary evacuation of station housing from Delta and Charlie rings...no, ma'am, we don't know for how long. This will only be until they can get systems repaired and make sure life support station-wide is safe and functional. Yes this is for your protection and wellbeing. They have opened up the commissary, recreation center, and cafeterias for you."

"Hey!" Soraya screamed, her much louder voice almost immediately catching one of the security officers' attention. He nudged his counterpart with an elbow and pointed in their direction.

The two men guided the personnel off down the hall, before turning and moving in their direction.

"Officers, please, we need your help!" Anna called, a stitch forming in her side.

"Woe-woe-woe, wait just a moment, ladies. Where did you two come from, and in such a hurry? Haven't you heard...?" the shorter of the two men said, leaning to one side and puffing out his chest. Anna ignored his posturing. They just didn't have time.

"Please, you have to listen. There is something going on...uh..." Anna stammered, a creeping sensation crawling up her back.

"...there is something happening...something wrong with people. A sickness...it's changing them, turning them into something else. They're hurting people...killing them. One of them, my...my husband, he attacked us," Soraya said, chiming in right where Anna left off. Anna took her hand, but Soraya's usual strength wasn't there. Instead, all she felt was bone-chilling fear. She felt the need to move, but the two men blocked the hall.

"Wow...wow. Slow down, ladies," the officer on the left said, turning and sharing a smile with his counterpart. The tag on his armor read "Blake", while his taller counterpart's name appeared to be "Garrett".

"Did you say your husband attacked you? Where is he now? Have you reported this yet?" Blake, the shorter man, said. The white and gray padded armor didn't quite conceal the bulge of his belly. His graying hair was short, but combed neatly over to the side. Anna's gaze flicked from his dark brown eyes, to a baton hanging at his waist, over to his counterpart, and to the other man's hazel eyes. She could feel it. They didn't believe them.

"No, you need to listen. It wasn't him! Something happened to him. It changed him. He was bleeding, and coughing, like really sick. He got suspicious, but then just snapped and sort of went crazy. His bones...his bones were...moving, but it was his face...the skin on his face..." Anna said, but realized how crazy it sounded. Hell, she wouldn't believe it if random strangers ran up to her and started spouting off similar gibberish.

"Communications are still down station-wide, so you wouldn't have been able to report it even if you'd have tried," Garrett, the taller of the two, said. The elevator dinged somewhere behind them, the tone sharp and abrupt. Anna and Soraya both stopped and turned.

"We need to go...now! They're dangerous," she said just as the lights flickered, the power cascade flowing all the way down the hall in a wave, before stabilizing again.

"This shit bucket is really fucked now," Blake cursed, then swatted his baton and moved between Anna and Soraya. "Station code requires we check on and report any threat of domestic violence. Is he down here, your husband? Was anyone else involved?"

"Wait, no. Don't go back there. Please. We just need to go," Soraya said, but Garrett moved around her.

"It's okay, miss. You're safe now. You just stay behind us," the larger man said, moving to follow his counterpart.

"No...please. We just need to get out of here. You don't understand," Soraya argued, but the men wouldn't listen.

Anna grabbed her hand and held her back, turning to look down the long, curving hallway. The people that had left their quarters stopped before disappearing around the bend, stacking up behind what appeared to be a sizable line.

"They're evacuating the habitation rings, sending people down to public sectors on A ring. That means they have to shuttle everyone in the transit elevators. You can only fit what, twenty in at a time?" Soraya asked.

"What if someone down there is infected?" Anna asked, watching the two security officers walk away.

"We need to stop them!" Soraya hissed, and before Anna could argue, she pulled her after the two men.

"...we get a lot of these calls, surprisingly. I guess being way out here doesn't stop people from bringing their spouses, or keep them from fighting. Is he close? Are you on this floor?" Blake asked, evidently unaware that the two women hadn't immediately followed when they walked away.

The two men turned left and disappeared into the elevator corridor, the shorter man's voice echoing behind him.

"What...in...the...shit-stained sheets?" Blake cursed just as Anna and Soraya slipped around the corner. The two men pulled the batons free from their belts, the pronged ends crackling blue in the dim corridor.

"Soraya, we need to go," Anna whispered as they cleared the wall. The service hatch came into view, the door swung wide against the far wall.

"Call it in, man. Call this shit in right...now!" Blake said. Garrett hovered in the doorway for a long moment, the baton twitching at his side, before finally moving off to the side. He fumbled for a mic built into the chest pad of his armored suit.

As soon as he moved aside Anna saw what they did, and a sour pit formed in her stomach. The elevator doors were half-open, the single, dim interior light swinging by a wire from the ceiling. The white light flickered dimly, stretching shadows over dark spatters on the walls. A large smear ran down the elevator's right wall, swirling in a mess of footprints and puddles on the floor. Long, stretched fingerprints marked both doors, as if someone had grabbed on and been pulled free.

"Security alarm station," Garrett said, talking into his mic. "Say again, I can't understand you."

A buzzing sensation crept over Anna's skin, crawling down into her arms and legs, like squirming bugs were dumped all over her. She looked to Soraya, the other woman turning at the same time. She felt it, too.

"Ain't right. Nothing right about it," Blake mumbled, leaning tentatively towards the elevator. Then he spun on Anna and Soraya. "Was this you? Did he do this...your husband? Where'd all the...who's blood is that?"

"Security alarm station, come in! This is Officer Garrett. We've got a situation here and need immediate support, over."

The buzzing sensation grew more intense, fluttering her stomach. She felt sick, but why?

"That wasn't there. I don't know...I don't know who's blood that is," Soraya said, and pulled Anna back. "This is bad. I feel it. Feel the bad. It's close. We shouldn't be here. Any of us. We need to get out of here." Soraya and Anna backed away from the grisly elevator.

"You two stop right there! We've got a fuckin' killer on the goddamn station, and until we figure out *who* is responsible and *what* is going on, no one is leaving this spot!" He circled around, tapping his counterpart on the shoulder, before settling in the hall behind them, cutting them off. "No one leaves until we get ahold of someone."

"You don't understand, officer-" Soraya argued, turning to face him.

"I think I understand pretty fuckin' good. It's simple. It always is. You cushy folk hob knob your way to a juicy contract out here in the black, come out and soak up an ass-load of company credits, act like the rules don't apply to you while you're here, and when your contract is up, just leave. What happened? Did he catch you in bed with another guy? Freak out and break some stuff, scream a lot? Is that it? Well, look at this," Blake said, jabbing his baton at the bloody interior of the elevator. "You people are all the same. Don't think about the consequences...until someone ends up with their guts smeared all over the inside of a lift. Then we have to clean up the mess."

Anna slapped her arms as the crawling, sickening feeling intensified. She massaged her forearms, the sensation so strong it made her want to pull her skin off. Soraya shuddered next to her. They could both feel it.

"No! We just need to go...now!" Anna gasped.

"I can't get the alarm station on the freaking radio, man. It's all static...just static. The network is down, too...no data point connectivity," Garrett said, cutting off Blake's tirade and moving directly outside the elevator doors.

"What's wrong with her? Is she tweaking out?" Blake asked, looking to Soraya, then back to Anna. "Are you brain boiling, honey? Oh, this is rich. Were you all tweaking together and he lost his shit? Is that it?"

The elevator car shook violently, the light swaying from side to side.

"What in the hell was that...?" Garrett asked, turning back to the doors.

A shudder vibrated the ground beneath their feet a heartbeat before a massive, dark form dropped through the elevator. The ceiling exploded in a shower of broken metal and shattered plastic, the light crashing against the wall and going dark. Garrett pitched back as something lashed out of the darkness, hitting him with a startlingly loud and wet crunch.

The security officer picked up his baton and staggered to a knee, but a long, white shape shot out of the dark elevator and hit him square in the chest. It punched clean through his back, a perfect line of pulpy gore splattering the ground behind him.

Garrett fell back and started to flop about, his baton dropping out of his hand and rolling towards Soraya's feet. A long, bone-white shape pulled back from the fallen man, folding in on itself and disappearing into the dark lift.

"Garrett! Man, get up! What in the fuck was that?" Blake cursed and jumped around them. He kicked Garrett's body, but the officer just twitched and jerked. He hadn't seen what Anna did...hadn't seen the spear-like shape plunge right through him.

"Weapons are prohibited on the station, asshole! Throw it down and step out of the lift! Now! Do it, and get on the fucking ground!" Blake growled, widening his feet and snapping his baton out to full length. He snapped something on the handle and the glowing end shone brighter in the dim hallway, electricity snapping off the prong.

"I said step out of the goddamn lift! Now! Do it or I'll fry your ass crispy and then dump you in an airlock! I'll space you, motherfucker!" He swept his baton through the air just outside the door, the blue flash flickering off something dark and moving inside.

"Garrett, get up, man!" Blake nudged his counterpart, and the man moved in response. He coughed, gagged, and started to roll over.

Long, boney fingers appeared around the lift doors, and with a grinding crash, they slid open the rest of the way.

"Got ya," Blake snarled as the man-sized form moved out of the lift. He jabbed his baton straight ahead, but staggered back as two long, pale appendages streaked out the darkness and punched clean through his shoulders.

A wave of sickness washed over Anna, her knees giving way and sending them both tumbling back to the ground. She tried to cry out, to scream and deny the horror, but she knew the sound wouldn't come out.

Blake shook and convulsed, his angry curses devolving into pathetic, twisted cries. He slumped towards the ground, but immediately started to rise, his feet lifting clear of the ground.

Anna fumbled over Soraya and managed to get her feet straightened. The sickening churn in her stomach, the almost slimy crawling feeling over her skin, intensified. It radiated out of the elevator, from the darkness, washing over them like putrid, loamy rain.

The creature slid slowly out of the elevator, long, skeletal arms bending and propelling it between the doors. It stomped forward on long, muscular legs, another entirely different set of limbs sprouting out of its pelvis. A foot fell free, landing on the ground as it moved. The hall light gleamed off the human skull, what had formerly been Soraya's husband. The skin and jaw was now gone, his frayed tongue flicking and lashing at the air.

It held Blake off the ground with long, sinewy appendages, the air filled with the creak, rattle, and crunch of grinding bone and popping cartilage.

"W-W-What...the f-f-f..." Blake groaned and sputtered.

Soraya got her feet under her first and heaved Anna up with her. They staggered back, falling against the wall as the creature's chest opened, sharp ribs splayed like curving teeth. A human-shaped head appeared from the within the chest cavity, its jaw working silently and its eyes milky white.

Anna rolled against the wall and pushed off, but Soraya lurched forward before she could stop her and scooped the fallen batons off the ground. She turned as two smaller boney appendages unfolded from the creature's chest cavity, rose up like bent spider legs, and snapped down, plunging violently into Blake's chest and face. They pulled back in a flash and lanced out again and again.

They were running down the hall then, the sickening *crunch* and *thump* of bone sinking into flesh and muscle filling the space.

"Who were you talking to?" Doctor Reeds asked, shifting his weight from one foot to the other.

Manis stared back, his blue-gray eyes heavily lidded and unblinking. Jacoby watched the lanky man's Adam's apple bob as he swallowed, the faintest hint of a twitch pulling at the corner of his lips.

"What was Layla doing with these people down here? Why were they taken from the hospital block? What is your interest in all of it?" the physical followed up quickly, the questions piling up.

"You are a physician. I am an administrator. Your job is to see after my employees. Mine is see to the proper operation of this station," Manis snapped back, but Jacoby saw the twitch in his lip again.

"You saw what those people did? You saw what they were capable of? What happens if they get out into the station proper? If they are infected with something, we could..." Reeds stopped suddenly, and paused. "This station is like a big, sealed can. The air, we're all breathing it. We're all at risk."

"I don't...uh," Manis stammered, his eyes twitching from Reeds to the ground and back again.

"How did Layla find out about this? Better yet, what data was she able to collect? What was the premise for her observations?" Reeds asked, pulling a data point out of the pocket of his coat.

"Administration streams and monitors all data collected on this station. We see everything. It is our job. Then we decide what is appropriate for you to see."

"How...how were you...?" Reeds stuttered, and turned, searching the air as if looking for a word. "Goodness gracious, that word escaped me. We saw you using a data point. How? I haven't been able to connect for some time now," Reeds asked, animatedly waving his device between them.

Manis eyed it but looked away quickly. Beads of sweat had formed on his forehead, the twitch in his lip more pronounced. Jacoby could smell it on the air. He was terrified.

"Administrative privileges, which don't extend to you. I have status, you know – protections unavailable to just anyone. If something happens to this station, I'm taken care of."

"You're unwillingness to help is putting every person on this station at risk," Reeds said.

"The only one putting this station at risk is standing behind you. You let him out of containment, and now we're probably all, uh, contaminated or infected," Manis shot back, his eyes fluttering to Jacoby and away again.

False. Liar. Paper man playing like he is real. Fold him over and watch his true nature reveal itself. Peel him open! Expose the coward. The voice accompanied an unequaled wave of anger – the heat and angst bubbling up and setting his hair on edge.

Jacoby didn't necessarily disagree, although the idea of peeling someone open made his stomach squirm.

"Doctor Misra has had administration filtering all medical data coming out of the clinic and the hospital block for some time now. It was her directive...uh, from corporate, I believe. She also had access to alter records and save others on her private server here in the lab," a woman said, speaking up behind them.

Jacoby turned to find a nurse standing between two men in lab coats. She looked Asian, perhaps Japanese. She was short, with a slight build and dark hair pulled back in a ponytail. The two men immediately looked at her and stepped away.

"Hey, you can't tell them that! You shut up! You signed a full non-disclosure agreeme..." Manis pushed around the desk. The nurse immediately cowered, but before Jacoby could cut him off, Lex slid in front of the woman.

"Back off," she growled, her bruised cheek and cut lip only adding to her intimidating presence.

"Officer, I order you to take this woman into custody. Cuff her...gag her!" Manis demanded, reaching over Lex's shoulder to jab a finger at the nurse. Lex eyed his finger for a moment, and shook her head.

"Answer the doc's question. What did Misra know? Why did she have these people down here? What is happening to them?"

"I can't tell you that! I'm just doing my job. Now I gave you an order, officer," Manis snapped, spittle flying as he talked. The tall man cleared his throat and made an effort to stand taller, before jabbing an index finger into Lex's chest. She reacted in a flash, twisting his arm aside, capturing his thumb in her right hand, and wrenching it back towards his body.

She is magnificent, the voice chimed in, a part of Jacoby watching with rapt interest.

"Don't touch me," she snarled, her left fist driving hard into the pocket of his shoulder. Manis cried out and fell back, stumbling and dropping ungainly into the office chair.

"Don't! No, get away," Manis shrieked as Lex came forward, his hands and feet twitching up towards his body. Lex grabbed his wrist, wrenched his data point free, and stepped back out of the office. She slapped the door close button, and locked it without a second look.

"Doc, I think our nurse friend will feel a little more comfortable talking now...unless anyone else has an issue with the doc trying to save lives," Lex said, looking around the handful of lab assistants. The group shook their heads animatedly.

"Thank you...thank you," Reeds said, nodding to Lex and moving towards the nurse. "Your name?"

"Emiko," the nurse offered, throwing Lex an appreciative smile, before following Reeds back out into the lab.

"Okay. Perfect. Yes. Perfect. Show me everything. And this, I...I don't know if it can be done, but can you see if the data on this Palmer Module is still intact?" Reeds bobbed the damaged device in the air between them, talking faster than Jacoby had ever heard him.

"Yes, Doctor. Right this way, Doctor," Emiko said, nodding.

Jacoby casually followed Reeds and the nurse back out amidst the tables, consciously trying to pull his hospital gown closed behind him. The cold draft was horrible and he felt like his ass was hanging out.

"You...Peter," he said, pointing at one of the young men in lab coats, and reading his name badge. "How safe are we in here?"

"Uh...well," the young man stammered.

"The entire lab is sealed off from the rest of the station," an older man with a beard said, stepping forward, "but this part of the lab was built with strict biological safety in mind. It is completely isolated and has its own dedicated climate control and air purification systems. The only way in or out is through that door. And she locked us in."

"So you're saying, we're relatively safe in here," Jacoby asked. The bearded man turned and considered the door.

"That door is four inches thick and hermetically sealed. As long as no one opens that door, we're safe," he said, turning back.

"Alright, good..." Jacoby said, quickly scanning his nametag, "Yani".

Yani? the voice laughed in his mind.

"Yani... Jacoby said, and coughed, fighting to master a sudden impulse to snigger. It wasn't him...at least not the *him him*, but the other one. Damn, he silently wished for the day when he only had to worry about simple shit, like a hangover or making enough money to buy their next meal. Now his head was half-full of angry tirades, inappropriate jokes, and the kind of perverse horny ideas that would make a prostitute blush. "...is there somewhere I can clean up...maybe something I can wear besides," he said, catching the neckline of his flimsy gown with a thumb.

"Sure...yes. We have a locker room and showers. Right this way," Yani said, and waved him forward.

They moved back towards the front of a lab and passed by Reeds, the physician now hunched over a wide terminal, the screen's glow casting his face in a bluish glow. Emiko huddled next to him, reaching over to type on the keyboard and point at the screen.

"Anna...was she the young woman with you in the clinic?" Reeds asked, not looking up.

Jacoby stopped, his gown flying open as he turned around.

"Yes...why? What's wrong?"

"When is the last time you spoke with her?"

"Uh, well..." Jacoby sputtered and tried to think. "It would have been in the clinic. When, you know... is she okay? Tell me if she isn't!"

"Perfect. Yes, perfect," the doctor said, bobbing his head excitedly. "Emiko here has granted me access to Doctor Misra's notes. It says 'note two

– secured rock specimen from production floor before processing completed. Specimen moved to clean room. Collected subject personal affects'...I think she meant effects with an 'e' not an 'a' here though. Grammar, it is such a pain, as you know...just like sickness. As I always say, misery does love company."

"But what about Anna?" Jacoby interrupted as Reeds rambled.

"Yes sorry! 'note three – dispatched security team to habitation ring D level six to secure subject quarters and quarantine roommate – Anna Vullinova.' It says she dispatched them at just two fifty a.m. today," Reeds said, leaning in close to read off the screen. "But there is no follow up, which I guess makes sense since we're here now and she isn't. What does this mean, here?" he asked then, gesturing to the screen and turning to Emiko.

Jacoby hovered for another minute or two, but he could tell that Reeds was too absorbed in the data on the screen. He turned back to Yani and gestured him forward. They walked into a locker room, the outside walls covered with open-air cubbies. White coats and dark scrubs hung on hooks in some of the spaces, while athletic or personal clothes hung in others. Yani walked to the middle of the space and turned around.

"This is our locker room, obviously. Through there is the showers. You'll find soap and shampoo and all that stuff is already in there," he said, pointing to a set of glass double doors against the longest wall. Then he turned to another door on the right wall. "That door is the security team's ready room, but it's always locked. I don't know what they keep in there. If you need something to wear, I guess you can poke around in the lockers in here. Most of them won't need this stuff anymore."

Jacoby watched the young man, his dark eyes flitting from locker to locker, before crawling slowly up to him. There was a weight to his gaze, a sadness that Jacoby felt. He was mourning...grieving, even if he wouldn't say it out loud.

Yani slowly moved to walk out, but stopped by the door. "Oh, wait," he said, and pushed open a small door set just off the door to the lab. He reached in and waved on a light.

Jacoby followed him in, immediately taking in a small, rectangular room, the walls to his left and right both covered in floor to ceiling shelves. Yani walked in and pointed to a table set at the far end.

"So, yeah. This stuff is all yours. We took everything from your locker and your workstation on the production floor. It has all been swabbed and decontaminated. Didn't find anything on any of it, it was all clean. So, here you go."

Jacoby walked up to the table, almost every spare inch of space covered. He saw two heavy work suits, some modesty undergarments, gloves, boots, a protective scarf, safety glasses, his work helmet, and in the middle of it all, a shiny newish plasma saw. A stack of fusion plugs sat in a box next to it, the small charge indicators all glowing green.

"Don't worry, Janice, I'll take extra good care of this one," he whispered and pushed one of the plugs into the saw's cord port. The tool hummed in his hand, the small indicator lights on top all shifting from yellow, to blue, to green.

"What is all of that?"

Jacoby spun to find Lex standing in the doorway. She walked forward slowly, her hands wrapped protectively around her midsection, but didn't meet his gaze.

"It's all of my work gear from the production floor. I guess they snatched it all up to run some tests on it or something."

"So, you're a rock cracker?" she asked, picking up the protective scarf and running her thumb along the tight weave.

"It's what I do, but I wouldn't say it's necessarily what I am. I have ambitions beyond this place...this job. I always wanted to be a pilot...to explore places no one had ever seen before."

Lex nodded and set the scarf down. He watched her move as she settled her hands onto the table and leaned forward. She let her head sag a bit and reached back to rub her neck. His hand lifted halfway, but froze in the act.

Jacoby could feel her tension, the anxiousness bubbling just beneath the surface. She dropped her hand and drew in a breath through her nose, nostrils flaring ever so slightly. Then she grunted and coughed.

The next few heartbeats brought on a host of additional emotions and sensations. He felt Lex's doubt, a barely veiled insecurity, but below that, even deeper, a fear. And yet he couldn't quite tell what of.

"Out there...the doc said you've got a lady friend here with you...Anna?" Lex stared at the wall next to her, refusing to look his way.

"Yes. She's been my best friend since we were kids. We came out here together. She...she..." Jacoby stammered as Lex spun back around, her remarkable green eyes snapping up to his. He struggled with how much to tell her...to confide in her. Despite their few odd encounters, one of them ending with her shoving a stun baton in his face, Jacoby felt a significant connection to Lex. Some part of him needed her, wanted her, but the rest of him felt it, too. He wanted her to need him, and not just sexually, but deeper than that.

Tell her...show her who we truly are.

"Anna paid my way off earth when I didn't have two credits to rub together...when I ran away from home, my abusive, dickhead father, the booze, and the violence. She was my only friend in the world," Jacoby said, deciding on honesty.

He felt her hand slide overtop his - her skin soft but grip firm and strong. The contact elicited a spark inside him, his heart immediately starting to race. The voice didn't pop up in his mind, but he felt it, the pressure thrumming behind his eyes.

"I had friends like that once. We served together on a gunship. We were a crew - tight, as close as any people could be that didn't share blood. Mikey, Shawna, Ayo, and Liriano. We had engine troubles on a training mission...a turbine blade in the engine came loose, or something like that. Ayo flew the hell out of that bird, tried to get it on the ground safely, but we lost power and that thing dropped. I was thrown out of my gunner pod when we hit the tree canopy. I fell a hundred feet before my rig snagged on the branches and stopped my fall. I watched my gunship...my friends, go down, watched the fuel cell explode when it hit.

I hung in that tree for a day before they found me, broken ribs, dislocated foot, broken leg and arm. They fixed the broken stuff and my body healed, but the stuff inside, the loss of my friends...that never did," Lex said, clearing her throat at the end. When she met his gaze again, her eyes were wet.

Jacoby squeezed her hand back, but didn't speak. He understood she didn't want empty words.

"I...I don't know why, but I felt like I needed to tell you that. I never talk about them; just kind of keep their memory stuff inside. But you, I well..." she straightened and quickly swiped her eyes dry, and then held a data point up between them.

Jacoby accepted it slowly.

"It works...administrative privileges. Check on your friend. Even if she can't connect, you can leave her a message, so when the network comes up for everyone else, she'll know where you are and that you're all right." Lex threw him a crooked half-smile, and then promptly turned and walked out.

0500 HOURS

Anna turned back just before she turned the corner, only to see Garrett's body move, the larger of the two security officers pushing himself up onto his hands and knees. Soraya pulled Anna out into the main hall, the batons clutched under her left arm.

"He was getting up...he was still alive," Anna gasped. Even when her mind screamed at her that it was impossible...that no one would get up after being so violently impaled.

"He's already dead...even if he's still moving. We're alive. We run and keep it that way," Soraya grunted and propelled her forward.

They sprinted down the sweeping hall, the long queue of people appearing ahead. A man and woman turned as they stomped up, their wary smiles melting away as they searched Anna's eyes.

"What happened? Is it another malfunction? Is it worse than they say?" the woman asked. Anna gave her a cursory scan – Asian, most likely Korean, short, thin, perhaps mid-forties. Her mind reeled, collecting and collating the observations in the blink of an eye.

"Just move...we need to move," Soraya said, shrugging forward and urging the couple to crowd forward. They bumped into the people in front of them, who turned and immediately started to complain.

"Move forward. Please...move!" Soraya yelled, her voice clear and loud.

"We can't. There is a line for a reason. We're waiting our turn, and so should you!" a man yelled from just up the queue, his face appearing as he lifted onto his tiptoes.

Soraya didn't back down. She urged the couple in front of them forward, muscling the entire queue down the hall. They bunched up, shoved back and complained, but Soraya continued. Anna watched people shuffle together, pushing and shoving everyone in front of them. They piled up, filling the hall from wall to wall, but were moving.

"Soraya!" Anna yelled as she turned to look back down the hall. Garrett stood a dozen doors down, legs shaking as he wavered in place.

"Good! Come...you can make it!" Soraya called, waving him forward as she turned.

"No! Look at him!" Anna said, catching her arm and pulling it down.

Garrett twitched and shook, lumbering towards them in an awkward zigzag between walls. Blood and dark matter ran down his white and gray armor. A blurry form moved behind him, coming up the hall in a much faster, straighter line. Blake sprinted by Garrett, running right at Anna and Soraya, his armor even messier than his counterpart's.

"They're not right, Sor-" Anna started to say, pushing into the man behind her. He turned and caught sight of the two men approaching, and started to scream. Panic hit the crowd like wildfire, the former calm split by the churn of feet and pushing arms.

"I know...keep them moving!" Soraya pushed Anna back and propelled herself forward. She grunted and kicked out hard, catching Blake in the gut.

The security officer staggered back and doubled over, a black mess spilling out of his mouth. But he was up in an instant, screaming wildly and clawing forward.

The people in line reacted to his voice, turning and pushing, shoving and fighting by one another. Anna felt their panic, the energy flooding over and through her. She pulled a man back as he tried to crawl over a woman, but he turned on her, swinging his hands at her face. The whole queue smashed forward, shoving and trampling the people in front of them.

"Soraya, what do we do?" Anna yelled, falling back against the wall.

"I don't know...not let them kill us," she spat back as Blake came forward, arms splayed as he tried to tackle her to the ground. The former athlete dodged around him and jabbed one of the batons in his side. He staggered, tumbling head-first into the wall with a *crack.*

"This is crazy. These guys are supposed to be the ones keeping us safe!" Soraya said, jumping back between Anna and the two men and waving the batons. "Aren't these things supposed to, I don't know, zap them?"

"Hold them off long enough for people to get off the floor? I don't know, I work with maintenance," Anna hollered, pushing off the wall and pulling a woman out from the bottom of the churning pile. "Does the baton have a trigger or button? Look for a trigger."

"Get away from me!" Soraya growled as Garrett ambled in. She jumped clear of Blake and shoved the bigger man away.

"T-w-e-a-k..." Blake moaned and burst off the ground. He looked at Anna, his eyes milky-white and unblinking, and pitched forward.

He was on her before Soraya could react. Anna fell back onto several people, her weight tumbling them all to the ground. Blake fell onto a man next to her, the security officer clawing at his face and chest.

"Get him off me...please!" the man screamed, bloody scratches extending from his forehead all the way to his lips.

Anna rolled over a woman's legs and tried to stand. Blake clawed his way forward. Biting and clawing at anyone close by.

"Get up!" Soraya yelled and lunged in, driving a baton into the back of the officer's head like a club. Bone cracked, but he rolled to the side and latched onto another woman's ankle, biting clear through the pant leg of her suit and into the meat of her calf. The woman screamed and pitched forward, toppling even more people to the ground.

Anna pushed off a man's back and grabbed ahold of Blake's feet and pulled him back. He thrashed, flopping around but she managed to get him free of the crowd. He kicked up and lunged at her, but Soraya stepped in and jammed a baton into his side. The prong connected with an audible *crack* and *snap*. Blake pitched against the far wall, the whole right side of his body convulsing violently.

"Hey, I figured it out," Soraya yelled. She turned as Garrett lumbered in, jamming the other baton into his stomach. The man doubled over, a trickle of smoke rolling up where the prong struck, but he didn't fall back, or cry out.

Soraya jammed the other baton into his chest, the resulting arc flashing blue in the hallway. Anna immediately smelled ozone on the air, the sour, caustic tinge of burned flesh drifting in right after.

Garrett moaned and batted the baton away, lurching forward to wrap his arms around Soraya. She swatted his arms wide with the batons and jammed them both forward together, the combined force knocking him back just a few well-earned steps.

"I can't hold these fuckers off forever, Anna. Think of...something," Soraya yelled. She swung the right baton like a club, catching Garrett in the jaw and spinning him around. She turned, just as Blake surged off the ground, the weight of his body throwing her back into the opposite wall.

Anna managed a step forward, desperate to help, but Soraya shoved Blake back and caught him in the stomach with a baton, swinging the other across into his face. The last blow crackled with double the electricity of before, the flash of light burning a blind spot into Anna's vision.

Blake spun away and fell, half of his face blackened, his jaw hanging free on one side. Soraya was impressive to watch, an almost perfect amalgamation of grace and strength Anna could never match. That was her...it was who she was.

Think, Anna. Use your brain...that is what you are good at. Be smart, she thought and shook her head. She turned and looked up the hall. The people in the queue were frantic, smashing together en mass, but she could see her destination now, the side halls turning to the left and right. The black doors of the station's transit elevators stood just beyond. A chime sounded and she glimpsed the doors opening, someone standing next to the lift ushering the panicked people inside.

"Tell them to squeeze as many people in as they can. Fill it up! Tell them they need to get as many people in as they can! Get everyone off this floor!" she screamed, and then nodded to the people close by. She saw eyes flick from her, to Soraya and the two bloody men, and then they turned, repeating the message down the hall.

Anna stumbled forward as someone crashed into her back, and then she was falling, stumbling, and rolling down the hall. She caught her bearings and realized it wasn't Soraya, but Garrett. The former security man launched his body towards her, his jaw hanging on one side, his mouth a wide, bloody hole.

She rolled back and caught him with her feet, his weight immediately bending her knees. Anna could hear Soraya grunting and cursing, the batons cracking against skin, the violent *snap* of electricity splitting the air.

Garrett clawed his way forward, his hands raking against her legs. His tongue lolled out of his face, strange, dark tendrils weaving around it, slithering out of his body like frenzied snakes.

"Get off me!" Anna grunted and kicked him free. She rolled sideways and pushed to her knees as Garrett came back in. His eyes were dead, glassy orbs, but she didn't doubt that he, or whatever he was becoming, could see her.

Use your self-defense training...remember!

Anna closed the distance between them with a quick step and brought her knee up in a violent strike. Her kneecap hit Garrett squarely in the genitals, the padding of his armor absorbing some of the force. She reared back again and again, running her knee into the same spot, the former man's genitals smashing beneath the onslaught. The last kick cracked the his padded armor, but he didn't groan or cry. Hell, he didn't even seem to notice. A horrible groan issued from the ruined hole of his mouth and he grabbed onto her upper arms and started to pull her close.

His body was cracking, popping...shifting under the padded suit and segmented armor. She remembered Preston, the strange spines that shot out of his chest, and reacted. Anna chopped her right hand down on his right arm, and rolled his grip over.

She felt his grip break, slid her hand down, and twisted his hand into a perfectly executed wristlock. Garrett grunted, the force and leverage turning him away. Anna used the hold and pushed him across the hall, running his face into the wall.

The impact snapped his head back, dark, bloody fluid spattering the ceramic wall panels. Anna increased the pressure on his wrist, forcing him down to a knee.

She felt Soraya, her fear and need spiking, and looked back just as Blake knocked the batons from her grasp and caught her by the collar. Something pushed out from beneath his armored suit, sharp points digging and tearing through the fabric.

Long, boney appendages burst out of the man's body, hinged and curving, the ends tapered like a knife and dripping with dark, toxic bodily fluids. Blake pulled her arms wide, the cruel spear-like limbs twisting towards her exposed stomach and chest.

No!

Anna wrenched Garrett's wrist down hard, the bones in his arm breaking with a loud *snap*. She grasped him by the shoulder and heaved him back, before driving his head into the wall with all of her strength.

She jumped clear, letting Garrett's body fall away, and scooped one of the batons off the ground. She came forward with a roar and swung down, the heavy weapon hitting Blake's right arm with a satisfyingly solid *crack*.

He twisted from the blow as the boney limbs stabbed straight out, blood and skin spattering the ground all around them. They missed Soraya's stomach by an inch on either side. Anna brought the baton down on the other arm with all of her strength, the humerus breaking loudly. Soraya stumbled free as Blake's arm flopped towards the ground.

Anna recoiled as he swung her way, broken arms flailing at his sides. Her training kicked in and she lunged in close, narrowly avoiding a skewering stab and violently jammed the pronged end of her baton into the hole that used to be his mouth.

He groped for her, the jagged bones from his broken arms jutting out through the skin. The flesh tore, and his hand flopped to the ground, still grasping and clutching.

Her finger wrapped around the baton's trigger, an impulse firing like a gunshot in her mind. Her thumb flicked down to a small knob just down from the trigger. She felt a hand, not hers but so very familiar, push it in and turn it. Anna did the same, and then pulled the trigger.

The baton came alive in her hand, an angry crackling *buzz* filling the air. Blake's body went rigid, but Anna had to dance back as the boney limbs stabbed down at her legs. She held onto the baton, her finger smashing the trigger down.

Blake's left eye burst, a ropey tendril shooting out and waving frantically through the air. His right burst next, the man's face splitting open down the middle. The boney arms stabbed out again, banging into the floor between her feet, but she refused to let go. A horrible burned meat smell tinged the air as black spots appeared on his mutilated face. And then his head started to burn.

Anna shoved him back against the wall and yanked the baton free, jumping back as the stabbing arms jabbed for her midsection. Blake's body thrashed from one wall to another and crashed onto the ground. Anna helped Soraya up and they dodged around Garrett, the tall man lunging at their feet.

Blake gave one final, violent flop and went still, dark smoke wafting off his smoldering skull. A heartbeat later, a shrill scream echoed from down the hall. Anna felt Soraya go rigid, and heard the people massed behind her go silent. A bang reverberated through the floor, another ear-splitting screech ringing out.

"What in the hell was that?" Soraya asked.

They turned together down the hall in time to see a massive, dark form moving slowly up the passage. Garrett flopped over onto his side, a broken chunk of skull sticking out of his scalp, and crawled back down the hall. Had Anna done that? There was no way she was that strong.

The transit elevator dinged behind them, and she felt the crowd of people move, shrinking behind her as the lucky piled in.

"Move...move!" Anna gasped involuntarily as the creature appeared fully around the bend. Long, segmented arms lashed out, cracking loudly into the walls and floor.

It pulled its bulk along slowly, shuffling forward and lashing out again for another hold. The walls shuddered as if it were punching holes clear through the ceramic and metal plating. Its head...Preston's head, swung from side to side, empty eye socks dark in the light. The hooked, teeth-like ribs curved and flexed on its wide-open torso, the head jutting out of what used to be a man's chest moaning and screaming. A pair of arms burst out of the mess of its abdomen, clawing at the ground, grasping and reaching, ready to pull something...anything into its embrace.

"We have to get out here now...like now...now...now!" Soraya screamed and immediately started to push the back of the pile towards the elevators.

Anna watched the horror move slowly down the hallway towards them, its body changing, blood and fluid spattering the ground beneath it. Each new appendage looked sharper and more deadly than the last, until it filled the hall like an alien insect, tearing the station apart as it moved to reach them. A spidery arm streaked up and cracked into the ceiling again and again, finally striking a light panel.

Think, damn you, girl, she thought, but choked back a scream as a spidery arm burst out of the beast's back and swung up into the ceiling, shattering the light. That section of hall fell into darkness. The *boom...smack* continued as it pulled itself forward into the next pool of light, but that light went dark as well.

She heard Soraya screaming at the people to move, their terrified responses, and her own beating heart. The floor vibrated with every thunderous step of the approaching monster, the subtle *ding* of the elevator almost lost in the din.

Anna's thoughts spun as she searched the walls, the doors, and the ceiling around her. She spun, catching sight of Garrett slowly, painfully crawling away from her, moving towards the ambling monstrosity, moving like a child to its parent.

Her breath caught, and she pushed back into Soraya, but they weren't moving anymore. The crowd's energy was toxic, crashing over her like suffocating, urine-tinged waves of dread. She stepped on someone's ankle and almost fell back, but caught herself.

The creature appeared in another light, as if jumping from shadow to shadow. A crack split the air, and the shadows drew even closer.

Her eyes shot up to the ceiling, catching on a yellow strip of caution paint right above her. It framed in a two-inch strip of metal. Anna's gaze crawled down the wall, following a track running all the way to the ground. A small service panel sat right next to it.

"It's a fire door. A fire door," Anna gasped pushing off and sliding to her knees. It was a fired door, or a pressure door. She couldn't remember exactly which. All that mattered was that it was designed to close and seal off the passage.

"What...what does that mean?" Soraya asked, still pushing the crowd.

Anna hooked her fingers into the maintenance port, but the cover refused to open. She slid both hands under the lip and pulled, grunting and pulling. Her arms strained, and the metal groaned, but finally popped and swung outward.

She fumbled her code scanner out of her pocket, pulled the plug out, and jammed it into the port. The scanner booted up, the small screen glowing to life as lines of boot code scrolled down over the screen.

Another light cracked, plastic raining down noisily in the hall. Anna couldn't bear to look up. She could feel the darkness getting closer, the skeletal arms breaking and crushing, the mouths opening and closing...the death.

The scanner menu popped up and Anna fumbled with the cheap buttons on the side. The icon refused to move, so she smashed it in hard. The little square of white moved down once, and then twice.

Anna connected, the door control driver popping up, designated only by a massive string of letters and numbers. It connected right away.

Bang Bang Crash...the darkness drew closer. Anna could smell it – sour, like stomach acid. The ill feeling was back, too, bubbling inside and settling like a greasy film on her skin. She didn't want to feel the thing, or be anywhere near it for that matter. She wanted to run, but her instincts told her that if she did, they would all die.

"My god, Anna. Move...It's coming. Move...move!" Soraya screamed. She was further down the passage, moving people.

"I can't. What if there isn't another door further down...there will be no..." she yelled back, flipping through the menus one after another, her fingers moving faster than her eyes could track. But she couldn't finish her sentence...it felt like she would be sick.

"It's too close...Anna, please move!" Soraya screamed.

Anna shook her head, swallowing hard. A bead of sweat ran down her forehead, saliva filling her mouth. Her mind spun in frantic circles as she flipped through command prompt after command prompt, but she couldn't find a direct way to just close the damn door. She was running out of time. A foul breeze wafted over her, and she knew it was close, the darkness crawling on the floor just beyond her knees.

Boots stomped onto the floor next to her and she heard Soraya snap the stun batons out to full length. The other woman's presence sent a jolt of strength charging through her.

"Go, Soraya...please, just go!" Anna gasped, spinning through another dozen menus. Sweat dripped off her face and onto the screen.

"I'm not leaving you," Soraya snarled, and Anna heard her turn the knobs on the weapons, the electric hum increasing in intensity. They were both going to die because she wasn't smart enough, not quick enough.

"Just go, you don't need to..." Anna hiccupped, as she was about to say *you don't need to die, too,* but the truth hit her. She didn't need to command the door to close, it only mattered that it closed. She pushed back through a dozen menus and found the one she was looking for.

{{Root-test_menu}}

Anna opened it, found another prompt, and immediately found what she needed.

{{_menu – scan door for error code(s)}}
[Pressure door test -_]
[open – status_]
[alt-close-test_]
[close]

Bang Bang Crash. The darkness flooded over her and Soraya growled, but Anna screamed, "I got it! I got it!" and smashed the button. She dropped the scanner, and rolled back.

An ear-splitting claxon sounded, a line of yellow lights flashing all the way up the wall. Anna pushed off the ground, hooked an arm around Soraya's waist, and yanked her back.

The beast was right on top of them. The spidery arms swung in and hit the wall above her code scanner with a sharp *crack,* punching clear through the ceramic panels. They jumped back as another set of arms crashed down, punching through the textured metal at their feet. They reared back to stab out again, but the door dropped, shiny stainless steel sinking from the ceiling.

Anna shoved back with her hands and feet, Soraya wrenching her body back as the monster's arms stabbed at them. The door hit the boney arms with a *crunch,* the hallway filling with a horrible screech.

Something vibrated from inside Soraya's pocked just as Anna flinched into her. The door groaned, the hydraulics whining loudly. Bones snapped and broke as metal ground against metal. The claxon abruptly stopped wailing, replaced by a slightly less intrusive beeping.

"Anna...Anna, it worked," Soraya gasped, nudging her.

She opened her eyes, lowering her hands from her face. The shiny, partitioned door was closed...most of the way. The creature's long arm lay on the ground before them, trapped and broken under the door's bulk, like the twisted branches of some long-dead tree.

Her code scanner beeped, a message flashing on the screen. Anna scuttled over on her hands and knees and scooped the small device off the ground.

[Error-door closure failure_]
[-Test failed-00001432-]
[-Open door to service_]
[Open]

The error button continued to flash, the device prompting her to open the door again and again. Anna carefully set the code scanner down and backed away. She didn't dare unplug it – what if the door opened automatically if she did? What if it would time out and open again anyways?

"Anna," Soraya whispered behind her.

She looked from the code scanner to the door, and over to the horrible arms. The creature was moving on the other side of the door. She could see it in the small gap between the bottom and the floor. Something heavy and hard struck the door, the shiny metal shaking in the light.

0600 HOURS

Jacoby picked up the data point off the table, the screen coming alive in the underwhelming glow of the single, small overhead light. The home screen was fairly similar to his, although the network i.d. was different.

He opened the network directory, a flashing microphone icon appeared, and said "Anna Vullinova." The network icon spun and a weighted moment later, her name appeared on the screen.

Jacoby clicked on her name and the icon spun for another long moment. A message popped up.

[Hidden Network] Network cannot find device–device not online or transponder is powered off. Error in connection.

"Damnit!" Jacoby cursed, and tried again. The network searched again, but popped up the same error. He slapped the data point against his leg.

Stop thinking, and start feeling. You can feel the truth, the voice chimed in his head suddenly.

"What in the hell does that mean?" he growled irritably.

She is okay. If something had happened to her, we would have felt it. But perhaps something did happen to her data point. If you cannot connect with her, try connecting with someone that might be close by.

"That makes sense," Jacoby muttered, and thought for a moment. Anna didn't socialize with many of their neighbors, except Soraya. After their strange run in, he decided opening that particular can might not be the best idea. What if Soraya told Preston?

The voice laughed quietly somewhere in his mind after his imagination turned dark, an image of his imposing neighbor punching his teeth in filling his head.

But he didn't know his neighbors that well, at least not well enough to randomly connect with and ask to run down his friend. Realizing he didn't have any other options, Jacoby pushed the microphone icon and said "Soraya Graeves".

The network id spun for a moment, before a message popped up, the text flashing green.

[Hidden Network] Transponder SG45021 located. DP device on primary station server - error - device network not responding. Do you wish to migrate device to {Administrative / Hidden Network}?_

A separate dialogue box appeared with a yes and no button flashing below. Jacoby pressed yes. The network i.d. spun and then flashed green.

[Hidden Network] Transponder SG45021 successfully migrated onto network.

Jacoby almost dropped the data point as he fumbled back to the home screen and pushed video call. It rang for several moments, before returning a no response icon.

He pressed audio message, and the microphone icon reappeared.

"Soraya it's...Jacoby," he stammered, before swallowing, sucking in a breath, and continuing. "Soraya, I was wondering if you've seen or talked to Anna. I am stuck in a, well, it's a lab somewhere on A ring, I think. I was in the hospital block, but then they moved me. I just want to make sure everything is okay. You can contact me on this data point. Thanks, bye. Oh, hey, if you see Anna or know where she is please let her know that I'm okay and that...well, have her contact me if she can. Bad things are happening on the station and I want to make sure she's okay." He hit end and watched the file zoom away as it was sent.

So eloquent.

"Shut up," Jacoby muttered, and set the data point down.

She came onto us. We shouldn't feel awkward about the fact that she couldn't control herself.

"But why?" Jacoby asked picking up a flashlight off a shelf to his left. He walked wearily out of the storage room, his eyes naturally gravitating towards the dark corners. He pushed through into a locker room, the open cubbies so unrealistically clean and organized.

Do you really want to know why? Some questions are better left unasked – some secrets left buried. Trust...us.

He walked down the row to his left. White coats and scrubs hung in the open spaces, while digital photo frames, personal hygiene products, and even a few paperback books filled the shelves above.

"Trust is a thing one earns, and after all I've seen recently, I'm not sure I'll ever be able to do it again..."

The glass double doors to the showers opened as he approached, automatic lights blinking on in the space beyond. Jacoby walked slowly into the showers, letting the flashlight play over both walls all the way to the back.

The space was oblong, forming a figure-8 rimmed by smooth, tiled benches. Two towers sat equidistant in the middle of the space, like silver Christmas trees covered in shower nozzles.

Nonsense. You feel it when you're around people. We can feel...them. It is growing, deepening. Soon we will be able to tear away their defenses and see all of their secrets.

"That sounds horrible. I don't like my own thoughts sometimes, let alone everyone else's...if you know what is happening to us, tell me and stop being so cryptic."

He let the light play over the ceiling, taking a small bit of comfort in the lack of ventilation ducts. Jacoby stepped fully into the showers and reached behind him, struggling to untie the hospital gown's drawstring. After a moment of struggling, he pulled it up over his head and threw it to the far side.

The voice laughed suddenly, its mirth making him unintentionally chuckle out loud.

"Okay, that's creepy," he whispered.

I know what you know, nothing else. But perhaps I can feel it better than you – the strength, the wonderful power growing and making us more...perfect.

Jacoby pulled the grip socks off, tossed them by the gown and moved over to the far showers. The water turned on, the drenching spray almost immediately hot. He stepped under the water, letting it wet his hair and cascade down his back.

He rubbed his face, scrubbing the dried blood free from around his nose, mouth, and eye. He bent over, wiping the steam from the mirror sticking out between nozzles, turning his face one direction and then the other.

"Broken nose, eye socket, and severe concussion," he said, quietly, remembering what doctor Misra told him after waking. He pushed on his face, but nothing hurt. Hell, not even his nose, and it looked straighter than ever.

He lifted his hands, letting the water run over the burn marks snaking over his hands and around both wrists. His mind wandered over everything that had happened over the last few tumultuous days, settling on the moment he decided to ignore the void warning and crack that rock.

Yes, that changed life for both of us, the voice chimed in suddenly.

"But how? That is what I want to know. I can hear and feel you. My heart beats six times faster than it is supposed to, and I'm healing in almost no time. That arc flash from that baton should have killed me. Is this some kind of side effect of the tumor growing in my brain?" Jacoby whispered, rubbing the burn marks on his wrists. The blackened skin broke loose, exposing fresh, pink skin underneath.

You only call it that because that is what the doctor called it. What if the thing growing in our brain is something else...a blessing and not a deathly curse? Look at the burned skin peeling off our hands, the broken bones magically pulled back together and healed.

"Do you know something?" Jacoby repeated the question, his quiet voice echoing in the voluminous shower. There was something it knew and wasn't sharing, he just had a feeling.

We see with the same eyes, and hear with the same ears. I know only that my voice was lost to you until the other day, when you cracked that rock.

"This is impossible. Are you me?" Jacoby groaned and lathered up his hair with shampoo.

A part of you, perhaps. Perhaps you were whole once, in the beginning, and when mother left and father's drinking and anger turned to you, things changed. Perhaps I am a splinter, a sliver broken away from the larger piece. I am the suppressed anger and unrealized lust of an abused boy. I've been here through it all, you just didn't realize it. The part of you not content with absorbing a broken man's rage. Now I can speak in more than whispers, help you outside of your dreams. Whatever was in that rock changed us both, made you better, and gave me a louder voice. I know you can feel it – the strength in your heart and muscles, the power in your lungs. Just look at us, the voice said.

Jacoby finished scrubbing his hair and rinsed, the remaining dead skin falling away and washing down the drain in the process. Besides the pink flesh, there was no evidence that he'd been hit with over ten thousand volts of scorching electricity.

He looked down. The muscles in his arms and chest were thicker, but he'd always been strong. His midsection showed the most change, however, as the plush padding that formerly covered his stomach was gone. His skin was tight, following the lines of his pelvis, forming a V right down to his privates.

Jacoby worked a hand down his stomach, following the well-defined, almost chiseled lines. He stopped on the old scar by his beltline, and moved down to find another on his thigh, both born from his father's impatience and inflexibility.

A fuzzy sensation crawled up his back. A heartbeat later, the doors opened. Jacoby didn't need to turn to know who walked in behind him. He could feel, smell, and taste her.

He pumped some soap into his hand and started to scrub his body, fighting the almost undeniable desire to turn to her...to let her see him. Jacoby heard Lex undo a zipper and his heart started to race.

Mind your own business, he thought, but felt the other part of him laugh at the notion. It didn't have to speak for him to know what it wanted. Intense warmth spread to his groin and the air around him filled with his peculiar musk, like fragrant flowers and baking bread. The scent cut through the soap and water, filling the showers like invisible steam.

He heard her approach, the pad of bare feet on the tiled floor barely perceptible over the raging cadence of his beating heart. The showerhead next to his turned on. He saw her feet and ankles, and was very aware of the blood flowing into his groin, but it's not like he could turn away and hide it now, so he continued his shower.

"I'm not going to pretend for a moment that I know what's going on," Lex said, her voice cutting the silence between them.

Jacoby lifted his eyes, letting his gaze crawl deliberately up her calves to her thighs, hips, and to her slim, muscular stomach. A large scar ran from just beneath her belly button, and around her side, before disappearing to her back. His gaze crawled up to her large, full breasts, where another, smaller scar overlapped her right collarbone and ran up and over her arm. Her mouth pulled into a crooked smile, her green eyes sparkling.

Lex took a deep breath, her breasts heaving, and moved towards him, the water from his shower nozzle now falling over them both.

"I've seen bad shit, the worst of people, and come through all of it, because I keep my head and stay in control. But I need to be straight with you. That back there, with that woman. I don't know what that was...or what is happening to those people. I only know that it scares me. I also saw you lift a man half again your weight off the ground with a single arm and smack him against the wall," she said, sniffling and reaching up to pull her red hair out of her face. Then she moved a little closer, her feet right next to his.

A primal need rose up inside Jacoby, his right hand trembling slightly. Part of him wanted to reach out and trace a finger over the scar on her belly, to kiss it. They resonated with a piece of him...the broken, scarred young man cowering at his father's feet – the naked man scarred from a parent's abuse. Lex's scars only made her more beautiful to him, more complete. It was that part of him, perhaps the voice he'd been speaking with, sliding in and quietly merging with the rest of him.

"I've never seen someone get hit so many times with a baton and not go down. That's not extraordinary...it's fucking crazy," she said, lifting a hand and running her fingertips down his chest. "No burn marks, not even a bruise. Crazy. You're not normal...stronger than any I've seen before. But I...I can't get those people out of my head. The way their bodies peeled open, the way their bones moved, and..."

"I don't understand any of it..." Jacoby said softly, but Lex cut him off.

"I'm used to order, structure – do this, or do that. The simplicity of it all. But it's all breaking down here. Nothing is certain, except for you. And I don't know why or how that makes sense, but that woman...she tried to...she would have killed me. You didn't have to, but you helped...me. I've seen it. You're different somehow. I can feel it, too," Lex faltered, moving up and brushing against him.

The spark turned to a full-blown inferno inside Jacoby, the warm contact of her skin almost more than he could take. She leaned in, her supple breasts pressing against him. She leaned even further, until her mouth hovered next to his cheek, her breath hot against his neck. He felt her hand glide gently over his stomach, coming to rest just above his manhood.

"I felt it when I first saw you in the commissary – a need, an urge, so strong it seemed to resonate within my bones, like we'd known each other before but parted for a long time. My...my whole body seemed to vibrate with it. It made me dizzy. I saw things, felt things...intimate, sensual things. You felt familiar and safe. I feel it right now, like I'm breathing you in. You make my skin tingle, my heart flutter, and–" she said, but Jacoby pulled her close and kissed her.

Lex hooked an arm around his back and pulled him close, returning his kiss. Jacoby took control. He reached up and ran his fingers through her thick, red hair, and moved them down over the smooth, short-cropped hair on the sides of her head. He kissed her again, his tongue dancing over her lips before meeting hers.

Jacoby tilted her head back and ran his tongue down her neck, stopping to kiss the scar just over her right breast. Lex grabbed ahold of his manhood, her grip strong but not rough, and slowly started to work it back and forth. He eased his way down, kissing and then playfully biting at her pink nipples.

Lex tried to follow him down, but Jacoby pushed her back upright and slid down to his knees. Driven by a fire he could barely contain, he eased her feet apart, and moved in to kiss her thigh. She obliged, lifting her left leg and letting it rest on his shoulder.

The hot water cascaded down Lex's body, spattering his head in heavy droplets as the steam rose up in swirling clouds. The muscles in her legs shook as he eased her apart with his tongue, her sex warm and soft. She moaned, first running her fingers through his hair, and then grabbing handfuls to provide gentle encouragement.

Jacoby lost himself to her embrace – the warmth of their bodies, the swirling and intoxicating redolence of their lust. He worked his tongue lovingly back, easing it just inside her, and she shook in response. He felt the rhythm of her body, a vibration passing from her flesh to his, a hum he could feel but not hear. Jacoby explored her with his tongue and lips, her excitement evident almost immediately.

Lex grew tense as he teased her apart again, matching his tempo to the subtle energy coursing through her body. It grew...the feedback almost electric as he touched her.

Lex pulled him away, lifting him from his knees almost completely by his hair. She kissed him hard, the water flooding over them anew. He savored her taste – a thing both new and familiar at the same time.

Jacoby was moving backwards then, Lex pushing him back forcefully onto the tiled bench. She crawled into his lap, sliding forward on her knees, and eased down, first finding the tip of his penis, and then slowly, methodically, letting her weight drop until his full length slid inside her.

Jacoby groaned as she rose up again and unhurriedly eased back down, her body hot and wet, but almost painfully tight around him. He ran his hands over her muscular rump and up her back, the soft skin broken by several scars.

"You're so...big. It feels so...right," Lex moaned softly and slid them together again. She leaned forward and dropped her hands to his shoulders, her breasts bouncing teasingly before his face.

Jacoby buried his face between them, his fingers crawling over and mapping the network of scars on her back. They weren't flaws, but beauty marks earned through sacrifice and pain. The thought added to his fire, his manhood swelling further. Lex seemed to notice, a shiver running down her back. She drove her hips down hard and slid back, dropping to kiss him.

Her lips were full and wet, her arms and legs contracting strongly around him. She kissed him with determination, each brush of the lips or tongue measured and exact. Jacoby grabbed her hips and pulled her down hard into his lap. She ground forward, the motion bottoming him out inside her. Lex kissed him, her breathing urgent and fast, but pulled away a moment later and groaned loudly. Her voice filled the shower, echoing off the walls.

"Stand up," Jacoby said as she pulled away, stopping a moment to smooth her hair back. Lex's green eyes locked onto his and she slid back and then forward again, one corner of her mouth lifting in that crooked, mischievous half-smile. She held his gaze and clamped both hands onto his upper arms, rocking him deeper and deeper inside.

She likes strength...she likes a challenge, he realized, reading the sparkle in her green eyes.

She groaned loudly as he rocked forward suddenly, hefting her completely off the ground. He carried her over to the shower and set her down.

"Bend over," he said, standing and pointing to the column of the shower nozzles. Lex cocked an eyebrow and licked her lips, but didn't move.

Challenge her.

Jacoby led her to the column of shower nozzles. He took both of her hands and lifted them to the pole.

"Keep them there," he said, watching her carefully, and then slowly walked behind her. Lex turned her head to watch him, the tip of her tongue pressed into the corner of her mouth.

Jacoby grabbed her hips and pulled back. She walked her feet back, twitching her butt as she lowered her head. He edged forward and rocked up onto the balls of his feet, Lex's long legs almost putting her out of reach.

"Deeper...harder," Lex moaned, still clinging to the shower pole.

She groaned as he slid back inside. He thrust forward hard, his hips slapping against her bottom. Jacoby set an even pace, pulling almost completely out and savoring the following thrust. Lex responded vocally, moaning and crying out until the shower echoed with the slapping of their bodies and her cries of pleasure.

"Harder. I'm close. Harder!" she growled, pushing back as he thrust forward. Jacoby obliged, clamping onto her hips and rocking forward hard.

The air grew thicker around Jacoby, the pronounced muscles of his torso coiling and flexing. Lex's body hummed as they slid together, the luscious curves of her hips and back gleaming in the shower's spray. Fire grew in his loins, the heat building and spreading into his chest and legs. The pressure was there in his mind, too, coiling and pressing behind his eyes.

He closed his eyes and thrust again and again, Lex's body so hot and soft around him. He felt her climax, a ripple coursing through almost her entire body. She cried out a moment later, the muscles in her arms and shoulders flexing as her whole body shook.

Jacoby thrust harder, his fire rising violently inside, until he hung on the very precipice. He slid his hands up to her waist and plunged himself forward as hard as his body would allow, the pressure in his mind and his orgasm tearing loose at the same time.

He rocked back and slid forward, the tremors of his orgasm still echoing throughout his body. It seemed to go on forever, the hum, the chorus of their conjoined bodies.

Jacoby finally slumped back, the afterglow of his orgasm fading until it was a barely perceptible warmth in his loins. Lex stood, her legs shaking, an oddly orange glow framing her body.

She is ours now. All ours, the voice said, sliding forth from the depths of his mind.

She came forward and sank into his embrace.

0700 HOURS

"Anna," Soraya hissed again.

"I don't know how long it will stay closed. I mean, I just ran a root door closure test, but it might be programed to automatically open if it jams, or there might be a timer built into the test. It might...I just don't know..." she said, turning, but found Soraya standing above her. She accepted her hand and stood. Soraya lifted a data point between them.

"Where did you get that? Mine broke back there and I didn't think you...?" Anna asked.

"I scooped it off the counter when we stopped to get my boots...just kind of did it by habit...but that's not important. Well, it is, but here...just listen." Soraya pressed a button on the screen and held it up between them so they both could hear.

"Soraya it's...Jacoby..." the voice crackled out of the device's small speaker, but Anna knew it was him before he even said his name. She listened to the entire message, Jacoby's voice and outward awkwardness the most beautiful thing she'd ever heard.

"He's in a lab? We have to find him!"

Soraya nodded and together they turned back and jogged to the back of the queue waiting for the transit elevators. The crowd was small now, barely a few dozen people – perhaps enough to fit into the two large lifts at once.

Anna pressed record and lifted the data point to her mouth.

"Jacoby, it's Anna. Oh my god. I can't believe it. I'm so glad you're all right! Soraya and I are still on D ring, but we're about to hop on a transit elevator down to A. Where are you? We'll come to you! Tell me and we'll find you. Hurry!"

The pressure door shuddered behind them, the metal groaning and shifting. She ended the recording and hit send, and then against her better judgement, looked behind her.

The horrible boney arms trapped under the massive, shiny door were still moving...somehow. They tapped against the floor, before curving up and off the ground, their segments clicking together. They curled up to the door and started tapping, almost as if they were feeling or searching the door.

"Soraya!" she hissed, and pulled her around to point, "look!"

"What the...hell?"

The arms snaked back down the door, clicking, crawling like snakes, searching and feeling their way to the ground.

"It's almost like it's searching for something..." Soraya breathed.

"But what?" Anna whispered, as her gaze flicked to her code scanner. The small black device lay on the ground just to the right of the door, the cord still plugged into the service port. The arms seemed to follow her eyes, flicking towards the black device. "No...that's impossible!"

"Why didn't you unplug it?" Soraya asked.

Anna spun and closed the distance to the back of the queue. "I was afraid that it would abort the test...that it would open the door if I unplugged it! I didn't know...just didn't want to be the reason why it got through."

The elevator on the right was open and people were streaming inside, flooding into the overly bright space.

"Go! Fill it up! Get everyone in!" Anna screamed.

The queue was shrinking, but the lift was filling up quickly. Her gaze flitted to the lift on the left. The glowing indicator was moving as the elevator approached the ring.

"You did good, Anna...better than good. I never would have thought of that. You gave us time!"

The lift doors on the right were closing, but Anna could see open space. There was room for so many people.

"Wait, no! You have to squeeze as many people..." Anna yelled, but it was too late. The doors closed and the lift started to move.

The lift on the left opened a moment later, the flood of people pushing and shoving to get inside. Soraya cut forward, knifing between two women and pushing almost completely up to the elevator itself.

"Get everyone inside...don't let the doors close!" she yelled, muscling a man aside.

Anna flinched back and saw the door shudder. The arms slapped the ground, stabbing down into the ground. Her code scanner flopped to the side, and then shattered in a shower of black plastic.

Someone pulled her forward, and she turned to the bright elevator interior. People were packing inside, hugging and squeezing together to fit into the space.

"Get everyone inside!" Soraya yelled, pushing everyone forward.

"It's full. Wait until the next one comes!" a man said, and jumped forward, slapping a button on the inside. A chime sounded and the lift doors started to close.

"No!" Anna screamed.

Soraya shoved a woman out of the way and slid into the gap before the door could slide closed. The chime sounded again and the door opened.

"It's full! It's overloaded! You're going to get us all killed! Hit the button...hit it!" the man screamed and came forward. He balled up his fists and pushed Soraya back.

The crawling sensation tickled her back. Anna turned to find the pressure door slowly rising. A host of boney, spear-like arms snapped through the growing space between the bottom and the floor, and then the door buckled, bending and peeling out of the way.

"We all go, or no one goes!" Soraya growled and came forward, grabbing the man by his shirt and bringing a knee up into his groin. She shoved him back into the crowded lift, his eyes wide and face crimson.

"Everyone on!" Anna yelled, pushing the last few people forward. They shuffled in, smashing together, the cramped space filled wall to wall.

"I can't breathe...there isn't room," someone shouted, but Anna threw herself forward. She was outside the door, then even with it. Someone reached out, a woman, her arms groping around her midsection. She pulled Anna in close, the mass of bodies crushing together.

She turned and sucked in her breath, pushing back, smashing her body into the others. The creature was moving towards them...twenty feet away, then a dozen, an impossible mass of slashing, stabbing legs tearing the ceramic panels from the walls and puncturing the metal floor. It had three faces now, the padding of Garrett's armor somehow melded with its flesh. Human arms reached and clutched, groping for her, hungry for her.

The doors closed, sliding just past her face, the cool metal catching and squeaking against her hot cheek. They closed, the bright interior light fading to blue as the chime sounded, and then Anna felt gravity shift and the lift started to move.

Lex fell asleep in his arms, their bodies warm and pressed together. He held her for a long while, her peaceful, deep breathing soothing his own flyaway thoughts.

Jacoby's thoughts drifted from Anna, to the guilt associated with his run in with Soraya, to Janice, and finally back to Lex. Part of him wanted to wake her up and kiss her, just to experience the deep and complicated bond growing between them.

The doors to the shower opened, interrupting his thoughts. Doctor Reeds stepped into the showers, the automatic lights blinking on overhead.

Jacoby covered his eyes and Lex groaned, turning to bury her face in his chest. The physician turned left, then right. He spotted them and half-stepped forward.

"There you are, I have unearthed some interesting...oh," he said and then seemed to realize they were naked, and abruptly turned around.

"What's up, doc," Lex grunted, and started to laugh. Jacoby chuckled as well, catching the reference from the cartoon's he used to watch with Anna after class. They'd been bootlegged videos she bought from a friend of a friend. He struggled to remember what the cartoon series was called.

"I didn't mean to interrupt. I, uh, mean...sorry," Reeds said, his cheeks flushing red. He gawked for a moment and then turned away awkwardly. "I just think you might want to get dressed and come out here. I've collected some rather interesting, and quite fascinating information from Doctor Misra's findings. You should see them," Reeds said, now talking to the empty side of the shower.

"We'll be right out," Jacoby said as Lex pushed away and stretched. His gaze crawled down her back, the muscles flexing impressively in the light.

"Uh, quickly please," he said and turned to leave, but stopped halfway out the doors. "It's really none of my business, but you know, I'm a doctor. I hope you two used protection." Then he was gone.

Lex laughed and turned, throwing her arms around him. Jacoby returned the embrace, leaned in to kiss her neck, and pressed her close. She leaned back and kissed his cheek, before pulling his earlobe between her teeth.

Lex bit hard at first, a jolt of pain shooting through his ear, but then nibbled it affectionately, her tongue sweeping in, warm and wet, right after.

We have time. The doctor can wait, the voice chimed in, the thrill quickly hitting his groin.

Jacoby pulled Lex around into a strong kiss. She returned it, before biting his lip.

"I think the doc was jealous," Lex whispered into his ear, and then slowly pulled away. With her crooked smile firmly in place, she ran her fingers over his lap, just brushing against his privates.

We had time for more fun. She wanted it. You could see it in her eyes.

"There will be time later," Jacoby whispered and watched Lex walk away. Her hips swayed as she walked, a confidence and sexuality in her step that wasn't there before.

Lex scooped her clothes off the far bench and walked out, turning and giving him the faintest hint of a wink before disappearing through the doors.

Jacoby followed Lex out, but didn't stop in the locker room. He closed the storage room door behind him and dressed in his spare modesties, before pulling on a pair of work coveralls. The boots were brand new, the reinforced soles and leather uppers stiff and unyielding around his feet.

He rolled up his sleeves, scooped a pair of hand wraps and the chip guard off the table, and turned to leave. Something buzzed angrily behind him, vibrating against the table.

Jacoby spun, scooped the data point off the table, and woke up the screen. More than a dozen connection requests showed in the notifications, at least as many text format messages waiting to be read. A solitary audio recording icon flashed in the middle of them all. He pressed play and smashed it to his ear.

"Jacoby, its Anna. Oh my god...glad you're all right! Soraya and I are still on...ring. Where are you? We'll come...tell me...and we'll find you."

Jacoby's heart leapt, an electric buzz shooting over his skin at the sound of Anna's voice. The recording faded in and out, a chorus of shouts and screams drowning out her voice. A loud, hollow boom filled the data point's small speaker, before he could understand Anna again.

"...there's something happening to the people. Preston is...we think he's dead....monsters...horrible. We're waiting to...transit elevator down to A...their evacuating...habitat rings...find you!"

The recording ended and Jacoby pulled the data point away from his ear, shaking it in frustration. Anna said "monsters" and "horrible". Somehow what had happened to Janice and the others in the clinic had spread.

If it is an infection, it could be anywhere.

Jacoby spun, lifting the data point to his mouth.

"Anna, get to A ring. Go someplace public, with a lot of people...the commissary. I'll meet you there as soon as I can. Send me a message when you get there! Stay safe...I'm coming."

Jacoby dropped the data point into a pocket and pushed out of the storage, immediately turning right and walking back out into the lab. Lex sat on a table to his left, combing through her hair with her fingers.

"Glad to see you finally found some clothes," she said, and hopped off to follow him.

They found Doctor Reeds at a computer terminal halfway up the long room, two nurses in scrubs and a single young man in a lab coat standing around him.

"Where are the others?"

Reeds spun to meet him as he walked up. His mismatched eyes were glassy and red, the skin underneath puffy and dark. He looked exhausted.

"Emiko, Erica, and Yani here are the only members of Layla's team that felt compelled to help. So, we locked the others in the office with Mr. Nazzar."

"Smart," Lex said, settling in next to him.

Jacoby glanced down at the workstation. The shattered Palmer Module he'd pulled off his arm sat to the left, another broken and bloodied unit sitting next to it. Both devices were connected to the terminal by long, glowing cords.

"So, what was Doctor Misra doing? Did you find out what is going on?"

"Find out?" Reeds scoffed, reaching up and wiping his forehead on a sleeve. "Rarely do these things follow such linear or simple paths. Medicine and science, as they say is more akin to mice navigating a maze in the long hope of finding some cheese. Now, mind you, I'm not a clinician, and I have spent the majority of my time practicing general medicine. So, you could say, I doll out antibiotics and immune boosters for a living. You know? Misery does love company, and it has kept me busy!"

Jacoby nodded and smiled, silently urging him to continue.

"We've been able to gather enough information to start piecing together the puzzle, I believe. I'm afraid the implications will affect all of us, but you, Jacoby, and well, now you, too." Reeds glanced to Lex, but the redhead didn't look sheepish or embarrassed. If anything, she stood up a little straighter.

"What are you saying, doc? I'm not sick like Janice and those other people," Jacoby argued.

"No you aren't, but that doesn't mean you aren't affected. Infections manifest in people differently, and by that I mean symptoms. That much I do know. And I think now, thanks to your congenial time in the showers, she will be affected, as well," Reeds said, looking at Lex.

"I'm an adult, doc, and can make my own decisions. Were you spying on us? Do you like to watch? Is that it?" Lex argued, her voice raising several octaves.

Reeds chuckled awkwardly and stammered.

"The showers echo really bad. Trust me, it's loud. We hated it most when particular coworkers would sing during their showers," Emiko said, speaking up.

"Oh," Lex said, shrinking back a bit.

"But what do you mean? What is affecting us? If you know, spit it out! You tested me in the clinic and said I was clear, that I wasn't sick," Jacoby spoke out, more worried and frustrated then embarrassed.

"Thanks to Miss Emiko and Jani's help, I've determined that Doctor Misra wasn't just using the Palmer Modules to keep you and the other patients sedated. She was also using their sensory and artificial intelligence to gather data...a lot of data, in fact. You see, she knew that you had cracked an asteroid and hit a void, but her suspicions went deeper than my own. She believed that you were possibly infected by something...well, something biological trapped inside that rock. Well, I mean, I would have known, but it looks like that information had been filtered out when the report was sent up to me from production."

"It was a gas pocket," Jacoby blurted, even though his heart wasn't in it. "How could something live...sealed in a rock and floating in space? There is no air and it's like negative a thousand degrees out there."

"Ha ha, yes, cold, but not quite that cold, I think. There are forms of life on earth that have adapted to live in the harshest of environments...in very low or high temperatures, without light, some even in almost oxygen deficient conditions. Some bacteria has adapted to live within swirling eddies of sulfur-polluted water. But that is not my field of study. Like I said, I can only look at the data they were collecting and make educated guesses."

Jacoby lifted his hand for the doctor to continue.

"Through these Palmer Modules we've been able to learn some...well, I can only call them 'startling truths'," Reed said, lifting his fingers into air quotes. "First, that the mass I identified on your cranial scans is not a tumor, at least we do not believe that it is. It isn't growing, you see. The testing equipment in my clinic is designed to evaluate and identify key compounds and only very basic blood and fluid tests. It was flagging your blood with incredibly high levels of androstadienone, but it turns out that it isn't that at all. Yes, the compound in your blood is similar, and in reality it may end up being a derivative of Testosterone, too but it is unlike anything Doctor Misra had ever seen before. Or, that's what she wrote in her notes at least. We managed to isolate some from blood samples trapped in your Palmer Module and analyzed it under an electron microscope," Doctor Reeds said, clicking through to a series of images on the computer.

Jacoby shifted, moving forward to look over the doctor's shoulder. Emiko and the other staff edged away from him. It was subtle, but he noticed.

"Okay, now here is a skin cell we managed to extract from the torn catheter at five hundred times magnification."

Jacoby watched the cell, which just looked like a blob in the middle of the screen, suddenly split in two.

"Fascinating, isn't it? I haven't studied cellular activity since medical school. The power of these microscop..." Reeds said, pointing excitedly and swiveling in his chair, but Jacoby cleared his throat, interrupting him.

"Sorry. There," he said, pointing at the screen.

"And...? Lex asked. She was next to Jacoby now, squinting at the image.

"Doctor Misra documented in her notes that your cellular division rate was off the charts...easily twice that of a normal person. This cell has been removed from your body for hours now. It should be dead, and yet it continues to divide. And that is not all. We have detected abnormalities within the plasma membrane of your skin, tissue, and red blood cells. Those membranes are semi-permeable boundaries, only yours are not. Something is creating an almost unbreakable barrier around the building blocks in your body. And...and the compound flooding your blood to an almost toxic degree? It is a chemoreceptor, but unlike any we've ever seen or documented. Your body's pheromone release and olfactory sensitivity are off the charts. I mean, to a crazy degree." The doctor swung around in his chair again, his face pulled into a look of almost manic excitement. "Do you know that dogs have a sense of smell one hundred thousand times more powerful than humans?"

"Yeah, sure, I think I'd heard something like that before. But what does that have to do with me?" Jacoby responded, taken off guard by the doctor's seemingly random change in direction.

"Your body, it appears, has become similarly efficient. Goodness gracious, with these numbers, it could almost be hypothesized that you might be able to feel a person's mood, or...or make them feel yours. Shit, you might even be able to alter another person's disposition! There have been documented studies supporting how some 'hyper sensitive' individuals can suffer dramatic up or down swings in moods due to the presence of some external hormonal stimuli. Women can sync menstruation cycles with other women living in close proximity."

Jacoby's mind reeled as he tried to make sense of everything Doctor Reeds said, but he talked so fast, turning logical corners with every breath.

"But...but why? I mean I feel fine...and those people. Janice...what was wrong with them? Is it...the same thing?"

Reeds expression darkened, while Emiko and the other medical staff shared a look. There was something there, something Jacoby wasn't sure he wanted to learn.

"Their blood samples show some startling things. Some things that we...just...don't..." Reeds began, but faltered. He turned back to the computer and started to flip between screens. Lex coughed quietly, while Emiko leaned back against the desk and shared a look with Yani, but no one spoke.

Breaking bones and boiling blood, what was inside became outside, and known unknown. Do you feel it...beyond the lust, the heat from the computer equipment, and the stench from their industrial cleaner? Do you feel their fear? There is something...some knowledge that scares them...these people of logic and science, of mathematics and measurement. If it scares them, then it should scare us. Make him tell us!

"Is it the same thing that's happening to me?" Jacoby asked, voicing an unspoken doubt building in his mind.

"It's just...it's just," Reeds stammered, clicking through another series of screens. Jacoby spotted pages upon pages labeled blood panels and other data, but it flipped by so quickly he couldn't imagine how anyone could actually read it.

"Doc?!" Jacoby said loudly. Reeds jumped, his eyes snapping up from the screen at the sound of his voice. "What is it, doc?"

"It's just so very bizarre...very bizarre. The blood workup from the sick individuals showed marked similarities...except for significant and rising levels of certain hormones not present in your labs...mostly cortisol and adrenaline. And they all tested positive for the one thing you didn't...the influenza virus."

Emiko jumped as a crash sounded down the lab behind them. Jacoby spun, but Lex slid over the table behind her, and moved down the row of tables towards the door.

He followed Reeds down the aisle, moving slowly, but paused as another loud crash sounded beyond the door. The sound was muffled and distant, definitely not in the room with them.

Beyond the door...in the dark, where the monsters lie waiting.

Lex stood just before the lab's solitary door, the white and gray pads of her armor floating as her dark bodysuit seemingly disappeared in the shadows.

"What is it?" Emiko asked, hovering tentatively behind them.

Lex leaned into the small windows on the metal door, cupping her hands around her face to block out the ambient light.

"I don't see anything..." she started to say.

We are trapped. You...we will need to fight.

"Wait. I see something moving, but it's so dark out there. Can we turn out some of the lights in here so I can see...?" she turned to ask, but a violent tremor shook the door. Jacoby jumped forward and pulled her back, another violent impact jarring the portal and shaking the floor.

Jacoby pulled Reeds back as something struck the door again and again, the metal frame rattling loudly.

"You said they all tested positive for the virus. Why is that significant? Tell me!" Jacoby said, hooking Reeds under the arm and turning him around.

"Layla's observations were still very early, but she was a brilliant clinician. She completed a fellowship in virology at John's Hopkins. These are her observations, not mine. Whatever is living within your brain is changing you...refining you at a cellular level. Hell, the ability to accelerate the cellular division rate within a person could be worth billions on the pharmaceutical market. But the other people? Well, a virus is a simple organism. It invades a body, and when not warded off by the immune system, attaches to a person's cells. The cell accepts it in, and the virus takes it over, forcing a person's own body to start replicating and creating more virus cells. You see? It takes over, invading and turning a person's body against them. Something...I don't know, let's call it an alien, bacterium, or symbiotic organism...yes I like that, is streamlining, strengthening, and improving the cells in your body. What if that same organism came into contact with tissue infected with this virus? What would something with that capability due to a microscopic organism designed to do one thing...invade and reproduce?"

Jacoby knew the doctor had stumbled onto at least a fragment of the truth, he could feel it in his gut – just like he could feel the things moving just beyond the lab door. They that used to be human like him. He felt them inside, a gut-cramping, spine-tingling reaction, as if his body recoiled and disapproved of their proximity.

As if in answer to the doctor's question, the door shuddered. Jacoby threw his arms around Lex and heaved her back as the small window exploded inwards, shards of glass raining over the floor.

"Get back!" he yelled and pushed Emiko out of the way.

Jacoby spun to find an impossibly long and boney arm stuck through the small window – segmented, hinged, and ending in a sharp point.

"My god...they have weapons! Where did they get weapons?" Yani asked frantically, after the spidery leg pulled back through the glass.

"They didn't find them. They grew them," Jacoby surmised, and looked to Doctor Reeds.

Lex cursed as the door shook again and again, shuddering as if a breaching ram was striking the other side. Reeds nodded grimly and swallowed.

"How long will that door keep them out?" Lex asked, recovering quickly and moving into their midst.

Reeds looked to Yani and said, "You said that door was designed to seal the lab, correct? How, uh, strong is it?"

Yani jumped as the door shuddered again, metal starting to grind in the walls. He shook his head, his mouth starting to move well before he could form words.

"I-I-I don't know. I mean, they said it was designed to hermetically seal the lab in case of a biological release. Seal it against fire and vacuum. Strong? Yes. But I don't think they designed it to hold out monsters!"

"And that door is our only egress route, correct?" Lex asked, moving directly before the bearded man and gathering his focus. Yani nodded.

"It's a choke point. But...we have no weapons. So, we're screwed–"

"Yani," Jacoby said, cutting Lex off.

The lab tech flinched as the door shuddered again, the grinding noise growing in intensity. Was it the mechanical workings of the door failing? Would it just slide open and let them in if it gave way completely?

"You said the other door in the locker room is for Doctor Misra's security team, correct? Their ready room?"

"Uh, yes..." the young man sputtered, but seemed to gain confidence with the realization. "Yes! They have weapons in there! We've seen them, long black ones."

Another crash sounded outside, the glass in the left side door shattering in. The boney arm pulled back and bent, latching onto the door. Then Jacoby watched as another appendage eased in through the other window and hooked onto the other side. They snapped out, wrenching on the doors. A small crack appeared in the center, as the doors started to pull apart.

Jacoby spun around and made for the locker room, but Lex was already moving. She hit the door with a boot and smashed it open violently. By the time he ran into the locker room, she was already at the door.

"It's locked, and there is some kind of hand scanner. It's not letting me open it!" she yelled. He moved in behind her, and caught sight of her right hand pressed up against a glossy, black panel. A red silhouette flashed around her hand and the door buzzed.

"Access restricted. Step away," a cool voice intoned.

"I'm station security! How do I not have fucking access?" Lex growled angrily and kicked the door.

"It's biometrically coded to her security team members only. That's how the directorate wanted it, or at least that's what I heard Doctor Misra say once," Emiko said, appearing through the locker room door.

"Hey-hey-hey! Whatever you are going to do...please do it fast!" Reeds screamed from the lab. Jacoby could hear metal bending, breaking. Lex screamed and threw herself at the door, clawing for a grip as she tried to wrench it open.

We can give her what she needs. But you need to move...now! the voice said, booming in his mind.

Jacoby spun before he knew where he was going, but by his second step he was cursing himself for not thinking of it sooner. He ran right by Emiko and Yani, the young woman's eyes wide with fear.

"Is he leaving us? Where is he going?" he heard her cry, but Jacoby wasn't really paying attention.

The storeroom light blinked on but he was already halfway to the back table, his gaze locked on his goal. Lex continued to scream and pound on the door in the room behind him as he scooped up the pile of fusion plugs and jammed them into a pocket. He flung the chip guard around his neck, snugged on his gloves, and threw his safety glasses on.

Jacoby wrenched the plasma saw off the table, twisting the plug, and clicking on the power button, all in one, economical movement.

The tool vibrated in his hand, the capacitors whining softly. The contact points on the blade were already hot by the time he stepped out of the storeroom, the blade beginning to spool.

"Clear the door! Clear a path!" he shouted. Emiko and Yani yelled and jumped back, the saw's almost amber glow filling the room with light.

"Lex!" he shouted, lifting the saw as he approached the door. She spun, mouth opened in a half-formed curse, and her eyes shot wide.

"Will that cut it?" she asked, jumping out of the way.

"It cuts through rock and ore like butter," Jacoby shouted over the saw's whine. Janice's voice cut into his thoughts just as he brought the glowing blade up to the shiny metal.

Don't fuck around with MY saws. They cut rock, not metal. They cut ROCK!

The blade bit, the saw jumping in his hands, glowing sparks immediately bathing his legs and the ground beneath him.

"Please...cut," he grunted, tightening his grip and forcing the blade fully into the thick metal.

We don't ask it to cut, Jacky! We make it cut!

The plasma saw whined loudly, the blade sinking hungrily into the metal a foot below the door's centerline. Jacoby eased it sideways. Hot slag flowed out from around the blade and dribbled down the door to pool on the floor.

He could hear Lex behind him, feel her anxious energy. Someone else was shouting, too. It sounded like Doctor Reeds, but he couldn't turn away to be sure. The blade reached the doorjamb and he slowly eased it out, being careful to keep the blade spinning.

Jacoby lifted the saw and started a new cut a foot above the centerline, moving it slowly to cut parallel to his previous cut. His arms shook, and the saw vibrated, but it was familiar. Damn he missed running a saw. There was indeed something honest about mining – perhaps the act of breaking lumps of lifeless rock down into its building blocks and allowing them to be purified and molded into something new and useful.

He finished his second cut and pulled the saw out, the blade barely clearing the door before the motor powered down and the fusion plug turned and popped free.

"Shit," he cursed, and then let the hot blade dip towards the ground. Jacoby yanked the spent fusion plug out of the port. He jammed his hand into his pocket and fished around for a fresh plug, but glanced up.

"They're breaking through the door! They're breaking through!" Doctor Reeds yelled, running into the locker room and slamming the door behind him. Yani ran to his side. Both men threw their bodies against the door as a loud and violent crash sounded out in the lab.

"Go! Go! Go!" Lex urged. She bounced on the balls of her feet, her hands grasping at the air, as if clutching for a weapon.

The new fusion plug slapped home and twisted, the saw, already hot, spun back to life in an instant. Jacoby changed the cut vector, the blade head rotating until it was straight up and down.

The hot blade punched into the steel, more molten metal sliding out. Flames spurted in glowing bursts as the paint covering the steel ignited.

"Jacoby!" Lex yelled behind him, but he couldn't stop. Hell, he couldn't even make the saw cut faster. At this point he was just holding it in place.

A crash sounded behind him, the locker room falling into chaos. He had six inches left to cut...four...two. And then the blade broke through. He felt Lex behind him, prepared, like a coiled spring ready to break.

Jacoby ripped the blade free and dropped to the side. Lex jumped forward and kicked the door hard, sending it swinging into the darkness. The glowing cutout in the middle of the door hung in the space, now fused to the sturdy locking bar.

Lex leapt over the puddles of molten steel and disappeared inside, automatic lights blinking on and filling the doorway with light.

Jacoby spun and found Reeds falling over a bench, and Emiko teetered by the farthest row of benches, a monstrous form breaking through the door. Yani jumped over the benches, hooked Emiko and swung her back towards Jacoby. The nurse screamed and tumbled. Yani took a single step to follow, but pitched sideways as an impossibly long object flashed across and skewered him, pinning him to a locker.

Jacoby managed to catch Emiko and hefted her off a knee. He pulled her behind him, spooling the saw at the same time. Jacoby ran right at the monster, breaking every O.S.H.A rule he'd ever been taught in the process.

He lifted the saw up over his head, but couldn't get to Yani before the creature snapped another arm forward, punching it right into the man's throat with a loud, wet *crunch*.

The glowing saw blade came down, cutting through the closest arm with only a hint of resistance. The blade rotated around and he brought it back up, quickly severing the other arm. The creature staggered back, squealing loudly, the smell of burned flesh and bone filling the air.

It was definitely one of the people from the clinic, or more than one of them. The flesh had darkened, but he could clearly see a woman's torso sticking out of the side of a man's ribcage. The two heads stuck together, as if the flesh was slowly trying to merge them into one.

Jacoby pushed off of Yani's body, the man pinned in place by the severed limbs, and brought the saw around. The creature jumped back onto the bench, another long appendage stabbing into the lockers behind it for balance.

"Come on, you ugly sack of rotten guts," Jacoby growled, leveling the glowing-hot saw between them.

It lashed out without a sound, the two long appendages stabbing from its torso and hitting him in a blur. Jacoby swung the saw around, but caught only air. The creature's attack hit him hard, violently knocking him back into the locker.

Duck!

Jacoby lurched to the side as a boney appendage burst from the creature's chest and stabbed into the locker above his shoulder. He brought the saw up, catching one of its human-shaped arms just below the shoulder, and cut clean through.

Another white shape burst from the body in a splatter of dark fluid and stabbed into his right arm, jarring it aside before he could bring the saw back down. His right hand knocked free, the saw swung down in his left, and the safety engaged, immediately spinning down the blade.

The creature shrieked and brought its long, severed limbs up, the burned and blunted ends poised to pummel and crush his face. A sharp crack split the air before the creature could strike, chunks of fleshy bone bursting into the air. Jacoby looked over as Lex stepped out of the ready room, a long, glossy rifle tucked tight against her shoulder.

"Get clear!" she yelled.

Jacoby grunted and kicked his boot up onto the creature's midsection and pushed. The skin and muscle squirmed beneath his boot, but it slid back, the spear-like appendage pulling free from his right arm. Free from its hold, Jacoby fell.

Lex pushed in, the barrel of the rifle flashing brightly. The creature spun around as the round punched through its chest, blood and bits of flesh blowing out its back. Both mouths screeching, it turned on Lex, horrible, insect-like arms lashing out.

Pop-Pop-Pop-Pop-Pop-Pop.

Jacoby covered his ears as the rifle came alive, the munitions splitting its flesh open from stomach to neck, organs, bones, and bodily fluid bursting out the back and all over the floor.

He pushed up onto his knees after the echoing reports faded to a dull ringing in his ears, and found the creature slumped to its knees, a gaping, smoking hole where its chest used to be.

A spent magazine dropped out of the rifle, Lex sliding a replacement in without pulling it from her shoulder. She slapped it for good measure, as a trickle of smoke drifted off the barrel. She stepped slowly forward, the weapon still trained on one of the creature's heads.

"Is it dead?" Emiko asked, rising from the floor beyond Lex.

"I uh...I uh," Reeds stammered, giving the creature a wide berth, before looking back at Jacoby and then Lex. "I do believe that Lex here did an incredibly efficient job of moving its guts from inside its body to over there on the floor. Thank you for that."

Jacoby eased up to his feet, the pain in his right arm flaring as he wrapped his fingers around the saw's grip. He squeezed the trigger, just enough to get the points to pre-heat, but not to engage the motor. Reeds approached the creature, leaning in to get a better look.

"Please don't...I don't think you should get that close to it, Doctor?" Emiko said, still hovering behind Lex.

"Doc," Jacoby warned, and shook his head. He tightened his grip on the saw. That creeping feeling still roiled his guts a bit. Either it wasn't dead, or there was another close by. Jacoby flicked his eyes up to Lex, and she nodded. Jacoby's finger tightened around the trigger, the motor engaging.

"I think it is quite dead now, Emiko. If we are to survive, I fear we need to gain a..."

The creature shuddered suddenly, its head snapping up, a wet, sucking noise issuing out of its body. Lex moved to fire, but Jacoby was faster. He fully engaged the blade and brought the plasma saw across at shoulder level, severing both necks in a single pass.

He kicked the decapitated body over as the heads came to rest at Reeds' feet, the stumps of its necks cauterized and smoking. He held the saw, ready to plunge it down at the first sign of movement, but the sickly sensation was already lifting. The body was still...dead.

"Do you think they know who or what they are anymore? Even feel pain? Jacoby cut off three of its...arms?" Lex asked. She kept the rifle trained on the creature's body, and lifted one of the long, boney appendages with a boot toe. "And after, I pumped an entire magazine of sonic cavitation rounds through it, dead center-fucking mass, and that still didn't kill it."

Jacoby felt the truth of her words. They'd just killed someone. Well, several people, as their bodies had somehow melted and grown together.

"Yes...yes. Truly horrific," Reeds muttered, glancing over to Yani's body pinned against the lockers, and quickly looked away, "able to break through a sturdier-than-most metal door, exceedingly aggressive, exceedingly adept at killing, and frustratingly hard to kill. I think the only thing we know about these things might just be...well, might just be that we don't know anything about them. Not much humanity left in it, I think."

"I think it's time we get out of here, doc. Maybe find someplace a little safer, eh?" Jacoby suggested.

Reeds nodded, his eyes remaining locked on the dead creature at their feet. Then he hooked an arm around Emiko's back and guided her out of the locker room.

Jacoby set the saw on a nearby bench and rolled his right sleeve up to expose a bloody wound on his bicep. Not just a wound, actually. The creature had punched its needle-like arm right through. And yet, it was already closing, the new, pink flesh growing in as he watched.

"Doc said it was a virus? Does that mean it can spread?" Lex asked, her gaze dropping form his eyes to his arm. He read the underlying question – if you're infected with something, does that mean that I am now, too?

Jacoby rolled the sleeve back down and scooped the saw off the bench, careful to avoid stepping in the mess of guts and blood on the floor. Lex nodded, taking his unspoken response.

"How many of those things do you think are out there?" she asked, "I grabbed the rest of their ammunition, but there was only so much. If I blow through that many rounds to *almost* kill one of them..."

"We'll have to find a more efficient way to kill them," Jacoby said, finishing her thought. Lex nodded, and they left the locker room together.

They found Manis and the rest of Doctor Misra's staff still locked in the office. They poured out, faces red and fists raised, until Lex stepped forward.

"Shut up!" she yelled, the rifle whirring as she tightened her grip. The group, two women and three men, immediately went quiet.

"We're leaving. It's time for you to unseal the lab doors," Reeds said, as Jacoby pulled the data point out of his pocket. There were no new audio messages from Soraya's phone.

Damn! he thought. He closed his eyes for a moment and concentrated. The pressure in his head intensified, and somewhere, deep in the fog of his mind, he thought that he felt her.

Yes, I feel them, too, the voice chimed in as he opened his eyes again.

"Them?"

Yes, both of them. Don't be slow.

"I can't do that. Can't unseal the lab, not after what we just saw. Layla's order went to administration offices. Once the door is sealed, only they can unseal it," Manis said.

Jacoby lifted the data point between them. "So, have them unseal it. Tell them whatever they want to hear. Tell them it was a test, or a false alarm. But do it, now!"

"I don't take orders from you! You're the reason why we're in this whole mess in the first place. If it weren't for you..."

Lex stepped forward, the people around Manis parting like an opening book. The rifle barrel snapped up, hovering right before the administrator's face.

"We weren't asking. You call, you get it done. That's the easy way. You don't? My finger twitches and I have Jacoby cut that door open with his saw. Either way, we get out of here. Only one of those options sees you leaving with us," Lex said and ever so gently pressed the barrel against Manis' cheek.

The color drained from Manis's face and his eyes went glassy and wide. His mouth worked for a moment, but Jacoby stepped forward, holding the data point against his chest before he could condemn himself.

"I can see you're scared. We all are. But I'll tell you now, if you don't think she'll do it, then you're just wrong. One of those things broke through the lab door on its own and she took it down without flinching. If they can get in here, they've probably already made it out into the station. The longer we stand around, the more people die. Don't believe me? Go in the locker room and look for yourself. But be careful where you step," Jacoby said.

Manis stared at him for a long moment, but let out a shuddering breath and dropped his gaze to the floor. Lex dropped the rifle as he accepted the data point and immediately made for the mangled door. Jacoby hung back, dropping into line behind Manis and the others.

When it came time for him to move through the bent and broken door, Jacoby paused. Strips of skin and muscle hung from the jagged metal.

"I guess that answers that question," he whispered, bending out of the way to avoid the mess.

A virus works to supplant its host. Perhaps this is what happens if nothing gets in its way.

"That's a horrifying thought," Jacoby whispered as he straightened on the other side of the door.

"What's that?" Lex asked.

"Oh, just thinking out loud," he lied, and tried to hide his surprise.

Tell her about me...about us, the voice said, and Jacoby immediately shook his head.

Lex turned and moved away from him, her rifle tight against her shoulder, the barrel scanning the ruined beds and dark corners.

She is clever. She will figure it out. And then what will you tell her?

"That I have conversations with a little voice in my head? That you're a fractured part of my mind given an unreasonably loud voice by something that may or may not be an Alien organism living inside my brain," Jacoby mumbled under his breath.

Yes, perfect! Add that I like redheads, and you prefer blondes, so we establish the parameters of our relationship. I think she will understand. Let's tell her now before that twerp opens the doors and we all get torn apart!

"I don't think she will find it nearly as funny as you," Jacoby whispered, as Reeds pushed Manis up to the large, lab doors.

"Open it!" Jacoby said, walking up to stand next to him.

Manis swallowed, his eyes temporarily flitting to the ceiling.

"If you're worried about what they do to you, just tell them that I threatened you or something," Jacoby offered.

Manis closed his eyes but tapped on the data point. A moment later, the doors clicked loudly, and slowly opened.

"That's it? That's all you had to do?" Lex snorted behind him and pushed out in the hallway, sweeping the rifle left, before the passage to the right.

"Well, shit!" she swore.

Jacoby pulled the data point out of Manis' hand and pushed him into the hall, Reeds and the rest of the group shuffling along close behind. He turned to find Lex standing in the middle of the passage, her rifle lifted towards a massive hole in the ceiling.

"I think that answers our question, doc. They're out," Lex said, and skirted the jagged hole above.

Jacoby ushered the rest of them through, pulling anyone to the side that got too close to walking directly beneath the hole.

"Where to, Jacoby?" Lex asked.

"The commissary."

"One floor up, through the hospital and clinic, and we're basically there."

"You all are just going to make this whole mess worse. You've likely killed everyone on this station," Manis said, his eyes nervously scanning the hall.

"Misery loves company, sir, as I say. If you and Layla hadn't kept secrets, none of this would have happened in the first place. This is on your..." Reeds argued, but Lex swung around a corner and went rigid.

"Heh! You on the ground, can you hear me? Are you all right? Wait a minute...stay back!"

Jacoby's skin started to crawl, his insides bubbling.

"Lex, get back!" he yelled, just as someone appeared from the hall to their right. The rifle barked once, the muzzle flash filling the dark space with blue light. The man grunted and staggered to the side, but refused to go down. Lex managed one more shot before he was on her.

Jacoby moved to help but watched as she jabbed the weapon's barrel hard into his face, knocking him back a step. She fired two rounds in quick succession into his chest, and a third into his face. The man collapsed back and fell still, a dark pool spreading around his head.

She is impressive with the proper tools. An angel of death, the voice said, and Jacoby silently agreed.

They moved down the passage and Lex pushed through a door to the side, sweeping the rifle from corner to corner. Jacoby entered last, finding a dark stairwell. He clicked on his flashlight, closing the door behind him.

He climbed, refusing to let his finger come completely off the saw's trigger. The tight space filled with the sound of shuffling feet and loud breathing. He heard Lex open a door somewhere above him and waited for their small crowd to file out into the next passage.

He followed Emiko around the last corner, the group moving out through a door up and ahead. A door clicked and banged open below, the muffled sound echoing up and around the corner.

"Go!" he said, pushing her up the stairs. "Go...quickly!" Emiko nodded and turned, pushing the others up and telling them to hurry.

Jacoby clicked off the flashlight and stuffed it in his pocket, and then smashed the trigger, engaging the blade. He'd never be able to hold both at the same time.

A storm of footsteps echoed up the small stairwell, the noise quickly drowned out by the spooling saw blade. Jacoby backed up into the straight run of the stairwell, giving himself more room to maneuver.

A woman appeared in the landing below. She hit the wall and rolled sideways, grunting and moaning loudly. Her head flopped around, the strange, jerky movements even more mechanical and terrifying in the saw's orange dancing light. She spotted Jacoby, and screamed, a horrible mess of black sick tumbling out of her mouth and running down her chin.

"I'm sorry," he whispered, and brought the saw down. The blade caught her on the left shoulder and bit hard. She squealed and tried to jump back, but the super-heated blade points chewed through muscle, bone, and organs, burning and incinerating until pulling free above her right hip.

The woman flopped to the ground, her body effectively cut into two pieces. Her arms and legs thrashed and clawed, slapping the floor and walls. A man tumbled in next, the remains of a much smaller person stuck to his chest. Another body tumbled onto the landing behind him, and yet another.

"Shit!" Jacoby cursed and jumped up two steps. The man swung around, a long, boney arm stabbing into the wall to Jacoby's right. He brought the saw up, but it pulled free before he could strike, leaving a cracked and jagged hole in the wall.

"I hope you are all out up there!" he screamed.

Boney arms swung in, driving into the ground at Jacoby's feet. The man lunged forward, a mass of arms and mouths groping for him.

It wasn't the voice that popped up, but an urge, or a compulsion. Jacoby acted without second thought. He kicked the lunging man in the chest and knocked him back, and then leveled the saw blade at his chest and charged in.

The blade plunged deep into squirming flesh, the monster falling back under his weight. They tumbled onto the landing, Jacoby surfing atop the roiling bodies. He ripped the saw straight up, pulling it through the man's chest and cutting his neck and head clean in half.

The orange light danced as black fluid and severed flesh spattered the walls. Jacoby swung the saw blindly to his left and felt the blade cleave through something soft. It hit the corner of the wall and ignited the darkness in a shower of sparks.

A boney limb caught him in the left thigh, an explosion of fiery pain igniting all the way from his groin to his toes. He kicked out, catching one of the monsters with his right foot, their head crunching under the weight of his boot. The saw swung down and cut through the spear-like appendage stuck into his leg.

He jabbed and swung the saw over and over, the glowing blade biting and chewing through flesh and bone, the motor whining in a gleeful battle cry. A red light ignited in the darkness, flashing on the back of the saw, pulling Jacoby out of his frenzy. A rational part of his mind pushed in, and he managed to turn away from the churning, screaming pile of flailing monsters just before the fusion plug popped out, and the saw powered down.

Anna's throat tightened as the weight of people smashed her against the door. She tried to push back, but it was no use. A woman coughed and gagged somewhere in the group behind her, and then a man. A ripple passed through the crowd, vibrating through the people around her as if they were one. Her throat tightened a bit more, the air around her face heavy and closing in.

"Just...breathe," she gasped, trying to push every other thought away and focus only on her next breath. The lift would get there. It would. She would hear the chime and then the doors would open. It had to. She needed it to.

The elevator grew dim, and Anna tried to blink it away, but the murk remained. The woman coughed again – a wet, raspy, unhealthy sound.

"I need out...of...here. I'm sick...d-d-don't feel well at all. Please!"

Anna's skin crawled at the woman's words, an uncomfortable nausea bubbling up inside. Was it claustrophobia? No...she'd felt it above, when the monstrosity got close. The transit elevator dinged suddenly, but the sound was muffled as if she had cotton stuffed in her ears.

"You have arrived at A ring annex," a voice said overhead. Anna could barely breathe. The door slid open and she sprawled forward, forcing her hands out to cushion her fall.

She curled into a ball as a flood of bodies poured out above her – some fell on and around her, while other stepped over and on her. She felt their feet, elbows, and knees pound down, smashing into her back and sides. Something struck the side of her face, and her head bounced painfully against the ground.

A ringing filled her ears just as she felt a bit of the smothering weight pull away. A body was pulled free and Anna dared open her eyes as Soraya's face came into view through the pile of limbs.

"I said get the hell off of her!"

Another body pulled free and she felt Soraya's hands hook around her, and then she was standing.

"I thought they were going to crush me to death," Anna gasped, and threw her arms around Soraya, squeezing her hard. "You're the most wonderful thing I've ever seen!"

Soraya returned the embrace, holding her up and sheltering her as the crowd pushed and shoved by. They moved like a stampede, a mass of unthinking, unapologetic, and violent animals. But despite their chaos, their strength, Anna felt safe in Soraya's embrace. She was a mighty pillar of stone holding the crashing waves at bay.

"Just let them go," Soraya whispered.

They hung there together until the crowd from the elevator had all moved past. Anna accepted Soraya's strength, greedily taking in the cool, fresh air, and reveling in the strong heart beneath her breasts.

She opened her eyes after the noise of the crowd had faded to a distant echo. Her head was nestled in the crook of Soraya's neck, a familiar and almost intoxicating buzz passing between their skin. By some means, they could feel the gruesome monsters, as if their bodies were receptive to something foul the bastardized people emitted. And likewise, they were connected as well. But there was nothing threatening or dark about Soraya...quite the opposite, in fact.

Anna lifted her head, and before she realized what she was doing, leaned in and pressed their lips together. Soraya flinched at first, but didn't try to pull away. After a moment, she leaned in, accepting the embrace and pressing them closer together.

A spark ignited between them, flooding over Anna's skin from her lips, through her face, and down over the rest of her body. Soraya opened her mouth and their tongues momentarily brushed together.

Anna hadn't kissed another woman before, save a few friendly pecks with friends in school, but those weren't intimate. This was something wholly different. Soraya tasted sweet and warm, her mind immediately spinning up recollections of fragrant flowers and a tangerine-colored sunrise.

Their passion deepened and Anna moved her hands down Soraya's back, savoring each finely sculpted curve. Soraya reached up and cupped Anna's face, then slid her hands slowly down her neck. The electric buzz coursing through her body intensified as Soraya's hands gently slid over her breasts, the grip delicate and unlike any man she'd ever been with. Anna gasped, her chest heaving.

Soraya's warmth intensified suddenly, as her hand moved down onto her stomach, and lower. Anna's body hummed, the sunshine-like heat filling her completely, burning away the panic, the ache, and the weakness, leaving only warmth and the fresh fragrance of flowers in its wake.

Their lips separated and Anna dared open her eyes. Soraya watched her intently, her rich, chocolate-brown eyes speaking in a language far beyond the simple words they could form with their voices.

"Did you feel that?" Anna asked.

Soraya cocked a single eyebrow, but she didn't immediately speak. She didn't have to. Anna could feel that she did. And beyond the spark, the warmth of their connection, she could feel others as well - like pieces of herself floating somewhere in the station, waiting to be reclaimed...waiting to be made whole.

A scream echoed from somewhere far down the concourse. Anna and Soraya turned together and listened. It went silent, the gentle buzz of the station flooding back in its absence.

"Jacoby...he's close. And...someone else? I can feel them, too, but not quite as strong. I don't know how or why this is happening, but we need to find them and get out of here." Soraya's voice was quiet, her words slow and deliberate, as if she was rationalizing the strange experience as it happened.

Anna nodded. Soraya retrieved the stun batons from the floor by the lift doors, while Anna pulled the data point out of her pocket. A spidery crack covered the right side of the screen, a few small segments of the screen pixilating randomly, but it still worked.

She pulled up the number Jacoby had been sending them messages from and tried to bring it up on a voice call, and then a video chat, but the network continued to decline the requests.

[Hidden Network] -Error- Bandwidth insufficient. Improper permissions exist. -Error-.

"Stupid piece of crap. It's like we're playing Marco Polo," Anna cursed, and pressed record.

"Jacoby, we're here...in the A ring atrium. We just got off the transit elevator," Anna said, pausing to turn and consider the lift doors, "two. We just got off Transit lift number two and we're headed for the commissary now. If you can, meet us on the lower level by the exchange store...the one next to the noddle place we like."

Soraya watched, and nodded when she finished. They set off down the hall and turned onto the concourse. The long walkway was strangely empty, a number of the long, photo-organic light bars overhead intermittently blinking on and off again. The ground hummed and the plants clustered against the walls rippled and swayed in the gentle air currents.

"Where did they all go?" Soraya whispered.

A loud *bang* followed a *crash,* the noises echoing down the wide passage ahead of them. They moved quickly up the wide stairs, a mass of tools and workbags haphazardly strewn about the ground. Several floor panels had been removed, a series of snaking, glowing cables pulled out into wide loops.

Blood covered the floor – a spattered, swirling mess of surprisingly dark fluid. Anna stopped and quietly pointed to the nearest access panel in the floor. A man's arm stuck out of the hole, a clear technician's tablet sitting not six inches away from his still fingers.

"This is something different, right? They can't be down here already, right?" Soraya whispered, holding the two stun batons towards the open service panels.

"I think we'll be a whole lot safer if we assume that whatever is affecting people around here is everywhere," Anna whispered, and moved forward slowly.

She tread slowly forward, crouching down and picking her way through the puddles of blood. Soraya was right behind her, but she could feel the other woman's trepidation, the unanswered question that she couldn't quite spit out. *Why are you getting closer to the big, scary hole in the ground?*

Anna's eyes locked on the maintenance tablet, but it was more than her hunger for tech and knowledge this time. She knew what kind of permissions and privileges were granted to station maintenance workers. With that kind of power, they could go practically anywhere in the station.

Anna scooped the tablet off the ground, a large, bloody thumbprint smeared halfway across the shiny screen. She moved to slide away when her gaze caught on something on the man's arm. A glove covered his hand and stretched halfway up his forearm, several small optical cables glowing gentle blue. A small wave of nausea bubbled up in her gut, but she swallowed it down.

A neural interface glove! Anna thought, her gaze flicking from the high-tech glove, to the blood smeared all around her. Soraya tugged gently on her collar. The message was clear – *let's go now!*

Anna turned back and mouthed "one minute" before turning back and sliding forward. She tried to ignore the squirmy blood under her boots, but she couldn't ignore the smell – coppery, pungent, and invasive.

Her boots stuck to the ground, creating a sticky, tearing noise as she squirmed up to the edge of the maintenance panel. Anna reached forward gingerly and started to work the glove off the man's still arm. It slid free an inch and his fingers twitched. Anna froze, a shiver running down her back as the man moaned.

My god, he's still alive, she thought and looked back to Soraya. She shook her head, and mouthed "get away from there".

Anna swung back as the technician lifted his head, his eyes popping open. His pupil's expanded and contracted wildly before focusing on her. His mouth started to move, his breathing raspy and loud.

"It hurts...it hurts. Help...me," he groaned.

Then she saw it properly. Someone clung to the technician, their arms and legs wrapped so tightly around his midsection that she could barely tell where one began and the other ended.

"Help...me!" the man moaned as the other face, the one seemingly growing out of his back, hissed.

The technician sunk into the darkness then, the glove pulling free in Anna's grip. She hovered there for only a moment, her gaze unable to penetrate the dark service tunnel. And then she pushed back, slipping on the gooey, blood-coated floor. She stood quickly and followed Soraya, dancing through the puddles.

"What is that?"

"He was still alive, but..." Anna whispered back, unable to adequately explain what she saw. She knew Soraya was asking about the tablet and the glove, but the look on the man's face haunted her, the shock, confusion, and horrible pain.

"That was stupid-stupid-stupid," Anna hissed pulling the glove on. She felt it grow warm against her hand, and the tablet responded, a three-dimensional menu block glowing above the screen. The concourse curved around, and Soraya skidded to a stop. Three bodies lay sprawled against the right wall, their clothes torn and bloodied. Were they from the crowd in the elevator? Had this just happened?

A loud *pop* echoed somewhere around the corner ahead, followed by another, and then another.

"Is that a...gun?" Soraya asked. Anna shook her head.

They pushed over to the far wall, giving the bloody scene a wide berth. One woman lay draped over a box of cables. Her left arm was torn clean from her shoulder socket, but that wasn't all. A gaping hole had been punched in the side of her head, jagged fragments of bone and pulpy gray matter framing the wound.

Anna's thoughts immediately went back to the creature, and its long, spindly arms...how it punched clear through the tough ceramic and metal plating. Soraya flashed Anna a look, and promptly turned the knob on both stun batons, the hum and crackling electricity increasing in kind.

"Jacoby, we're on the concourse. There's blood everywhere. Those things...they're here, too. Where are you? I need to know you're okay. Mining administration offices are ahead, and then the clinic and hospital. I hope you're close, I need you to be okay!" Anna said, recording a quiet message into the data point and hitting send.

They ran along the wide concourse, following the gentle curve until offices appeared on the right. Glowing signs hung on both sides of the wide space. A woman screamed ahead, and then glass shattered.

Jacoby kicked off a squelchy body, thrust off the next firm step, and pulled himself up. Without the saw running, the stairwell was black – the black of cloudless nights, of the worst childhood nightmares. He couldn't see the next step, the creatures behind him, or his hands fumbling blindly before him.

Just climb!

"The door!" he screamed, fumbling for the handrail and finally finding it. "Open the door!"

The creatures thrashed in the darkness behind him, their boney limbs cracking violently into the floor and walls around him. A weight fell onto his back, but Jacoby rolled, bent his good leg, and managed to kick the slimy form away.

He kicked up another step, and then another. A slice of light appeared above and ahead, the doorway appearing like the gateway to heaven itself. A face appeared in the doorway, the eyes wide with shock and fear.

Jacoby muscled his way over the final step and threw his weight forward and through the doorway. He caught a glimpse, a flash, of a woman in black scrubs holding the door open, a bright hallway, and the massive barrel of a black rifle leveled right at him.

"Shit!" Lex cursed, a blue flash filling his vision right before the ear-splitting *crack.*

Jacoby tumbled to the ground, the doorframe exploding just over his head.

"You should have called out! I almost smoked you!" Lex cursed.

"They're right behind me. A lot of them!" Jacoby gasped and pushed off the ground. Emiko was there, helping him up, but he pushed her away, and yelled, "go!"

Lex lifted the rifle and fired into the dark stairwell, the sonic rounds echoing loudly in the tight hall. Jacoby ejected the spent fusion plug and snapped in a replacement, twisting it into place.

"We need to move, now!" Lex growled, as a creature emerged from the darkness, long, stabbing appendages flailing wildly.

Jacoby limped behind her, glancing up to the signs on the wall. An arrow pointed to the left and read **clinic**, and then behind him and to the right, **hospital**. He looked down when his left leg buckled. The boney stub was still lodged in his thigh, the cut end burned smooth by his saw blade. He pulled it out, the pain flaring and almost making his bladder release.

We will heal! Now repay the favor!

The plasma saw started to spool as the wave of bodies tumbled out of the doorway. He turned and ran, hobbling every other step on his gimpy leg. Lex spun ahead of him and dropped to a knee.

"Run!" she snarled, the rifle cracking in a short burst.

Don't leave her! the voice chimed in.

"I'm in no shape to leave anyone anywhere," he grunted and squeezed his leg. The group ran frantically ahead of them, crashing into automatic doors when they wouldn't open fast enough.

They moved through a narrow passage and then into a familiar hallway, the clinic exam rooms located on either side. He spotted a crack in the wall just above his head.

Yes, from Randall's head! Part of him laughed, despite the fact that nothing happening at the moment was funny. He didn't even think nearly choking an orderly to death was humorous, no matter how dangerous the man was.

"I'm out!" Lex shouted, and he heard an empty mag clatter to the ground.

The rifle wound up again, the *crack-crack-crack* hitting the walls and pounding his ears.

They pushed through into the waiting room, and Jacoby caught sight of their group, led by Doctor Reeds, scatter. He spun and spotted something as it dropped down from overhead.

"Get out of the way!" he screamed, waving the lab techs aside, but he couldn't get to the woman before she was ripped back up into the air vent. A man screamed out, and Jacoby turned just as his legs disappeared into a hole torn in the wall.

The creatures were everywhere, coming out of every air duct and wall panel around them. There was no way he could guard every approach at once.

Lex roared, her rifle rattling into an impressive chatter of almost automatic fire. He watched as a creature jerked backwards, the flashing sonic rounds snapping off its limbs, before cracking its large, misshapen head in two. She smacked another magazine in, and turned. The rifle flared as a half-melted looking person emerged from a broken wall panel to his left. The first shot hit it in the shoulder, blowing its arm off. The second and third rounds walked up its neck, the latter hitting it in the mouth. The creature's jaw and throat disappeared in a mist of ionized flesh and vaporized blood.

"I'm almost out. We need to move now! I don't care where, but we need to find somewhere safe! Three mags left and then I'm spitting on them!"

Reeds caught Jacoby's gaze and nodded, pulling the frantic lab techs together and shoving them towards the door.

"They're everywhere...everywhere! We need to get off the station. Get me to the docks safely and...and I'll make sure you're handsomely rewarded. Safe passage...safe passage!" Manis screamed, just as Reeds shoved him through the doors.

Jacoby slapped Lex on the shoulder and pulled her around.

"Go! Lead them down through the commissary. We can take the service lift there. The freighter crews use it to resupply. Save your ammo. We can't fight them all. We go quiet and fast and maybe we can sneak by the majority!" Jacoby said, and pushed her towards the door.

"But your leg?" she said, hesitating.

"I'll be fine! Please, go!"

Lex leaned in and kissed him hard, her green eyes sparkling in the light, and then she kicked the doors open, knocking the right door against the wall and shattering the glass.

"You stay close!" she growled, before turning.

"I'll be right behind you."

1000 HOURS

Anna watched the crowd of people tumble through the doors and into the concourse. Some wore white lab coats and other scrubs.

"That's the doctor!" she gasped, recognizing the short, middle-aged man as he appeared amidst the mass of people.

"Move-move-move!" a woman yelled, pushing through the doors last, a long, black weapon immediately rising to meet them.

"We're okay! We're not...them!" Anna screamed, holding her hands up. The redhead let the barrel of the large weapon dip ever so slightly towards the ground, but it didn't move far.

"Wait...I know you," the security officer said, suddenly, her green eyes opening in recognition. "You were in the clinic, with..."

"Jacoby! Yes...where is he?" Anna cried, relief flooding through her.

"He's coming. He'll catch up. We need to get out of here now. Trust me. Now go!"

Anna pulled Soraya forward and they both ran, merging into the small crowd. The offices ended, the wide concourse sweeping around the ring to their left. A wall appeared straight ahead, the glowing sign for the commissary shining just above the oval airlock door.

"All in! All in!" Anna screamed as the group started to pile in. She couldn't bear the thought of being crammed in another confined space with a bunch of people, but she hated the idea of waiting on the wrong side of an airlock when the monsters found them even more.

"Jacoby?" she asked, when the security officer stepped in last, holding the rifle down against her body to make it fit.

"He's coming. He'll make it!" she said.

The airlock started to cycle, the light above them slowly changing from red to green.

"You probably don't remember me...from the clinic. I'm Anna."

"Lex," she said, her green eyes meeting hers, before flicking back to the airlock door behind them. "He'll make it, Anna. He has to. We all have to get out of here." Lex nodded as she talked, swallowing hard. Anna knew the look well enough. She looked unsure, the way only guilt and indecision can make a person second-guess a decision.

"We're going to make our way through the second floor of the commissary, to the other end by the airlocks, make our way down the escalators to the first floor, and through the food vendor stations. There is a service entrance that will lead us down to the docks and allow us to bypass the production floor. We go fast, we go low, and–" Lex said, her voice rising above the chatter.

"That's halfway across the ring and then some. You expect us to run that whole way?" a woman complained from the front of the group, interrupting.

"You know how to use those?" Lex asked Soraya as she stepped out of the airlock.

"Hit them with the glowing end...hard!" Soraya said, lifting up one of the batons.

Lex nodded and swallowed hard, her mouth pulling tight. "You look strong. Can you lead?" she said, burping and holding her gut.

Anna flinched away, immediately looking for signs of sickness – a cough, the black drool...any of it.

"I'm okay. Just go!" Lex growled, seemingly mastering herself. Soraya nodded, and stepped out into the commissary. "Hey...wait?" Lex grunted, covering her mouth and pointing at her.

"I'm Soraya."

Lex nodded, swallowing hard. "Soraya...the dial...just below the handle. Don't turn it all the way up. There's a defect. They can arc. It could kill you if you're too close. They say it's one in a hundred thousand, but I've actually seen it happen. Trust me, you don't want to be holding one if it does. Be careful."

"Arc...kill me. Right!" Soraya grunted, and then looked down at the batons in her hands. "Not all the way up...right," she muttered again and quietly turned the nobs on either baton.

The airlock cycled, the light flashed green, and the wide, half egg-shaped door opened. Soraya immediately set off at a jog.

The commissary was half-lit, the overhead lighting on the ceiling sprawling like a giant, curved checkerboard. She followed Doctor Reeds and Emiko out of the airlock, snugging the interface glove into place.

Glowing signs reached out from the walls on either side, a waist-high handrail stretching around the middle, where the floor dropped off to reveal the level below. The shops all appeared to be open, the security gates that dropped every night pulled up and out of sight. The space looked perfectly normal, aside from displays and merchandise toppled over and scattered out into the walkways.

A buzz filled the air, like a crowd of talking and shouting people, but she couldn't see anyone.

"Where is everyone?" Anna whispered.

Soraya slowed a bit, her head sweeping from side to side. They moved in a tight group down the middle of the walkway, an essential oil and bio-mod supplement vendor to their immediate left. A digital travel agency sat on the opposite wall, a holo-projector playing a flashy and loud advertisement for a "Rings of Saturn Cruise Vacation".

"They told people to come down here. They said they were evacuating the habitat rings and sending them all down here. Where is...?" Soraya started to ask just as a crash sounded from a shop ahead and across from them.

"There's someone in the vents! Oh my god, they're coming out!" a woman screamed, and then a crowd of people burst from a shop.

People tripped and fell over displays, tumbling into the open, their panicked screams echoing loudly. A man ambled out after them, his body bloody and disfigured. A long, flexing shape pushed slowly out through his shirt, dark fluid spattering down his pants and onto the floor.

"Hey you!" Lex screamed, shoving through the group and bringing the rifle up to her shoulder.

Anna's head snapped around. People appeared in all of the shops around them, their faces poking out through displays or pressed up against glass. They materialized from hiding, heads and eyes swiveling to track the source of the noise.

The rifle cracked, the blue muzzle flash reflecting off the glossy floor and handrail. The sick man pitched backwards, the shot catching him just above the sternum. Bits of gore spattered the display behind him, but he didn't go down.

"Damn it!" Lex cursed, tracking him with the weapon as he took off at a run after the group of fleeing people. "Stay away from him! Run! Don't let him grab you!"

Anna ran as the commissary fell into chaos. People burst out of every shop, some crawling out from under kiosks, tripping others and tumbling awkwardly. A woman appeared to their left, screaming and throwing herself over a crowd and knocking them all to the ground.

"Move! Move!" Soraya screamed, wading into their midst. She pulled people out of the way and shoved them down the path. Anna ran in and found the bloody woman, wrestling an older man to the ground, pinning his arms to his body and wrapping her legs around him.

"Get off him!" she screamed and kicked her squarely in the face. Soraya lunged in as she fell away, driving a baton into her midsection.

The rifle cracked loudly behind them, the sound mixing with the screams and the searing *pop* of the stun baton. Anna glanced into the shop, and spotted another person squirming through a jagged hole in a ventilation duct just above the desk. The metal tore and bent outward, snagging his clothing and tearing into his skin, but he didn't seem to notice.

"Push her inside!" Anna screamed.

Soraya hit the woman again and again, electricity flaring and sending her toppling over a short display of bio-mod nutritional supplements. Anna slapped the glove onto the security panel on the wall and immediately felt it tingle against her fingers. She'd seen countless techs use them, but hadn't had the chance to get one on her hand before. It was simple tech, a touch-activated voice to code maintenance interface. Simple but powerful.

"Axos," she said, after reading the designated system name off the screen, "close security gate!" Small colorful holograms appeared above the glove as the device interpreted her voice quickly into code. The panel on the wall beeped and the security gate appeared from the top of the doorway, shaking and rattling in the track as it descended.

The infected woman screamed and jumped off the ground as the other tumbled free from the ruined vent. They ran forward as the gate hit the ground, clawing and pounding like animals to break through.

"Unless you can close all of them from here, we need to move!" Lex yelled.

Anna swung around and caught the older man by the arms, turning and pointing him in the right direction. "Run. You have to run. Go to the lower level. There is an access passage to the docks. We have to get off the station," she yelled, fighting to get the panicked people to move in the right direction.

She stopped at the next shop and the next, closing the gates, but watched as infected people streamed out of the shops ahead and behind them. Lex was right. Even with the ridiculously fast interface of the glove, she'd never get them all closed in time. There was likely a panel to control all of them at once, but she hardly had time to go poking around for it.

They moved as a group, Soraya aside them and Lex at their lead. An infected man burst out of a shop to their left. Soraya hit him with a baton. He staggered but kept his feet, sprinting right at Anna, arms extended and mouth agape. She jumped back, hitting the handrail, and then ducked and spun under his arms. He tumbled over the handrail and out of sight.

Anna kicked forward into a run and caught up with the group. She saw more people appear from the shops, spurred from hiding, but spotted more infected, too. They were everywhere, a few even dropping from overhead vents, bursting through the ducting like scurrying rats.

Lex yelled, stopping periodically to rattle off a shot or two, but there were too many to stop and fight. They simply had to run. They wove around and over people as they were knocked to the ground or pulled back into side passages. Anna wanted to stop and help them, but knew that if she did, she'd have no chance of fighting her way free again.

They reached the end of the commissary, the crowd around her red-faced and out of breath. Doctor Reeds ushered people down onto the escalators, his mismatched eyes scanning over the crowd as if counting, tallying everyone that passed. He spotted Anna and squeezed her shoulder, before pushing her onto the moving stair.

"Keep moving...don't stop!" Soraya screamed ahead, urging the people along. Anna leaned around the crowd behind her. She spotted Lex and Reeds jumping on last, the security officer yelling, her massive rifle flashing a deadly counterpoint.

Anna jumped off at the bottom and stepped to the side. Soraya fought two men off, smashing a baton into a third as the crowd filed around and ran behind her.

Lex fired point blank into a man's head as he sprinted down the escalator after them. His head peeled open and he went down, but another took his place. Another appeared beyond that, and then another, their bodies stuck together, the horrible gangly appendages appearing through their clothing. They burst through the gates closing off the other lanes, spilling down the lanes before Lex could take them down.

"Come on! Move! Move!" Anna screamed, pulling the people off and shoving them down the path. Reeds scrambled down. He met her gaze, his look saying, "you need to run", but she took his arm and guided him around the corner.

"You need to move, now!" Lex screamed, backing down the escalator, swinging the riffle around, the barrel flashing in conservative, well-aimed shots. But then it clicked.

"Shit! I'm out!"

"Go, I'll slow them down," Anna yelled and slid her hand onto the escalator display panel. Her fingers tingled, the air above the glove coming alive.

"Axos, reverse all lanes," she said, the small glowing shapes changing shape and color as the code reconfigured. A claxon sounded and the entire escalator assembly shuddered to a stop. A dozen running, screaming terrors staggered forward as it abruptly stopped, tumbling and rolling face first downhill.

"Axos, increase speed," she said, watching the stairs start to rotate away from her. The monsters clawed over one another to get to their feet. They didn't seem to feel pain, let alone fear it. How could she slow something down that didn't...fear?

"Axos, increase speed to maximum," she said, and once the holograms turned and changed color she pulled her hand away. The escalators whined, spinning like an out of control treadmill, knocking and carrying a handful of their pursuers up and away.

Lex staggered against the wall, a hand snapping up to her mouth. Anna hooked her under the arm and pulled her around. They ran left around the corner, passing food vendor carts. Soraya stood just ahead, waving her arms, screaming Anna's name. A man in a flight suit stood in a doorway just behind her. He pulled the last few stragglers through, looked up at Anna, and gestured for them to hurry.

A monster crawled up and over a cream roll cart to Anna's left, half of his face stark white, his mouth and nose covered in a black mess. He leapt off, jumping at them, jagged shapes squirming beneath his clothes.

Soraya ran forward and hit him with a baton, but there was no crackle, or flash of light. He grabbed the baton in one hand and struck out with the other. Soraya's head snapped back and she staggered.

Anna let go of Lex and made it to Soraya just as the infected man was hooking his arms around her. She threw an arm around his neck and wrenched his head back hard, squeezing his throat with all of her strength. Lex was there, wrenching on his hands. She heard his fingers snap like dry twigs, and then Soraya fell free.

Anna staggered back. The man flailed, wrenching around, somehow twisting his body in her hold. A sharp pain stabbed into her belly and then the man's head cracked violently to the side. She released her hold and pushed away.

Lex growled and drove the butt of her rifle into the man's face, his bones popping loudly. He wailed and staggered back. Soraya was waiting, and clubbed him back in the other direction with a baton.

"Anna!"

She caught the baton out of the air. She didn't even see Soraya throw it. She just knew it would be there. The glowing end hit him just under the chin, his face pulling tight and every visible muscle knotting up. Anna held it there another second for good measure, before pulling it away and letting him drop.

They ran together, and slipped through the service door. Lex sagged between them as the man in the flight suit pulled the doors closed.

"I hope you're it. I'm Gil...part of the Nielson's flight crew. They're loading people on board now, but we need to go!" the man in the flight suit gasped.

"Jacoby!" Anna spun, catching a glimpse of him wedging something through the handles of the door. "Jacoby is still out there! He is coming, don't block the door!"

"I hate to break it to you, but if he ain't here now, he's gone, honey!"

"He's coming..." Anna yelled, her anger spiking, just as Lex tipped forward, gagging and coughing. She jumped back and reached down, expecting pain to flare in her belly. There was a hole in her jumpsuit, just to the left of her bellybutton. She'd felt it keenly when wrestling the infected man off Soraya, the sharp bite, and yet when her finger worked through the hole in the fabric, she found no cut, hole, or blemish in her skin.

"Hey-hey-hey, she doesn't look so good! Is she...is she...like them? Infected?"

"No, she's just sick, uh she's fine," Anna growled. He wasn't listening, wasn't even meeting her eyes. He wedged another long bar through the handles.

"But...but, how do you know? They said that's what happened to the others, too. That they were just sick, but then...well, I don't know. Freaky shit started to happen to them. They went crazy. We can't let those people anywhere near the freighters," Gil said, walking back behind Soraya and over to a mesh gate down the hall.

Something hit the doors hard, like fists or palms smacking against the metal.

Anna glanced between the door and Gil. "Please, unblock the door! That could be him now. Please, let him in!" She could feel Jacoby, somewhere...somehow, but could feel the creatures as well – their poisonous anxiety, skin-tingling creep, and gut turning presence dulling even Soraya's warm spark.

Anna eyed the door, looked to Lex, and glanced up, trying to pick through the mess of it all, desperate to feel Jacoby, to know he was still alive. The ceiling over her head was made out of some sort of metal grating, the holes big enough to see through to the space above.

"I can't do that, honey. If one of those things gets in here, it could be the end for all of us. You just follow me, and I'll make sure you pretty things are taken care of."

"Ugh, my stomach," Lex gasped, her rifle clattering to the ground.

Anna's anger flared and her arm snapped out, her fingers bunching up in Gil's flight suit. All of the fear, frustration, and helplessness broke loose at once.

"We've seen people we care about pulled apart and turned into monsters. I still smell them, hear them crying – their sobs, their pain, their desperate pleas for help. They're never coming back. Do you understand that?" Anna growled, and slammed Gil back against the wall. Her fist tightened, the fabric tearing beneath her fingers.

"Please...she's...sick!" Gil gasped, his eyes wide and locked on Lex.

"Anna!" Soraya said, her eyes snapping down to Gil's feet. Anna looked down to find the man's boots hovering clear off the ground, and her arm barely shaking from the effort.

Soraya leaned back as Lex pitched forward suddenly and vomited onto the ground.

"Gack...get away from her. Come on, we have...to...go!" Gil grunted.

Anna released her grip, and held her hand out in front of her face. Her arm looked as it always did, except for the sad state of her nails. Somehow she'd just lifted a grown man into the air with one arm, and not broken a sweat doing it.

Gil slumped against the wall, coughing and cursing. The smell of sick washed over her as Lex staggered back and sucked in a shuddering breath. Then she wiped her mouth. Anna watched as a large red bubble formed in the strikingly blue mess at Lex's feet, and then popped.

"She'll go crazy and hurt you!" Gil yelled, running down the hall and through an open gate.

Anna met Lex's gaze, an energetic sparkle quickly filling the redhead's eyes.

"Jacoby..." Soraya whispered, smirking as she looked up from the mess on the floor.

"...Jacoby," Anna quietly agreed.

Anna and Soraya reached down and each took one of Lex's hands. The spark ignited inside, an electric, enervating pulse shooting from Lex's hand throughout the rest of Anna's body.

She felt Soraya, that familiar strength and resolve, but felt Lex now, too. She felt bright, lively, and unpredictable, a swirling mix of lust and aggression.

"Shit! I can feel you. Like really feel you, both of you, as if a part of you is inside me," Lex gasped.

"I'm sorry! I told you not to touch her!" Gil yelled. Anna's head snapped around as hinges groaned loudly. They jumped forward as one, all sharing the same impulse. The gate crashed closed with a loud *bang,* Gil turning the lock and jumping back.

"Gil...open this gate!"

"Shit!" he sputtered, staggering back. "Can't you see? I'm sorry. You're infected now...you're probably infected. If I let you through, it...you could kill...could kill everyone. It's for the best. I'm...I'm sorry!" Gil yelled.

Soraya cursed and grabbed the heavy bars and pulled. The metal groaned, the wall cracking next to them. But then she staggered away. A wave of creeping cold pushed over Anna's skin, the familiar dread bubbling up inside. A shadow passed overhead, like a cloud sliding before a warm sun, its chill settling over her skin like a blanket.

"What is that...?" Lex gasped. They looked up. A massive dark form moved across the grated-metal ceiling, and then they were peeling it open, tearing through the metal as if it were wet cardboard.

Gil looked up, screamed, and turned to run. He made it two steps before the first dropped behind him. Another tumbled down after, and then another. They swarmed the hallway, screaming, horrible limbs snapping and smashing.

Soraya pushed away from the gate as Gil screamed, his cries dying away in the storm of thrashing bodies and screaming voices. Lex turned and scooped her rifle off the ground as the doors behind them shuddered violently, a boney limb breaking through the metal.

1030 HOURS

We are healing, but you'll never be able to keep up. You can feel them. They are converging. They feel us. You cannot fight all of them! They are only growing stronger and will not stop! They can never stop.

Jacoby limped through the broken door and turned around, spooling the saw and taking a deep breath. He could indeed feel them all around, the sickly sensation seemingly creeping in from all sides.

"It's spreading like an infection...taking over the station. How do we stop something like that?" he gasped, pounding a fist against his throbbing leg. The pain was dimming, the strength slowly returning, but it wasn't fast enough. He needed to run.

Cut it, burn it, scoop it out.

"We're in a damn space station. How do you...?" Jacoby started to ask as a monstrous gangly creature streaked through the clinic and shoved through the broken doorway after him, its long, spidery legs stabbing and swinging into the walls and ceiling. Jacoby jumped back, wincing as his leg almost buckled. The beast had a single pelvis, but what looked like three human torsos melded together. Two, withered and skeletal heads hung limp on the two outside bodies, but the torso in the middle had only a mound of flesh where the neck should be. Its ribs grew out through its darkened, mottled flesh, and flexed, moving like the spines on some horrible, human-shaped fish.

Infected people stacked up behind the creature, seething, grunting, and coughing. They pulled and pushed around it and through its legs, but the creature snapped a hook-like arm down, pinning the first to break through to the ground. It stabbed another through the face, and promptly pulled its body apart. Jacoby watched as the dissected person's limbs started to melt and grow into the larger creature's body.

The plasma saw came up and waved before him, the brightly glowing blade throwing angry sparks into the air.

The creature screeched loudly as slender, boney appendages burst out of its disfigured body. They slammed into the walls and floor all around him, hooks bursting out of its back and stabbing into the ceiling, until it filled the narrow space with a web work of churning, limbs.

The infected people suddenly shrunk back, stepping into the clinic and going quiet. He spotted dozens of them – some wearing admin suits, maintenance jumpers, while others wore hospital gowns or scrubs.

"That's new," Jacoby muttered and limped back another step.

Do you feel it?

Jacoby nodded, wincing as he limped back another step. He could feel a great many things – the fibers of his leg stitching back together, Anna, Soraya, and Lex running scared, but also the corrupted, vile things crowding in around him. And yet, none of the myriad of sensations was as strong as the one radiating off the massive, bastardized creature in front of him.

We cannot fight something like that. Not with just a saw, and not without our full strength, the voice said, the pressure building behind his eyes. It was prodding around in his skull, as if someone's hands were gently pulling the different parts of his brain aside, looking, searching for something.

"I feel you in my head!" Jacoby grunted, his right eye twitching. "You seem to know more about what is happening in my brain than I do. It's making me heal faster, feel things I never could before. I can't seem to control it. But you...can't you use it? Can't you heal my leg? Or, make me stronger, faster?"

The creature ripped its multitude of limbs free, showering the hall with debris and came forward, hooking and ripping to pull its bulk along. A short arm swung at him, but the hallway was too narrow, and the long legs folded awkwardly in the narrow space. Jacoby caught the limb before it could pull away, the saw severing it cleanly just above a joint.

You can hear me, and I you, but there is something blocking us...keeping us from coming together. I can feel the thing growing in your brain, like a fiery and powerful energy source, begging to be used. It has and continues to change us. It gave me a voice and the strength to take a sliver of control, but I do not know why or how. All I know is that I can feel it, that you can feel it, but there is something holding it back.

Jacoby hobbled and ducked as the shortened leg swung around at his head. The saw came up and took the limb off at the body. He swept the tool back at waist level, catching the middle torso with the tip of the blade. Black flesh and muscle sprayed the wall next to him, a coil of looping, stinking intestines spilling out of the cut.

"What do you mean 'holding it back'?"

Two spear-like arms cut straight down at his head. Jacoby twisted and turned. He dodged the first, but the second caught his right shoulder, his collarbone popping loudly in respond.

"Argh!" Jacoby cried out and swept the saw back in response. The blade caught the creature's leg, biting deep into the muscle and tendons, and swung back out the other side. But it didn't fall, nor had he cut deep enough to catch bone. A horrible, numb ache shot down his right arm and his finger slipped off the trigger.

I am your right hand...but you don't know why, so I don't know why. There is something in you, in your mind, splitting us apart. You need to break through it...tear it down. Make us whole! Make us whole! Then maybe we can take control and seize its true strength...

Jacoby staggered back against the wall, barely keeping his one-handed grip on the saw. He threw himself against the other wall, a spiny arm clawing against his back. The blow tore his suit and spun him around, red-hot pain stretching across both shoulder blades.

He lurched painfully for the doors. They were just half a dozen steps away. He caught movement out of the corner of his eye. The creature reared back with the broken limb, and Jacoby could only watch as it shot towards him. The impact knocked his breath away and sent him tumbling through the doors, and out into the concourse hallway.

Jacoby landed flat on his back, the saw clattering free from his hand and sliding across the floor. He saw people running down the wide concourse to his left, their forms just distant, blurry shapes.

Go! he silently begged them.

The doorway bowed and then shattered outward as the creature pushed through, its multitude of legs spilling into the hallway.

Jacoby pushed away and stood, but only made it a few steps. His feet were pulled out from under him, the ground painfully embracing him. He rolled over as he started to slide back, a ropey tendril wrapped around both of his ankles.

It hadn't been intestines that spilled out of its body when he cut it open, but squirming, churning tentacles. Boney arms slammed down on either side of his legs, breaking the floor panels. He reached for the saw, but it was well out of reach.

Break free!

"I can't," Jacoby grunted, kicking his feet, and then he stopped fighting as the creature moaned. The noise was disturbingly human and distantly familiar – a strangled, almost drunken cry, muffled by a cocoon of writhing flesh.

Two arms speared out, stabbing hard into his shoulders, plunging deep into muscle and bone. The pain was so intense he didn't feel it at first, just a white-hot wall that washed every other thought and concern away. He felt his body wrenched up and off the ground, his feet kicking pathetically.

Jacoby grunted and gagged, struggling for breath. He picked up his head as the middle torso shuddered, and then the mound sitting atop the shoulders split open. Goopy black liquid spilled out over the chest and writhing spines, the skin pulling apart as if someone had grasped a zipper and pulled down. A face pushed forth, the human head emerging into the light as if birthed by the monster itself.

Muddy brown eyes slid open slowly, the crow's feet and papery flesh pulling tight as the mouth opened to reveal jagged, coffee-stained teeth. Janice's nostril's flared, her grayed red hair plastered to her head.

"Jack-Jack-Jack," she chattered, her dark, emotionless eyes locking on him. The skin pulled away under her face, revealing the handle of the stun baton, the metal and flesh surrounding it scorched and black.

"No...fucking...way!" Jacoby grunted, fighting to lift his hand and pull free from the skewering limbs.

"Jack-Jack-Jack," Janice's face continued to chatter over and over again. But there was no comfort in seeing her face. It wasn't really her, just a monster wearing her skin.

She reveals her true form.

The opening under Janice's head flexed open, exposing a wide hole, covered in curved, flexing teeth. She began to draw him in, pulling him towards the gaping mouth.

Break free! Tear down the barrier and make us whole! Find the hole in your memory, and remember! the voice screamed in his mind. The tentacle wrapped around his right leg pulled tight.

"Hole in my memory? Remember what?" Jacoby gasped, fighting and pulling to free his leg, but the pain burned like scorching fire in his shoulders. The pressure was too great, cutting into him, pinning him into place. No, not pressure. It was weight...crushing him.

Something stirred in Jacoby's mind, but it wasn't the voice. He wrenched his left leg free and kicked against the creature's body. Janice's face contorted, and the manic chatter grew more intense.

"Jack-Jack-Jack-Jack!"

"Stop!" he screamed as the tentacle pulled harder on his right leg. A strange odor drifted over his face – stale cigarettes and synth alcohol. The monster's shadow and weight grew stifling. He caught a flash of movement, a distant part of his mind swelling in response, the pressure pushing out on his skull, his eyes, and his ears.

A small, white shape stabbed out of Janice's body, flashing like a dagger at his face. His right hand snapped up, the muscles and tendons tearing around the boney intrusion in his shoulder. He caught the sharp bone weapon, somehow, his knuckles turning white as a gray tinge washed over his skin.

"Dad stop...please!" He heard the voice. The young man sounded scared, small, and far away. It wasn't in his head. It wasn't.

Jacoby's gaze snapped to the sharp bone arm, his right arm shaking, the small part of him fighting back, struggling to keep the point from jamming into his face and ending his life.

Remember...remember what he did to you! Remember what you did! That is the key. You have to remember!

The young man screamed out again, but Jacoby couldn't hear what they said. Another voice responded in kind, angrier than the first. The pressure suddenly doubled, and something snapped in his head.

Jacoby was toppling through darkness, a swirling mist and noxious aromas burning his nose. He felt pain cut into his body. A fist struck his mouth, then the side of his head. He felt it crack into his arm again and again and again.

"Stop it. It hurts. It hurts," he said, but it wasn't his voice. It was the young man.

Jacoby blinked but he didn't see Janice's monstrous form anymore, but his father. He held a knife in his fist, his nose reddened from too much drink. Hot spittle and alcohol spattered Jacoby's face as he screamed.

"You took my knife! I told you to never touch my stuff!" his father screamed. His eyes bulged, the whites stained with yellow and red.

"I...I just," Jacoby heard himself say, but his father's open palm snapped up into his mouth. He tasted blood, felt his teeth knocked loose.

"Yeah I saw the mess you made, whittling on that stick. Was it for that little rich girl you insist on talking to? Well, is it? What we are and got ain't good enough now? I know you sneak out to see her, know you lie to me about it! Lie...to...me!" his father screamed, his fist snapping into his mouth, then his nose, and finally the side of his head.

"Dad stop...please!" Jacoby sputtered, choking on a mouthful of blood. His vision went blurry as a pain flared inside his head.

"She doesn't like you for you. She lifts her nose up at the thought of who you are and where we come from. Those people think you're nothing," his father screamed and drove the knife into the wall. "You're nothing, Jack. Nothing! You're supposed to love me, Jack! Not them!" The knife stabbed into the wall next to his head again and again. His father's face grew redder, the knife cutting into his ear. It pulled back again, but his father's arm was wavering, the gleaming blade poised to come down right on his face.

Jacoby caught his father's wrist with his both hands, his arms shaking as the knife inched closer and closer to his face. The blade danced against his cheek, the dulled tip biting into his skin, the pain burning as it slowly pushed through.

"Dad stop...please!" he croaked, his right hand snapping out and catching him in the face. Jacoby tried to push him away, his hand sliding down his nose and over his chin. He squeezed, pushing on anything in reach to make the pain stop. His hand slid down around his father's throat, and the man gagged.

"You make me so angry I could just...rip and tear, bite and gnash my own flesh and blood," his father grunted, and then stumbled back, the blade pulling away.

Jacoby fell with him, one hand pushing the knife out wide so he wouldn't fall on it.

"Dad...please...stop!" he cried, hot tears filling his eyes and running down his cheeks. They hit the cuts on his face and lips, burning like fire.

"Kill...you...worthless boy! You're not mine...fake flesh and blood. Fake!" his father growled, eyes gone wide, his arm jerking and trying to pull the knife free. Jacoby dropped his whole weight onto his father's chest and squeezed as hard as he could, desperate to keep the knife from biting into his flesh again, desperate for his father to calm enough for him to get away.

The man struggled beneath him, gurgling and sputtering, "worthless" over and over, until finally, after what felt like an eternity, he stopped fighting.

Jacoby coughed and sputtered, his tears flowing freely, and looked up. He recoiled. His father was motionless, his face a deep shade of purple, his eyes bulging and lifeless. He pulled his hand away from his throat, his whole arm turned an almost gray shade of white in the struggle, his fingers and nails cracked and bloody.

I...I...killed him. I killed my father, and then I ran away, Jacoby thought, the realization stampeding into his head like a crushing mountain of stone. The pressure filled his thoughts and pitched him end over end in a swirling mess of light and dark, of blazing fire and freezing cold.

Forgive yourself. He would have killed you...us.

He snapped to clarity, his hand still trembling in the air, the boney limb starting to cut into his cheek. Just like the knife.

Jacoby felt his mind pull together, the broken pieces of him melding into the whole. He felt the horrible moments – the fear, doubt, and pain...all of it, flood back in.

We...are...whole.

The pressure swept through his mind, but it wasn't a voice anymore, but a feeling, an all-encompassing sensation. Lively, kinetic energy rushed out to every synapsis of his brain, down his neck and into his chest. It struck his heart like a billowing cloud of pure fire, erupting into the rest of his body.

"My...name...isn't...Jack!" he growled and shoved the boney appendage away. Jacoby reached out, grasped the handle of the damaged stun baton, and tore it free.

He wrenched the boney appendage back, a length breaking free in his grasp. He jammed the fractured piece into Janice's head, piercing skin and bone, and swung the baton down, smashing it clear through the other side.

Janice shrieked, the other heads crying out angrily. Jacoby twisted and tore free. He fell and hit hard, but immediately rolled away, the clicking arms smashing down to skewer him. He pushed off the ground, his broken collarbone snapping back together. Blood dribbled from his punctured shoulders, but he could already feel his muscle and flesh knitting themselves back together.

Jacoby rolled under a stabbing strike and scooped the plasma saw off the ground. He ejected the spent plug, smashed a new one in and turned it, all in one surprisingly dexterous movement.

The monster bore down on him as the saw spooled, its bulk almost filling the concourse. Jacoby danced right, and then left. He swiped the saw across in a flash, catching two boney legs at once. The blade flipped around and he lunged forward, the glowing mass of spinning, super-heated points ripping clean through one of the woman's formerly human legs.

The creature shrieked and toppled over, spiny legs lashing out to catch its bulk. Jacoby jumped onto one of the limbs, pinning it to the ground, and severed it cleanly, then jumped away before another could lash out.

He spun, cutting a human arm free, the saw almost weightless in his hand. He felt powerful and fast, his muscles coiling and flexing almost before his brain could tell them what to do.

The monster ambled sideways, the gyrating spines flexing. He ran in, swept the saw down low, and brought it straight across. The blade bit just beneath the monster's ribs. Jacoby ripped it sideways, hard, churning metal and searing heat chewing through flesh and bone in an instant. The saw broke through the other side, and Jacoby wheeled around on a heel, the strength behind the strike spinning him fully around.

He brought the saw up again, but the monster gurgled, and promptly fell over. Then its upper body slowly slid free and fell in a heap. Janice's head flopped out as it came to a rest, her dark eyes wide and vacant.

"I am sorry, Janice. For my part," Jacoby said, quietly and let the saw spool down. He turned down the passage, towards the commissary and paused.

The creatures were everywhere. He spun like a compass, their presence burning like the dark smudges on the canvas of his mind. He could feel them crawling through vents, breaking down doors, harvesting prey and feeding, growing and becoming stronger. Then he felt Anna, Soraya, and Lex. They burned like bright stars against that same canvas, radiating warmth and life where the monsters cast only shadow and cold. There was something else there, floating amongst his thoughts, pulsing in and out of every thought and emotion – an energy, binding all of them together.

Jacoby concentrated on them, a fiery tingle filling his mind. The hall shrunk around him and then expanded. He felt Anna, her silvery glow ahead and down, but she was surrounded by so much darkness. It was crowding in, moving hungrily and threatening to swallow her whole.

"No!" he growled and kicked forward into a run. Jacoby cycled the airlock, jumped inside, and waited for it to process.

"Hurry..." he muttered, his hands bunching up into fists. The creatures continued to converge as the light shifted from red to green. They were going to hurt Anna, Lex, and Soraya, violate and tear their flesh...turn them into something unnatural.

The thought of Anna's crystal blue eyes turned lifeless and dark sparked a profound anger inside him. The idea of her genuine smile and flawless skin marred and melted into some grotesque and mindless beast triggered something inside him he'd never felt before. No, he had. He'd felt it in the clinic, when Randall tried to smash his brains in. His hands started to shake, the unseen wall of energy binding him to the three women igniting in a sudden maelstrom of strength, determination, and almost unbridled rage.

When the airlock finally started to open, Jacoby grabbed the door and propelled himself through, the metal giving way under his grip. He bounded forward, each stride covering what he'd been lucky to accomplish in five before.

The commissary was a mess of debris, vendor carts, and bodies strewn across the floor. Some moved, dragging themselves along, while others lay twitching, their arms and legs latched around their victims.

Jacoby felt the dark creatures massing closer and closer to Anna, until he struggled to differentiate where her light ended and their darkness began. They were like his father – both foul and parasitic creatures, smothering any light and happiness in his life with their insufferable darkness.

Anna, Lex, and Soraya felt like a part of him now. They were his family, his blood, and he was damned if he would let anyone or anything harm them.

The fire burning through his body deepened, a gold hue sliding over his vision. An infected burst from the ground and ran at him, a multitude of different limbs waving and reaching out to claim him. Jacoby ignored the saw and jumped right at him. He swung a fist into the man's jaw. His impact knocked the creature back, clear off its feet, tumbling head over feet. And then it landed in a pile against the wall.

Jacoby lifted his fist. He'd felt no pain. Shit, he'd barely registered the contact. His knuckles shimmered in the air, the strange gold cast surging brighter around his body.

He ran as fast as his legs would carry him, shouldering aside anything that got in his way. He approached the end of the commissary and skidded to a stop. A mass of screaming, churning creatures pooled above the escalators. They fought and clawed over one another, but tipped and tumbled back. Then he spotted the moving stairs. They were all spinning up and fast.

"Smart girl, Anna," Jacoby beamed, and ran to the handrail. He jumped over, his heart jumping up into his throat. He dropped twenty feet and landed, the impact barely registering in his legs.

"I could get used to this," he grinned, and ran forward, weaving and ducking through vendor carts.

Anna, Lex, and Soraya were close. He could feel them. Shit, he'd almost be able to smell them, if not for the creature's acrid taint on the air.

A cluster of churning bodies appeared off to his left, hovering behind a massive creature, its boney arms banging and thudding loudly into...Jacoby couldn't quite see what.

"Hey!" he shouted. The monsters chattered and screeched, wheeling about at the sound of his voice. The gold sheen shimmered across his vision. It cast the creatures in an entirely different light, and Jacoby didn't see them as sick, mutilated people. He saw them as they truly were, horrific and alien – beings that would end all life if given the chance.

"You can't have them," Jacoby growled as the creatures swarmed in, the saw coming to life in his hand.

Anna pulled Soraya and Lex close as the monsters pressed against the gate. The heavy metal shuddered, the lock banging back and forth violently. Boney limbs stabbed through the gaps, clattering against the ground by their feet.

A hand slid through, reaching and clutching for her, the fingers melding into something more claw than fingers. She felt their mouths, their hunger, their stifling need to consume and spread. It was all they wanted...all that they were. They would never rest, turn back, or give up.

Anna pulled the two women into her, their combined spark the only thing keeping her from crumbling to the ground. The door shook behind them. Dark shapes punched through the metal, before pulling clear and stabbing back in. The bars Gil had wedged through the handles shook and bounced, bending in with the pressure.

Lex shook her rifle angrily and tossed it to the ground, swearing under her breath. Soraya lifted the stun batons, but one was dead, and the other had just a few good uses left in it.

"We don't go down without a fight," Lex said, her voice a defiant growl, "we hit, and we tear, and we crush everything we can get our hands on."

The door shuddered again, a hinge popping loudly and bouncing to the ground by their feet. Anna balled up her fists, met Lex's gaze, and nodded.

The chorus of screams and shrieks rose in a sudden fervor, the gate tearing partially away from the wall behind them. The door bent and broke, metal shattering and raining across the floor.

Anna wanted to fight, she wanted to be strong, but there were so many of them, their dark and sickly corruption smashing down all around her. She only hoped that the others made it to the docks below and were headed to safety.

Anna's back abruptly straightened a bit. A trickle of warmth spread over her skin, the new sensation breaking through the monsters' blight.

"Do you feel that?" Soraya gasped.

"I do...it feels like," Anna said.

"...a storm is coming straight for us," Lex gasped. Anna felt it, too. Her scalp tingled, the hair on her arms standing straight up. It felt like a tornado, or a hurricane was bearing down on them.

"Get down." Anna wrenched the two women to the ground just as the doors exploded. A massive monster surged through the opening, its tangle of boney legs crashing into the walls and floor. She flinched, waiting for it to lash out, the pain to fill her, and everything to end. But it didn't move right.

The massive creature jerked as a brilliant flash appeared through its skin, and it split in two, flesh and bones smoldering and red-hot. Anna ducked as something bright barreled right over them, hit the ground a few feet away, and smashed through the remnants of the heavy gate.

She felt the metal give way, the wall panels rending as hinges tore loose. The floor shook as orange light flared, a loud, angry buzz merging with the monsters' chorus-screams. The beasts converged on the light, their boney spider arms thrashing and stabbing.

The closest beast tore in half, its upper body tumbling through the air in a spectacular shower of fire and blood. It landed against Anna's feet, the head still twitching and arms flailing. The bright light flashed again. It spun, and she saw it clear. It was a person, their outline cast in a gold glow. The light spun in a tight arc and a crowd of flailing monsters burst apart, their bodies torn violently in half.

More infected people ran in, their blood and flesh spattering the walls. An arm landed next to her. Anna tried to push it clear, but something heavy and horribly wet fell on top of her. Soraya and Lex pulled her close, the three women huddling together.

The buzzing noise grew closer and she felt the weight atop them grow. The smell of blood and tainted flesh filled her nose. A bright light burned through the tangle of bodies covering them as a hot, salty odor crept into the mix.

A creature screeched, its voice strangled, hoarse, and animalistic, and then it abruptly went quiet. Anna squeezed Lex and Soraya's hands, breathing, fighting to stay calm, and listening. A heartbeat later, something moved amidst the bodies.

"Anna!" a man yelled, his voice resonating throughout her entire body.

* * *

Jacoby ripped the saw straight up, catching the last monster between its legs, and severing it cleanly in half. Its manic screams died away in a gurgling, bubbling mess.

He looked around the hallway, but saw only the death and destruction he'd wrought. Bodies and their severed parts covered the floor, blood and their infected, black sick peppering the walls all the way to the ceiling.

"Anna..." Jacoby yelled. He was too late, but how? He'd felt them...so close, their presences burning so bright.

There was only death...no Anna, Lex, or Soraya. His anger bled away, the fire pumping through his veins cooling and the gold hue starting to dim. Despair washed in, replacing the heat and almost uncontrollable strength he'd felt just a moment ago with a cold, dark pit.

A creature stirred straight ahead, its macabre, folded limbs straightening. It rose, grunting and straining. Another moved beneath it, and then another. The pile churned, the monster on top lifting to face him.

Jacoby growled and pulled the spent fusion plug out of the saw, jammed the last one in and twisted it hard. The saw started to spool, bits of blood and meat almost instantly burning off the blade.

"You took her! I will cut every...single...one of you to pieces. Until there is nothing left!" Jacoby snarled, stepping forward and preparing to strike.

The monster tipped up and then suddenly toppled forward, tumbling clear from its severed lower half. Another fell away to the side, and then a pale face appeared amidst the carnage, blue eyes shining.

Anna looked so small, huddled with Lex and Soraya, her hair stained red.

"Coby!" she gasped, jumping to her feet.

"Anna?" he whispered, and dropped the saw. He jumped forward and caught her, squeezing her close and lifting her off the ground.

She sobbed, coughed, and sputtered into his neck. Lex and Soraya smashed into them. Jacoby hooked his arms around them all, pulling all three women into a crushing hug.

Before he could stop himself, Jacoby leaned in and kissed each of them. He felt the wonderful pulse of their energies, buzzing inside and all round him.

"We have to go!" Soraya grunted, and begrudgingly, they separated.

Jacoby scooped the plasma saw off the ground and led the three women through the mess of bodies. They picked their way through the door at the far end of the passage. Jacoby slammed it behind them, while Lex and Soraya pulled down everything within reach – boxes, crates, an old and battered four-wheeled cart, and stacked it all up in a barricade.

Two old and battered elevators sat behind them, blackened tracks worn into the floor leading up to both doors. Jacoby pressed the old-fashioned button, the elevator to their right chiming. The doors rattled open.

They piled inside, Soraya hitting the down button repeatedly. The doors closed slowly, rattling shut before the old lift started to move.

"This thing is ancient!" Anna whispered, eyeing the scratched and dented walls warily.

"As old as the station, probably. Everything else has been replaced or upgraded since, but not these. Why bother if the only people that use them are freighter crews," he said, reaching out and squeezing her hand.

Jacoby felt her relief, but it was clouded by anxiety, fear, and a blanket of exhaustion so profound he was surprised that she could still stand. He felt the same from Lex and Soraya, but struggled to sort all of it out.

I struggle understanding what I feel most of the time, and now I have to worry about others, too, he thought, as the old lift moved down its vacuum tube.

After a quiet ride, the elevator slowed, and dinged again. There was no flashy arrival light or voice greeting. This was his part of the station, where things were simple, rugged, and beat up from constant use.

"I'll go first, just in case," Jacoby offered, and lifted the plasma saw before him. The three women nodded in unison, none visibly eager to argue the point.

The saw started to hum as he stepped out into the hall. The overhead lights were out, the only glow coming from a battery backup unit mounted high on the wall to his right. He squeezed the trigger down a little further, the contact points throbbing red in the darkness.

They moved slowly down the hall, more battered carts lining the wall to his left. Garbage and refuse covered the floor, flowing from an overflowing bin. The doors opened onto a wide ramp running down and away, the floor and walls covered with the familiar patina of rock dust and grease.

Jacoby led them quickly down the ramp, the airlock door at the bottom leading out to the half-dozen docking bays. He turned left, his gaze quickly sweeping the corridor. The five round hatches closest to them were closed, red lights glowing against the ceiling above them. But the furthest door was open, the light from inside casting a long, dark shadow onto the floor. A person leaned out, spotted them, and shouted.

Jacoby ran, Anna and Lex on either side of him, and Soraya pacing just behind. Two people ran forward, meeting them just outside the lit hatch.

"You're alive!" Emiko yelled, her mouth turning up into a wide smile. "There were so many people, and it was so confusing. They all crowded onto the freighters, pushing and shoving. Then the crews just left, but Doctor Reeds made the last ship stay. He said you would make it. He knew."

Jacoby looked from Emiko to Doctor Reeds, the physician's differently colored eyes studying him.

"Thanks, doc," Jacoby said.

"Of course. Of course. We've got a lot to talk about, to figure out, I think, but why don't we do it in there?" he asked, and gestured back towards the open hatch.

"Solid plan," Lex agreed and they moved as one. Jacoby squeezed Anna's hand again as they approached the light, their spirits both lifting as one. But the hatch hissed loudly, the round door suddenly rolling shut.

"What the...?" Reeds yelled, but Jacoby reached the hatch first. He looked through the small window, and found a tall man stooped over just inside.

Manis turned and looked out the door, and their eyes met.

"Open this door! Do it now!" Jacoby yelled, pounding his fists against the metal.

Manis said something, but he couldn't make it out. The hatch was too thick. He pointed behind him at the freighter's airlock and shrugged his shoulders. Then he mouthed "sorry" and turned and walked away.

"Open this hatch, you fucking coward!" Jacoby raged, pounding his fists against the stout door again. He felt the anger spark once again, the fire sliding down into his muscles. He curled his fingers over the lip, kicked a foot onto the frame and pulled. His muscles bunched and knotted, the door groaning in response, but felt the outer hatch slide shut. The gold hue slid slowly over his vision, the dark passage brightening considerably.

"Don't leave us here!" he screamed, but a tremor shook the floor. Anna and the others ran to a wide window set in the wall, but Jacoby could see well enough through the windows in the hatch.

The ship's dull-gray hull was moving, floating away, jetted thrusters firing and pushing the large vessel into the black. He slammed his fist into the hatch, his knuckles sinking into the metal. The ship's engines fired, the pulsing *thrum* vibrating through the deck plating beneath his feet.

The freighter gained momentum as it slid out of sight. Manis' wide, watery eyes and shrugged shoulders popped into Jacoby's head and he punched the hatch again, the metal ringing from the impact.

"Jacoby!" Anna yelled.

"That weasel left us! He left us to die," he growled, spinning around.

Anna, Lex, and Soraya stood side by side, but Reeds and Emiko were backing away.

"What?" he yelled.

"Coby, you're...glowing!" Anna whispered. He looked down, but his hands and arms looked normal enough, save for the gold tint.

"No...look!" Lex said, pointing at the window.

Jacoby slid between them and stood before the exterior window. His reflection shone back at him, a surprisingly warm and bright halo framing his body. He took a deep breath, forcing the anger away, fighting back to a calmer place. The glow flickered and started to die away, just as the energizing fire receded in his muscles.

"F-F-Fascinating," Reeds whispered. He was behind him, at the hatch, running his fingers through knuckle-shaped dents in the hard metal.

"We've got to find another way off the station," Lex said.

"But how? There were five freighters down here. Two were scheduled to depart this week, two more next week, and the fifth just arrived. We don't have any ships due for arrival for at least a month! Our spot in the orbit right now puts us further away from Jupiter and Mars than any time this solar orbit. Trust me, I'm a...was a scheduler. There is a relay station on Ceres, the habitat domes on Europa, but they're resupply ships run on a completely different schedule than ours do," Soraya shot back.

A thought popped up into Jacoby's head, locking into place with almost photo-quality recall.

"What do you think Manis meant when he said, 'If something happens to this station, I'm taken care of?'"

"Wait, I remember that? How did you...how can I? My memory usually sucks, but I can picture that in my head perfectly," Lex said, trailing off.

"Maybe it's that," Anna said, pointing to the now closed airlock door. "Maybe he was planning on jumping ship the whole time."

"I don't know," Jacoby said, shaking his head. "Is it possible they have a ship docked someplace else on the station? Someplace we don't know about? Something small, like a shuttle, or rock jumper?"

"You mean, besides the gravity tugs they use to haul rocks back to the station?" Soraya asked.

"Yes. And if there is one, how would we find it? I mean, the rest of the station could be filled with those...things," Emiko said. She stood by the opposite wall, her arms hugging her midsection.

"The question we should be asking ourselves is: should we get off the station at all? Our most prudent move right now might just be to establish outside communication. There are dozens, maybe hundreds of people on those freighters, and any number of them could be infected. What would happen if those things got to Mars, the lunar colony, or any of the other dozen or so off-world settlements? What would those things do if they reached Earth?" Reeds asked, stepping tentatively forward and looking to them each in turn.

A shiver coursed through Jacoby's body. Anna, Lex, and Soraya all trembled visibly at the same time.

"We can't...won't let that happen," Jacoby muttered, and met Anna's crystal blue eyes.

"That's the spirit, Jacky," a man said, stepping out of the shadows next to Emiko.

Jacoby flinched, his hand jumping to the saw handle. Anna, Lex, and Soraya spun, following his eyes.

"Who is...there? How did you get in here?" Anna asked, her gaze locking onto the shadowy figure.

"What in the hell?" Lex growled, "That's..."

The stranger stepped back into the shadow next to the airlock and appeared again next to Reeds.

"Jacoby, what...err, who are you talking to?" the physician asked and swiveled about. He looked right at the stranger, but didn't seem to see them.

"Jacoby?" Soraya asked, pointing as the stranger stepped fully into the light.

"What the shit?" Lex cursed.

"Stop it, you're scaring me," Emiko cried, jumping forward and wheeling about.

Jacoby squeezed the saw's trigger as the stranger's face clarified. It was him...somehow, another Jacoby.

"What is it, Jacoby? I see it in your eyes, on all of your faces. You four see something that Emiko and I obviously don't," the doctor said, his voice pulled tight in alarm.

"Honestly, doc. I don't think you'd believe me."

"Yep. He'll think you've gone bat-shit nuts, Jacky! Well, because you kinda are. But heh, I'm outta your head now, so you've got that going for you. But let me tell you, now that you and the girls can see me, we're going to have so much fun together!"

NecroVerse will continue in...

EXODUS

Coming soon.

Lightning Source UK Ltd.
Milton Keynes UK
UKHW020653251022
411061UK00015B/956